# The Moonlight Cavalry

BECOMING THE GREATEST GENERATION BOOK TWO

# THE
# MOONLIGHT
# CAVALRY

A World War II Novel

Lynn Ellen Doxon

Artemesia
Publishing

ISBN: 978-1-951122-83-6 (paperback)
ISBN: 978-1-951122-84-3 (ebook)
LCCN: 2023947438

Artemesia Publishing
9 Mockingbird Hill Rd
Tijeras, New Mexico 87059
www.apbooks.net
info@artemesiapublishing.com

Content Notice: This book contains descriptions of war and trauma that may be disturbing to some people. The book also uses racial slurs that were in use at the time that this book is set. We have kept this language to reflect its usage at the time, but the author and the publisher condemn the usage of such language whether it was used in the past or today.

Dedicated to
Lieutenant Colonel Kermit Lynn Doxon, U.S. Army Retired
1914 - 1995

# CHAPTER 1

## OUT OF AUSTRALIA

**E**VERY OFFICE I CHECKED was locked. I looked around nervously for the right office. I'd arrived at the Southwest Pacific Headquarters in Brisbane two days late because an autumn storm had delayed the ship from Townsville, and now everything seemed to be shut down for the noon hour. I climbed to the next floor, where I heard voices from a room down the hall. That must be it. I rushed in. US Army General Walter Krueger and several other officers glanced up from the papers spread out on a table as I burst in. I stopped dead in my tracks and saluted.

"Lieutenant Sinclair, reporting for duty, sir!"

General Kreuger raised his eyebrows slightly, returned my salute, and then turned to a major who stood behind him.

"Hamilton, get this boy where he belongs."

I trotted back downstairs behind the lanky major. As we walked, he asked me. "What were you thinking barging in on the general?"

"All the other offices were empty or locked."

"You had better thank your lucky stars it was Kreuger and not MacArthur," he puffed, a little winded from the speed with which he was taking the stairs. "How much field training experience have you had?"

"I've been executive officer of my battery as we trained at Fort Bliss and Townsend for the past year. Before that, I taught school for three years. Physics and chemistry."

The major found a captain in a cafeteria on the first floor of the converted office building.

"This lieutenant will lead that radar platoon to Kiriwina," the major said, then he turned on his heel and left without another word.

"Have you had anything to eat?" the captain asked.

"No, sir."

"Grab some grub and sit down. We'll discuss your orders."

In a few minutes I dropped my tray, heaped with food, on the table.

"You ever been in the field?" the captain asked.

"No, sir. I just completed jungle warfare training."

"How much experience on the SCR-584?" The food made me think of Mom's Sunday dinner, distracting me slightly from his question. I hadn't had food this good since leaving home.

Swallowing, I replied, "I operated a prototype unit demonstrated at Bliss."

"How did you come to be separated from your battery?"

"They sent me to Darwin for malaria officer training. The Japs attacked the city, wounding me. My unit left while I was recovering."

"A lieutenant as malaria officer?" he mused. "Seems the field officers aren't taking this as seriously as MacArthur planned. At least you've been under fire. You'll have to do."

Shoveling some more delicious food into my mouth, I said, impolitely talking with my mouth full, "I would like to get the radar unit set up and run through the operation a few times before we leave for the island."

"No. You're leaving this evening."

Pausing with a forkful of food, I replied, "Yes, sir."

After I inhaled the rest of my lunch, the captain called for a driver, and we headed for the field where my new platoon waited. On the way, he explained the arrangement.

"This platoon is made up of select recruits fresh from Camp Davis. They came here to train previously deployed troops on the SCR-584 with a Lieutenant as green as they were. One of those Ninety-Day Wonders. Don't know how they think they can make an officer of a college kid in three months."

I didn't mention that I, too, was a Ninety-Day Wonder, graduating with the first class at Camp Davis. But, of course, by now, I had been in the army for nearly two years, which qualified me as an old hand.

"They did fine training the old hands on the new equipment. The lieutenant had been a schoolteacher, so he knew how to do that. Then the plan was to send the platoon out as replacements. The poor boy broke down during the first week of jungle training. That's what you get for sending a schoolteacher to do a soldier's job."

I shuddered and kept my mouth shut.

"Anyway, you'll take on this platoon, give 'em some additional training, and prepare 'em for combat duty while on the island. We've kept 'em in the dark until we knew we could go through with it. You'll have a very short time to get 'em packed up and ready."

"You're sending a bunch of inexperienced troops who still need training onto an island with no artillery or infantry support?"

"There aren't any Japs there, but we aren't telling the troops that. We want 'em to feel like it's the real thing. You're going in with an Aussie Air Corps radar unit. Their captain will be in charge overall, but you'll be second in command and train the Aussies on the 584. This is the first time we've tried something like this. We're counting on you to make it work."

"What about my former unit?"

"When your battalion arrives at the island, these boys will become replacements. They'll be assigned wherever the battalion has lost troops."

"If there aren't any Japs on the island, why would we need replacements?" I asked.

"We expect to lose at least a few men from each platoon to disease. After all, it's a jungle out there," he laughed at his joke. I opened my mouth to reply to his cavalier attitude as the driver slammed on the brakes, and the captain jumped out of the jeep. Several soldiers lounged in front of their tents.

"Platoon, fall in," he shouted to the men. The platoon quickly formed ranks.

"This is Lieutenant Sinclair. He's taking command of your platoon." The captain paused, apparently waiting for me to say something.

I stepped forward. "Good afternoon, men. I'm very pleased to be here. We've been temporarily posted to the RAAF," I said. "They're sending us to an island with one of their field radar stations. We'll train the Aussie radarmen on the SCR-584 while we're there and gain a bit of field experience ourselves. Pack up the equipment and your gear. We leave at 1700. Fall out."

The captain drove off and the men turned and began packing their lockers and duffels but didn't seem too eager. A staff sergeant, he looked like a career army man and was about ten years older than me, stepped up and saluted. "Staff Sergeant Bridger, sir."

"Good to meet you, Sergeant."

He looked at me and seemed to take my expression for worry. "We'll be ready by 1700, sir."

"I would expect nothing less, Sergeant." He started to turn away and I asked, "Why are they sending a full platoon and support personnel with one radar unit to train the Australians? A platoon usually has three searchlights and two radar."

He hesitated, then replied formally, "There has been some bad blood between Lieutenant McCarthy, our previous CO, and the men. Things got a little out of hand. I think Cap wants you to calm the men down. They sent McCarthy home. The captain told us you were selected for your strong, even-handed leadership skills."

I didn't set him straight about how I got the assignment. I knew I could lead the platoon, but there had been no selection process.

***

I had no idea of the lay of the land, but the captain had pointed north when he told me to join the RAAF unit, so when the men and equipment were packed up, I pointed my jeep in that direction. The men followed me in the trucks. Assuming the Aussie radar unit would be somewhere close to the airstrip where I saw RAAF planes taking off, I approached the surrounding encampment. The guard was expecting us and directed us to the command tent.

"Lieutenant Sinclair, US Army reporting, sir," I told the CO, a broad-shouldered, prematurely grey colonel.

"You blokes are a welcome sight," he replied. "How did you come to have one of those fancy new radar?"

"It was sent here for training purposes," I replied. "We're lucky to have it. There aren't enough of them yet for general distribution."

"And when there are, they'll all go to Europe. Can't understand that Europe First policy. We're fighting a war here, too, and against a very aggressive enemy," he growled.

"I hear you," I replied.

"The blokes in the radar station are excited to use that kit, though. I'm assigning your platoon to radar station two. Captain Wilson is in charge. We're sending you in to warn us of any airborne threats as we start this new island-hopping campaign. I'm pleased General Kreuger agreed to let you train our men on the equipment."

"Yes, sir. May I ask what this island-hopping campaign is all about?"

He looked me up and down, obviously considering whether a first lieutenant should be let in on overall war strategy, and just as obviously decided against it.

"Corporal Taylor," he ordered, "take this platoon to join RAAF radar station two."

***

"Howdy, Mates. You the Yanks who're going in with us?" the unit Captain asked as I hopped out of the jeep.

"We are. I'm Lieutenant Sinclair, CO of this platoon."

"Glad to meet you, Sinclair. Captain Will Wilson. Call me Willy. I head up the Aussies on this trip."

He was about my height and weight with the same sandy hair and ruddy complexion. The two of us headed for his tent.

"Willy, have you found a long-lost brother?" one of his men shouted.

"Maybe distant cousin," he shouted back.

Turning to me, he said, "D-Day for this invasion hasn't been scheduled. We'll be on the island until they get the invasion force together and get 'em there."

"Where is the island?" I asked, hoping to get more details from a captain than the colonel.

"Ah, our lovely holiday spot is called Kiriwina. It's a tiny island off the coast of New Guinea. We have food, tents, and other supplies enough for your platoon. We're planning for a month's stay. Make sure your medic has enough Atabrine, anti-fungal, and other meds. Bring your own arms, ammo, and fuel. Other than that, we're set to go. Be ready to board the transports in three hours."

Rejoining my platoon, I spotted the combat medic. "What's your name. Corporal?" I asked.

He turned to stare at me. "Lance, sir. Corporal Lance,"

"Corporal Lance, get us a month's supply of Atabrine," I said, then called the Quartermaster Corps to request fuel and ammo. The sergeant said he would have the supplies to us in two hours. Lance was soon back with additional medications.

"I got everything but the antimalarials," he said.

"We need that damn Atabrine!" I shouted. Corporal Lance looked frightened. "Don't worry, I'm not blaming you. Let's see what we can do."

I drove back to the medical unit with him.

"You are supposed to have a three-day supply," the pharmacist on duty told me.

I showed him our orders and told him we would be on the island for at least a month before anyone else arrived. He called his superior, who finally showed up and called his superior, who sent me to his superior. Eventually, I stood in front of the mobile hospital commander, explaining my situation.

"Troops are moving into the staging area now. They should be able to get there within a week," he said.

"I doubt it," I replied. "Nobody has mentioned a landing date before late June, and it's not even the middle of May yet. Until D-day, my platoon is on its own. I need a month's supply."

"Not enough to go around," he said as he wrote an order for two weeks of medication.

"Pick this up," I told Lance, handing him the order. I returned to the platoon. The quartermaster's corps had delivered the ammo, fuel, and other necessary supplies. The men and the precious SCR-584 were ready to go, thanks to Sergeant Bridger. As soon as Lance returned with the medication, I drove toward the dock where I had arrived in Brisbane only five hours before, this time with an undertrained platoon and, to the Aussies, an unfamiliar radar unit in tow.

\*\*\*

Two British Landing Craft Tank, which we called LCTs, approached the dock. The big, ugly flatboats, thirty feet wide and a hundred fifty feet long, dropped their bow ramps. Captain Willy motioned for us to board first. We backed our vehicles up the ramp and to the rear of LCT, where we tied down the trucks and equipment with navy personnel's help. I ordered my platoon to sit against the big, square engine house at the back of the boat to be out of the way as the Aussies boarded. The two pom-pom guns mounted on either side of the engine house were unlikely to protect us from a full-scale attack, but at least we had some protection.

"Open your C rations, boys," Sergeant Bridger barked. "You never want to miss a meal if you can help it, and it'll probably go down better if you eat before we get out on the water."

The Australians still hadn't started loading their equipment.

"Lieutenant," called the captain of the craft. "Where's the rest of your equipment?"

"This is it," I told him. "The first truck is for troop transport and tows the radar unit with our personal equipment inside, the second truck carries the fuel and pulls the power unit, and the third is for troop transport and additional supplies. Just three trucks, two trailers, and a jeep are all we have."

"What?"

"It's new equipment, smaller, faster to set up. We have everything we need."

"What do you know?" he marveled, signaling the Australian forces to begin boarding.

***

As we got underway, the Aussies gathered around, asking questions about the SCR-584. We promised to show them how it worked once we set up on the island. I hoped that would give me time to review the manual and get in a bit more practice since I hadn't used this equipment in a while.

The LCT, not set up to transport troops on long trips, offered no hammocks or cots. Several of the Australians strung their own hammocks between the trucks. My men and I sprawled out on the deck, rolling in our blankets as the sea swells rocked the boat. We finally fell asleep as the landing craft moved around the rocky island protecting the bay, then headed north toward the island of Kiriwina.

At sunrise, the Aussie mess team handed out ration packs. I opened mine to find some uncooked oatmeal cereal with nuts and dried fruit. I watched the Aussies. They dumped the cereal into their tin plates, scattered the powdered milk packet over it, and poured water over the whole mess. I demonstrated the process to my men. They thought I knew what I was doing even though I had never eaten uncooked oatmeal like this. The oatmeal and the cup of coffee the navy provided turned out to be a pretty filling meal.

After breakfast, the men played craps or poker, talked, smoked, and watched the clouds and sea—whatever they could find to while away the time. I pulled out Sarah Gale's most recent letter to read.

*April 25, 1943*

*Dear Gene,*

*I don't know if you should make your letters to me so mushy. You do know that censors read all of our letters, don't you? I do love you, but I try really hard not to put anything embarrassing in the letters.*

*I did make it to Des Moines just fine. I looked up your Captain Henderson's mother when I got here. At first, she was a little standoffish, wondering why a WAAC recruit knocked on the base commander's door. But when I explained that I was only in the WAACs for the duration of the war and that the man I intend to marry was her son's executive officer, she was very friendly and helpful. She invited me in, and I met Captain Henderson's wife and son. She is a bit more passive than expected, but maybe Henderson wanted someone who would behave as ordered. Somehow, your descriptions of him make me think that might be true.*

*Tomorrow we start training. I have already met some very interesting girls in the barracks. I hope I can keep up with them on academic subjects. I can run circles around some of them on the exercise field.*

*Last night, some of them invited me to go with them to a bar near the base. They were really surprised when I told them I had just turned twenty-one and would love to go to my first bar with them. It turned out that Iowa doesn't allow places to sell alcohol by the drink except for beer, which is less than 5% alcohol. They wanted to get me a martini, but we drank a beer and returned to base. I had fun, but it was not as exciting as some of them expected.*

*I need to get a good night's sleep tonight so I will be ready for training.*

*I love you and miss you a whole lot.*

*Love*

*Sarah Gale*

Willy walked up behind me as I tucked the letter into my pocket.

"You got a Sheila back home?"

"Sure do. The cutest little red-haired, green-eyed beauty you ever saw."

"You have to watch out for those redheads. They've got spirit."

"She sure does. She joined the WAACS as soon as possible and is now in their officers' candidate school."

"My mom was one of those green-eyed, red-headed Scottish girls.

Dad was a much more reserved Englishman. Couldn't hardly keep up with her."

"Really? In my family, my Dad is a Scotsman, and my Mom is English. Dad's family went to America after the battle of Culloden, and my mom's family came on the Mayflower."

"Probably works better for the Sheila to be English and the bloke Scottish. My people got to Australia at about the same time. After Culloden, I believe."

Willy and I spent the rest of the day getting better acquainted. He had chosen a military career while I had been drafted into it. We were both thirty years old, but he was an experienced captain, and I was an inexperienced lieutenant. By our second night on board, we felt like old friends.

# CHAPTER 2

## LANDING

**A**FTER SEVERAL ENDLESS DAYS on a boat not meant for sea crossings, we spotted our destination one morning. The long, low island curved around a large natural bay. Coconut palms and a dense jungle backed a narrow strip of beach. Not mountainous like other islands we had seen around New Guinea, with only two real hills. Captain Wilson and I studied the island as we approached.

"There's a relatively flat spot on that hill to the north. Do you think we could set up there?" I asked.

"If we can get there, it would be an excellent site. It looks like the highest point, although that ridge on the neck there might be higher. But the northern site faces open water on three sides, so we could see what's coming from New Guinea, the Bismarck Islands, and the Solomons. The plantation overseer will know if we can get up there."

"It looks like grass on the steepest part. We can probably do it."

"Hope it isn't sawgrass."

\*\*\*

As we neared the island, a dark-skinned seaman came forward, climbed on the frame of the landing craft, and began calling out directions. I climbed up on the other side, spotting bright fish darting in and out of the many coral formations in the crystal-clear water.

"Your first view of a coral reef?" he asked. "Ten degrees starboard!" he shouted behind him.

"Yes. Stunning! The water's so clear, the coral so bright."

"And it can take out the bottom of the boat in a second if we don't follow the channel. This is my home island. He turned away and shouted, "Five degrees port."

"Why does the channel wind so much?"

"It's a natural channel that we've followed for generations. Unfortunately, they will have to blast out a bit more for the troop landing to fit the bigger ships."

"Too bad they have to destroy any part of this beautiful reef."

"This reef is only a tiny bit of the destruction this war is causing, both to my people and yours."

I nodded in agreement.

Slowly, the boat moved toward the island, winding through the narrow channel as the seaman called out directions. On the beach, palm trees waved in the breeze.

"It's a tropical paradise barely disturbed by man," I reveled. The seaman gave me a funny look but didn't say anything. I wondered if he saw something I didn't.

The LCT dropped its ramp onto the clear, sandy beach. Across the sand, we saw a road that the local seaman said led to the one plantation on the island.

The Australians quickly released the tie-downs and drove their first truck onto the beach. It immediately bogged down in the sand. The Aussies rushed to the jungle and cut palm and tree fern fronds to lay in front of the truck's wheels, making a path to the road.

"Push," shouted Willy.

Ten men put their shoulders to the back of a truck and managed to push it onto the path of fronds. Other men stood on the beach with machine guns and bazookas, watching the jungle and cliffs nervously. I wished I could tell then that there were no Japs on the island.

We moved the other trucks, trailers, and jeeps across the sand one by one. Then, as the skipper of the LCT raised the ramp, we waved and headed up the road. We made excellent progress through the palm trees on the well-maintained dirt road for a mile or so. At the plantation house, the British proprietor greeted us and assured us, ironically, that the island was free of Japanese. He introduced himself as The Reverend Mister Reynolds.

"Can we get up to the top of that rise?" Willy asked, pointing northwest.

"It won't be easy. There's a ridge that slopes to the southeast from the top. A narrow track at the end of this road will lead you there. Might take a bit of chopping to get the trucks through. Take the track until you see an even narrower track leading to the right. Past that point, making your road along the escarpment's edge will be easier than following the native trail."

We moved out on the plantation road.

On the other side of the plantation, the road suddenly gave way to a narrow footpath. The Australians pulled out axes and machetes without an order. A sergeant cut a pole barely longer than the trucks' width and laid it with its center at the beginning of the track. One man started chopping at one end of the pole and another at the other. Another man began chopping in the center when the first two were six feet in. Two others followed him, clearing the strips that were left. The Australians traded off much more often than we Americans had in jungle training. Workers alternated between Australians and Americans, switching off every two to three minutes to avoid exhaustion in the miserable heat and humidity.

The jungle fought back. Vines, thorns, and sawtooth leaves snagged our uniforms and clawed at our faces. Giant rhododendron bushes filled the spaces where the towering trees let light through. Tree ferns and thick bamboo blocked the path, and vines knit the trees together in a solid mass of vegetation. Colorful orchids bloomed all around us, and overhead, a bright array of birds twittered, seeming to laugh at us for thinking we could drive through the jungle. Insects, rodents, and snakes scampered and slithered out of the leaf litter at our feet, startling more than one man as we moved forward.

We stayed on the high ground, which was all of six feet above the level of the swamps and marshes we detoured around. Soon, a rough, winding road appeared through the jungle along the formerly narrow track. Generally, we avoided chopping down large trees, but occasionally, we had to cut down a tree to make room for the trucks to pass.

"Chop it down!" came the call and two American men moved forward with axes. The men wielding the axes didn't appear to have any experience chopping down trees. I moved forward and called for them to stop. They turned toward me with surprised and somewhat fearful expressions on their faces. I simply took one ax, waved them back, and started chopping.

"First, you chop a wedge out of the side toward which you want the tree fall," I explained. "It has to be low to the ground so the trucks can drive over it. Cut about a quarter of the way through the tree." With the newly sharpened ax, it took me about five minutes. It was one of the smaller jungle trees. "Then move to the other side and chop through to the wedge." I handed the ax back to the watching private. "Stand back, one on either side, and take turns with your swings," I watched until they got it right.

Bridger walked up beside me. "First time I ever saw a Lewie so eager to do grunt work."

"Those two were going to kill each other and take a few others out with them if I didn't teach them the right way," I replied.

The trucks crawled behind the sweating machete and ax wielders, moving forward to drag a fallen log away when necessary.

"This is what he meant by a bit of chopping?" I asked Willy as we inched forward.

"British!" Willy spat as he swung the machete through the trunk of a tree fern.

After five hours of backbreaking work, we reached the point where the narrow trail branched upward to follow the ridge to the hilltop. We stopped for lunch and a rest break.

Here, the ridge was a gently rounded hill. Farther up, a sharp-edged sixty-foot cliff fell from the south side of our proposed route.

"Crickey, it's all sawgrass," Willy exclaimed.

"The alternative is to try to go over those rock outcroppings and chop down dozens of trees," I said. "Here, all we have to do is mash down the grass."

"Right, that's all," Willy nodded.

Four Aussies pulled leather chaps and gloves out of their gear, took the truck-width pole, and stepped up the steep incline, mowing down the sawgrass with their machetes. When they called out "pothole" or "rocks," men scrambled up behind them with shovels or sledgehammers to smooth out the path enough that the trucks could pass. The trail rose gradually to about sixty feet above the swamps and jungle in the first mile. I realized why they called it sawgrass when I wandered too close to the edge of our trail, and a leaf caught my hand, ripping a gash in it as I pulled loose. I wrapped it in a bandage and trudged upward. Then we arrived suddenly at a rough coral outcropping that rose about forty feet, surrounded by different species of jungle plants, but they were just as thick as in the swamps below.

"Hold back!" Willy called. "No trucks will start climbing the hill until the road is cut to the level spot up there. We'll do some scouting for the best path up tomorrow. But, for now, hunker down here."

The sudden dark of the tropics descended. We set up camp between the jungle and the cliff. A cool breeze wafted in from the ocean, drying sweat and lifting the oppressive humidity. However, inside the tents, the temperature remained a balmy eighty degrees all night, the humidity still oppressive. Fortunately, my flashlight didn't reveal mosquitoes or other insects, snakes, rodents, or animals inside my tent as I prepared my bedroll.

*** 

We had barely begun widening the track the next morning when a tall man in a British uniform from the Great War came down the narrow trail, followed by a line of natives. One man had a large feather headdress, face painted with black, red, and white designs, a flower lei around his neck, and flowers tucked into grass bands on his upper arms. Other men wore flower crowns and less elaborate face paint.

"G'day," said the man in the uniform. "Welcome to Kiriwina. I'm Kevin Armstrong-Davis, and these fellows are part of my little army of coast watchers."

"G'day," responded Willy. "We're an advanced radar station, here to watch for aircraft. We plan to set up on the rise over there."

"Come visit their village," Armstrong-Davis said, gesturing at his entourage. "After you meet the chief, the natives can show you the best path to the rise."

"We appreciate that," Willy said. "This man is not the chief?" he asked, gesturing to the man with the feathered headdress.

"He's the emissary," said Armstrong-Davis, "sent in place of the leader. So if you attacked these blokes, the leader would still be alive."

I didn't envy this poor guy, sent as a sacrifice if we were hostile.

The natives helped us widen the path through the jungle until we reached a fork in the footpath. We left the trucks and equipment with a few guards and walked to the village. The Aussies and Americans stopped and stared. Women went about their work wearing short, brightly colored grass skirts tied around their hips, coral necklaces, and flower leis draped between their naked breasts. When I could pry my eyes off the women, I looked around the village. Children ran everywhere. Tiny thatched roofed houses, elevated on poles, surrounded a central yard. In the shade beneath the most prominent house, an old man sat on a chair made of a log.

"Come pay your respects to the chief," Armstrong-Davis invited Willy and me. "Don't let your head be higher than his. Do you have anything for a gift?"

"No. What would he want?" asked Willy.

"Empty shell casings, tin cans, food."

Willy turned to his supply chief, Corporal Rankin, while I asked, "Why would they want casings and tin cans?"

"They can make things out of them. Necklaces, little oil lamps, cut tin decorations. Shiny metal is scarce and valuable here."

Corporal Rankin soon trotted back from the trucks, lugging a case of canned peaches.

Two for one, I thought, food and cans. Clever!

We duck-walked toward the chief and presented him with the peaches, opening the box so he could see the cans. He repeatedly turned a can in his hand, confused about what it was. Finally, I took another can from the box, opened it with my knife, and speared a peach. As I lifted the peach slice from the can, Armstrong-Davis said, "Don't eat that. Eating in public is taboo here. People eat at their own hearths with their backs turned to each other."

"What in the world?" exclaimed Corporal Rankin.

"Food is scarce. They talk a lot about food, but they eat privately."

I pantomimed eating the peach, then dropped it back into the can, giving the open can to the chief. Willy and I backed away from the chief, and the group that had greeted us led us out of the village. I looked back as we left and saw the chief entering his home with the case of peaches under one arm, the open can held high in the other hand.

*** 

With the natives' help, we chopped and cut our way through another half-mile of rocks and jungle. Finally, circling a coral knob, then following a ravine up the last slight rise, we found ourselves on the highest point on the island.

"You set your unit up here," Willy said, choosing a small grassy clearing near the top of the ravine. "We'll go a little farther and see if we can find good spots for our stations."

The men pulled the trucks and trailers into position. Then, as I reviewed the manual, they leveled and stabilized the trailer, unfolded our pre-assembled antennae, connected the generator, and fired it up. Next, I worked with the radar operators to relearn the radar's operation while the other men set up tents and prepared to crawl into them for a break. Then I looked up the ridge, where the Australians still assembled their equipment and would for the next four or five hours.

"Let's give the Aussies a hand, men," I said.

The men groaned but followed me up the road.

"Blimey, you blokes set up already?" asked one of the Aussies. "Where's your equipment?"

"That's the new SCR-584 antenna," I told them, pointing to the round receiver on top of the equipment trailer, visible through the trees. "It folds flat for transport, then we just unfold it and hook it up. Takes about fifteen minutes. All the operational equipment is inside the trailer. We sit in there and monitor everything."

"And we sit out here, rain or shine, watching through these viewers. That is, once we get the bloody things set up." He sounded unhappy!

We laid cables, carried parts, and helped assemble the three Aussie radar units in record time—only three hours and forty-five minutes. The Aussies loudly and somewhat vulgarly expressed their appreciation, slapping their helpers on the back.

I had assigned several men to put up the Aussie tents while the rest helped with the radar. When the Aussies saw the fully erected camp, they cheered and broke out cases of beer to share with my men. I noticed several men were watching to see how I would react. I took a bottle myself and sat down with Willy. We shared a meal of cold C-rations, then returned to our camp in the dark.

***

I considered how I would deploy the men. Four men on the radar, four sentries, and two manning machine guns would give me six crews, provided I took a shift myself. They had all trained on the radar, but only fifteen were experienced radar operators. I set up a four-hour rotation for the men and took the first shift, feeling slightly slap-happy from fatigue. I had the radar operators give a refresher on the radar's operation to the entire shift, then sent the gunners and sentries out. When the midnight shift arrived, I repeated the process. I plied the replacements, groggy from just four hours' sleep, with leftover coffee brewed during the first shift.

Despite the late hour, I had trouble falling asleep, the air heavy with impending rain, and my mind churning over my first combat assignment. I felt the pressure of my duty, responsible for the lives and welfare of sixty men inexplicably sent to this remote island with one radar unit. Although quiet now, I couldn't help worrying about what would happen when the infantry landed. I finally dozed off and slept through a torrential downpour, the men later told me, before my alarm woke me. I checked on the new shift, then walked up the road toward the newly erected mess tent. As I approached, I saw case after case of peaches. We would be eating peaches at every meal.

# CHAPTER 3

## THE SHOWER CAMP

**I**S THERE ANY WAY we can at least get a fan in here?" asked Private Hanks. "I'm sweating like a pig. I don't know how you expect us to work under these conditions."

"Sure, I'll just run down to the Kiriwina Five and Dime and pick one up." I gave Hanks a "what the bloody hell" look.

He looked at me, his eyes wide like maybe I was dangerously crazy.

"That was a joke," I said.

"Oh. I'm not used to officers joking around. Could that be fraternization?"

"It wasn't that much of a joke," I replied. "This heat is the reason I keep the shifts at four hours. I don't want anyone to succumb to heatstroke from sitting in this metal box. Make sure you drink water and take salt pills."

"You actually thought of that?"

"Of course. We all have to look after each other. Even though I'm the one calling the shots, we are out here alone, and we have to depend on each other. We must do everything we reasonably can to stay healthy and combat ready."

The radio crackled to life.

"We've detected something to the west," an Australian voice said. "Do you see it? About two hundred eighty degrees."

"What do you see at two eighty?" I asked Hanks.

"A pretty significant rain squall," he replied.

"Just a rain squall. You can relax."

About fifteen minutes later, Captain Wilson and several men came slogging down the road through the rain.

"How could you determine that was a rain squall so quickly?" Willy asked.

"Here's another to the south," Hanks said. "Look at the pattern. Planes come in regular formations. This is just a blurry mass."

"We can't tell the difference on our screens. After we watch for a while and determine speed and direction, we realize it's a storm. But we waste a lot of time watching rainstorms."

"Our bandwidth is narrower, and the resolution of the scopes much better," I told him. "These new units give us a much clearer picture."

"When can we start training on this unit," Willy asked. "After all, that's why you're here."

"Why don't you send down one man per shift. I'll send someone to replace him, so you'll keep a full complement."

The arrangement worked out well for both contingents. Willy's men soon got up to speed on the new radar, and the men of both units began to interact more with each other, another good outcome. No aircraft appeared, but we spent hours tracking rain squalls and could predict almost every afternoon storm. Between shifts, I had the men pulverize coral rock to make paths, then put a thick layer of grass and leaves on top to protect our shoes and feet from any coral with sharp edges.

After relieving myself at the latrine that evening, I walked past Bridger's tent. Inside, several men were talking.

"He has no right to make us crush rock like we are on a chain gang," one of the men said.

"You're right," Bridger replied. "You're radar specialists, gunners, technical specialists, not some Negro service platoon."

"He's not such a bad guy," Private Hanks said. "It is kind of nice to have the camp looking neat and trim,"

The others laughed at him.

I walked to the closed flap and called, "Sergeant Bridger, could I see you in the HQ tent?"

"Now, sir?" Bridger asked.

"Now, Sergeant!" I shouted.

Bridger ducked out of the tent and followed me to the HQ tent.

He refused the seat I offered him, so we stood face to face.

"Sergeant Bridger," I said firmly, "I am aware that you have a few more years in the army than I have." He grinned as though I was about to put him in charge. "Which means that you should know full well what it means that you are a staff sergeant and I am a lieutenant. I am the CO of this platoon. I make the decisions, and your job is to support me in seeing that the men are prepared to carry out those decisions."

The grin disappeared, and Bridger said, "Yes, sir."

"With the number of men we have on one radar, they each work four hours a day. I'm sure you understand the kinds of trouble young men can get into when they have nothing to do, especially with a village full of half-naked women just down the hill. We have no maintenance crew with us on this island. Therefore, these soldiers will serve as both radar specialists and maintenance crew. Understood?"

"Yes, sir."

"And you will make sure that this is the most orderly, cleanest, and safest camp you have ever seen. Understood?"

"Yes, sir."

"You will also refrain from encouraging the enlisted men to engage in insubordination, disparaging their officers, or engaging in cruelty while encouraging healthy forms of release of the frustration at the less pleasant aspects of this assignment."

"Yes, sir,"

"Please see that all the men are using their mosquito nets properly before you retire. Dismissed."

He saluted and left. I stood, shaking in anger for some time before I retired for the night.

*** 

The Aussies worked hard. Perhaps unsurprisingly, about half their provisions were cases of beer. In just a couple of days, routines developed between them and us. When not on radar or rock duty, most of my men hurried to one of the three Aussie encampments. I decided to check what drew them there, aside from the beer.

Around the first radar installation, Camp One seemed deserted except for the men on duty.

"Where is everybody? I asked.

"The ones who aren't sleeping are in the poker tent," replied the sentry. "Third one on your right."

I ducked into the tent. The three US men at the table and those watching from the sidelines looked a little nervous at being caught playing poker, but the Australian corporal running the game said, "A dollar to get in, Lieutenant. We take either American dollars or Australian pounds."

"I'm just on a little tour," I replied. "I wanted to know where my men were off to."

"I'm out," Lance said. Another waiting American player stepped in as he stood, and the game continued.

"Be careful not to lose your entire paycheck," I told the Americans.

"Don't worry," said the corporal, "we don't let anybody lose more than three pounds in a week. Willy would shut us down otherwise."

"Yesterday, I won five, so I am still a bit ahead," Lance said, popping something into his mouth. I noticed his teeth and tongue were red.

"Are you chewing Betel?" I asked. "You know that's not good for you."

"It's just a little stimulant, like drinking coffee. It helps me stay alert."

"Be careful," I warned. My spirits sank a bit. I didn't want my men to rely on a stimulant. I knew it could have the opposite effect under some circumstances.

Before I reached Camp Two, I noticed a trail through the underbrush and down a steep incline. From below, I heard shouting. Carefully descending the path, I peered through the jungle vines. A naked man ran and jumped off a worn coral outcropping. A few seconds later, I heard a splash. Walking to the edge of the outcropping, I saw a sparkling pool surrounded by flowering hibiscus, gardenias, passion vines, and rhododendron, visited by brightly colored butterflies. Tea trees shaded the pool, birds of paradise flashing between their branches. A waterfall flowed from beneath the coral I stood on, splashing into the pool.

"Come on in, Lieutenant," several Australian swimmers called to me. My own men turned their backs when they realized I was there.

"Maybe later. It does look like a lot of fun."

"Fun and cool," they called back.

I longed to jump in and cool off, but I wanted to check out the third camp.

Several men chopped away at the jungle at the very end of the road. Willy among them.

"Willy, what are you doing?" I asked. He frowned and walked toward me a little stiffly.

"Making a Cricket pitch," he said.

"You must be avid players to work this hard to make a space to play."

"One of my men is a leading professional player in Australia. He doesn't want to get out of practice. First game is scheduled for Tuesday. Send up any players you have who might be interested."

"I don't think any of my men even know what cricket is. It's something like baseball, right?"

"Only that it involves a ball and a bat."

"I'll see if anyone is interested," I promised. "Could I have a word with you?"

"Yes," he replied guardedly.

We walked a little way up the hill. "Some of the training experiences your men have talked about are very upsetting," he began.

"My platoon was under the leadership of a lieutenant who ruled by fear. They've come to expect tyranny from officers. I've been trying to build rapport in the few days I've been their commander, but I haven't made much progress."

Willy visibly loosened up. "You aren't the bugger I been hearin' about? Your blokes've been tellin' horror stories about their CO, and I thought I'd totally got you wrong. How long were they under this tyrant?"

"Just short of a year."

"How long have you had the platoon?"

"Five days. I took command hours before we boarded the LCTs."

"You made a wise choice by taking a shift on the radar for yourself. Talk to the men, play with 'em. This is the lightest duty you or any of us will get in this war, and it'll give you a chance to get to know 'em. Get something going in your camp to interest the men. What're your interests?"

"I doubt the things I like would interest too many of the men. I like reading. I would love to have the time to study the local people's culture and the island's botany. I bake cakes and cookies when I have the chance."

"Well, try to spend more time with 'em, just larkin. They'll come around. By the way, I noticed you had some books in your tent. How 'bout we trade after you read them?"

"I'd love to."

Each camp became known for its different diversions. The library was in my tent, a constant poker game went on in RAAF Camp One, swimming in RAAF Camp Two, and cricket in RAAF Camp Three. My men were standoffish when I first joined them for swimming or cricket lessons, but they began to come around.

Willy regularly visited the tent for books throughout our stay on the island, and as we talked, we realized we were very much like long-lost brothers. Like me, he was a little more on the intellectual side than the average soldier. We spent hours sharing experiences and ideas.

***

One Sunday, a young native boy came to camp, inviting us to a worship service at the plantation house. Sixteen of my men jumped at the opportunity. We pulled out our dress uniforms, brushed them off, cleaned up as much as possible, and headed down. Twenty Aussies joined us, and we picked up seven natives in the village.

Overjoyed to move his service from the parlor to the big lawn in front of the house, The Reverend Mister Reynolds read the scripture in a booming voice. *"And ye shall hear of wars and rumors of wars: see that ye be not troubled: for all these things must come to pass, but the end is not yet. For nation shall rise against nation, and kingdom against kingdom: and there shall be famines, pestilences, and earthquakes, in diverse places."*

"War has come to our world! Yes, war has come to the very shores of this island. Yet our savior lives on and cares for us through all that may come from man."

He continued, but I tuned out, thinking of attending Sarah Gales' little backwoods church in North Carolina.

Mrs. Reynolds led us in "Onward Christian Soldiers," after which The Reverend dismissed us with a traditional benediction.

Following the service, the household servants served a delicious roast pork feast with various familiar vegetables and native foods. This being the first home-cooked meal we had eaten in some time, we "tucked in," as the Aussies said, and finished it in no time. Willy and I approached Mrs. Reynolds to thank her.

"Oh, we're so happy you're here!" she gushed. "We came to New Guinea as missionaries but had such terrible experiences trying to witness the cannibals. Donations stopped coming when the war started in England, so Cliff took this position as a plantation manager. The only time we've seen anybody from outside in the last three years is when the ship comes to take the copra. Won't you have some more sweet potato pie?"

"Thank you so much, but I can't eat another bite."

"Why don't you take some to the men on duty on the ridge. We have two whole pies left."

"Between the Australians and us, we have over a hundred more men on the ridge. It would cause some real problems to try to feed two pies to a hundred men."

"Oh, I see. I didn't realize you had that many men up there. We've seen very little of any of you."

"We have work to do, Ma'am," Willy said. "Between watching the radar and setting up camp."

He didn't mention the strict orders not to leave the ridge unless on armed reconnaissance missions. Attending Sunday service was the first exception.

Armstrong-Davis came over to discuss how he had set up the coast watch for the island.

"Most of the villages participate," he said. "I had to convince the matriarch of each village. That was more difficult than recruiting men. Each village watches its own portion of the coast, but they could all assemble into an army. Trobrianders are very warlike people. The government forbade intertribal warfare, which they've missed, so they're very excited about the possibility of fighting our enemies. They're vigilant and an excellent watch force."

"How did you come to be on the island?" I asked.

"I was the overseer before Cliff Reynolds. The company decided I was too old for the job, but I had nowhere to go. The Reverend and Mrs. Reynolds graciously allowed me to stay in the guest house. It was a boring existence until these latest hostilities broke out. Now I know that there was a reason I needed to stay. Only I know the island well enough to protect it from invasion."

Mrs. Reynolds rolled her eyes and looked heavenward but didn't say anything.

A muscular young native approached us. "You play cricket?"

On the verge of saying yes, Willy stopped when Cliff said, "Oh no. Don't play cricket with them. You'll lose. They have their own rules, which are violent and inappropriate. Your men might get slaughtered, possibly literally."

"We have some pretty good cricket players with us," Willy said.

"No, you don't understand. In Trobriand cricket, the home team always wins. If they don't, it can lead to violence. The game of cricket has replaced traditional warfare. The rules are so different you wouldn't recognize them. They will field forty men against you. And the game involves hours, or even days, of chanting and dancing."

"Perhaps we could watch a game of Trobriand cricket first," Willy suggested to the islander.

I turned to Cliff and Armstrong-Davis. "A little business. Colonel Squires radioed that D-Day for this operation has been set for June thirtieth. We hoped it would be earlier, but it was delayed due to the difficulty of gathering troops from around the Pacific. Apparently, they can't prepare the forces before the end of June. He also asked for a report on the coast watch from a military point of view. Could I meet some of your men?"

"I'll make the arrangements immediately," Armstrong-Davies promised, quickly striding off.

"We'd better get back up the ridge, too. Thank you so much for our hospitality," Willy said to Mrs. Reynolds.

\*\*\*

We heard men yelling as we approached camp in the slanting sunlight of late afternoon. Willy and I ran up the trail. Sergeant Bridger was attempting to break up a brawl in the center of camp.

"At ease, men," Willy shouted. The Australians stopped fighting immediately. Two Americans kept swinging, but Bridger and Lance pinned their arms behind their backs. I strode to the center of the crowd.

"What is the meaning of this?" I spat.

"He called me a bloody bastard," Private Jenkins replied, trying to break loose of Bridger's stronghold.

"Why?"

"Don't have no idea. I just beat him in a rasslin' match. Maybe he don't like to lose."

"In Australia, basturd means a tough guy. It was a compliment, not an insult," said Willy.

"Well, nobody's gonna call me a bastard no matter what language they speak."

"He just said it was a compliment, Jenkins," I said sternly. "You're confined to camp for the next ten days, and you will re-read the Pocket Guide to Australia section that deals with Australian slang."

Jenkins seemed about to argue, but when I stood taller and gave him the 'sit down and shut up' look I had used in high school, he said, "Yes, sir."

Lance took him and Corporal Rawlins to the medical tent to get patched up. Willy ordered the Australians back to their own camps. The rest of the platoon stood around, eyeing me warily.

"Men, we're on a primitive island with no medical facilities except Lance, the witch doctor in the village, and Mrs. Reynolds, a trained nurse without a clinic or supplies. We have to work with the Australians and with each other. Now, police the area and study up on Australian slang. No one leaves this camp for the rest of the afternoon."

I picked up litter with them and helped cover the paths with fresh grass. Sergeant Bridger worked beside me, acknowledging his acceptance of my leadership. The men were gradually coming to accept that I was not the enemy.

***

On Wednesday, four servants from the plantation arrived at the ridge carrying boxes. Inside the boxes were twenty-five sweet potato pies. I took ten for us and sent the rest up the trail to the Aussies. The men ran to their tents to pull out their kits while I hid pieces for the men on duty and set the rest of the pies on camp tables outside my tent, covering them with a mosquito net. Then, with the men assembled, I pulled off the net. Whooping and laughing, the men crowded in to get their pie. Within five minutes, only crumbs were left.

"I swear," Rawlins drawled. "My Mama couldn't make a better sweet tater pie than that."

When Jenkins, among the smaller group that had been on duty when the pies were served, came to get his pie, I asked him how he was doing on the Australian slang. He looked at the ground and mumbled something.

"Speak up, private! What did you say?"

"I said I cain't read," he replied.

"How on earth did you get into the army? Your draft board should've had you read a paragraph before they accepted you."

"I cain't read, but I got a mighty memory. So I just said what the guy in front of me said."

"And all through training?"

"Corporal Rawlins been readin' to me, sir."

"Well, you've shown remarkable abilities on the radar. So rather than just read to you, I will assign Rawlins to teach you to read."

"Sir, many a teacher has tried to teach me to read, but readin's beyond me."

"Nonsense! Anybody can learn to read if they try hard enough. A girl with Down's syndrome in my class in college could read. You're a lot smarter than she is."

"Maybe she learned to read, but I cain't."

"You work with Rawlins, or I'll send you home," I warned. I took a risk with that threat. The heat and rain were so disagreeable that he might want to go home, but he took it as a warning.

"Yes, Sir."

***

Empty fuel barrels began to pile up in our camp. Then, one day, I had an inspiration.

"Bridger, get some men to scrub out those barrels. Take the tops off and make sure the barrels are as clean as they can possibly get them."

I scoured the camp for parts.

"Who has some mechanical aptitude?" I asked Bridger.

"Jenkins is the best we have," he replied.

I sent for Jenkins.

"I'm sorry, sir, I haven't made much progress on those readin' lessons. I look at a word once, and it says cat, but the next time I look at it, the word is act. I really did try, sir. Please don't send me home. My folks need the money I'm sendin', and this's my only chance at a job."

"That's not why I asked you to come. See these barrels? If we can rig a valve in the tap on the lower side that can be opened by pulling on a rope from below, then put them on a platform in the sun, we'll have showers,"

Jenkins quickly grasped what I was thinking and had valves in six barrels before his next shift on the radar. Other men built an elevated platform from tree branches and pallets and placed the barrels on it. Then, they put more pallets on the ground under the valves.

"If we stretch tarps to those trees and collect water with them, we'll fill the barrels a lot faster," Jenkins said as he emerged from the trailer after his shift. "And if we tilt the barrels just a little, we can get more water out."

"Get some tarps and more rope," I told the men. "And cut some branches and vines to make an enclosure."

The next rainstorm filled the barrels, and from then on, we had lukewarm showers, sometimes hotter. Australians came down regularly, and we had a new designation. The Shower Camp.

# CHAPTER 4

## THE TOUR DE FORCE

**O**UR **ATABRINE RAN OUT.** Also, the pile of empty fuel barrels grew larger than the stack of full ones, with almost a month to go before D-Day. I visited the Australian camp to see how their supplies were holding up.

"We have fuel," Willy told me. "Bring your drums up, and we'll fill 'em. Unfortunately, I can't help you out with Atabrine. Our supply is running low, too."

I assembled the men. "No one leaves the tents without insect repellent. Always sleep under your mosquito nets. Without Atabrine, some of us are certain to get malaria, but if we're careful, maybe only a few of us."

Our camp reeked of the sweet chemical odor of insect repellent, and every cot had a mosquito net above it. I puffed on my pipe whenever I sat outside, hoping the smoke would supplement the insect repellent, and I encouraged my men to do the same with their pipes, cigars, or cigarettes. We had plenty of the latter.

Some of the men gathered the leaves of the tea tree the native girls recommended and either burned them in small fires near where they sat to create aromatic smoke or crushed them and hung them at the entrance to their tents or around their necks.

The men were listening to me, I realized with a smile. Their distrust of officers—well, one particular officer—had faded.

I decided to make another overture.

Willy had given me an exciting Australian novel, but I tore myself away from it to visit the poker tent. They were playing five-card draw.

"Deal me in," I said.

I got three kings on the deal. I did my best to keep a poker face as I drew two eights, giving me a full house. After raising the bet, I won the hand. On the next hand, I folded early with nothing. Two hours later, I remained in the game, not winning or losing more than the $3 limit.

As the days wore on, I watched few cricket matches, although I never really caught on to all the rules. Swimming became my favorite off-duty diversion. I relaxed completely when floating in that pool, hearing the waterfall splash out of the cave, smelling the gardenias and tea trees as sunlight filtered green through the canopy. I seemed to live in the tropical paradise my gal, Sarah Gale, had teased me about.

So long since her last letter, I wrote to her regularly, filling a large manila envelope in my tent to be sent when the invasion force arrived. Floating in the cool water, I felt sure she wrote to me as often. Hopefully, her letters would come with my battery. Thinking of her as I floated naked and alone in the pool, I began to get aroused.

A shout from above startled me. I opened my eyes and saw Armstrong-Davis standing on the cliff. "Do you want to tour the villages where I have coast watch groups?" he shouted.

"Sure!" I called, hoping he hadn't noticed the erection.

I grabbed my uniform and quickly pulled it on over my wet body. As I climbed the little cliff, I heard rustling in the bushes beside the trail. I must have scared off an animal that had come for a drink.

On the way back to our camp, Armstrong-Davis explained the tour.

"We'll visit the five largest villages. Each is a bit different from the others. You should bring some gifts for the war chiefs and matriarchs. Any shiny trinket will do in four of the villages, but a bit more will be required in the village by the bay. Some type of western food would be good."

In my tent, I packed a change of underwear and a few other items in my backpack, then gathered some gifts.

"Bridger!" I called. The Sergeant emerged from the radar trailer as I returned from the supply tent, "I'm going to inspect the coast watcher system. Can you hold down the fort here?"

"It'll be a couple of days before I bring him back," Armstrong-Davis said.

"Yes, sir," Bridger replied.

***

We stopped first at the village just down the hill from our camp, the women still working topless. Naked children splashed in the mud puddles, but this time, I noticed more. The thatched huts surrounded a broad central courtyard decorated with carvings and painted designs. Men lounged around the courtyard, stripping leaves from vines and braiding the vines into ropes. Several young women made stacks of banana leaves.

"What's with the banana leaves?" I asked.

"They use them for money and to make skirts. First, they scrape the leaves, inscribe designs on them, and finally bleach them in the sun. Those girls are gathering up the bleached leaves and tying them into bundles of fifty leaves."

"How much is a bundle of banana leaves worth?"

"About three pounds of pork. Depends on the season and current supply. Your peaches are bringing a high price right now. Two bundles per can."

"You have to be kidding! One can of peaches worth six pounds of pork?"

"The law of supply and demand."

Everyone looked up as we entered the courtyard, stopping their work. The war chief approached us, inviting us to sit under his stilt house. Armstrong-Davis translated as the chief described his coast watch activities. Every day, he sent different men to check his section of the island. One of them had reported seeing a ship in the distance. Another had spotted a man from another village in their part of the island. They had challenged his village to a cricket match to start immediately after the yam harvest.

"I'll let Willy know he'll have the opportunity to watch," I told Armstrong -Davis. "When will it be?"

"The yam harvest will be getting underway soon. First, there'll be the traditional celebration, then the Cricket match will start. It will probably be a big one. Maybe last until planting season. The yam harvest looks good, and the upper village chief is paying for the festivities. He has become quite wealthy by having his boys go through your garbage heaps."

"When is planting season?" I asked.

"November."

"A four-month cricket game?"

"I told you their rules were different."

We thanked the chief for his work, gave him an empty tin can, and backed out from under his house.

"Now we have to offer a gift to the matriarch," Armstrong Davies said. "Nobody does anything except on the orders of the matriarch."

The matriarch met us in front of her home. We thanked her for allowing the villagers to participate in the coast watch. I gave her a handful of metal washers I had found among our supplies. I thought the washers could be used to make jewelry. When I handed them to the matriarch, she beamed, gave them to her daughter, and ordered her to take them inside the house.

***

I walked silently toward the coast and the next village.

"Something bothering you?" Armstrong-Davis asked.

"Those children were playing games that seemed, well…"

"Erotic?" he asked.

"Yes."

"They encourage sexual play. Teenagers have special night hous-es where young couples go to have sex. That's how the girls decide who they'll marry."

"The girls? Don't the boys have anything to say about it?"

"They can avoid having sex with girls they don't like, but the girls decide. It's a matrilineal and matriarchal society. You belong to your moth-er's clan, and your mother owns the house and fields."

"But they have tribal chiefs."

"War chiefs. They fight wars, grow yams, and carve wood, but the women run things."

"So those teenage boys don't have to provide for all the illegitimate babies they father."

"There aren't that many babies because they eat so many yams. Yams have something in them that keeps the girls from getting pregnant. Wom-en also make some sort of herbal tea just for teenage girls. It wouldn't sur-prise me if the tea had some baby-stopping property. Of course, they don't have any venereal disease, either, so that's not a problem."

"Do they ever get married, or do they just keep sleeping around?"

"If the girl stays in the morning instead of going home at sunrise, they're married. It's as simple as that. The man gives her mother some sort of gift. He also has to give her brother or uncle a gift for the yams he provides. Men use yams for money like women use the decorated banana leaves, but a man's not responsible for his wife's children."

"So, who supports all those children I see running around?"

"A woman's brother, the child's uncle. He also grows yams for the woman's married daughters until their brothers are old enough, as uncles, to take over. When the yams are delivered, the husband slaughters a pig if he decides the yam supply is generous enough, and everybody celebrates. It's quite a ceremony, with some exciting dances."

When we arrived at the next village, all activity stopped like in the first, and the people gathered around us.

"Can they afford to stop what they are doing because we're here?" I asked.

"They don't have the same concept of time as Westerners. There's only now. And right now, the most exciting thing around is us."

"Don't they have to keep track of time so they know when to plant and harvest the crops?"

"The new year starts when a certain worm appears in the fields. Then, when the rain is right, they plant. They harvest when the yams reach the ripe stage. They have different words for an immature yam, a growing yam, and a ripe yam. But they don't plan, except to decide that the cricket match will follow the harvest festival. Things like that."

We met with the village war chief and talked about the observations of his warriors. They had seen nothing of consequence except the LCTs that had dropped us off. I presented the chief and matriarch the empty cans from the C rations I had been eating. With all the C rations being consumed, empty tin cans would soon decrease in value, but today, the natives still consider them a treasure.

The matriarch offered us a hut for the night. A pubescent girl took my hand and tried to lead me toward the sex house.

"How do you say no?" I asked Armstrong-Davis, and he doubled over in laughter at the expression on my face.

"Just pull your hand away," he said. "She won't be offended. They've been watching through the bushes at the pool. She must have concluded you were well endowed."

The heat rose in my face, and I pulled away as the girl and her friends giggled and pointed at me. I fell asleep quickly on the grass mat in the hut, exhausted from the long walk along the jungle path, and dreamt of Sarah Gale.

*** 

In the morning, we followed a path south to a larger village close to the bay. The youngest war chief we had met so far came out from under his hut as we approached. He startled me by shaking our hands and saying, in perfect Australian English, "G'day, major. Welcome. I see you've brought the American officer with you. Is the invasion near?"

"I don't know that you would call it an invasion," I said. "The landing is scheduled for the last day of June."

"I understand you're bringing over two thousand troops to the island in the first wave and potentially six to eight thousand more after that. We definitely consider that an invasion."

"I can see your point of view," I replied.

Some residents wore Western clothes, and the women cooked in metal pots.

"You notice the differences between our village and some of the others. My grandmother felt we should learn more about your ways after the first missionaries came to the island. When the anthropologists started coming, she studied them as much as they studied her. Then she sent my aunt, and later me, to be educated in Australian and English schools so we could understand some of your bizarre customs. Things like obsessively watching your calendars and watches but practically ignoring the rising and setting of the sun and the passing of the stars and seasons. After I graduated from college, I served with the major here in your last war."

He didn't look nearly as old as Armstrong-Davis.

Our visit with the chief revealed no enemy activity. I realized this matriarch would probably not be happy with washers or empty tin cans, so I pulled out the rest of the C rations I carried and handed them over to her. The peaches delighted her, as did the Spam.

The story stayed much the same in the other two villages we visited that day. No action, but the duty made the warriors feel essential. On the way back to camp, I asked Armstrong-Davis if we should have a feast for the coast watchers to thank them for their job.

"Gifts of food would be very welcome, but the tradition of gift-giving and feasting is extremely complex on these islands. It's all tied up with political power and status. You're probably better off just giving small gifts here and there. That way, you don't accidentally become obligated in ways you don't understand. There's a very complicated interisland trading ring in which the war chiefs try to one-up each other. It is best to leave that alone."

***

"What did you learn?" Bridger asked when I returned.

"For one thing, the teenage girls from the village have been watching us swim from behind the bushes."

"Most of the men know that already. They sneak down to the village sex house at night and have a little fun with the girls?"

"What?!" I exclaimed. "We have to stop that!"

"Why?" he asked. "The girls like it, the men like it, and the parents don't seem to have a problem with it. The matriarch and the war chief don't see any problem with it. I say, 'When in Rome, do as the Romans do.'"

This news concerned me a great deal. So, I went to talk with Willy about it.

"It's the custom here. The matriarchs are encouraging it because they believe when the spirit of the Australian or American man enters the woman, it produces strong, healthy babies. They've probably interbred for so long that they could use some new blood."

My science and pharmacy background kicked in. "But our men might carry venereal diseases. Those are unknown here and will spread rampantly once they're introduced because of the encouraged promiscuity."

"We can take care of that with penicillin, you know," Willy said.

"Provided they know they have venereal disease and come in for a shot," I countered.

"We'll get all the young blokes to report to the clinic for exams when the field hospital arrives. It will only be a couple of weeks now. I wouldn't worry about it."

"But what about the girls?"

"The little Sheilas will get their big healthy babies; if they need it, we can get a shot for them too. So it isn't as big a problem as you're making it out. Under ten percent of the boys in the whole army have any venereal disease, and it's higher in Europe than here, so I think you're overestimating the chances."

"We are lucky to have miracle drugs like penicillin, aren't we," I responded. "It puts our conventional mores in a whole new light. "

# CHAPTER 5

## TYPHOON

**A** WEEK LATER, THE sentry woke me before midnight. "Sir, we saw lights winding through the bay. Probably three boats out there."

"I bet the advance party has arrived," I said.

"How do you know it's the advance party?"

"The enemy would bring more boats and at least try to be secretive. They wouldn't light up the bay and make themselves obvious." I brought out a telescope to watch. We were three days past the full moon, the light still bright enough to make out a large ship beyond the reef with two PT escorts and two landing craft in the bay. With the scope, I read the large letters on the side of the landing craft nearest the beach.

"American!" I declared. "It's that new landing craft, vehicle, and personnel. LCVP."

We passed the telescope around as the LCVPs pointed spotlights at the beach, and soldiers poured off, looking like ants crawling across the beach. The plan called for constructing a causeway, so they must be engineers with some infantry to protect them.

Close to shore, one of the landing craft crossed the path of the other one. They crashed into each other. One plywood side of the hastily built craft collapsed, and the damaged craft took on water. A few men swam for the beach, and others clung to the LCVP, calling for help, evidently unable to swim. The two PT boats moved in to rescue them.

"Blimey, don't your navy know how to bring a landing party to shore?" asked the Australian radar operator who had just finished his shift with us.

"It's dark, and maybe there was a riptide," said Mike Mitchell, a gunner from California.

I took back the telescope. One landing craft remained tethered to the transport ship, apparently loading men and equipment, while another floated, empty, around it.

"I don't think they have much experience with this. The Australian navy has always managed the landings before," I said.

We watched for a couple of hours, but it looked like it would take all night to get these men off the transport and onto the beach. I ordered everyone not on duty back to bed and told the sentries to wake me again if there were any new developments.

*** 

"Sir, sir, the wind shifted, and there seems to be a storm brewing," the sentry said, shaking me awake. Salmon-colored clouds rimmed the horizon.

Private Jenkins came running from the radar trailer as I stepped out of the tent.

"Sir, there's a huge storm coming. It might be a typhoon."

The wind continued to pick up. Finally loaded with men, all three remaining landing craft bobbed near the reef.

Corporal Rawlins showed up. "I confirmed. It's a typhoon. Could be three hundred miles across."

Coming from tornado country, I told him to get all the men into the cave from which the waterfall fell into the pool.

"No sir," Rawlins replied in his Mississippi drawl, "the typhoon will bring heavy rain flowing through these porous rocks and filling that cave with water. We could drown. We'd be best off staying here, away from the flooding and storm surge. But we better warn the ships to get away from the reef."

I got on the radio and adjusted the frequency. "This is Alpha Alpha Alpha Two Two Seven. Major storm approaching at sixty degrees. Over."

Nothing. I repeated myself.

"Who the hell is this?" a voice full of authority replied.

"The radar unit on the island. A typhoon is coming. Move away from the reef. Over."

"I'll check our barometer. Over." The voice seemed to sneer.

The landing continued, the pilots of the LCVPs struggling to get them through the natural opening in the reef as the winds ahead of the typhoon increased.

"I don't think they have the equipment they need to build that causeway," said MacDougal, a driver for our platoon.

"They didn't get any communication equipment unloaded, either," our radio operator, Sims, added, handing the scope to me. "I saw it on an LCVP that turned back."

"I hope they move away from the shoreline," I said as I returned the radio to Sims, who scrambled into the radar trailer to get it out of the oncoming rain. "But we can't stand here watching. Pick up anything that's loose and get it into a truck or trailer."

"Look! I think Armstrong-Davis has the Coast Watch assembled to attack." Jenkins warned.

"Jenkins, Rawlins, get down there and tell him they are American allies."

"Seems to have figured it out himself," Jenkins said.

I peered through the scope to see Armstrong-Davis and the leader of the landing party shaking hands. Armstrong-Davis pointed toward the plantation, and they marched off in that direction.

\*\*\*

"Move the trucks and trailer around to the leeward side of the knob, where we'll be protected!" I shouted over the rising wind. "Put the radar trailer up against the rocks with the trucks around it! I'll have hell to pay if I let that thing blow away. Tie it down good!"

"Get some C-rations into the trailer and trucks. Take down the antenna. We don't want to lose that. Flatten the tents and put something heavy on top of them. Tie down everything you can. Use every rope or chain you can find. Take down the water collection tarps and use them to hold supplies in place. Weigh down the edges."

Men scurried around the camp, following my orders.

"Bridger, take a squad to the Australian camps and help them dismantle their antennae! Take shelter in their vehicles. They have more trucks."

"You expectin' us to sit out a hurricane up here on this ridge?" Sergeant Bridger asked me.

"What choice do we have?" I asked. "Rawlins nixed the cave and seemed to know what he was talking about. Where can we go otherwise in this weather?"

He walked away, shaking his head. I wondered if he knew anything else that might save us. Surely he would have told me anything he knew since it would save his butt and the platoon he had protected for so long.

The men scrambled to prepare our camp for the typhoon, blowing full force by midday.

"Get your packs and take them into the vehicles with you," I shouted as sheets of rain fell. "Lance, make sure you have all the medical supplies with you."

As I climbed into the driver's seat of the fuel truck and put a tarp between me and the windshield, I knew we would not be completely safe anywhere. A falling tree might still smash any one of the vehicles, but the tarp in ours would protect against broken glass. I wished I had thought to tell all the men to put a tarp up. Lance climbed in beside me.

"This is our most dangerous spot," I told him. "I want you in the trailer where you'll be safest so you can take care of anyone injured by the storm. Send a couple of other guys up here."

Three privates soon joined me, overflowing the cab.

"We were losing our minds in the trailer," Jenkins told me as he squeezed in. "We were packed in like sardines. It's pitch black with the door closed and the radar off. And it's rocking like crazy. Lance told us to come up here."

"We have the trailer braced and tied down. I doubt it will tip, but we can at least see what's coming here."

We sat in the rocking truck, listening to the wind. We watched the rack holding the shower barrels blow over, and the barrels bounced out of sight over the cliff. Leaves and twigs slashed through the air, plastering the truck windows in green. I kept talking, trying to keep the claustrophobic privates from panicking.

"In Kansas, we have tornadoes. The winds are much faster than this but don't last as long. They just blow through and take what they want with them. Once, I saw a tornado go through my uncle's pig farm and take the pig houses into the air. They went twirling around just like the house in *The Wizard of Oz.* Have you seen that movie?"

"Can you stop talking about storms and houses blowing away? That's not helping," one of the men said.

"How about singing?" I asked.

"As long as it is not 'Over the Rainbow.'"

We sang every silly and patriotic song I could think of until the dim light faded to darkness. Then we curled up the best we could, falling into a fitful, often interrupted slumber.

By morning, the wind had died down a lot, no longer hurricane force. I climbed out of the truck, surveying the damage. The camp was a mess of fallen leaves and branches, all sopping wet. However, birds chirped, and rushing water indicated that the little stream that dropped into the pool had become a raging torrent, and the cave filled with water, as Rawlins predicted. I felt relief that I had followed his suggestion and horror that I might not have. We could all have drowned if I had my way.

The men set to work gathering our scattered supplies. Aside from our shower barrels, we found everything. Unfortunately, a large branch had blown down on several of the tents and punctured one of them. Men collected our small supply of food and repitched the undamaged tents. Others moved the vehicles back to their original positions.

"Myers, take your squad and get the radar operational again. Hughes, take a couple of men and check on the Aussies. I'm going down to talk with the leader of the advance party."

***

I scooped the water off the floor of my jeep, cleared the windshield of leaves, then bumped and slid down the rough path to the plantation. The wind buffeted the jeep, and water dripping from the trees soaked me to the skin.

I saw Cliff Reynolds first.

"Some storm," I said.

"It was a doozie. We have one about every two or three years. The natives predicted it a couple of days ago. The Lieutenant Colonel said you warned them off. I assume someone from the village up there told you about it."

"No, we saw it on the radar."

Reynolds lifted his eyebrows.

"Where's the Lieutenant Colonel?" I asked.

"Around the front lawn, blowing hard as though the typhoon came intentionally to spoil his landing."

I strode around the plantation house, spotting Armstrong-Davis speaking with the agitated Lieutenant Colonel as the native servants dragged fallen branches away.

"There are sixty men on coast watch, but we can deliver over three hundred capable soldiers if necessary," Armstrong-Davis said.

The red-faced colonel puffed out his cheeks, blustering like the wind in the aftermath of the typhoon. "You have just said there are not any Japanese on the island. We're here to build an airbase as a jumping-off point for missions to New Guinea. Why would we need your spear chuckers? We'll have over two thousand highly trained troops here within the week, and there isn't any enemy to fight. If the Japs decide to notice this island, we'll let you know. In the meantime, you can continue having your little platoon watch the coast, but we won't need regular reports. Just come to us if you see anything unusual."

He watched Armstrong-Davis walk away. I think he had just burned a bridge, if not a causeway. He turned to the major next to him. "Damn Brits and Aussies, always wanting to provide redundant information. We're here to save their asses. Why do they think they know more than we do."

*Because sometimes they do,* I thought. I approached the Colonel and saluted.

"Where did you come from?" he asked, looking at my soaked uniform and AAA patch on my shoulder.

"The radar unit on the ridge."

"You're with the Aussies?"

"Yes, sir. My platoon is attached to their unit. We've been here for over a month and haven't seen any Japanese activity."

"That's why we chose this island. A nice, Jap free jumping off place for the next operation. If we can ever get it underway."

"We were led to expect that the Japanese might show up."

"Never can tell; they still might. Never know what those bastards're up to. We didn't inform the men that there weren't any Japs. We wanted them to come ashore as though they were under fire. Makes 'em better prepared for the real deal on the next island."

"I understand," I said. "They obviously needed the practice. So how did everyone make do through the typhoon."

"Are you the one that informed the Navy folks about that? You said you saw it on the radar, right? Aren't you supposed to be watching for aircraft? If you hadn't scared the Squids off, we could have at least gotten some of the equipment unloaded before the storm blew in."

"Yes, sir, I informed them. Didn't want your equipment and the landing craft on the bottom of the ocean or shipwrecked on the reef. We have the new SCR-584. With it, we can track storms and see any incoming aircraft simultaneously in scan mode. Have you seen this radar?"

"No, and I don't particularly care to as long as you men keep us informed of what's coming."

"Did you bring additional malaria prophylactics?" I asked.

He looked at me with a blank stare.

"Anti-malaria pills."

"We don't have any. We took ours this morning and will take 'em again when the medics come to hand 'em out."

"I only brought a two-week supply for my men when we came. I specifically asked that additional pills be sent with the advance party. Did no one talk to you about that?"

"What difference can a week without the pills make?" he asked. "It takes more than a week to come down with malaria."

"We've been without them for almost three weeks already, and mosquitoes carrying malaria have bitten us numerous times. Without the pills, we have an eighty percent chance of developing the disease."

"Well, we just have to take our chances," he said. "Those damn pills just make us all look like yellow-faced Japs. Don't know why we have to take them. We don't even have the necessary equipment to start building the causeway. I have a whole damn company here with nothing to do. At least your men can do what they were trained for. Now get back up that hill and get them to doing it."

"Yes, sir!"

He walked away, not caring who overheard what he said: "Half the crew still on the transport ship, a whole company of infantry with nobody to fight. And why does this kid think we should provide him with pills?"

I drove back up the slick track to the ridge, cursing about the army's ineptitude, and grew angrier as I climbed. As I neared the top, I gunned the engine to get through a puddle. The jeep jolted out of the puddle, hit a rock, spun half circle, slid off the track, and landed sideways against a tree clinging to the rocks below. I flew another ten feet down the ridge and rolled under a fallen log. I could not find the energy to move. As I lay, chills and shaking battered my body.

# CHAPTER 6

## A DIFFERENT WAR ALTOGETHER

**I** **AWOKE WITH MY** left ear in a marsh and a sharp pain in my left foot. I pushed myself up and lifted the pained limb from the muck to find that a broken branch had punctured my boot. But what sort of boots were these? Definitely not my army-issued combat boots. I'd never worn such boots. I pulled the branch out of my foot, and blood poured from the hole. Not good!

I looked around for a medic. Instead, I saw a ring of men in a motley assortment of homespun shirts, blue or green uniform coats, and leather jerkins. Colonial uniforms. Was I dreaming?

"Has anyone got a bandage?" I asked.

"Tear a piece off your shirt, Colonel," one of the men said. "The surgeon and supply wagons ain't been seen."

*Colonel?* I pulled my linen shirt from the once-white breeches and cut a strip from the bottom with the hunting knife hanging from my belt. Then, pulling off my boot, I wrapped the wound, sure it would be infected by the end of the day.

Although I believe I appeared resolute to the men following me, even as I limped along on my throbbing foot, my mind churned. How did I become a colonel in the Revolutionary War? How did I know these woods? And most of all, should I have taken command, or would I be court-martialed for ordering a retreat when General Thompson had said attack?

"Proceed upriver to the village of Berthier, across the St. Laurence from Sorel. From there, we can cross to rejoin General Sullivan." I ordered.

As we ran, more American soldiers joined us. I led a growing band of men toward Berthier, where I hoped we could cross to Sorel and rejoin General Sullivan's forces. The pain in my foot increased. I began to fall behind. A small group of junior officers surrounded me, urging me on. I began to feel dizzy and finally collapsed, unable to continue.

\*\*\*

A few minutes later, I came to be surrounded by bare, dark-skinned feet among the ferns. In addition to the sounds of excited Trobianders, I heard Australian and American English curses and what sounded like a herd of elephants crashing through the brush.

"Lieutenant, Lieutenant, wake up!" I heard an Australian voice call to me.

A group of khaki-clothed legs swam into view.

"Hold on while we get you out of here," another voice said. I lost consciousness again as they lifted me.

I came to slowly, with the world spinning around me.

I groaned.

\*\*\*

A face appeared above me. "You're awake. We've been so worried. You've been babbling about islands. We can't get to any of the islands. The British hold all the river crossings."

Not again! Above me, oak leaves waved in the breeze. A woodpecker tapped an insistent rhythm on a nearby tree. Gradually, I became aware of throbbing pain in my foot and gunfire in the distance. Two men in dirty blue coats worked to cover the branches above me with dry leaves.

"Where are we?" I asked.

"We really don't know. You're the only one who's been here before. You told us you followed this trail in the French-Indian War, but once you became incoherent, we got hopelessly lost. The British are almost upon us.

I realized I lay in a hollow under the roots of a large tree that had blown over. As the gunfire approached, the two men crawled into the damp cavity where I lay and nestled into the leaves.

"Lie still, Colonel. They're coming closer."

I lay back, losing consciousness again.

\*\*\*

"Here you go, Lieutenant. Drink this."

I swallowed a couple of times, then choked, coughing up the water.

"What do we do?" asked an American voice.

"Not much we can do until we get some medicine," replied an Australian. "I sent Lance down for some. He shoulda been back already. We may have to send a search party after him." A hand touched my shoulder. "Hold on, Sinclair. Help is on the way."

Again, I faded out.

\*\*\*

Someone shook me awake. The captain in the blue coat spoke softly.

"Coast clear." We climbed out of the hole. "Which way, Colonel?"

I looked around, breaking a relatively straight branch off the dead tree for a walking stick. Even though I felt confused and disoriented, the men seemed to be counting on me. Taking my bearings from the stars, I pointed, and we began warily creeping through the woods, skirting British encampments and searching for the French village where I knew we could ford the river. Night became day. We rested briefly, then proceeded with the sun well up, neither seeing nor hearing any sign of the British.

My mind functioned in dual mode. One part, Colonel Arthur St. Clair of the Continental army of 1776, knew that I had ordered a retreat from Quebec after General Thompson's disappearance, just ahead of the British forces. In another part of my mind, Eugene Sinclair, lieutenant, US Army, knew Canada had never joined the Revolution and would, for some time, remain a British colony.

We finally found a road churned by the feet of the troops I had sent in this direction two days earlier. Voices approached, and we darted into the underbrush at the side of the road.

"They're speaking French," I whispered to the captain. "I'm going to ask them for something to eat."

I stepped out of the brush and said, "Bonjour."

The three men approached us in clothing that was even more worn than our own uniforms, carrying ancient weapons. They stopped and greeted me, first in French, then in English.

"Do you possibly have any food you could spare?" I asked.

"Come, come. We will take you to our village," one of the men said. "My name is Henri. You must refresh yourselves before you continue on."

We followed them, turning onto a path several hundred yards up the road. About ten houses stood in a clearing not far from the road, surrounded by corrals and small fields. A girl in the nearest garden saw us coming and ran inside to alert her mother. The woman greeted us at the door with cold water from the well.

"My wife, Mary," Henri said.

"Welcome. Supper is almost ready," she told us in British-accented English. "You look as though you could use something to eat. Please wash up at the barrel out back."

After washing I limped toward a seat by the fire. Mary asked, "Has your foot been injured? May I cleanse and bandage it?"

I nodded, uncertain what she could do, and sat on the settle. It was aching with the early effects of infection, so any cleansing and a bandage other than a scrap of sweat-soaked shirt would undoubtedly help.

She pulled off my boot, unwrapped the wound, and whispered, "Oh dear!"

Her daughter stood by with a basin and a bottle of something.

"I'll clean it with a tincture of herbs in alcohol," she informed me. "It'll sting, but it's necessary."

As she poured the alcohol over the wound, I cried out. She stopped.

"Continue," I said, gritting my teeth.

She thoroughly scrubbed my foot, then spread a thick layer of honey on a clean cloth and bound it around the wound.

After supper, Mary rolled out clean pallets on the cabin floor, and we fell asleep as soon as we lay down.

I drifted toward consciousness during the night, seeing a US Army private's fresh, clean face. "You're safe, sir. Calm down. Drink a little of this."

I drifted off again.

*** 

Henri delivered us to Sorel in his bateau the next morning, where the remnants of the army had gathered. General Sullivan greeted me as I limped into the fort, although Mary's herbs and honey seemed to have stopped the infection.

"St Clair, congratulations. You managed to get over sixteen hundred men back safely. Without your guidance, the whole of the Canadian Branch of the Continental Army would have been lost."

"Thank you, sir. Unfortunately, General Thompson's been captured."

"Along with seventeen or eighteen other officers," Sullivan replied. "We feared you might also have been captured, but we're pleased to see you back here. We leave for Crown Point in the morning."

After their long march back to Sorel, I returned to my Pennsylvania regiment, exhausted and hungry. I gave them a moving speech about their part in creating a new nation, forgetting that the Declaration of Independence would not be signed for another couple of weeks, and sent them to their tents to prepare for the march to Crown Point. They grumbled about having nothing to eat.

*** 

Over the next few days, I drifted between riding horseback through the woods in the eighteenth century and tossing and turning on a cot in the twentieth. Then, there was a period with neither dreams nor consciousness. When I woke, I discovered my regiment had moved to Fort Ticonderoga at the opposite end of Lake Champlain. General Horatio Gates arrived to take charge of the fort and the remnant of the Northern army.

"St. Clair, your voice carries well. Please read this document to the men," ordered Gates.

My twentieth-century mind came to the forefront. I had memorized the Declaration of Independence in fourth grade and recited it at our little town's Fourth of July celebration. Holding the handwritten document copied from the original only days before, my heart beating fast and my hand shaking. I began.

"In Congress July Fourth Seventeen Seventy Six. The Unanimous Declaration of the thirteen United States of America.

"When in the course of human events it becomes necessary for one people to dissolve the political bands which have connected them with another and assume among the powers of earth the separate and equal station to which the Laws of Nature and of Nature's God entitle them... And for the support of this Declaration, with a firm reliance on the protection of Divine Providence, we mutually pledge to each other our Lives, Fortunes, and Sacred Honor."

The men cheered wildly.

"You are now the Army of the United States of America," Gates declared. "We are fighting for the continued existence of our new nation."

# CHAPTER 7

## RECOVERY

**A** **BRIGHT BEAM OF** sunlight landed on my face as someone opened the flap of my tent. I moaned.

"Lieutenant Sinclair, you're awake!" exclaimed Corporal Rawlings.

"Lieutenant?" I mumbled.

"Sir, you've been down with malaria. We think you've been hallucinating. You kept talking about hogs and muskets and getting supplies loaded."

I tried to sit up, but I felt incredibly shaky and failed.

"How long?" I asked.

"Five days, sir."

I had lived a whole summer in my dreams.

"You seem to have had some rather vivid hallucinations," he said.

"They didn't seem like hallucinations. I became a different person. It was bizarre."

"Good to have you back, sir."

"Has there been any sign of enemy aircraft?"

"No, sir."

"I should see to the duty roster."

"That's all being handled. It'll be a while before you're strong enough to stay out of bed for very long."

Corporal Rawlings brought me an egg purchased from Mrs. Reynolds, which he had fried. A real, fresh egg, straight from the chicken. It took almost more energy than I could muster to eat it.

"Has anyone else had malaria?" I asked Lance when he came in a little later.

"Four others, but you were by far the worst case. The others were each confined to their cots for less than forty-eight hours."

I lay in my cot, trying to remember life in the twentieth century on this Pacific Island ridge. I had begun to think like St. Clair, to react like St. Clair. This war moved much more quickly than the Revolutionary War. We drove mechanical "beasts" on land, flew through the air, and crossed the seas in ships, rarely at the mercy of the wind. I spent the day trying to prepare my mind for that quickness.

*\*\**

Early the following day, I made my way to a camp chair overlooking the bay. The engineers worked quickly. A broad coral and concrete causeway now obliterated the center of the reef. Bulldozers had decimated the coral near the beach and churned up sand all around the bay.

Two destroyers anchored offshore. Twelve LCIs approached the causeway, each one rapidly discharging its passengers. Infantrymen disembarked quickly, charged up the causeway, across the beach, and into the cover of the palm trees as though under fire. Their superiors must also have told them to expect a Japanese barrage. Artillery units towed heavy guns ashore, unrolled wire tracks across the beach to keep their vehicles from bogging down in the sand and headed inland.

I watched the activities below all day. Lance brought me some soup for lunch, which tasted delicious. My strength slowly increased as I sat watching the activity in the bay. I spotted more ships off the coast late in the afternoon, but the usual afternoon storm prevented them from landing.

*\*\**

Rawlings drove me down to the encampment as additional landing craft delivered more men and equipment the following day. We pulled up in front of the newly erected hospital tent as chills overcame me. Two nurses ran out of the tent to help me out of the jeep.

"You look like hell, lieutenant," one of them said.

"Malaria," I replied. "But I'm past the worst of it. I just need Atabrine."

The nurses helped me out of the jeep and led me toward a bed in the tent.

"No!" I pulled away. "I need to speak to the doctor in charge. My men and I have been without prophylactics for more than a month. I need to get some pills up to them on the ridge."

"More than a month?" the doctor shouted when I asked for the pills. "We passed them out as we were boarding the ships. How did you manage to miss them?"

"We were already here, Major. Up on that ridge." I pointed through the tent wall. "We came with the advance reconnaissance team in the middle of May. They only gave us a two-week supply before we left Australia, and I had to fight for that. The doctor there said two weeks was all he could spare, and he would send more with the advance party, but he didn't."

"What? That's murder sending you men out here without the proper medication."

"Believe me, after my recent experience, I am prepared to go as far as necessary to get my men what they need."

"Good. Morris, give this man 300 mg. of Atabrine, then give him enough 100 mg tablets for his unit for two weeks."

I looked at Nurse Morris.

"Are you Tom Morris's little sister?" I asked.

"Yes," she said.

"Tom was my best friend in Boot Camp and at Fort Worden before the war. You're the reason we met in the first place. When you and my little brother broke up at that football game during college."

"You're Robert's big brother?" she exclaimed.

"I am."

"We'll have to catch up later. Right now, I'm too busy helping get this hospital set up, and you're too weak to stand here any longer. Come with me."

Nurse Morris took me to the opposite end of the tent and opened the drug cabinet.

"This will probably turn your skin yellow and give you diarrhea," she said as she handed me three tablets. Then, she turned to Corporal Rawlings. "Bring him back if he has psychotic symptoms," she said.

"He's been a raving lunatic for a week already," he said. "But I'll keep an eye on him."

As we left the hospital tent with our jar of pills, Captain Harding, from the advance landing party, spotted us.

"Sinclair!" he shouted. "One of the supply ships managed to get some mail on board. Stop by HQ and see if they have any for your platoon."

At HQ, I reported to Colonel Herndon, who knew about our deployment and camp location. After debriefing, I entered the supply office, where several soldiers organized things.

"Is there any mail for the First Platoon, Battery A, 227th AAA?"

The sergeant barked, "All mail had been distributed. If you didn't get it, ain't none to get."

"Wait a minute," said a corporal behind him. "There is a packet here for the Aussies on the ridge. Are you the platoon assigned to them?"

I nodded.

He handed a large packet to Rawlings. "Must've been a while since you got mail."

"Quite a while," I said.

I opened the packet on the way back up the ridge, shuffled through it, and pulled out a handful of letters from Sarah Gale, tied together with string.

"Better watch that," warned Rawlings. "Wouldn't want anyone's mail to blow away."

A sudden tropical rainstorm broke out. I quickly covered the packet as Rawlings worked to keep the jeep on the rough track up the ridge. My gut began to rumble and knot.

Back at camp, Rawlings grabbed the mail packet, hunched over it, and ran into my tent as I ran for the latrine. Nurse Morris had been right about the Atabrine. While I sat in the latrine, my bowels tying themselves in knots, the rain stopped. Finally, I returned to my tent, wobbling on legs that seemed made of rubber. Rawlings had sorted the mail and opened his own two letters.

"Better assemble the men," I told him.

"You going to be able to stand that long?" he asked.

"I'm not sure, but the men need their Atabrine and mail."

He unfolded my chair in front of the tent, put the Atabrine on a camp table next to the chair, pulled the bullhorn from under my bed, and called the men. When everyone except those on duty had assembled, I had them file past me to get the pills, then Rawlings handed them their mail.

"Take the mail and pills to the men on duty," I told him. "Then run the Aussie's mail up to them."

I should have made the men wait until they were off duty to give them their mail, but I knew how anxiously they wanted it. I stood but fell back into my chair. Hanks and Jenkins grabbed me by either arm and hauled me to bed. I tried to open my letters but fell asleep before I could manage the task.

***

I dreamed of running along the beach in Florida with Sarah Gale. It had a dream's soft, misty quality, not the harsh reality of the hallucinations. We ran along the beach until we fell onto the sand, holding hands. I could smell her auburn hair's fresh, clean scent mingling with the ocean breeze. I rolled toward her and kissed her. The dream faded as raindrops on the roof of my tent lulled me into a deeper, relaxed sleep. I slept soundly until late the next morning.

I walked under my own power to the radar trailer, offering to take my shift, but the men waved me away.

"You just rest, lieutenant," they said. "We can handle this."

After eating breakfast, I returned to my tent and grabbed Sarah Gale's letters off the lid of my trunk, where I had put them before falling asleep.

May 8, 1943
Dear Gene,
OTC is fascinating. There are Negro candidates in my class, just like there were in yours. They are a little wary of me because of my southern accent, but I think I can work with them better than the women from Nebraska or the locals who have never met a Negro before. I'm not saying I don't sometimes do or say things I shouldn't, but at least I've worked with Negros before in the laundry at Camp Davis.

Most of the officer's candidates have more education than I have, but I hold my own thanks to the reading you had me do and the training I received on the job. I did pass that exam and got my high school diploma. Everyone in the family was impressed. I'm the first one in my immediate family to get a diploma. Aunt Lily graduated from high school, which helped me believe I could. Most candidates are college-educated professionals, like schoolteachers and journalists, who have just joined up. Being in the Corps for almost a year gives me a different perspective.

Physical fitness is essential, and it's a little harder for me this time. I got soft, spending my days analyzing photos. They are teaching us how to develop our own personal fitness plan so we can stay in shape after training and be excellent examples to enlisted women. There is also more emphasis on appearance than there was in basic. Not too much makeup, not too little. I think all the negative publicity made that necessary.

The most fun thing was learning to drive. Only a few of the candidates knew how to drive, and most of them had never driven a jeep before. They said that was a little harder than the cars they learned to drive. But now all of us can drive a jeep and even keep it on a muddy, bumpy test course. Daddy will be amazed when I go home, jump in the truck, and drive it straight to town.

We are also learning leadership skills. And we spend a lot of time learning all the skills that WAACs generally do so we can ensure the enlisted personnel perform their jobs correctly. I know I'll be working in photo interpretation, and the other candidates are impressed that I already have top-secret security clearance. So, a lot of the training is really dull to me, but I am paying attention so I can get a better job when the war is over. There will probably be more opportunities for switchboard operators or stenographers than photo interpreters after the war. I hope you won't mind if I keep working after the war. I have found that I really like working.

Enjoy your time in your tropical paradise – but not too much. I really miss you.
Love,
Sarah Gale

Lance interrupted me.

"Sir, we've been invited to a Fourth of July celebration at the main camp. Do you think you are up to it?"

"I certainly am, I replied."

Willy sent a crew of Australians down to man the radar while the rest of us went down the hill to the celebration. Some of the men climbed onto our troop transport truck. The rest walked, taking a shortcut the native girls had shown them. Corporal Rawlings drove me down in the jeep. He dropped me off at the tent marked Officers Club.

Inside, I spotted the officers from my Battery.

"Sinclair, you certainly look the worse for wear," Captain Henderson said. "I didn't realize your injuries were so severe."

"It was more malaria than the injuries in Darwin," I said. "The doc there held me for observation, but I could easily have come with you if he'd let me."

"Wish he had," said Henderson as Lieutenant Edelstein approached.

"Sinclair, wait until you see the improvements I made to your filing system," Edelstein said as he shook my hand. "I really cleaned up the mess you made."

"We do have three enlisted clerical personnel," I said. "I generally left the filing to them. They managed to do a pretty good job as long as I gave them clear instructions."

"They had no idea what they were doing until I took over, "Edelstein insisted.

Henderson turned his back on Edelstein and walked away. He seemed as tired of Edelstein's egotistical self-aggrandizement as I had been when we were roommates at Fort Bliss. Carson, Brasseux, and Douglas approached, rescuing me from a detailed description of how Edelstein had improved office procedures.

"Sinclair, welcome back!" Brasseux exclaimed.

"I should say welcome to the island," I said. "Maybe I can show you around."

"For now, come wet your whistle. I bet you haven't had a beer in weeks," Carson invited.

"I've been with the Aussies. They don't travel without beer," I told him. "But I wouldn't mind joining you. Everyone's here except Wright. Where's he."

"You know Wright," Douglas said. "Mr. Social Secretary. He's putting together the evening's celebration. You should go find him after we have a drink. He wished you had been here earlier."

After catching up with the others, I found the stage set up for the evening's festivities. Wright was there supervising the installation of a podium.

"Still in charge of the entertainment, I see," I called to him.

"Sinclair, it's a miracle. Just the man I need. You have the perfect voice

for reading the Declaration of Independence at the beginning of the celebration."

***

As the sun set, a band Wright had managed to put together played
the Star Spangled Banner as I followed the Color guard up the aisle between rows of soldiers onto the stage. After the song and the Posting of
the Colors, I stepped to the podium.

"When in the course of human events..." I began from memory, the
battle for that independence fresh in my mind.

# CHAPTER 8

## REASSIGNED

**I**REALIZED THE FOLLOWING day that I had partied much too hard in my weakened state. I served my shift in the radar room, after which I only had enough energy to return to my tent and read Sarah Gale's next letter.

*May 22, 1943*
*Dear Gene,*

*I got your letter about your injuries in Darwin. I have always been afraid you would be injured or killed in the war, and you were before you even got out of Australia, which I assumed would be safe. I had not heard anything about the Japanese bombing Darwin. I am glad it was only a minor injury, and you are back on duty. Please be careful. I don't know how I could go on without you. I have hardly been able to concentrate on anything else since I found out you were injured.*

*It is interesting to me how they could so easily reassign you. I do hope your new assignment works out. What little you could say made it sound like a very unusual assignment.*

*We are deep into our officer's training now. It is forcing me to grow up quickly, learning about all the responsibilities I could have as an officer. I know I will still have the same job I had before, but it may involve more responsibility. It is definitely more responsibility than working in the laundry, which is the only other job I have ever had.*

*Joey just turned eighteen and wants to join the Air Corps. Mama is really upset. When Johnny joined the army, she was proud. It wasn't too bad when Jeb joined the Marines, especially since he became a cook. Then, I joined the WAACs, and Robby joined the Navy. She said she had provided enough children to the service then. Now Joey wants to join, and she is beside herself.*

*I thought I was the only one who wanted to get out of the backwoods, but it looks like we have a whole generation of adventurers in an otherwise unadventurous family. Joey has always been the quiet, unpretentious one, so I am a little surprised he wants to join the Air Corps. Most Air Corps pilots I have met are pretty full of themselves. But maybe he will become a mechanic or something.*

*I haven't seen much of Captain Henderson's wife. She was glad to have some-one younger to talk with, but our lives are so different, and the training keeps me busy. However, we did go shopping together last Saturday to buy clothes for her little boy. He is growing so fast. Tell Captain Henderson that he is a fine young man there.*

*Love,*
*Sarah Gale*

I dozed off until Willy came down from the Australian camp around noon.

"Sinclair, you look much better than last week when I visited. Then, you were a sorry-looking bloke, tossing and turning on your cot, going on about General Thompson. I don't know any General Thompson."

"An American Revolutionary War General," I said.

"American Revolution? You were hallucinating?" he asked. "Well, welcome back to the twentieth century. Glad to see you up and around. You had your medic concerned."

"I'd have been concerned myself if I'd been conscious," I said. "Do you know anything about malaria?"

"Once you have it, it can come back any time. Make sure you keep taking those pills."

"Now that the supplies are here, that shouldn't be a problem."

"Speaking of which, we are low on petrol after what we gave you. Can you get the US Army to replace it?"

"That shouldn't be a problem," I said.

I took the jeep down to the supply tent and explained the situation to the sergeant.

"I can't just give gasoline to the Aussies," he said. "They will have to get it from Aussie supplies."

"Isn't it all allied supplies?" I asked. "They gave us gasoline when we asked. Why can't we just replace what they gave us?"

"We have to account for everything. If you can document what you borrowed from them, we should be able to give that to you, and you can give it to them."

I radioed the ridge, found out how many gallons we had gotten, filled out a requisition form, and returned to the supply tent.

"You don't have the proper signatures. You need to have the swap approved by an officer in both forces. Someone above your grade."

I searched for the AAA camp, finally finding it at one of the lowest points, right next to a swamp. I found Edelstein in the HQ tent.

"Who chose your campsite," I asked. Edelstein looked up from his filing, frowning at the disturbance. I saw a massive pile of loose paper on the desk.

"The plans called for the airstrip to be over there," he said, pointing to the south. "But when we got here, it turned out to be a swamp."

I asked him to type up the request for a swap. "Better do that yourself," he said. "I'm so far behind. Henderson threatened to demote me if I didn't get caught up."

"Just how do you demote a second lieutenant? Where is Henderson?" I asked as I dug the typewriter out of the paperwork.

"Meeting with the colonel," Edelstein said, returning to his filing as I typed up the request, attached the requisition, and headed off to Battalion HQ. The meeting had just ended, and I asked Captain Henderson to sign the request. Colonel Squires overheard me and said, "They'll probably be more cooperative with my signature. He signed with a flourish at the bottom of the page. Henderson stalked away grumpily.

As I walked into the supply tent, the sergeant looked up from his paperwork.

"That was fast," he said, looking at the request. "You will need an Aussie Colonel to sign it, too."

"At the moment, there isn't an Aussie colonel within five hundred miles of here."

"Well, I need some Aussie commander to sign it," he responded.

"I'll get a captain's signature." I hopped in my jeep, drove back to the ridge, had Willy sign the paper, and returned to the supply tent. A new sergeant sat at the desk.

"What's all this?" he asked.

I explained the situation.

"You don't need all this paperwork. Giles just can't get his mind around what wartime footing means. He was within two months of retirement when the war began and is frustrated that his retirement was delayed. I'll see that the gasoline is delivered to the ridge first thing in the morning."

I thanked him and returned to the ridge, barely arriving in time to get supper at the Aussie camp, thoroughly frustrated at the useless runaround that had gobbled up my afternoon.

I read the final letter from Sarah Gale by the light of my flashlight back at my tent.

June 6, 1943
Dear Gene,
 I have completed officer's training and am now officially an officer. I just arrived in Washington, DC, and will find out tomorrow what I will be doing here. Not that I will be able to tell you.

*The trip to DC was by far the fastest one I have taken. It was a quick hop to Chicago from Des Moines, then a direct express train to DC. I spent a day in Chicago looking at the tall buildings and seeing the city so you wouldn't tease me about thinking a ten-story building is tall. I went with a group of navy men, so you don't need to worry about me being safe. They were lots of fun but made me miss you even more. The wind off the lake was really something. I can see why they call it the windy city. I am glad I didn't come through in the middle of the winter like you did. The temperature was at least above freezing when I was there.*

*I found your last letter really interesting. It had not occurred to me that winter in the United States is summer in Australia. Your explanation made it very clear why that is so. It was just very strange to me.*

*By now, you are probably where the seasons are just rainy and not rainy. Is it the rainy season or the dry season? I imagine the islands are beautiful, although I know from pictures I have seen that the fighting can destroy the beauty, and the conditions can be horrid. I really hope you are staying safe and healthy. Please write as soon as you can.*

*Love,*
*Sarah Gale*

Apparently, Sarah Gale did understand the actual conditions we experienced but was teasing me about the tropical paradise. I worried about her spending time with Navy men. What if she found someone else? She had so little experience with men, having spent her life in rural North Carolina, where the only males she had regular contact with were her brothers and a few nearby farm boys. She says she loves me but regularly sees and works with so many other men. I lay in my cot, growing increasingly worried that Sarah Gale would fall for someone else.

# CHAPTER 9

## CONSTRUCTION

**W**E ASSUMED CONSTRUCTION OF the airfield would begin immediately, but something delayed its start. Even though more men arrived every day, construction still didn't start. By the end of the week, we realized why: the heavy equipment, giant bulldozers, hadn't arrived. Finally, midweek, a ship arrived and began unloading. The heavy equipment moved slowly across the wire on the beach. Then we watched as the bulldozers moved mysteriously from one site to another. One bulldozer got mired so deeply in a swamp that it took three others a full day to pull it out. Still no construction.

After two weeks of this, General Kruger showed up. From the ridge, we saw him arguing with Colonel Herndon. Two days later, Colonel Murray arrived, and Colonel Herndon left. Sunday, the day after Murray's arrival, I finally felt I could make it through one of Cliff Reynold's worship services. We went down to find the plantation in turmoil.

"The Colonel says the men should worship in the tent with the army chaplain," Cliff explained. "Frankly, I don't care about that. Thousands of soldiers are overrunning the island, destroying everything, stealing coconuts, and more. Their behavior is extremely uncouth. I had to send all the female workers home to their villages. I just didn't think they were safe."

I went to the official army worship service. After the service, I approached the Colonel.

"Colonel Murray, there seems to be a problem with the island residents. Cliff Reynolds, the plantation manager, has sent his female employees back to the village because of their frequent liaisons with the soldiers. Of course, customs are different here, but I'd hate for our men to spread disease among the people. Do you think you can do something about it?"

"Lieutenant, do you have any idea what you're asking? These beautiful women invite red-blooded American boys to their beds every night. These boys have been without companionship for months. How do you think I can stop it?"

"May I at least explain the customs of the people? Sexual relations mean different things here than they do in our culture."

"You can teach sociology classes when you get back stateside. We have a war to win here. Top priority is finding a decent place to build an airstrip among all these swamps."

I sighed.

"You can get a pretty good island view from our radar encampment on the ridge. Just follow that track over there."

"Let's go now, Lieutenant." He ordered his aid to radio a couple of other officers and call for some jeeps, and we headed up the track.

On the ridge, he surveyed the island and found a likely spot for the runway. I will say one thing for Colonel Murray: he was a man of action. By mid-afternoon, the equipment had arrived at the selected location, trees toppling and burning. Within two days, we could see where the airstrip would cut across the coral rock.

My platoon received orders to relocate to a camp near the airstrip where we would rejoin my former battalion. Already, twenty men had been sent back to Australia with serious illnesses. The platoon from the ridge would be split up and be assigned as replacements for those men and extra staff to fill in as needed.

Another shipment of supplies brought more mail, and I settled into my camp chair to read it after handing out mail to the troops and relaying the message that we would be moving downhill the next day. Before I could start, Sergent Bridger stormed up the path.

"What's to become of me if this platoon is to be disbanded," he shouted. "I've brought these boys all the way from the States. We've been through a lot together. You can't take them from me now."

"I'm not supposed to know this yet, but I spotted a paper in Captain Henderson's office that indicated you might be up for a promotion. I can't guarantee it until it is signed, sealed, and delivered, and who knows when that will happen with Edelstein processing the paperwork, but the paper was there."

Bridger beamed and walked back to his tent as I turned to Sarah Gale's letter.

*June 20, 1943*

*Dear Gene,*

*Washington is not that far from home, at least not compared to Des Moines, but it sure is different from my tiny North Carolina hometown. First of all, it's so big. The biggest town I have ever been in, except for passing through Chicago. It is incredibly busy, too. People are always coming or going, no matter the time of day. There are sailors and soldiers and men in business suits, but there are also a lot of women out on the streets because they are all working. The streetcars are* driven by women; women cut meat and check people out in the grocery stores. They are doing all sorts of jobs. I met a woman who worked at the Washington Naval Gun Factory the other day. I guess everyone is working all over the country now, but since I can't remember much of anything before the depression, it seems a little strange.

I am staying in a boarding house for government workers. I share a room with a girl named Marge from Colorado who works as some sort of assistant to someone in Congress, I think. Neither of us can talk about our work, so we talk about home and family and, of course, you and her husband, who is in the navy, on a ship off some European coast.

We love going to movies, soda fountains, and out to eat together. They have some great restaurants in Washington. Of course, I can't afford the best ones, but even the ones I can afford are pretty good.

Here at the boarding house, the meals are hearty but rather boring. I think it is because so many items are either scarce or rationed. Marcy, our landlady, isn't very good at making do. She loves to bake but can't bake much, even with all our sugar rations. We all turn over our ration books to her, and she buys and cooks for all of us. Marge said she thinks Marcy drinks more than her share of coffee, but I don't really care because I don't like coffee.

I planted a little Victory Garden in front of the boarding house. Lots of people are growing Victory Gardens in the little bits of ground between the sidewalk and the street and in their tiny front yards. They can't grow much, but even a few tomatoes, greens, and squash can help. I put cucumbers in because they are my favorite, even though they take up more room than some things. Marge wanted me to put in some melons, but that just takes too much space for our little postage stamp garden. Eleanor Roosevelt even has a victory garden at the White House. It is bigger than ours.

I am so glad you got to Australia safely and are on an island where there is not much activity. I want you to be safe all the time. I love the flower pictures you sent me, and the picture of you swimming in the pool is great. That looks like so much fun.

Stay safe, and write soon.
Love, Sarah Gale

# CHAPTER 10

## SWAMPED

**W**E HADN'T REALIZED HOW good we had it up on the ridge. Our ridgetop camp got muddy with every rain, but the rainwater drained away down the slopes or through the porous coral in a matter of hours. Cool breezes blew every morning and evening. Radar site lines were clear for miles in all directions, and we were free to arrange our days in ways that worked most effectively rather than follow procedures designed by armchair generals in Washington.

Below, located at the least desirable edge of a tent city of three thousand men, we were mired in the foul drainage from the rest of the camp and regularly swarmed by insects and other vermin from the swamps immediately behind us. I warned the men to check their boots for poisonous insects before putting them on and their cots for venomous snakes before turning in. The men started complaining the minute they saw the place.

"Don't worry. You will be reassigned as soon as the paperwork is completed," I told the men. "Think of this as a temporary inconvenience."

"Doesn't look too temporary to me," grumbled corporal Rawlings, "The other platoons in this company aren't in much better positions."

"We'll soon be moving closer to the airstrip," I told him. "Our main job is to light the airstrip until the Corps of Engineers can install permanent lights."

There was more grumbling about moving too many times.

"We want to move frequently," I told the men. "We aren't going to defeat the Japs sitting around here."

The platoon had just gotten set up when Lieutenant Edelstein showed up with his duffel bag.

"Sinclair, Captain Henderson wants you back at HQ. Hopefully, you can keep up with him."

"So, you aren't staying on as XO?" I asked.

"No, I'm back to platoon CO, and boy am I glad! Henderson is such a taskmaster. I couldn't keep up with all his orders and demands." It surprised me that Edelstein hadn't worked out. He was such a stickler for proper military procedure. As platoon CO, he punished his men harshly for the slightest infraction. Hopefully, Henderson helped him calm down while he worked as XO.

"I'm not worried about keeping up with Henderson, although he can be rough around the edges," I replied. "It's the reports and clerical work I don't like."

"Well, that should all be in order. I'll show you my system."

Edelstein returned with me to HQ and showed me the elaborate system he had created to ensure all reports were filed appropriately before returning to his platoon. The necessary forms and papers were easily accessible in clearly labeled boxes. I knew I wouldn't keep it as organized as he had, but he'd developed an ingenious system. His boxes could quickly be loaded into trucks, moved, and unloaded without any resorting. The clerical staff looked on. As soon as Edelstein left, the senior office clerk, Corporal Feltner, said, "We certainly are glad you're back, sir. He yelled at us for almost everything we did, so we stopped doing anything."

"Do you think you can follow his system? It does look like it would make moving easier."

"Can do, sir."

"Well, then get at it and see if we can clean up this mess by tomorrow.

\*\*\*

"Sinclair, welcome back," boomed Captain Henderson as he entered the tent.

"Welcome to the island, sir! I can show you the best beaches, introduce you to the supreme war chief and matriarch, show you a cave with crystal clear, cool water for swimming."

"How about an introduction to some of these beautiful island girls?" he asked.

"Women choose men here," I replied with raised eyebrows. "If a woman stays past sunrise, it means you're married. They're a bit lax on ceremony, but that doesn't mean you won't get a spear through your middle if you insult them. I'd be careful if I were you. I wouldn't want to have to report to your wife that you'd been speared for refusing the advances of an island girl."

"Here," he said, ignoring my warning and handing me a sheaf of papers. "Reassign the men you brought to platoons. There's a list of sick and injured that we need replacements for somewhere in there. Get these reports ready ASAP, then type up your report on the time you were here."

I spent the day at my desk sorting out new assignments and then working through the pile of incomplete orders, reports, and requisition forms. Edelstein must have spent all his time organizing already completed paperwork. As evening approached, I shoved the remaining pile into the inbox and walked to the officer's mess.

As I entered, I heard raised voices across the room. Carson and Brasseux were arguing. "They're still at it? ," I asked Captain Sessions, the man I had replaced as XO at Fort Bliss when he was promoted. He had arrived at the officer's mess right behind me.

"Just leave them to it," Sessions said. "They love sparring with each other."

I waved at them from across the room and got in line for my dinner.

I worked on the backlogged papers for two days, then wrote my own report, happy to be back in HQ despite the paperwork. Though I'd enjoyed comradery on the ridgetop, I liked being in the center of things, seeing the bigger picture. In typing up the orders and reports, I learned that this island and Woodlark, about a hundred miles southeast of us, would be jumping off places for a kind of leapfrog campaign up the coast of New Guinea; Americans would be based on Woodlark and the Australian Air Force here on Kiriwina.

***

Captain Henderson stormed into the tent as I put the finishing touches on my report.

"What the hell do you think you're doing, going over my head to the Colonel? I'm the CO of this battery, not you! You will not speak to the Colonel again without my express permission!"

I stared at him, totally confused.

"You talked to the Colonel about keeping the men away from the women, which we all know is impossible, then you took him to the ridge and showed him where to build the runway."

I stood up. "Sir, the civilians on the island came to me with a problem, and I felt he was the only one who could take care of it. I wasn't even assigned to this battery at the time."

"Do you understand the line of command, Lieutenant?" he shouted.

"Yes, sir,"

"Good. Now get to HQ and find out how they want to redistribute the lights."

"Yes, sir."

Although normally overprotective of his position, that tirade was unusual even for Henderson. I walked into HQ and found Captain Sessions rolling up a map.

"Sinclair! I wondered how Henderson would deal with the little row with the Colonel."

"The little row?"

"He's upset that I got the HQ position and he's still with the battery. Being at HQ is usually a better route to promotion, and he wants a promotion more than anything. The argument didn't last long, but yelling at the Colonel is not the best way to get promoted."

"Henderson just reamed me out for talking to the Colonel without consulting him. I wasn't even reassigned to the battalion when I did. Then he sent me over to find out where we should station the lights. Strange behavior even for him."

"Keep an eye on him. Wouldn't want him to crack." Sessions said. "We need to redistribute our units to protect the seaplane and PT base they're starting to build, as well as the camp and runway. The RAAF will be here soon in force. Henderson was so angry when he left that he forgot his map."

Sessions handed me the map. I asked for directions to the post exchange to check for mail. It turned out to be a little wooden shack made of shipping crates. One thing about so many people coming and going is that the mail got through more often. I had another letter from Sarah Gale.

After delivering the map to Henderson and having him sign all the reports and orders I had typed up, I distributed the mail to the various platoons and returned to my tent to read my letter from Sarah Gale.

July 4, 1943

Dear Gene,

Happy Independence Day. Of course, by the time you read this, it will be way past Independence Day. You said you haven't celebrated holidays very much since you have been there, but I hope you had a chance to think about the freedom you are fighting for. We won't have any fireworks because all the gunpowder is going to the war effort, but we planned a special party in the park. Marcy has been saving up the sugar rations for weeks so she can bake, and we have eaten a lot of rice and beans, so we have plenty of sausages for today. I am really looking forward to the party.

You will never guess what is going to happen. I will be going overseas! I can't say how soon, but they want me to work there. Remember how you said I probably would not get to see the world? Well, you were wrong. I am so excited.

Another really exciting thing is that the WAACs became part of the regular army. We are called WACs now, the Women's Army Corps. I am officially a second lieutenant and will soon be a first lieutenant, the same as you unless you get promoted before I do. I get the same pay as a male officer, too. I am sending money home to Mama and Daddy. They are saving to buy a car. Their lives have really changed because all of us are sending money home. They have actually moved into the twentieth century.

I picked a cucumber from my little victory garden. A lot of the girls think I should have planted tomatoes rather than cucumbers, but I really like cucumbers

*much better. Marge can't believe that. She is a real tomato lover.*
   *Stay safe and know that I love you.*
   *Love,*
   *Sarah Gale*

   Oh, for the simple life of deciding between tomatoes and cucumbers
   I folded the letters and put them in my pocket as Perry, the radioman assigned to the HQ platoon, scratched on the flap of my tent.
   "The Australian radar post picked up approaching aircraft," Perry said. "Looks like just one plane."
   I went outside and saw the Jap plane approaching. The gunners were ready, but the plane stayed just out of range.

# CHAPTER 11

## ACTION

**T**HE JAPS HAVE MADE a successful reconnaissance flight. Be extra vigilant. The next planes might be bombers." Henderson told us at the daily debriefing. "Keep the schedules tight and the men alert during their shifts. We're here to protect the airbase. Let's show 'em what we've got. Keep your feet dry and stay away from the Island girls." We could all tell his heart wasn't in that last part.

We returned to the schedule we had developed during training. I took command during the night as the crews searched the sky and lit up approaching aircraft. Then, after reporting to Henderson, I slept for six or seven hours before going to work in the HQ tent, seeing to my administrative duties.

Henderson was right. Three days later, just after sunset, the Aussies, still on the ridge, reported incoming aircraft. At about the same time, our radar picked them up and alerted the searchlights and gunners. Three bombers twenty miles out at two hundred forty degrees. As they approached, the gunners opened fire; the bombers turned away. So much for our first official enemy contact of the war. The next night, a lone bomber flew over but again turned away when the gunners fired.

By early August, the RAAF arrived in force, the island's military strength reaching almost seventeen thousand. We outnumbered the native population by nearly double.

Mrs. Reynolds came to me almost daily with a new complaint. I told her that, as a lieutenant, I couldn't change the situation and reminded her of the importance of the base for the New Guinea campaign. The next day, she would return with a new complaint—anything from destroying her flowerbeds to deflowering the (already deflowered) village girls. One day, Chaplain Marshall came for a visit just after she arrived.

"Dorothy? What in the world are you doing here? We didn't believe you had survived your mission to the Dani."

"Paul! Imagine meeting you here. I thought you would stay in the States and continue gathering support, yet here you are in a uniform."

"The army needed me. How do you happen to be here?"

"Cliff took a job as plantation manager. Come, he's at the plantation house."

They walked off, chatting. I was grateful that I didn't have to listen to another complaint.

I headed to the PX, picking up several letters. I opened the one from Mom first. Granny had died. Not unexpected, she had just turned ninety years old. Still, it felt like a rock had settled in the pit of my stomach. Granny and I had been incredibly close. She was the local herbalist and midwife. I had assisted her in formulating medicines and treating her male patients since I was a boy. It was because of Granny that I had planned on becoming a doctor until the war intervened. That plan was on hold now. It wouldn't be the same without Granny to share it with. I dragged myself from platoon to platoon that night, my mind on the Kansas prairie with Granny.

Returning to my tent at sunrise, having finally managed to bury my thoughts in radar screens and searchlight maintenance, I felt vaguely uneasy but couldn't remember what was wrong. Then, as I tried to fall asleep, I remembered that Granny had died, and I couldn't sleep. So I picked up Sarah Gale's letters and began reading.

July 18, 1943

Dear Gene,

I am writing to you on board the ship, crossing the ocean. I am really enjoying the trip, although the ship's captain seems to think the women on board will cause trouble. There is only me, another lieutenant, and five enlisted WACs, but we are constantly watched. I think he believes the rumors circulating about WAACs earlier this year. We can walk on the deck, surrounded by an armed guard, in the morning and evening. Otherwise, we have to stay out of sight of the soldiers and sailors. There is a little outside staircase near my cabin where we can sit, so I have been taking my pillow, putting it on the iron steps, and spending most of my time there. We even have to be escorted to the officers' dining room (they are letting the enlisted women eat in the officers' dining room), where we have to sit at our own table and not talk to any of the men for any reason. The other day, a male lieutenant asked if he could get me a piece of cake when he returned to the chow line, and he got in big trouble for even offering. I think this captain is going to have to change his policies. They are saying many more WACs will be coming over, and he can't keep them all cooped up like this.

I have spent a lot of time reading. I just finished Gone with the Wind, an excellent expose of your grandfather's contribution to the Civil War. When I am allowed my 'constitutional' this evening, I am going to try to slip into the library and see what else I can find. The other WAC lieutenant suggested looking for something by John Steinbeck. I don't know if they have any of his books in the little library on board.

I got the massive packet of letters you wrote while you were isolated on the island. The typhoon must have been terrifying. I'm glad they only come every year or two. I won't have to worry about you being blown away. I think of you swimming and relaxing in the pool, enjoying the tropical weather and ocean breezes. At least, I hope that is what you are doing right now.

Love,
Sarah Gale

It wasn't all tropical beaches and ocean breezes. There were so many men down with jungle fever, malaria, and jungle rot that I took regular shifts on radar or searchlights in addition to my executive duties. Japanese raids came in every night. Just a few planes per night, and most did not get close enough to drop their bombs. Nevertheless, watching and waiting was nerve-wracking.

I fell asleep thinking of Sarah Gale on the troop ship and longing for the breezes of the ridge. I read her next letter at breakfast the following day.

August 1, 1943
Dear Gene,
We spent a little time in London on the way to our station because our dormitory was not ready. It is still not really finished. More on that later.

I was surprised by the attitude of the people of London. So many of them have sent their children away but are staying in London themselves. We saw an astonishing number of buildings that were bombed in the Blitz, but the people kept on almost as if nothing had happened. There was one alert while we were there, but it came to nothing. The Brits responded to the air raid sirens, but it was almost like going to the pub for some of them. Not that they drink beer in the air raid shelter (although I think some of them do), but it was a chance to catch up with the neighbors and exchange gossip. They sat and talked until the all-clear came, then walked out and went home. They didn't show much fear of anything.

The King and Queen are still in London. I read about their tour of a hospital the other day. They stay in London or Windsor, which is not too far from London, but often visit hospitals, bombed-out neighborhoods, and military installations. If I were the Queen, I would want to be in the most isolated place I could find with my children, but she said she would not send the children away without her, she would not leave her husband, and he will not leave his people. I think the British are the bravest people around.

The place where I work is not in London. We got here yesterday and found that there is only one functioning toilet and no shower. Some men are working on *it, but they are all about as old as Methuselah, so I am not too sure how long it will take. I am trying to be patient because I know that all the able-bodied men are fighting the war, and both the men and the women are fighting here to keep vital services functioning and rebuild what they can. Yesterday, after work, I helped clean up the construction area. I would install the toilets if I knew how. That is the disadvantage of living in a house without indoor plumbing for most of my life.*

*I do know how to plant a garden. It's a little late to start summer vegetables, although I don't know how the seasons work here. It's cooler here now than in North Carolina, but they say the winters are mild. I'm just not sure how they interpret mild.*

*Anyway, I planted some cabbage, lettuce, spinach, kohlrabi, radishes, leeks, and onions. I haven't had kohlrabi or leeks before, but the lady I bought the seeds and sets from said they do very well here. I don't know if I will be here long enough to harvest anything. I only got one cucumber from my Washington, DC garden, and it was small. If not, I am sure someone else can use the vegetables.*

*Thank you so much for the pictures. I wish you could send me photos of the people, but since you say the island could be identified by their dress and war paint, I don't want you to do anything that might mean more attacks. Keep sending me pictures of flowers and trees. I think my favorite flower is still dogwood. I guess I'll never be anything other than a North Carolina girl, no matter where you take me when this war ends.*

*Love*
*Sarah Gale*

***

One morning, after a very long, uneventful night, I returned to camp to see enlisted men piling sandbags around several tents.

"What are you doing that for?" I asked.

"Don't know. Lieutenant Brasseux ordered us to, so we're doing it."

I went to Brasseux's tent, finding him pacing back and forth and wringing his hands.

"Do you know how much danger we're in?" he screeched. "It's typhoon season, deadly diseases all 'round, poisonous snakes and insects, and de Japs might show up any minute."

"Yes. We're fighting a war, living in a swamp on a Pacific island, and have no resistance to the diseases here. Growing up in the bayou, you should be used to this sort of thing."

"Dat's exactly why I know how dangerous it is," he said.

I asked O'Neill, the medic for his platoon, if any psychiatrists were on the island.

"Nope. Those psych guys are only at the general hospital in Australia. You got a problem?"

"I think Brasseux is suffering from battle fatigue."

"He can't have battle fatigue," O'Neill said. "There aren't any battles here. Probably just plain fatigue. I can get him some sleeping pills. Lots of guys haven't been sleeping well, which can make them a little crazy."

I told him that was a good idea and returned to Brasseux's tent.

"How have you been sleeping?" I asked.

"How can anybody sleep 'round here. We have to be awake all night to run de lights, den planes roar over all day. If it ain't planes, it's all dat construction.

O'Neill returned with a sleeping pill. "I'll give him one and put him to bed," he told me. "If it works, I can get more at the field hospital."

\*\*\*

Time seemed to drag on. Some nights we would spot a Jap plane or three; other nights, we watched empty skies or tracked thunderstorms. One morning at breakfast, Lieutenant Wright, our battery communications officer, said to me. "We need some entertainment. Why don't we put on a play?"

"Would anyone be interested in a play?" I asked.

"Sure. They show the same three movies for a month in the cinema, and USO shows don't come to this remote outpost. How about we do our own."

"A variety show like the USO or a serious play?'

"I doubt we have the audience for a serious play. Shall we put out a call for variety show acts?"

We put up notices in the PX, mess tents, RAAF HQ, enlisted and officer's clubs, and various other places. I was shocked! We got over two hundred acts.

"How do we make a show out of this?" I asked as I shuffled the stacks of paper on which people had described their acts.

"We make it into a weekly event, and we have auditions," Wright declared. I had not seen him so excited the entire time I knew him. Until now, he had seemed to be an insecure, reserved young officer, except, of course, when he was on the dance floor. But there hadn't been any dancing since we left the states.

We set up auditions: three hours each evening for the next week. Wright got up on the stage and seemed utterly at home as he spoke to the crowd.

"We'll be putting together a new show every week. Not being selected for the first show doesn't mean you haven't been accepted to perform. This is a variety show, so we need variety. We have many more comics and singers than other types of acts. We would appreciate it if some of you want to put together skits to add to the show.

"We won't be able to audition all of you this week. We'll hold auditions monthly as we continue to put shows together. Rehearsals will be every evening that we don't hold auditions.

"We've randomly chosen the acts we would like to audition today. We'll post those for tomorrow's auditions outside the theater later this evening and each evening after that. So, if you're not on our preliminary lists, don't worry; we'll get to you.

"If any of you, or someone you know, has other skills, like stage manager or lighting, we would appreciate the help.

"Now, let's begin. The first audition is of a Navy man doing a magic act. Ensign John Carson."

A skinny, dark-haired man stepped onto the stage and launched his performance.

"What do you think?" I asked Wright.

"He has some potential, but I want something better in our first show."

We put him down for a possible later show. We had eight acts that were sure things and a list of twelve maybes three hours later. The whole process had been tedious for me, but Wright seemed energized. Afterward, two guys with backstage experience approached us and volunteered. I bowed out of the remaining auditions, leaving it to Wright and his small crew.

When returning to my tent, I stopped at the PX and picked up Sarah Gale's latest letters.

*August 15, 1943*
*Dear Gene,*
*Guess what? I learned to ride a bicycle. We have to ride bikes to work. I asked if I could ride a mule because I knew how, but they just frowned. I don't think they have a very high opinion of mules. I don't know why. We rode Old Peg to school every day until she died when I was in fourth grade, and she got us there safely, rain or shine.*

*I am getting the hang of the bicycle, though. We ride them to work, and when we're not working, we ride them around the countryside sightseeing. There are some ancient houses here and lots of streams, rivers, and farms. There is even a castle not too far away. When I learn to ride a little better, one of the local girls said she would take me there to see it. I practice every day after work, riding a little farther each time. It shouldn't be long before I can ride well enough to get as far as the castle.*

*We have a few more toilets but don't have a shower yet. We also don't have any laundry, dry cleaning, shoe repair, or hat-blocking service. That is really dis-*

turbing to some of the officers who are not used to doing everything for themselves. They expect all those services because they have always had them. I can do all that for myself except repair my shoes, which don't need repair yet. I showed one of the women how to iron her summer uniform the other day. She didn't even know how to use an iron! Most of us can handle the washing, ironing, and that sort of thing. We won't need dry cleaning until we get our winter uniforms.

I am sorry. I am going on and on about the lack of toilets and dry cleaning when you are sitting in the mud on a tropical island somewhere and even having to scrounge your food from the jungle. I can't wait until the war ends and we can talk about our experiences face to face. Not that that is the first thing I want to do, of course, but having someone to talk to who understands when I don't have other WACs around will be good.

I hope there is some progress in the war there. I don't know how much news you get about what is happening here. We don't get too much about the Pacific here in England. The Germans surrendered to our forces in Tunisia. It looks like we have taken back northern Africa and are moving into the Mediterranean now. Our forces invaded the island of Sicily.

That may be where Jeb is. He was promoted to corporal and may soon be a mess sergeant in charge of his own kitchen. He was really put out at me being a lieutenant and him only a corporal. He writes most often, but then he is my twin. Occasionally I hear from my other brothers. I get news through Mama, so it is delayed about twice as long as news from you and Jeb.

I also hope you are keeping yourself safe and dry. The heat and humidity must be terrible. Keep swimming in your little pool and stay healthy.

Love,
Sarah Gale

.

# CHAPTER 12

## SLIPPERY SLOPES

**E**VEN AS I FILLED in for any number of sick personnel, working twice as hard as usual, time seemed to drag. The main highlight was Sarah Gale's letters. Her concerns seemed so mundane.

*August 29, 1943*
*Dear Gene,*
*We had a bit of an issue with food here. We get US Army rations, and it seemed our cook was pilfering them and replacing the meat, especially with the lowest quality beef and mutton she could find. The canned chipped beef and spam are nothing to get excited about, but they are well preserved and don't have maggots. Some of the girls were getting sick from what she fed us. I just picked out the worst of it and mainly ate vegetables. We do get a good variety of fresh vegetables from the local farms. Another officer and I have been going to a market to buy them and add them to our rations. Vegetables are not rationed, and several market gardens are within easy cycling distance.*

*Anyway, the cook was fired, and we now have an African woman doing our cooking. I showed her a few ways to make things so the American women would feel more at home, and we invented a few spam recipes. Of course, nobody really has any traditional spam recipes because it is so new, but I used some of the ingredients Mama used to make hash out of leftover ham.*

*Sicily's invasion, which I told you about last time, seems to be going well for us, and the Russians have liberated part of Ukraine from the Nazis. We did get some information about several battles won in the Solomons. If you were part of that, congratulations. I don't believe the war will last too much longer. We are making progress on all fronts.*

*Our living facility is still not finished. The lead contractor had a heart attack, so things came to a complete halt. The old men cannot figure out what to do without their leader, who I think is about sixty. They all just walked away from the half-finished work. It might be because they believe if they keep working, they will have heart attacks, too.*

*It is too bad that your men are fighting over the different ways words are*

used in the United States and Australia. I thought the English spoke the same language we do, but I am finding that there are a lot of differences in the words we use and how we pronounce some words. The other day, one of the guards called me a bird, and I thought he was crazy. And one of the girls said she liked my jumper when I was wearing a sweater. I couldn't figure out what she meant for the longest time. The worst misunderstanding was when one of the girls said she put a necklace her boyfriend had given her in her grandmother's casket. I told a long story about how my granny had died, and Mom and Dad had buried her under the big tulip tree. They don't have tulip trees here, just tulip bulbs, and they thought a tulip tree was a giant tulip. It took almost the whole dinner to get everything straightened out. To them, a casket is a jewelry box or just a box.
Love,
Sarah Gale

PS: August 31, 1943
Oh my darling, I just got your letter. I am so sorry that you got malaria. It must have been a severe case. The encyclopedia says the symptoms are fever, chills, and flu-like. The article also talked about malaria in the brain, and they said that it is often fatal. Is that what you have? Are you going to die? Please, if it is that bad, get them to send you home. I don't want you to die on some island, alone and lonely. Please send another letter soon to let me know you are all right.
Love
Sarah Gale

Fortunately, I had already sent that letter.

Mrs. Reynolds had not visited me in several weeks, so I stopped by the plantation house on Sunday to see what had changed. On the lawn, I saw several Australian airmen and a scattering of US Army enlisted men attending the worship service despite Colonel Murray's orders. I sat through another of Cliff Reynold's sermons and sang the songs Mrs. Reynolds led from the hymn book.

After the service, I approached the almost empty food table where Mrs. Reynolds stood with a tall, severe-looking European woman. I assumed the state of the table meant the plantation didn't have much in the way of food supplies.

"Gene, this is Mrs. Thompson," Mrs. Reynolds said before I even had a chance to say hello. "She's staying with us after escaping the island to the north where she and her husband lived. The Japanese took over the entire island, destroyed their plantation house, and captured her husband. She had to hide in the jungle for three days before the natives could get her off the island and send her down here. You have got to stop them and get her husband back."

Mrs. Thompson suddenly sobbed. The short, plump Mrs. Reynolds reached up to comfort her in what appeared to be an oft-repeated routine, and the women returned to the house.

Cliff approached from nearby. "She's in her element. She has a poor soul to care for and is putting her whole self into it," he said.

"I'm sorry about Mr. Thompson. I hope we can liberate him from the Japanese soon."

"The women believe he's a prisoner, but word is that he was killed defending the plantation. I just haven't had the heart to tell them." I nodded as we watched the mismatched pair enter the house. However, I wasn't sure withholding that information from Mrs. Thompson was a good idea. The sooner she knew about her husband, the sooner she could come to grips with it.

"I hear you're responsible for our reunion with Paul Marshall. He planned to join us in New Guinea before we gave up being missionaries and took over the plantation."

"Why did you switch from missionary to plantation manager?" I asked.

"The mission society sent us to the interior of New Guinea to savages who worshiped evil spirits and practiced cannibalism. They ran us off from every village in which I preached. Dorothy did make some inroads with her medical skills, but when the chief's daughter died in childbirth, they blamed Dorothy and attempted to kill her.

"I just couldn't justify risking Dorothy's life. So, we escaped from Papua's interior, joining a trading party of the coastal people. They brought us here in their canoes. Never gave the missionary society a complete explanation about why we left and ended up here. They seem to revel in being able to claim martyrs among their missionaries, but that's not what I signed up for.

"We started off as guests of Armstrong-Davis, then he became obsessed with keeping the Japanese off this island. He saw the dangers before any of the rest of us. When he neglected the job of running the plantation, I took over. My family had a farm in Cornwall. Running a tropical plantation is quite different, but I caught on."

Willy came striding across the lawn, a broad grin on his face. "G'day, mate. I see you're fully recovered. Why don't you come to the ridge for some cards this afternoon? Get out of this stinking miasma down here."

"I have to take a shift on the radar in a few hours. So many men are down with one disease or another that everyone is taking shifts, even our Captain. Why don't you come to the variety show with me before I have to report? The first matinee is today. It should be a terrific show. The seating is rough benches for the officers and nothing for the enlisted men, but it is live entertainment."

"Capital idea, old buddy. I haven't seen any entertainment in I don't know how long," Then he whispered in my ear, "Do you have any grub. They keep trying here, but they are almost out of provisions. The pig they were going to roast today disappeared during the night."

"Our mess isn't exactly the Ritz, but let's see what we can rustle up," I whispered.

We drove to the kitchen entrance at the officer's mess.

"Do you have any extra provisions you could share with the plantation?" I asked Sergeant Martin. "They might be able to trade some fresh fish or pork for a few staples."

"We got us a fine porker yesterday. I'm roasting it now," he replied.

"You stole one of the plantation's pigs?"

"That weren't just some wild boar?" I was surprised he looked surprised.

"No, it belonged to the plantation. You had better make it good before we have another war on our hands."

"Well, we must have all the strawberry jam in the entire Pacific on this island. I can give you some of that."

"Add some flour, sugar, and powdered milk," I said. He frowned at me but began pulling together a box of staples, adding salt, pepper, rice, and noodles to my request. After Martin finished, Willy and I put the two cases of staples and six cases of strawberry jam into the back of a jeep.

"Any chance I could get a load of that jam to take to the ridge?" Willy asked Martin. "We haven't had jam since the beginning of the war."

The sergeant tossed two more cases of strawberry jam into the jeep, and we drove back to the plantation. I knocked on the door and asked for Mrs. Reynolds.

"I'm sorry about that pig of yours going missing," I told her, presenting her with a case of jam." I hope these supplies can help overcome the loss." Willy sent the houseboy for the rest of the stores.

"Strawberry jam! I love strawberries. It's been so long since we had anything strawberry. Thank you so much!"

She put down the case of jam and threw her arms around me, then around Willy. "Won't you come in for some tea and toast?"

"We need to get back to get seats at the show," I told her. "Enjoy your jam."

As we drove toward the makeshift theater, Sergeant Hammond flagged us down. He said, "Some mail came in on the supply ship today. You got a letter from that gal of yours."

I turned toward our camp and retrieved the letter. Willy drove the jeep back to the theater while I read.

September 12, 1943

Dear Gene,

I was finally able to ride my bicycle to the castle this weekend. It's sixteen miles from where we are, so we rode thirty-two miles in all. We could only look at it from the outside, but it was very impressive. It's a really old castle, first built around the time of the Norman Conquest, with several additions after that. I wish you could have gone with me. I am sure you would find it interesting. We think we have some old buildings in North Carolina, but that castle was already ancient when the first North Carolina buildings were built.

Our dormitory still isn't finished, but they have brought in a new crew to work on it. It's an all-women crew, and they are working much faster than the old men. I would like to help them so I can learn some new skills, but work has been too busy. They are gone by the time I get back home every evening. I think almost everything will be done next week except the painting. Our closets are in, and the showers are almost ready. We may even be able to take showers tomorrow!

They are having so much trouble fixing up this place for us because, apparently, the US Army and UK Army have different rules. They agreed to follow the US rules for this place. I don't know the difference, but building American style seems complicated for them. Seeing what Daddy and my brothers built at Camp Davis, I don't think the American way is better; it is just different.

My garden is doing great, although I have had to water it a few times. It doesn't rain as much here as I'm used to. I think it's even less rain than you are used to. Maybe this is just a dry year here, but there was less than an inch of rain in August. I am on my second crop of radishes and spinach and am harvesting lettuce every evening.

I was wondering, what vegetables do you like? I have told you that cucumbers are my favorite, but you haven't mentioned anything about what you like. I won't know what to cook for you when we are married. Of course, you can bake. I don't particularly like baking. Maybe I could cook the meals, and you could cook the desserts. My brothers would think that is so funny. But you might not have time when you're a doctor. I might have to do all the cooking. I won't mind so much!

I am really tired and just going on and on without making too much sense. I had better get to bed. I love you so much. I just can't wait to see you again.

Love
Sarah Gale

Willy whipped the jeep around a corner in the newly created road and pulled in behind the entertainment tent. The place was already packed, and no room was left on the officer's benches. The sides of the tent had been rolled up, and men spilled out in all directions, trying to get a view of the stage. Willy positioned the jeep behind the waiting audience, directly in line with the center of the stage, providing an excellent view. But we were barely within hearing distance. We put his crates of jam on the front of the hood and sat on them.

The show began with a comedy team—one artilleryman and one PT boat captain—that had everyone laughing. After several singers and a magic show, Wright performed a tap dance with one of the nurses. Then one of the mess crew stumbled onto the stage, smiled shyly at everyone, and after a nod of encouragement from Wright, began a dynamic and flawless rendition of the Toreador Song from the opera Carmen in a fluid baritone. The audience stared, open-mouthed. We gave him a standing ovation after the song as he stood, grinning, then waved and left the stage.

This performance was followed by an intermission. The second half included a passable ventriloquist, several singers, and a dramatic skit. The quality of the performances Wright pulled together from the troops on the island impressed me. Unfortunately, the show didn't leave as good an impression on Willy. Maybe the Aussies had a different perspective about entertainment, or Willy wasn't into amateur performance.

"Would have been better if we could have heard everything," he grumbled. "Come up the ridge as soon as you can get some time off."

"Perhaps next week. We'll see how things go."

"Sure thing. It'll do you good to get some fresh air."

I felt nostalgic for the ocean breezes and quiet nights on the ridge.

\*\*\*

We repelled two or three small raids per night for several nights. The Japs seemed to be teasing us, sending bombers but turning back from our guns, seldom dropping a bomb. I began to think that they didn't want to lose any planes but wanted us to use as much ammo as possible, hoping we would run out. Fortunately, our ammo supply would take care of the Jap planes for a long time.

About three weeks later, after four nights without an attack, a relatively dry period allowed several sick men to recover enough to return to regular duty. I got leave from Henderson, picked up a couple of letters from Sarah Gale at the PX, and headed up to the ridge. Even in the driest month of the year, the humidity hovered around eighty percent, and the temperature was in the upper nineties day and night. The ridge wasn't much cooler, but the breeze made it more pleasant.

Willy met me at our former camp site when I arrived. "I'll get provisions, and we can swim at the waterfall," he said. A few minutes later, he returned with a backpack full of beer, chipped beef, and peaches.

We hiked along the jungle trail, Willy whistling an Australian song I hadn't heard before. Brightly colored birds darted around the tops of the trees. The scent of the tea tree leaves and various flowers lifted my spirits as we walked. Some varieties I hadn't seen before bloomed along the path, and I stopped to examine them.

"Hurry up," Willy called, "The pool will be empty by the time you get here."

The pool was shallower, and the waterfall trickled because of the reduced rain. We stripped to our skivvies at the waterfall and jumped into the pool. The water, crystal clear and pure, immediately washed away the stress and strain of the nightly air raids, the number of men in sick bay down among swamps, and the stench of the muck in our camp. We dove and splashed and laughed the morning away.

Finally, we climbed out of the pool, opened the cans of rations, and washed them down with Australian beer. I scanned Sarah Gale's letters and then read them to Willy.

*September 26, 1943*

*Dear Gene,*

*Finally, we have showers and sinks and paint on the walls! Everything is finished. I even got to pick my room's color—green or blue. I chose blue because I thought that would be a better color for relaxing and sleeping. I am pretty happy. Some officers aren't because we still don't have laundry service and are having trouble getting supplies. The US Army provides our supplies, even though we are working at a UK base, and they have not been very good at getting things to our small group of WACs. We are expecting a regiment of WACs to arrive soon. That should make a difference; surely, they can't forget about a whole regiment.*

*I assume you have heard that Italy surrendered. We are on the ground in mainland Europe. The big news here is that a group of British soldiers was sent to Italy as replacements for soldiers who had been lost in the invasion. They refused to be assigned to different units. I don't know how they could do that. They made it very clear to us that we would have to serve where we were assigned. Don't they do that in the UK army? Someone here told me it was because they were initially in Northumbrian and Highland units, and the Scots are very stubborn. I'm a Southerner, but I would serve with a unit from any state—even you Yankees!—to get this war over with. I don't quite understand their attitude.*

Willy interrupted. "She doesn't get how insular the Brits are. They are awfully particular about their differences for such a little island."

I nodded and continued reading the letter.

*I have been thinking about where we will live after the war. I see a large Victorian house with a wide porch. We should have four children, I think. I see them playing on the wide porch, riding their tricycles around and around. In the backyard,*

we can have a playhouse by the garden. I will grow all kinds of vegetables. We should have some fruit trees, too. Probably a cherry, a peach, and an apple with a grape arbor we can sit under to stay cool when you come home from work. Do you like dogs? I remember how gently you handled Beaufort when he was hurt, so I assume you do. We could have a dog for them to play with, too.
Love
Sarah Gale

"That sounds idyllic," Willy said. "I hope you get her that Victorian house and the four children."

"I'm planning on it," I said. "As soon as I finish med school."

I started the next letter.

October 3, 1943
Dear Gene,
I am not sure if I am comforted or frightened by your explanation of why you got hallucinations when you had malaria. Why would people in their twenties be more likely to get hallucinations than others? I can understand that you are stressed because you are, after all, in the middle of a war zone, and the fact that you have to stay awake a lot of the time because you are in a searchlight battery makes sense, too, so those two risk factors are understandable. You also said it could be caused by a combination of the drug you are taking and malaria, but you had not taken the medicine when you were hallucinating. The scariest thing was that you said you seem susceptible to hallucinations and drug side effects. Is this going to be a problem all our lives? Let me know what you think because we need to plan for it.

I thought that when the regiment of WACs arrived, they would remember that we were here and deliver supplies to us, but the problem has only gotten worse. We have plenty of green beans and tuna but not much else. Our African cook is much better than the mess crew the regiment brought, but I have to eat lunch at the mess hall. We still have our own cook for dinner, and she leaves things like sausage and biscuits—American-style biscuits, not cookies—for our breakfast.

Some of the other WACs have helped me enlarge the Victory Garden so that we have more like a field than a garden now, full of cool-season vegetables, but everything is growing slowly because of the cool weather. It is colder than home at this time of year. We get more rain in the late summer, but the cook told me the most rainfall comes in the winter here.

I'm looking forward to a bit of moisture. The cook is making delicious meals with the turnips I give her. One night, we had nothing but turnips and squash, and she made six different-tasting dishes from them.

The supply shortage includes a complete lack of fine stockings. Neither silk nor nylon stockings are available. My last pair gave up the ghost last week. We shave our legs and put pancake makeup on them to look like stockings. You should *see us lathering up our legs every morning, shaving them, then covering them with makeup. When the makeup is on, we pair up and draw seams down the back of each other's legs with eyebrow pencils. Some girls can make it last for three days if they don't take a shower, but I am always crossing my legs, working in the garden, brushing up against things, or splashing in the rain, so I have to apply it every day.*

*The local women can't get makeup at all, but it is one thing that always comes in the supply shipments from the States. I gave a tube of lipstick and some pancake makeup to the colonel in command of my unit as a birthday gift for his wife, and you would have thought I gave him a bar of gold.*

*Love,*
*Sarah Gale*

"I wish I had someone like that waiting for me when I get home," Willy said. "I haven't stayed in one place long enough to find anyone."

We heard thunder and looked up. A bank of dark clouds building up on the horizon forced us reluctantly back to camp. The storm overtook us on the way.

"Willy, over here," I said, spotting a slight overhang of coral rock. He slashed off some taro leaves as we ran toward the overhang. We waited out the brief but violent storm there, using the taro leaves as umbrellas.

As we emerged from the overhang, a loud rumbling rose from the ridge. We watched a large section tumbling into the valley as the coral gave way. Only jagged coral remained where the jeep track had been. We ran under the dripping trees back to the radar encampment.

"I radioed the main camp," a young lieutenant, Hastings, told Willy after we reported what we had seen. "They're starting the repairs on the track immediately. The engineers are glad to have something to do again."

"I need to get back down," I said. "I told Captain Henderson I would be back before taps."

"Hastings, get Captain Henderson on the horn."

Willy took the microphone from Hastings when Henderson had been located.

After explaining the situation, he said, "Your man could hike down but wouldn't be there before dark. He would likely get lost in the jungle, and you'd never see him again. A new track'll be done by noon tomorrow. We'll keep him up here tonight."

"Let me talk to Sinclair," Henderson shouted.

I took the microphone. "Sinclair here."

"What do you mean taking off on me like this. Who is going to take your duty tonight?"

"I would suggest Douglas. Wright will be too tired after the show."

"Don't get smart with me," he shouted. "You hardly seem to realize we are trying to win a war here."

"Just trying not to kill myself on that rockslide," I said. "I'll be there for night duty tomorrow."

He signed off.

We played poker well into the night. Not being on duty, I slept late the following day for the first time in longer than I could remember. When I emerged from the tent to the catcalls of the men policing the camp, I went to the chow tent and asked for an Atabrine tablet.

"All out," the mess sergeant told me. "Our supply sergeant went down yesterday to get some and couldn't make it back up the ridge. You should be fine. They're making good progress on the road."

I found a vantage point where I could see the engineers surveying, bulldozers parked behind them to build the road. This would be a real road up the ridge, not just the narrow, rough jeep path we had cut a few months before. We had made it up to the spine in a little over twenty-four hours of brutal slashing. The bulldozers should be able to cut a road in about two hours.

I watched the heavy equipment cut a swath through the jungle and start up the ridge. The bulldozer began to tip when they neared the spot where the old track had crumbled. The operator jumped off as the whole machine fell into a chasm in the coral. My heart sank. As the engineer corps swarmed the fallen machine, I returned to camp and told Willy I would walk down.

"That's crazy," he said. "They'll find a more stable route and cut a new road by tomorrow."

"I can't wait that long," I said. "I need to get back."

"I'm sure Henderson can get by without you. You can get back to writing reports when they get the road built."

"It isn't the reports I'm worried about," I said. "It is the Atabrine."

"You can last for a week without it," he told me.

"I am not so sure. I don't feel so good right now. I'm going," I insisted. "I'll follow the track as far as possible, then detour around it. Even with the detour, it can't take that long. The camp is less than nine miles from here; it's all downhill, and there's a road most of the way. I should be there in two or three hours."

"Radio us when you get there, so we know you aren't lying in some gully somewhere," Willy said.

"Right-O," I replied, loading some rations in my knapsack. Then, I headed down the track.

I approached the upper portion of the washout. Uphill was a vertical cliff, almost impossible to climb. A loose pile of rubble covered the downhill side for at least thirty feet. There wasn't enough area between the cliff and the fallen earth to walk. I decided to risk crossing the rubble.

I walked cautiously across the rubble just below the cliff, clinging to the few trees and brush still poking out from the base of the cliff. Then I came to a steep slope of bare rock, but I felt sure I could get across. As I maneuvered out on the rock, like a crab edging sideways, I suddenly skidded downhill. I dropped to my hands and knees and crawled most of the way across. Even then, I slipped a little with each movement but made more progress across than down. Finally, about three feet from the other side, I lunged for the trees.

Keeping my right knee on the rock, I lifted the other leg and immediately slid toward the precipice. I dropped to my knees again but found nothing to hold onto. The coral cut through my trousers and into my knees and hands as I skidded down the face of the rock, tumbling off into dense jungle underbrush about fifteen feet below me, which cushioned my fall. When I stood and tried to walk, my ankle, weakened in an earlier accident at Fort Worden, buckled under me. I slid deeper down the slope into a stand of sawgrass, which sliced into my face as I rolled. A boulder stopped my descent. I lay there looking through the grey-green leaves as something dark and round approached me, silhouetted against the sun. As it drew closer, I made out thin legs and a long, red neck. I watched as it stepped closer, the feet, with their daggerlike claws, stopping inches from my face. The bird lowered its bright blue head with a sizeable bony crest on top to stare at my chest. Then, as it drew back to strike, my vision faded to darkness.

# CHAPTER 13

## WITH WASHINGTON

**F**IRST, I BECAME AWARE of the cold. Then, as my vision adjusted, I realized I stood in a stone house. A small fire burned in the fireplace. In front of me, a group of men gathered around a rough wooden table. Sitting at the table, I recognized General George Washington.

Oh no, not again...

"St. Clair! Welcome. What say you of the trip south?"

"Uneventful for the most part," I said, wondering how I knew this. "Upon setting foot in New Jersey, the New Jersey soldiers immediately went home. They were the men who were captured in the sea battle and held for a time by the British. Their enlistments ran out, and they were convinced the British had a far superior force."

Washington sighed. Half his men were too ill or weak to fight, barely surviving. The army quartered in houses around the area, and the women did their best to feed and care for them. The tents, clothing, and equipment lost at Fort Washington and Fort Lee in the recent retreat from New York were sorely needed.

"The British do have superior numbers and arms. But they are far from home, and even some of their generals are not convinced that our cause is entirely unfounded. So we simply have to avoid being beaten." Washington replied.

"Easier said than done," General Greene said. "That heavily armed British army isn't far behind us. We should retreat quickly and destroy as much as possible."

"We'll destroy boats and bridges, but we won't destroy farms," Washington insisted. "We're trying to gain independence for the colonists. They can't maintain independence with nothing to eat. But where will we retreat to? They hold New Jersey and Rhode Island, and our support in Pennsylvania is dropping. So, should we cross the mountains?"

"There are even more loyalists on the frontier," I said, having lived in the Alleghenies for the past sixteen years.

"How about Virginia?" asked Washington.

"That would be abandoning half the country to the British without a fight," said Colonel Cadwalader.

"There is a little Pennsylvania village not too far from here where I believe we can still count on support," I said. "It's easily defensible if the British did decide to cross the Delaware and the farmers have adequate supplies. We could launch an attack from there after building up our forces." Washington turned to me.

"Go north to McConkey's Ferry, cross the river, and talk with William Keith," I told him. "He has a large farm in the area and might be able to provide a campsite."

"Pennsylvania it is then," announced Washington. "We will march tomorrow for Keith's farm.

Livingston, my aide de camp, had my tent set up when I returned to camp. "My bones ache like never before," I complained to him. "Can you ride ahead to William Keith's farm first thing in the morning and find a house we can rent in the vicinity where I can sleep in a warm bed next to a fire?"

"Yes, sir," he replied.

I woke in the night, shaking so hard I thought my cot would fall apart.

"I don't know why he is shivering like this in this heat," someone said as another blanket was dropped on top of me.

"He is going into shock," a female voice said. "Keep him as still as possible. We haven't gotten an X-ray yet and don't know how severe his injuries are."

Another form appeared in the faint light.

"Hold him still. I need to get this needle in his vein and get some plasma started."

Someone held down my shoulder while someone else grabbed my left arm. I felt a jab inside my elbow, then something was taped to my arm. The shivering gradually diminished, and I fell asleep.

I woke in a stone house in Pennsylvania.

"Sir," Livingston said to me. "General Washington has called a conference of the general staff."

As I approached the house where Washington was staying General Sullivan joined me. Generals Lee and Gates were already inside the farmhouse sitting in front of the fire. Colonel Cadwalader, acting commander of the Pennsylvania force and General Greene joined us.

"Congress is pushing for a winter campaign," Washington told us. "I am planning to attack the Hessians at Trenton and Princeton. What is the condition of the troops we have here?"

We each discussed the troops we had under our various commands Adding up the total, we had about six thousand, several hundred of whom were sick or injured.

"We must leave some men here to guard the sick. A goodly supply of material has been gathered at Newtown," said Gates. "That will also need to be guarded, leaving us less than three thousand men to attack over five thousand seasoned troops. And in the dead of winter. We shouldn't do it."

I added my opinion. "The new recruits are in relatively good shape but will decline if we remain in camp all winter. Most of the other enlistments expire at the end of the year. Given their current condition and the lack of morale, we need to make a move now if we are to have an army."

"'Tis still folly," said Gates.

"Intelligence indicates they plan to attack us as soon as the river freezes. I would prefer the benefit of surprise over waiting like sitting ducks," said Washington. "They will least expect an attack on Christmas Day. That's when we will strike."

We planned a three-pronged attack, Colonel Cadwalader leading the Pennsylvanians across at Dunks Ferry, the main force with Washington crossing at McConkey's Ferry, and James Ewing crossing at Trenton's Ferry with the artillery.

On Christmas afternoon, the men assembled. Some expected a Christmas surprise, and others hoped for new uniforms or more food. Washington addressed them.

"We will soon leave on a secret mission. Pack three days of food, put fresh flints in your pieces, and be prepared to march. All personnel should be prepared to fight. Even officers and musicians will carry muskets and be prepared to use them. Whatever you do, men, keep by your officers. For God's sake, keep by your officers."

Washington had ordered senior officers to read a new pamphlet by Thomas Payne, called *The American Crisis*, to the men before moving out. I stood before my men, shivering, holding the paper in both my gloved hands to keep it from blowing away in the rising wind.

I read, "These are times that try men's souls. The summer soldier and the sunshine patriot will, in this crisis, shrink from the service of their country, but he that stands it now deserves the love and thanks of man and woman..."

Payne's words gave the men courage. They cheered as I mounted my horse and ordered them to move out. We marched into a light rain under the darkening sky. The rain turned to sleet, then snow as the wind approached gale force. Some of the men strode with rags tied around their feet, others with feet bare and bleeding, but we continued forward. I knew we approached the crossing when I heard Henry Knox shouting and cursing. We finally stumbled into the ferry landing two hours after sunset.

Across the river, I could see Washington on his big Arabian riding up and down the bank, encouraging the troops. Beyond the meandering crowd of soldiers, I thought I could see the Virginia troops of General Adam Stephan in their indigo-dyed coats with scarlet facing forming a sentry line. My men crowded onto the long, narrow, flat-bottom Durham boats borrowed from the nearby ironworks. As the boatmen rowed us across the river, we fended off chunks of ice floating down the river.

By the time all the troops and artillery had crossed the river, we were almost two hours behind schedule, with an eight-mile march through a blinding blizzard ahead of us.

"What say you of our chances?" I asked Washington.

"We've lost the cover of darkness, but this storm may be better cover. They won't be able to see us approaching, and the wind will prevent them from hearing us."

We moved out under the command of General Sullivan. With all the noise and confusion of our crossing, the Hessian patrols should have heard us, but we saw no sign that they had been alerted. Our men traveled more quietly than a regular army. Fatigue, lack of boots, and snow's muffling effect had as much to do with it as their experience hunting deer and turkey.

Washington caught up with us. I rode with him to the front line, where General Sullivan picked his way along the snow-covered road. "Sullivan, take your men south along the river road. Push into the town immediately when you arrive. Cut off the bridge across the Assunpink so they cannot retreat. St. Clair, tell that French officer Congress sent us to march with Sullivan and cut off any attempted retreat. Then you push your regiment toward the center of town."

I found General Matthias Alexis Roche de Fermoy and translated Washington's orders into French. He rallied his men and rode off after Sullivan.

A lone Hessian fired at us as we approached the town, then ran back to his guardhouse, alerting the other men. We got off three volleys before they turned tail and ran. Soon, we heard gunfire from Washington's troops on the other side of the town and, incongruously, a Hessian band playing loud German martial music. Civilians ran into the streets, screaming. I jumped from my horse and stopped one well-dressed woman.

"Return to your house, Ma'am. You'll be safer there. Please try to get all the civilians inside."

Realizing I could not stop the general panic among the civilians, I formed up the young men of my untrained regiment. I feared for them as they faced battle-toughened mercenaries. We marched unopposed almost to the center of town before the Hessians managed to form up and march toward us, flags flying, drums, and bugles playing. The Hessians retook the cannon General Mercer's men had captured, but the powder seemed to have gotten wet, and their guns wouldn't fire. Knox ordered six men to charge the cannons. Their lieutenant, a young man named James Monroe, fell, a bullet to his chest, but the men wrestled the cannon away from the remaining Hessians.

My regiment had taken cover in houses and other buildings, firing on the Hessians from three directions. Finally, the Hessians retreated to a nearby orchard. Some of the German-speaking Pennsylvanians yelled at them to surrender. They immediately put down their arms. We surrounded them, taking over eight hundred captives. I set the older men of the regiment to guard them and returned with the younger ones to the Hessian stockade.

Washington rode by and ordered me to a war council.

"Cadwalader and Ewing were unable to cross due to the weather," he announced. "We cannot go on to capture Princeton without those men and guns. St. Clair has captured eight hundred men and Sullivan another two hundred. "Load up all the supplies you can find. We'll return to Pennsylvania and regroup. General Learned, march the prisoners to Philadelphia."

By noon, we were back across the Delaware, distributing blankets and clothing to keep the men warm and ale to celebrate the victory. It turned out that only five men were wounded, although two were officers, William Washington, the General's cousin, and Lieutenant James Monroe.

I dozed as I sat by the fire during the celebration until a sharp pain in my chest roused me. I started awake to find myself on a cot elevated just a few inches above the floor.

"Hold still, lieutenant. We're trying to get an X-ray," a medic said. "This cassette holds the film. I will slip it under the cot and position the X-ray machine above it. When I signal you, hold your breath until I tell you to release it."

Suddenly, a generator was fired up, and I couldn't hear anything the medic said. He mouthed the word "now", and I held my breath until I passed out again and found myself back in Pennsylvania in 1776.

Washington appeared at my quarters.

"I was driven out of my quarters by the cannonade. We'll hold a general conference here if you're amenable. I have sent for the other Generals.

"We can't win this battle. We're trapped here, between the creek and the river. All is lost," insisted General Gage.

"We can. The British soldiers are fighting because they are told to fight. We are fighting for our homes, rights, and freedom!" Arnold spoke for a frontal attack.

"War is never predictable," Washington said. "We must be prepared to take advantage of any opportunity we can discover and make new plans at the spur of the moment."

"We could regain the element of surprise," I said. "As I was riding through this country last month, I spotted a back road to Princeton. We leave some men here to keep the campfires burning. They must make it look like the whole army is still here. Then we take the back road to Princeton and take the garrison."

I drew a rough map of the area as I remembered it.

"We take Quaker Bridge Road up to Stony Brook. After following the stream for about a mile, we can cut off on this old, abandoned road through Thomas Clark's farm. It's close to the Post Road, but the woods are so thick the British won't see us. If we are quiet, we can reach Princeton without being detected. We'll take the garrison there before Cornwallis even knows we have left."

"Agreed!" Washington declared. "Make sure all the men understand the need for secrecy."

We left five hundred men to keep the campfires burning. The rest of the army marched silently toward Princeton. We could hear British troops marching on the Post Road as we approached the town, but our men walked quietly enough that we were not detected.

As dawn broke, we were still about two miles from town. Washington sent General Mercer to destroy the bridge across Stony Brook to delay Cornwallis' return. Behind General Sullivan, Isaak Sherman and I led our regiments toward Princeton. We could hear the pitched battle toward Post Road near Stony Brook. Mercer must have run into those troops we had heard.

When we emerged from the woods and rejoined the Post Road, a British regiment marched in front of us. They must have been marching toward Cornwallis's camp but returned on hearing the fighting at Stony Brook. They turned to face us.

After a couple of volleys, it was a standoff, neither army moving for fear of exposing their flank. Then suddenly, the British retreated toward Princeton. As we chased them, they took up a position at the edge of a ravine on the north side of town. A platoon moved to flank us.

"Fire on that platoon!" I yelled. Both sides turned their muskets toward each other and there was a deafening explosion.

# CHAPTER 14

## UP AND AWAY

**I** **WOKE LYING ON** a cot, a brown canvas roof swimming into view. Around me, other men lay moaning. Malaria? I felt that and worse.

A plane roared overhead, and I turned to see a khaki-clad medic going from bed to bed. Antiaircraft guns blasted in the distance.

"Are we under attack?' I asked.

"Welcome back, Sinclair. You had quite a severe attack of malaria along with your other injuries."

Another burst of antiaircraft fire, closer this time.

"This is just another one of their flyovers. They haven't gotten close enough to drop bombs on the airfield. Word is they're concentrating their efforts on some town in southern New Guinea."

I took account of my body. My muscles were even weaker than the first time I had malaria. My head ached, and my left leg had some fantastically colorful bruises—blue, red, brown, yellow-green—not to mention the cuts and scrapes on my hands and knees. Raising my head created a throbbing pain in my chest, and the room swam. I dropped back down to my pillow.

"Do you know what happened?" I asked the medic.

"That Aussie captain said you tried to walk down from the ridge after the track collapsed. Near as we can tell, part of the coral gave way under you, and you fell quite a ways down the cliff. It took us three days to find you among the sawgrass. It wasn't easy getting you out. Some locals joined the search, and they were the ones who found you. Said they followed the tracks of some bird. They pulled you out and brought you partway down. You were burning with fever and had cuts and bruises all over your body. Somehow, the buttons and insignia had been ripped off your uniform, the trousers pretty much shredded. After they brought you in, you raved about Benedict Arnold, Aaron Burr, and General Washington for another week. Were you dreaming or what?"

I nodded, barely able to move my head.

"You're going to have to stay here for a while. Doc thinks you got a concussion and said he wanted to observe you after you regained consciousness."

I lay on the cot, just glad to be warm and resting. For most of the next three days, I slept.

Hearing I was awake, Captain Henderson came to visit. "Sinclair," he boomed, "Glad to see you up and around." I really wasn't up and around. "You need to stop sneaking off on these adventures that almost get you killed," Henderson continued. "We need you back on your feet quick. The paperwork is piling up."

"I'm ready to come back. It's hard to sleep with all these sick guys around."

"I brought you some letters from that gal of yours. You check and see when the Doc thinks you can come back."

I opened the envelope as soon as he turned away.

*October 17, 1943*

*Dear Gene,*

*I am really down in the dumps right now. I got word last week that Jeb was injured in Italy. He is alive but was sent home and is still in a hospital in Virginia. I have asked for more details but haven't gotten a reply yet. Mama thought he was less likely to get injured because he was a cook, but look what happened. If a cook can get injured anyone can.*

*It doesn't look to me like we are making any progress in this war. The Germans have taken back some of the territory we took earlier, and we have not heard any news from the Pacific. I have realized that in this war, no news is bad news. And I haven't had a letter from you in over a month. Are you alive?*

*We've had rain every day for two weeks, and the temperature is quite chilly. It generally isn't hard rain. It just comes every day. It rains a lot in the summer at home, but it rains hard and then clears up, so there are fewer really dreary days. I'm glad we are able to wear our winter uniforms. The wool overcoat is the best coat I have ever owned. But, of course, I wouldn't have been able to wear a wool overcoat too often at home, even if we had been able to afford one.*

*Please, please, please write to me.*

*Love*

*Sarah Gale*

I usually sent a letter to Sarah Gale weekly, though for the last couple of weeks I had been in the hospital, so I could not understand why she hadn't gotten them. The mail had been going out regularly since we came down from the ridge. I know how much I cherished her letters to me, and it made me boil to think the army could not get my letters to her. I would have thought it would be much easier to deliver letters in England than to find us as we hopped from island to island and get our mail, wherever it came from, to us. I occasionally got a letter within two weeks of the day she wrote it, although it often took longer.

Brasseux came to visit me before I could read the next letter. He looked worn and haggard. Before deployment, he had problems maintaining his weight below the 175-pound maximum for his height. Now, he looked like he didn't weigh much more than me, and at the moment, I would have been rejected as underweight.

"You mark my word, one o dese days dere gonna make it trough our defenses and drop a bomb on us. Dey jus been teasin us so far, but one day dat bomb gonna come and kill us all."

"All the more reason to be extra vigilant on the job. Have you been taking your sleeping pills?" His accent got much thicker when he wasn't sleeping, and it was deep bayou today.

"Dat's what I came to get, an tot I'd stop by ta visit while I was here."

"Well, you make sure you get enough sleep so you'll be ready when they come," I told him.

"An you get better quick, you hear?" he said.

The doctor stopped by my bedside. "I need to examine this man now. The visit is over." He told Brasseux. To me, he said, "You are one of the luckiest men I've ever encountered. You survive a thirty-foot fall with no broken bones, a cassowary, the deadliest bird in the world attacks you, and you live to tell about it, then you have a severe malaria attack and come out of it with no brain damage."

"I don't feel all that lucky," I told him. "And I couldn't tell you much about the cassowary attack. I lost consciousness before it struck. That's probably why it didn't kill me. No sport in attacking something that doesn't move."

He checked my bruises, had me follow his finger with my eyes, and had Nurse Morris help me into a sitting position before he listened to my heart and lungs.

"Well, you're still among the living. We'll probably send you for R and R as soon as you can stand. In the meantime, get some more sleep."

Rather than go back to sleep, I turned to Sarah Gale's next letter.

*October 31, 1943*

*Dear Gene*

*Today is Halloween. They made a really big deal about not lighting bonfires because of the blackouts that are in effect. I didn't know anything about lighting bonfires for Halloween, but a girl from Scotland I work with told me it was an important tradition there. She told me about how the whole Halloween thing got started. It was called Samhain, which was a sort of pagan fall festival. They* believed that the boundaries between this world and the Otherworld thinned so that spirits and fairies could come through. She said jack-o-lanterns were made to scare off unwanted spirits. I never knew that. Did you?

Anyway, they can't have bonfires, but there is a dance that will probably last past midnight. I went, but it reminded me of the dances we attended at Camp Davis and the Orlando Air Force Base. After that, I got terribly lonely, so I decided to come back and write you.

I have not gotten any letters from anyone in over a month. I want to know what is going on with Jeb. I still have not heard how serious his injuries were. And, of course, I want to know how you are doing. It actually makes me feel better that I have not gotten any letters. If I had gotten letters from home but none from you, I would think something had happened to you. Not getting any letters means something has probably happened to the letters. Whatever it is, I hope they get it figured out soon.

Love,
Sarah Gale

I wondered what was happening with her letters not being delivered.

Nurse Morris approached my bed. "You tolerated sitting up rather well while the doctor was here. He wants you to sit up a bit every day." She helped me sit, and I managed about five minutes before I started swaying, and a medic helped me lie down again.

I read the final letter from Sarah Gale laying down.

November 14, 1943
Dear Gene,
I am getting just like the other WACs. I am upset that I'm not getting my laundry done quickly enough.

The other day, our laundry girl turned eighteen. I arranged a birthday party for her. Her parents were killed in the blitz, so we are all she has. Then, as soon as she could, she joined the Women's Auxiliary Service, and we were without a laundry girl. I was so upset. I had formed a bond with her because she was so much like me — obviously. Up until now, I had no idea why Mrs. McCurdy and Sergeant Brown at the Camp Davis laundry were upset when I joined the WACs.

We found someone else to do the laundry. She is an older woman, and I have not yet learned her name. We have to coordinate things because she is a little slow and swamped with work. We send our laundry on different days because she cannot handle it all at once. My turn hasn't come yet.

I am not sure how things are going in Italy, but there has been a lot of progress on the Eastern front. The Russians have taken Kiev back and seem to be moving forward nicely. I am so glad we don't live in a place like Kiev. The war keeps going back and forth through there and all sorts of beautiful buildings are de-

*stroyed. (At least, that is what the newsreels look like.) I also saw a newsreel on the battle in Bougainville. Those beautiful islands are getting really damaged, too.*

*Things are getting hectic for us here. Don't worry if you don't hear from me. Starting next week, I will be working seven days a week for a while. You can write to me even if you don't get my letter. I hope everything is OK. I am still not getting letters from you.*

*Love,*
*Sarah Gale*

Henderson's visits became more frequent.

"We need you back," he said one day. "Your color is almost back to normal. I'm going to talk to that Doc. It isn't like you do any heavy-duty work. Paper pushing can't be too taxing on you."

Doc let me return to the battery HQ tent the next day. I found scribbled daily reports to be typed, requisitions stacked on the desk undelivered to the supply sergeant, and essential and unimportant paper mixed together in piles on every surface. I added a new uniform and First Lieutenant's insignia to the first requisition. I asked the clerks, "What have you been doing while I was gone. Some of this is routine work that could have been taken care of by any of you."

"Henderson had us filling in on the radar because so many men were down," Private Cox said. "And he was at Battalion HQ more often than here, so we weren't sure what to do."

I thought they could have taken more initiative, but I realized that Henderson sometimes got angry when enlisted men did things without a direct order, and if they had made a mistake, he would have been irate.

I intensely disliked paperwork, but it had to be done. So, I worked my way through it quickly, despite my weakness. I wanted to go on to things I enjoyed more.

"Sinclair, you're a genius with that paperwork," Henderson said as I handed him the last report for his signature two days later. "They should give you a desk job. I'm sure you could keep this army functioning more efficiently."

"Please don't suggest it. I'm just trying to get it out of the way to get a more interesting assignment."

"Well then, you just might get your wish. Call an assembly of the battery. We have orders to move out to the big staging area on Goodenough Island. From there, we'll take on another of these little islands."

\*\*\*

Men scrambled to disassemble radar, take down tents, and prepare for our departure. They moved like a choreographed dance, which was very different from when we first moved the equipment from Fort Bliss. First, the men took apart the radar arms and loaded them neatly into the trucks and trailers. Then, they quickly hitched the searchlights to trucks and lined everything up in neat rows, ready to go in record time.

A rain squall came up just as we took our tents down. Rain had fallen every day since I woke up, the rainy season well on its way. The tents would have to be packed wet. The men got them into trucks, and we headed for the beach. As we parked the last vehicle on the sand, the transport ship appeared on the horizon.

"I'd like to say goodbye to the Aussies up on the ridge," I told Perry. "Can you call them?"

"Oh, the Aussies left while you were sick," he said. He reached into his pocket, taking out an envelope "Forgot to give you this till now. The captain left it for you."

I found a scrap of paper inside the envelope with Willy's APO address written on it.

# CHAPTER 15

## R AND R

**I**T SEEMED FOREVER BEFORE the transport neared the island, but finally, it dropped anchor next to the causeway, opened the bay door, and lowered a ramp. The ship bobbed in the water, constantly changing the ramp's angle. The replacement battery drove their equipment slowly off the vessel and inched up the causeway. I waited in a jeep to lead them to the campsite and give them a little orientation to the island.

When he saw the swampy, stirred-up mud where they were to pitch their tents, the captain turned to me wide-eyed.

"Welcome home," I said.

"How the hell are we supposed to keep our feet dry and our men healthy in this bog?" he asked.

"Mosquito nets, foot inspections, good hygiene, and luck," I said.

As his men pitched their tents on the level spots we had taken ours from, I drove him to the airstrip and pointed out the searchlight locations.

I returned to the beach just in time to follow the last truck up the causeway and onto the ship.

These big, cumbersome ships moved slowly. I settled on the deck for a bit of a nap. It didn't take long for the waves to rock me to sleep.

Perry woke me as the sun sank into the ocean, turning the clouds red and purple.

"Brought you some grub," he said. "We should be at Goodenough within the hour."

At the island, I drove my Jeep up the big concrete dock.

"Battery A, 227th AAA," I told the sentry. "Where do we park?"

He looked at the clipboard in the guard shack.

"Sector O, section 345." He pointed toward a distant field where equipment of all sorts had smashed acres of sawgrass. I drove over to locate sector O, section 345, then back at the dock, motioned the first of the trucks to follow me. Douglas arrived soon after the first truck. As he and the sergeants got the equipment appropriately parked, I went to the almost abandoned staging HQ and inquired about our campsite.

"You'll be breaking new territory," a young corporal told me. "The engineers put latrines and showers there this morning and cleared some tent pads, but there aren't any tents yet. We don't even have signs up, but I can show you. Do you think you can set up your tents in the dark?"

"We do everything in the dark. That's why they call us the moonlight cavalry."

Back at O-345, I assembled the men. Luckily, clouds covered the sky.

"Bring the tents and follow the corporal here. Searchlight team one, fire up your searchlight. We'll bounce the light off the clouds until the camp is set up."

The site, situated in a dense stand of trees well up the side of a dormant volcano in the middle of the island, seemed as quiet as night in a teaming tropical forest could be.

"I don't think your plan will work," Carson said.

"Let's give it a try. Perry, radio our coordinates to the men at the searchlight, and we'll see how this goes."

Soon, a faint greenish-white glow lit the campground. The men had enough light to pull out the damp tents and get them up.

*** 

We rolled out of bed in the morning to discover that we were in one of the most beautiful places in the world. Giant trees, maybe three hundred feet tall, with spiky leaves, towered over our campsite. Other broadleaf trees formed an understory. I examined the tree ferns between the tents, furry new fronds unfurling due to the increased rain of the season. Bromeliads and orchids added color everywhere we turned.

Sergeant Martin called me over. "Ain't these some of them shitty mushrooms they said we could eat?"

I examined the mushrooms growing from the fallen logs scattered around the campsite.

"Shiitake mushrooms. Yes, they are. Why don't you have your men pick them and dry them?"

I heard splashing and shouts. Following the sounds, I found a stream bubbling down the rocks. It fell into a pool where several of the men were already bathing. From here, we had a one-eighty-degree view of the ocean. Below, we could see the staging area where nearly sixty thousand men congregated for upcoming invasions. A narrow, winding road led down to the staging area, smoothly graveled with no mud or ruts. I spotted Henderson returning in a Jeep from below and walked back to camp.

"Get the men together," he said as he pulled to a stop in front of our tent.

I turned to the nearest NCO. "Hammond, get the men up here from the pool."

I called the assembly.

"We have one week R and R," Henderson announced. The men cheered. "We will not be leaving this island, but you are free of regular duty for the next week. All the usual amenities can be found in the staging camp below. You are free to go down there as much as you like, sleep as much as you like, swim, fish, or whatever. Sergeant Martin will be setting his kitchen up here. Anyone caught doing anything wrong will be assigned KP duty to relieve the men in the mess. Dismissed!"

"They call it R and R when we're stuck on this stinking little island," one man grumbled as they were dismissed. "They could have taken us to Australia for a while."

"Back to the swimming hole," shouted Perry.

About two dozen men followed him, pleased to have free time wherever they were. A larger number started down the path to the main camp. I followed them, first picking up the mail for our battery, which Henderson had forgotten to do. I would hand the mail to the men at morning assembly, but I dug through it immediately, looking for letters from Sarah Gale. There was one. I sat down to read it.

November 28, 1943

Dear Gene,

You will never guess what happened! My big brother Johnny came to see me. You probably recall me saying he was stationed in Great Britain, but then he went to North Africa. Now he is back in Britain. Of course, I can't say where or why, but we had a great time together. He thought our food was excellent and our living quarters beautiful. (Of course, I couldn't take him to my bedroom even though he is my brother.) He said his unit had been subjected to much worse conditions, although he thinks the officers get better treatment in some places. He thought it was ironic that of all the people in the family who joined the service, I am the only one who is an officer. He has been getting mail all along, and he told me that Jeb lost one of his fingers in a kitchen accident but is home now, doing well. Joey is in a program where he will eventually be trained as a pilot. He did a bunch of tests, and they decided he would be very good at it.

More and more Americans are arriving in England. We rarely spend time anywhere except our officer's quarters or the bunker where we work, but we see American servicemen whenever we get out. The USO is creating opportunities for American service members and British families to meet. Since the photo interpretation service combines personnel from all allied countries, I have already met the families of several of my coworkers and am living like a Brit. The people who work, train, and live on the American bases feel like they are still in America until they go to a pub or something. The programs were started to keep arguments from *happening, like the problems with your men over words and things.*

*I have been assigned a particular job that I can't tell you a thing about, but it fascinates me. Maybe someday I can tell you what I am doing. Even though I can't tell you what it is. I can tell you how excited I am about doing it. Do you remember when we first talked about what being a WAAC would be like? You said I would still be washing clothes in a different part of the country. Well, I am doing something much more interesting in a different part of the world.*

*Love,*
*Sarah Gale*

So Sarah Gale got to see her family, and here I was in the Pacific, surrounded by strangers. I brooded for a bit, then decided to visit the officer's club and get a drink.

As I walked into the officer's club tent, I saw that Willy had arrived ahead of me, and was dealing cards to a group of junior officers.

"Hey, Mate, join us for a friendly game!"

"Don't mind if I do," I said, pulling up a chair.

"Where do you hail from, Sinclair?" asked Mitchell, the cavalry lieutenant on my right.

"Kansas," I replied.

"National Guard?" he asked.

"Regular army. And you?"

"The 112th was a Texas National Guard Unit before the war. So far, we've provided security on New Caledonia and Woodlark but haven't seen much action."

"Weren't you on Kiriwina, Morrison?" I asked the man on my right, reading the name from his uniform. I thought I recalled him from one of Wright's talent shows.

"Sure was. 158th Infantry. Formerly Arizona National Guard. We spent some time in Panama before coming to the Pacific. Earned the Bushmasters nickname there, although the New Guinea bush has several challenges we didn't see in Panama."

"Like Japs hiding in caves," said Smith, an infantry officer sitting across the table. "We've been here since 1941," he said. "Headed for the Philippines but didn't make it before we were pushed back. We tried to defend Timor. Lost several ships and men getting back to Australia. The unit started as Idaho National Guard, but I'm from Utah. Those distinctions fade after a while here."

"Let's play cards," said Willy.

Several minutes later, an MP interrupted the card game.

"We just broke up a fight between an American search lighter and an Australian radar man. Any officers here who want to claim your men?"

Willy and I rose and went to find American Corporal Randy Rawlins and Australian Private Evelyn Downs sitting in the MP captain's office.

Willy and I started laughing.

"Fighting over your names?" I asked.

The men hung their heads.

"Want to trade?" Willy asked. I nodded. "Evelyn, report to the American camp with Sinclair for KP. Randy, come with me to our camp."

We dispatched the men to our camp kitchens and returned to the officers' club for a beer.

"Think they'll ever learn to accept that even English words can mean different things in different countries?" I asked.

"I hope so because we can't keep breaking up these fights when we're attacked by the Japs," Willy replied.

*** 

Returning from a swim in the pool, I heard something crashing through the tree branches near the path. Tilton dropped out of the tree right in front of me and lay unconscious.

"Medic!" I called and bent to examine him. Brasseux came running through the jungle.

"Merde!" he shouted.

"What was he doing in the tree?" I asked.

"We were tryin' to rig a radio antenna. We can probably get radio from the States if we rig a big enough antenna."

O'Neill arrived and examined Tilton.

"I think he may have a concussion and a few broken ribs. We need to get him to the hospital."

I rode down with them and waited outside as the doctors examined Tilton. Finally, O'Neill returned and said, "I was right about the broken ribs. Doc also thinks he has hairline fractures in both legs. They're going to keep him here for a few weeks."

I drove back up the hill to fill out paperwork on the accident and arrange for someone to take over searchlight officer duties. Henderson decided Douglas and I would share the responsibilities in addition to our regular jobs. So much for R and R!

# CHAPTER 16

## ENEMY FIRE

**O**UR WEEK OF R and R passed all too quickly. I didn't get much rest or relaxation with my extra assignments, although the men seemed reenergized.

I learned we would be part of the first significant amphibious landing in the Pacific entirely organized and commanded by the US Army. Given the resources employed to date, that situation surprised me. None of the senior officers had led a significant beach landing before. The navy, marines, or Australian forces had previously handled beach landings. So, the general scheduled a full-scale rehearsal before we left.

It didn't go well. Troops climbed down nets at about half the planned speed, ships and landing craft crossed paths, barely avoiding collision, men arrived at one section of beach and their equipment to another, and officers barked orders that troops did not understand. In the end, the pretend Jap troops annihilated the infantry. After the rehearsal, the senior officers met to debrief.

I saw Mitchell of the 112th Cavalry in the officer's mess. The Cavalry would be among the first on the beach. "Are your troops prepared for this?" I asked.

"Hell no. We just got issued new weapons we've never even fired. There's no time for training. We have to learn to use them in the field. The colonels and generals are meeting to replan the operation, and it starts the day after tomorrow. You and I will get instructions we don't know how to carry out, and the men will be scared to death after the fiasco today. I don't like to be in such an unpredictable situation."

"War is never predictable," I said. "We have to be prepared to take advantage of any opportunity we can discover and make new plans at the spur of the moment."

"I guess, but I was an accountant back home and can't calculate our odds as favorable."

In all honesty, I wasn't much more confident than Mitchell. Still, the safety of my searchlight unit depended on the actions of his cavalry and the artillery.

***

Orders came to begin boarding the ships around noon. Our battalion arrived at the docks in pouring rain. The confusion in getting all the men and equipment on board did not bode well for the departure. Sixteen hundred men, driving or carrying the equipment necessary for combat, antiaircraft operations, base construction, mess, and medical care, milled around on the docks, uncertain where to go due to the changes made at the last minute. Finally, the senior officers arrived from the briefing. The men stood in long lines, sweating despite the rain. Ammo belts and pack straps held the damp heat against their bodies. Rain dripped off helmets into their faces. Word came that the battery and company COs should report for a briefing.

"We'll be in the fourth wave onto the beach," Henderson told us after meeting with the colonel. "A marker on the docks should indicate where the fourth wave will assemble. Sinclair, find the marker." Then, he turned to the other lieutenants. "As soon as Sinclair radios the location, get the men moving in that direction." Apparently, the only thing that had changed was the order of the landing.

Perry and I drove down the crowded docks, asking questions until we found a couple of privates tacking a newly painted sign with a four on it to a pole. I reconnoitered the area to find landmarks.

"Tell them to return to the main road and follow it south until they come to the engineer's depot, then turn right," I told Perry. "There's no way they'll get here before tomorrow if they try to come down the docks."

Soon, Henderson appeared, leading the battery to our location. The transport ship was already in place. At least the Navy knew what they were doing.

"When you hear the order, get the equipment on board and find bunks for the men as quickly as possible!" Henderson barked. "I'm going to notify the rest of the battalion to come down the main road."

He could have radioed, but I gathered he wanted kudos for finding a more efficient way to get to the location.

The ship signaled its readiness. Douglas and the drivers moved out to the cargo loading ramps while I led the men up the gangplank and onto the foul-smelling ship. They had all claimed prime bunks before the next unit arrived but, before long, discovered that sleeping on deck in trucks or under our tarps would prove more comfortable.

When we left the dock at midnight, the weather remained rainy, the waning moon invisible behind heavy clouds. We plowed through choppy seas all night. At least a third of the men barfed their guts out. I felt fortunate I didn't suffer from that malady.

The sun peeked through the clouds as we rendezvoused with the four destroyers escorting us to the island. The movement of the ships provided some breeze, but the heat still bore down on us. To make matters worse, drinking water was only available three times a day. The men quickly lined up each time it was turned on to fill their canteens. In the officer's quarters, two-gallon water jugs were filled each time they were emptied, but we were only allowed to fill small paper cups, not canteens.

For most of the day, we sailed north, then, at sunset, turned abruptly toward the Arawe Peninsula on the island of New Britain. After eating reconstituted potatoes and chipped beef in gravy, I settled into my narrow bunk, falling asleep almost instantly. I woke to explosive gunfire.

"What's going on?" I shouted as I leaped out of the bunk, landing on Brasseux's backside as he jumped out of the bunk below me.

"Whatcha doin', man. Careful!" he complained.

We pulled on our pants and ran to the deck, pulling our shirts on. The destroyers bombarded the shore. Their guns flashed, sending one shell after another onto the beach where great clouds of smoke rose and the coconut trees burned. The bombardment went on and on. Then suddenly, it was quiet. We could see the decimated forest through the clearing smoke; many trees were still on fire.

The cavalry units climbed slowly onto the landing craft on the starboard side of the first transport. Something seemed to be wrong, though. Infantry and cavalry were supposed to approach while the smoke hung over the island. Instead, they couldn't seem to get going. We watched as the first wave struggled to move toward the beach.

"Why aren't they moving in?" I asked a navy lieutenant.

"Tides going out, and the Higgins boats can't buck the current. The engine isn't powerful enough to move a fully loaded craft against an outgoing tide, so they can't get into the proper formation," he said. "Damn army doesn't even look at the tide charts!"

"SNAFU," Brasseux said, straight-faced and serious.

"FUBAR," I nodded.

The navy man walked away, shaking his head.

I wondered why the navy hadn't said anything to the general or one of the colonels. Maybe they had.

Finally, the first wave approached the beach. The men ran off the LCT, trying to reach the cover of trees as machine gun fire burst from a cave in the cliffs, followed by heavy shelling from mountain guns we could see at the mouth of several caves. A barrage of rockets arched over the beach, collapsing the cave entrances and silencing the guns.

The next wave approached the beach slowly, the LCVPs moving a little faster as the tide lost force.

"Triple-A, onto the landing craft!"

Unlike the training fiasco, we swarmed down the nets and into the waiting landing craft in record time. We stood behind the high steel walls of the new, improved LCVP, gripping our rifles, the walls protecting us from enemy fire. The men in the center crouched to keep their balance. I leaned against the wall, my hand on the pocket where I had Sarah Gale's last letter. 'I'll come back,' I whispered.

The LCVP moved off toward the beach. The skipper and a gunner stood on a platform above us, exposed to fire from shore as the boat powered toward the beach. The tidal current no longer pulled as hard as it had when the first two waves moved in. We caught up with the wave in front of us. Behind us, the fifth wave came on fast.

About a yard from shore, the skipper dropped the ramp. We ran like crazy off the boat, all thoughts of anything else gone. The smell of smoke, gunpowder, and burning trees, the splashing water as we ran toward the beach, and the hope of making it to the trees before more gunshots came drove us forward.

On the beach, we ran into utter chaos. Four waves of personnel had arrived at essentially the same time. At least a thousand soldiers on the beach ran in fear toward the cover of the decimated coconut trees, trying to find their unit and take the island.

I led the men to the dubious shelter of the bombed trees and took stock of the situation. I tacked our HQ sign to the charred palm trunk facing the beach. Edelstein yelled at his men to get into formation and stand at attention. Carson's platoon dug shallow trenches under the trees, getting out of sight of Japanese rifles and machine guns. All the HQ and maintenance groups found us, but Brasseux's platoon and the drivers bringing our equipment ashore had veered off somewhere.

"Edelstein, since you have your men in formation, scout out a suitable location for the lights. Sinclair, find the missing platoon and equipment," Henderson ordered.

A large coconut plantation comprised most of the peninsula, with trees spaced widely and roads every mile. Enemy fire had ceased for the time being. I trudged over the sand, checking with each unit gathered at the former edge of the coconut grove. Soon, I located our missing platoon with an AAA gun battery gathering further down the beach.

"Brasseux, wrong battery."

"These are the guys with the guns," he said.

"All they have so far are machine guns and rifles. We have those, too. Get your men up and moving. We're about three hundred yards up the beach." So far, there has been no sign of the missing equipment.

When we heard aircraft approaching, the platoon had just begun moving: eight Aichi D3A dive-bombers, called Val's by the AAA, and at least fifty Zeros. The bombers came in low to drop their payload on the larger landing craft, bringing equipment and supplies ashore. Zeros strafed the beach. The skippers of the boats performed some impressive evasive maneuvers considering the unwieldy flat-bottom boats as the gunners fired their machine guns at the planes approaching the beach. We watched as one of the Zeros burst into flames and turned back, leaving a trail of smoke.

"You hit it!" shouted Brasseux. "You brought down a plane with nothing more than a machine gun."

"It's the only antiaircraft gun on the island at this point," said the gunner. "I didn't have much choice."

As the planes turned, another gunner shot a Zero, and it plummeted into the ocean. A PT boat moved in, plucking the pilots out of the water. The supply landing craft, all undamaged, landed quickly. The two direct hits without any heavy artillery landed yet seemed to have spooked the Japs, and they turned and left.

Farther down the beach, the Quartermaster's corps scurried among the boxes and piles like ants, sorting and organizing. Douglas stood among maintenance and supply officers on the beach, watching for our equipment.

I approached him. "We thought you took a wrong turn," I said. "When do you expect the equipment to arrive?"

"It's on those boats. They brought the tanks first so the Cavalry could move out. That's why the Jap gunfire stopped. The cavalry headed up the peninsula, taking out their pillboxes and mortaring the caves."

When the landing craft arrived, our battalion drivers, who had ridden ashore in their vehicles, quickly drove off the landing craft as the officers directed them to the correct location. The quartermaster's corps swarmed the supply trucks, loading supplies, food, and ammo from the piles on the beach into any empty spaces in the trucks or trailers. I described our temporary HQ site to Douglas, telling him to bring the equipment as soon as the supplies were loaded. All the equipment and supplies were on the beach, and the ships were out of sight within an hour.

***

Finally, Edelstein and his tired, mud-covered platoon appeared through the trees.

"This whole place is mostly coconut trees and swamps, but I did find a rocky outcropping that might serve," he reported to Henderson. "It's out of range of the remaining caves, good line of sight, and we can get our vehicles up there on the Jap roads.

His men sat down to scrape the mud from their boots, clearly exhausted from the tension of the landing and slogging through swamps in search of higher ground. Edelstein eyed them, but Henderson called for a more complete report on the lay of the land, so Edelstein's men had a reprieve.

Douglas and the drivers made their way slowly across the beach, the maintenance crew dragging the heavy chain tracks from the back to the front of the convoy. As they inched toward us, the bombardment from the cliffs resumed, and more Japanese Zeros approached.

"Brasseux, Carson, get your men out there and get those trucks moving," Henderson ordered. They had entered a grove of coconut trees about half a mile down the beach, partially left standing after our bombardment. We heard crashing as the trucks pushed through the fallen trees and bumped over the bombed-out ground. They raised a great deal of dust and ash, which the wind obligingly spread, effectively screening our exact location.

After an unbearably long time to those of us waiting under strafing Zeros and bombardment from the cliffs, the convoy appeared out of the cloud of ash and dust.

A quick inventory and roll call proved that the battery, equipment, and supplies were all present and accounted for.

# CHAPTER 17

## ARAWE

**T**HE CAVALRY MOVED UP the peninsula. Intense gunfire told us they had engaged the enemy once more.

We pushed through the coconut grove in the opposite direction, climbing a narrow road rounding the cliffs from which the firing had come during the landing. Edelstein led us toward the top of the cliffs, the best vantage point for spotting enemy aircraft. We moved cautiously, knowing this area had been occupied by the Japs only a few hours earlier. The path narrowed and became impassable to our trucks when we passed the level of the caves. We organized the men to cut a road from the track. It was much faster going than on Kiriwina. The vegetation was thinner, and the slope more gradual and broader.

Suddenly, Edelstein stopped, holding up his hand. We dropped to the ground and looked at where he pointed. He had spotted movement near the opening of a cave below us. Two machine gunners crawled toward it, guns at the ready. A private darted between them and tossed a grenade into the cave. We heard screams as the limestone crumbled, sealing off the cave. We would never know how many were interred there.

A few hundred feet further, we spotted a group of Japs running through the jungle. Several men fired at them, but none fell, and we did not pursue them. Our objective to get the radar set up took precedence.

Finally reaching the top, we posted sentries around the site as we deployed the radar. Within fifteen minutes, our single SCR-584 was operational. The men ran cables for the gun controllers down to a level area where the gun battery could position their equipment. We radioed that we were active and ready. I pulled the HQ tent and camp chairs off the truck and assigned some men to set it up. Sergeant Hammond arrived a short while later with two truckloads of supplies.

"The gun battalion's not far behind. They'll be setting up on that shelf about a third of the way down." He announced loudly. "But no 90-millimeter guns made it off the ships. The Japs will be able to bomb us off the island, and we won't be able to do a thing about it."

Several of the enlisted men stopped what they were doing and stared at him.

"Hammond, report to me in my tent," ordered Henderson.

They disappeared into the tent and stood arguing. Finally, when Hammond came out, he mumbled, "Well, it's true. We can't do our job under these conditions and will probably die trying."

"Maybe," I said. "But don't announce that to the enlisted men."

"They deserve to know if they will be blown off the earth. This isn't a very good site, anyway. Why did we set up here?"

"We can defend the beach from here, and there are still several shiploads of supplies to be unloaded, as you should know, being Supply Sergeant. We'll move to a more strategic spot once the island has been scouted and secured."

"Pack up and move, set up, tear down. That's all we do. You know this is just a diversion, so the main force can go into Cape Gloucester."

"If all we do is keep a couple of divisions busy while the Gloucester landing takes place, we have at least given them a chance. But this could become a strategic base for planes and PT boats."

"It's too swampy for the big planes, and the coast is either cliffs or reefs. So this place is totally useless."

Perry ran toward us.

"Another air raid is coming, but the guns aren't set up. What do we do?"

"Radio the coordinates to the Air Corps. There's a combat patrol out there somewhere." I replied.

He ran back to the radar as about twenty Zeros appeared on the horizon. They came in bombing and strafing the supply boats unloading on the beach. We watched the approaching vessels attempt evasive maneuvers, although one was hit before it reached the shore. The supply party on the beach took cover under the coconut trees. Then, the sixteen P38 Lightnings of the US combat air patrol moved in, and the Zeros turned away.

Edelstein's platoon set up to the northeast, Brasseux's platoon manned the SCR-584 in front of HQ, and Carson's men set up to the south, closest to the beach. We spent the afternoon setting up the older radar, monitoring the 584 radar, and watching the crews on the beach, still sorting the supplies. They were obviously inexperienced. This could be said for us, too. Sitting on Kiriwina, where there were no Japs on the ground and fewer than thirty in the air the entire time we were there, could not be considered preparation for a combat situation like this.

"I believe more training would have been helpful," I told Captain Henderson as we watched.

"There's nothing like getting in the game to make a man of a boy," he said. "All the training in the world doesn't prepare you for the real thing. We should have more boys down there, but we'll make do with what we have. I sent Hammond down with his men to help sort things out."

"That should make them feel better," I said grimly as I set out to inspect the radar, which would have been Tilton's job had he not been hospitalized on Goodenough Island.

We heard sporadic gunfire and the occasional sound of a bazooka firing into a cave. It seemed the cavalry had cleared out most of the opposition on this part of the peninsula.

Another thirty Zeros and twelve Sally and Betty bombers flew over, strafing and bombing the supply convoys and the men on the beach. The gun battery fired their machine guns and 40-millimeter guns at them but did not manage to down any more planes. We watched as many of the supplies that had made it to the shore were blown up. Medics and soldiers rushed from the cover of the palm trees to pull the injured off the beach.

*** 

By evening, we had set up communications with a network of Australian coast watchers on various islands around the area. Willy's company was on an island off the coast. They began giving us thirty to forty minutes' notice before planes arrived. The Japs soon learned that we did not have any 90-millimeter guns on the peninsula and came in just out of range of the smaller 40-millimeter guns. The frequent attacks took a terrible toll on the quartermasters and navy supply personnel.

Air attacks continued throughout our second day on the island. Most planes approached from the northeast, keeping Edelstein's men on constant alert. We watched, helpless, as at least fifty Jap planes continuously attacked the ships offshore, entirely out of reach of any gun we had and effectively evading the navy guns. One transport ship suffered a direct hit and sank within five minutes. A sub-chaser and minesweeper plus four LCTs were also hit and sustained damage. The PT boats in the escort dodged among the refuse, picking up survivors. In a briefing at HQ the following day, we learned that forty-two men had been killed or seriously wounded.

Once their equipment arrived onshore, the engineers quickly laid out a large rectangle near the beach. They established a partially underground field hospital, safe from continuing attacks, where the medical corps treated survivors. Everyone on the island was short on supplies. Too often, the landing craft left the beach before their cargo was unloaded. Sergeant Martin began sending his men out foraging, but the Japs had been on the island for some time, and even wild food was in short supply. Although we had landed in a coconut grove, there wasn't a ripe coconut to be found.

We watched, helpless and furious from our cliff, as planes came in, dropped their bombs on the boats, and left without our guns even having a chance at shooting them down. The air force boys had been called back to their bases to fly air raids on Rabaul, the home base of the Jap planes. The bombs kept coming every day, sometimes more, sometimes fewer. With constant attacks, short rations, and a lack of supplies, morale fell to a new low.

Henderson returned from the daily briefing. "The cavalry created a line of resistance at the head of the peninsula, about two miles up. We're safe from attack by land. They've placed landmines beyond the barbed wire. Make sure none of the men try to leave the peninsula."

They didn't need to worry that we would wander into their minefield. The constant threat of air attacks kept us busy day and night.

We could see a village across the bay from our cliff where additional troops had been stationed. They were beyond the resistance line, but there didn't seem to be much activity there.

\*\*\*

After we had survived a week of half rations, another supply convoy approached the landing site. We looked forward to better meals and plentiful ammunition. Suddenly, our radios came alive.

"About fifty planes approaching," the Aussies said.

"Looks like they've sent an entire wing your way," one of the coast watchers said.

"At least two hundred planes," said another.

We directed the radar toward their approach and alerted the gun battery and the Air Corps. We realized the estimated two hundred was closer to the truth as the aircraft came. The first wave attacked as the convoy made their way through the narrow straight between offshore islands. We could not determine the extent of the damage from our vantage point, but we saw smoke. The convoy sped up, trying to get within range of our guns before the planes could turn and approach them again. They didn't make it. The second pass disabled one of the supply ships, stopping the convoy behind it as it foundered near an offshore island. The US Air Corps swooped out of the clouds as the third pass approached the remaining ships. We watched as the US planes flew from above and behind the Jap planes, gunning them down one after the other. As the spectacular air battle continued, we counted the downed aircraft. The flyboys shot down sixteen planes without losing one themselves. Our entire battery stood on the cliff and cheered as the Japs took off to the northeast.

The remaining supply boats were able to land. They carried both food and mail. I don't know which was more welcome. I devoured Sarah

Gale's short letter while eating my first full meal in two weeks.

December 5, 1943
Dear Gene,
There was a meeting of the heads of state in Cairo. You probably heard about it because it was about Japan. Chiang Kai-shek was there, so Stalin didn't go. I don't think Russia is at war with Japan. I think they just declared war on Germany. I am not sure if that is right, but there was some reason Stalin wasn't there. I can't pretend to know what they talked about, but things may get more coordinated now. Every time you talked about your supply situation in the letters I got upset. You would think they would have it worked out by now, and you would get supplies more regularly.

My turn finally came to send my laundry to the new lady. She does an excellent job. She got some stains out that I didn't think would ever come out, and her ironing is perfect.

Huge numbers of planes are leaving every day now. We see them going late in the day. They come back when we are asleep. I think perhaps the tide has turned in Europe. I don't know much about the big picture, but I think we are bombing there now more than they are here.

Working seven days a week is really exhausting. I am going to bed.
Love
Sarah Gale

\*\*\*

A few days later, I looked at the date as I signed and dated the daily report.

"Hey, it's Christmas," I said to Henderson.

"So it is. Merry Christmas."

We went back to work. Suddenly, we heard intense gunfire. The Japs had attacked the village across the bay. The night crew woke from sleep and nervously lined up among the trees close to the cliff's edge to watch the battle. It subsided quickly, although two other attacks during the day kept us on edge.

That evening, Sergeant Martin served a delicious fish dinner with a shiitake mushroom sauce. Afterward, everyone not on duty gathered in the mess tent to sing Christmas carols, listening carefully for any renewed gunfire from the village or defensive lines.

The land battle continued through the end of December without much progress. Finally, on the last day of the month, the cavalry forced the Japs back to an abandoned airfield farther up the island. The cavalry officer reported seven casualties among US troops and at least fifty Japanese casualties. He was confident they would have the Japs on the run in another week.

On New Year's Eve, I had just finished the daily report and was on my way to check with Douglas about some repair parts he needed before catching some shuteye when the most damaging air raid yet bore down on us. A few of the planes came in low to strafe the beaches, hitting a supply of ammunition, which blew up, destroying several cases of food stacked nearby. The gunners shot all they had at those targets, downing two. We cheered with the gunners and the men in the trees near the beach.

On New Year's Day, almost as many planes attacked as on D-day. This time, they stayed higher, although the gunners shot at them, and one left trailing smoke.

"That one will surely go down before it gets back," Henderson said. "Do we have anything around here for toenail fungus?"

I handed him a little bottle of potassium permanganate powder I kept in my kit.

"Put about half a teaspoon in a gallon of water and soak your feet in it twice a day."

He opened the bottle, frowned at the purple crystals, replaced the cap, and pocketed the bottle.

After New Year's, the raids continued daily, but significantly fewer aircraft approached in each raid. Word was that the air attacks on Rabaul had reduced the Japanese air fleet, and they had only thirty to fifty planes left to harass us. With fewer attacks, the supply convoys began to get through. Martin started to cook larger, tastier, more rounded meals, Douglas's crew repaired all the vehicles and lights, and we even got a few new tents to replace those most severely damaged by fungus when we put them away wet.

I noticed Captain Henderson limping as he climbed the muddy track to HQ.

"What's the problem?" I asked.

"Just a bit of jungle rot. It'll be fine."

"Did you use that solution I gave you? You should take your shoes and socks off and soak your feet at least twice daily."

"Stop trying to be my Mama, Sinclair. We have a war to fight, and I intend to fight it to the end."

I turned back to my work, knowing I could not sway Henderson.

Brasseux was not sleeping again. I sent O'Neill for more sleeping pills from the hospital, but it did not help this time. He continued to be delusional and paranoid. The doctor confined him to the hospital, putting him on more potent drugs to see if he could get back on track. Henderson assigned Wright, Douglas, and me to lead his platoon on rotating shifts. My duties, half of Tilton's and a third of Brasseux's, meant about four hours of sleep a day.

To make matters worse, Henderson had been called to battalion HQ, helping out while Sessions was down with malaria. For a good part of the day, I served as Battery Commander. Everyone operated on adrenalin and coffee. The medics passed out bennies to men pulling double shifts.

Edelstein's platoon had the fewest men report for sick call. As I trudged up to their site, not driving the jeep to save gas for the generators that ran the lights and radar, I wondered if it was because they were farther from the swamps and a bit higher in elevation. When I got there, I noticed an unusual number of men were up and scurrying about the camp. I approached a group of men who should have been sleeping at this time of day. I noticed hand tremors among some of them, and they chattered away without listening to each other. All of them had dark circles under their eyes.

"Good afternoon, men," I said.

They turned, seemed surprised to see me, then burst out laughing.

"Shouldn't you be sleeping so you can work the night shift?"

"Oh, we don't sleep much anymore. Lance gives us those bennies; we do just fine without much sleep. You should try some. They make you feel so fine!" a private told me, grinning widely.

"I don't think so," I barked, striding off to find Lance and Edelstein.

I found them both at Edelstein's tent.

"How many bennies do you give the men?" I asked Corporal Lance.

"As many as they want," he replied.

"Are you here to interfere with the discipline of my platoon again, Sinclair? Those pills keep them on duty when all the other soldiers are dropping like flies," Edelstein demanded.

"I just wanted to make sure you know that the pills can keep the men functioning, but if they get too many, they can become anxious, irritable, or even show signs of psychosis," I said. "Lance, keep track of how many each man gets. Try to keep it under twenty milligrams per day."

"Yes, sir," Lance replied.

***

Despite heavy cavalry attacks, the Jap regiment was securely dug in and had not budged from their position near the airstrip. General Cunningham moved cautiously, not knowing how strong the Jap forces were and wanting to keep this regiment pinned down until the more significant battle at Cape Gloucester had been completed.

The ninety-millimeter guns arrived on January tenth, along with a company of Marines. I was pleased we finally had our big guns. Two letters from Sarah Gale also came on the transport, which pleased me more.

December 19, 1943
Dear Gene,
I am getting really lonely at the thought of being so far from you and my family at Christmas. Johnny can't get leave to come see me, and I can't go to where he is. All the radio stations are playing "White Christmas" right now, perfectly designed to make us all feel homesick. Bing Crosby has a new song this year that is even worse. It is called "I'll be Home for Christmas." Have you heard it? It makes me want to cry every time I listen to it. The Colonel made us stop playing the radio in our photo room because he said he needed us to pay attention to what we were seeing, not cry our eyes out over some sentimental song. The thing is, I saw tears in his eyes the last time they played "I'll Be Home for Christmas." And his wife and kids are here in this country. I have never asked him where his home is, but it is in England.
We might have to work on Christmas, but we are planning a little celebration. We drew names and are giving each other gifts. I will have to think hard to decide what to give the girl whose name I drew. She is a wealthy heiress from Atlanta whose family sends her anything she asks for. She is friendly to the rest of us, but she is the one who led the complaints about not having the accepted level of service. She could not believe it when I told her I had always washed and ironed my own clothes. Some other girls said they did, too, which amazed her. Her name is Sylvia.
I wish you were able to join me for Christmas.
Love,
Sarah Gale

I wished I could have done anything other than work for twenty hours on Christmas, but most of all, I wished I could have spent it with her. I thought back to the December day when the Japs attacked Pearl Harbor. At that time, I had served half of what was supposed to be my one-year stint in the army. We thought on Christmas of 1941 that with the United States in the war, it would end in no time. Now I could see that we were overconfident then.

I opened the second letter.

December 26, 1943
Dear Gene,
We did get two days off, yesterday for Christmas and today for something they call Boxing Day. I thought maybe everybody got together to fight out the arguments that started on Christmas, but it is really a time when people give gifts to their servants. We Americans found out almost too late that we were expected to give something to our cook, washing woman and the people who clean the office.

*Fortunately, they expect money and other small gifts, so we each made a donation, and Jenny and I picked up a few things from the PX that we put in the boxes with the rest of the money.*

*I don't think I have told you about Jenny. She is from Ohio and works at the desk next to me. I am the youngest working there because everybody else went to college. Jenny helps me out sometimes when I don't know something, but she doesn't make me feel stupid or immature. We have lots of fun together even though we don't have much time for anything but work lately, and we have to ride our bicycles to and from work in the dark because of the short winter days; we find games to play along the way.*

*Still no letters from you. Why aren't you writing? I am getting really worried.*

*Love,*
*Sarah Gale*

I had no idea why she was not getting the many letters I was writing. Something had to be seriously wrong. I asked the private in the mail room if they sent them out regularly.

"Oh, yes, sir! You aint the only one with a gal across the water. We'd have hell to pay if we didn't send out those letters."

"Has your gal been getting the letters?" I asked.

"There was one she missed, but for the most part, she has, sir."

"Then why haven't my letters gotten through to England? I asked.

"No idea, sir."

***

I was filling in for Brasseux when news came from a coast watcher that three Vals were approaching, about half an hour out.

"Notify the radar and gunners," I instructed the crew. "Report back to me on the status of the big guns."

The report came back. "Guns are up and ready. Communication with radar established."

"The Japs are in for a surprise today," I said.

We watched as the Vals approached. They flew directly over the guns, believing they were out of range. The big ninety millimeters boomed, and two Vals fell out of the sky.

"Did you see that?" asked the sharpshooter on sentry duty. "Two at once. They will know we mean business now."

"Sure will," shouted the men.

There were no raids for three days after that. We were beginning to think the worst was over when the attacks started up again. Two planes, five planes, six, seven. Never the fifty that had bombed and strafed us as we landed or the hundred and fifty the week after landing, but continuous harassment, so we could never relax.

General Cunningham had requested reinforcements as the cavalry was down by at least ten percent. Tilton arrived with the relief troops.

"Tilton, you have no idea how glad I am that you're back!" I called out when I saw him approaching the HQ tent. "I've been trying to do triple duty: your job as radar officer, manage Brasseux's platoon, and my own."

"What happened to Brasseux?" he asked, apprehensive.

"He wasn't sleeping again, and Doc hospitalized him for a while. He's back up and around now. Everything should be fine if the two of you don't get any wild hairs up your butts.

# CHAPTER 18

## FRIENDLY FIRE

**I** **MOVED MY LITTLE** camp desk and chair outside the HQ tent. I could no longer tolerate the burning of my nose and eyes. Birds flitted around the site, exploring these new inhabitants and picking up everything from bits of food the men had dropped to broken shoestrings and brown paper that had wrapped a package from home. I breathed deeply of the thick swamp smell and deemed it better than the chemical smell inside the tent. I could no longer tolerate the burning of my nose and eyes. Between the stifling heat and noxious fumes of whatever Henderson was using on his jungle rot, I could not get anything done.

"Sinclair!" Henderson sat with his shoes off, pouring a bitter-smelling solution on his feet. I picked up the bottle. Picric acid. While the acid had been used during the Great War as an antiseptic and treatment for trench foot, it was far better known as an explosive. Artillery shells had been filled with picric acid for the past hundred years. Only recently had TNT taken over as the most common explosive. TNT was less powerful but much safer to handle.

"Do you know what this is?" I asked.

"It's trench foot medicine Sergeant Hammond gave me."

"Poisonous, explosive, outdated trench foot medicine."

I watched him pour more of the solution on his feet. His toes were swollen beyond recognition, the flesh slowly being eaten away. There was an enormous seeping ulcer on the heel of his right foot. He flinched as the acid hit his inflamed skin.

"Colonel Squires needs to talk to someone from the battery. Go see what he wants."

"Yes, sir. And I will bring back some silver nitrate from the medical tent. It's not explosive or poisonous like that picric acid you're using."

"I don't want any of that pink stuff. I am not going to run around with pink feet."

"As far as I'm concerned, pink feet are better than no feet, but potassium permanganate is the one that will turn your skin pink. Silver nitrate is more effective and will turn them grey. Let me dispose of this picric acid. It is old and probably unstable. It could explode any time."

"Give me back my medicine and go meet with Squires."

"Yes, sir."

***

"Where is Henderson," Colonel Squires asked as I entered the tent. The other battery commanders were already gathered.

"Can't walk because of jungle rot."

"Get that fool down to the hospital right after this meeting. Tell him it's an order."

"I will, Colonel."

"The Cavalry and Infantry have made it to the airfield where the Japs are dug in. It's located in a valley northeast of the peninsula. The runways are too short, the coral too soft, and the field too overgrown to be of use to us, but they have two divisions of Japs pinned down there. The fighting is intense, and they can't help us out if the Japs decide to attack down here. We have orders to flush out any Japs still hiding in the caves and forests. Each battery will form two ten-man patrols per day. These patrols will seek out and destroy enemy personnel remaining in the assigned sector. Colonel Brewer said there were only isolated pockets of Japs left. We want them all eradicated. Perkins, the orders."

Perkins handed out orders, and we gathered around the map and aerial photos, surveying our sectors.

"We should each start on the northern section of our patrol area," Captain Hawkins said. "Wouldn't want to run into one of our patrols and think they're Japs."

"If we're going to have personnel out, we should coordinate that with the gun batteries," I said.

"Get your XOs on that," Colonel Squires ordered. "Questions?"

"Do we search swamps and marshes or just the uplands and cliffs?" asked Captain Gill.

"You search every inch of the peninsula. If you can get to it, the Japs can get to it, and they probably can get to some places you wouldn't consider going. Anyone else?"

When we did not answer, he barked, "Dismissed."

I stopped on the way back up to our ledge to work things out with the gun battery. We agreed that the guns associated with radar unit three would be unmanned. Back on the ridge, I gave Henderson the orders to report to the hospital.

"Damn, damn, damn," he shouted. "Get Douglas over here with a jeep."

The fact that he didn't fight made it obvious how serious the situation was. Wright and I helped him hobble out to the jeep. His face was grey with the pain and exertion.

The camp began waking up around 1500 hours. Our practice was to do roll call at 1600 hours after the night shift woke up and before the day shift turned in. I called for volunteers to join the patrols.

"You will be searching for enemy soldiers, who may be hiding in caves, pillboxes, or just in the jungle or swamp. Both jungle and swamp are so dense you won't be able to see them until you are upon them. They could be a few feet away on your flank and be invisible."

Several men stepped forward. I formed two patrols from the volunteers, one led by Edelstein and one by Brasseux.

"Get a good night's sleep. You'll head out first thing in the morning. Edelstein, go along the ridge looking for caves. Brasseux, take the northern edge of the swamp. Don't go too far south because Battery B will be patrolling there. We'll leave searchlights two and eleven and radar unit three unmanned tonight. The rest of you need to be extra vigilant and be prepared to handle any action we have overnight." A single plane flew over that night, staying well out of range of the ninety-millimeter guns.

Both patrols set out at first light, loudly bragging that they were finally in the real war. The lieutenants in charge hushed them, even though Edelstein, at least, agreed with them. We listened carefully for action, but both jungle and ridge were quiet. Most of the men in camp returned to their tents to sleep. We were all back to our usual daytime duties when suddenly we heard machine gun fire from up the mountain. It was followed by bazooka fire, the explosion of three hand grenades, and several rifle shots. Several minutes later, Edelstein's patrol emerged from the forest, carrying Edelstein.

"He was shot," one of the men called out.

I rushed to examine him. Several bullets had caught him in his right hip and abdomen. It was badly mangled."

"Just a little flesh wound," Edelstein whispered.

"A lot of flesh is wounded," Lance said. "We need to get this man to the hospital."

Lance and I loaded him onto a stretcher mounted on a jeep. Then, as Lance kept pressure on the wound and I made sure the stretcher stayed on the jeep, Douglas took off on his second hospital trip in as many days.

"Tilton, take charge of this patrol and complete the search of this area," I shouted as we left.

"Who are you to order me around? I have years more experience than you."

"I'm XO; the CO is not present. I asked you to do it precisely because of your experience. You might be able to keep yourself from getting shot."

Tilton led the men out of camp, frowning at me as we passed the patrol.

Edelstein moaned as we bumped along the track.

"He's bleeding too much. I can't stop it!" cried Lance. "I think one bullet went through his femoral artery."

I could see a trail of blood behind the jeep.

"Give me one of those bandages," I said.

I pressed the bandage on the most extensive wound, then lifted Edelstein. A massive exit wound poured blood out of the back of his upper thigh. Lance packed the wound as best he could, but the blood kept coming. Edelstein's skin paled and turned grey. We continued to hold bandages on the wounds.

"It's stopping, finally," Lance said as we approached the hospital.

"I'm afraid it is stopping because that is all the blood there is. I think he bled out." I said.

Lance bent over the body sobbing.

At the hospital, two medics came and carried Edelstein's body away. Another led Lance and me to a washing station so we could remove as much blood as possible. A doctor found us there.

"Could I speak with you, lieutenant?" he asked.

I followed him to the little office set up near the hospital.

The doctor offered me a chair and sat at the desk across from me.

"Your lieutenant appears to have been hit by friendly fire."

I didn't know what to say. I stared at him for a moment, then nodded and stood.

"Your CO will need to investigate."

"Yes, sir. My CO is currently here with jungle rot. I guess that investigation will fall to me." I turned and left.

As I emerged, Douglas drove the freshly washed jeep toward the office, jaw set, gripping the steering wheel. Lance rode in back with his arms flung high, his fingers making the V for Victory. His face was flushed, and his eyes glazed. He was babbling about the battle being won.

Douglas said grimly. "This one stuffed his mouth full of those betel things he chews, and before I knew it, he had flipped his wig."

"Get someone here to take charge of Lance," I ordered. "He needs to be treated in the hospital."

"I don't think so," Douglas said. "That would remind him of Edelstein's death. We should keep him in camp until we send him to Australia for R and R."

I found Henderson in the hospital, emerging from the anesthesia they had given him when they had debrided the dead tissue on his feet. I reported on recent events.

"Get me back up to that camp!" he shouted.

"Sir, you are ordered on bed rest for a week," a nearby nurse told him.

"Then I will rest in my own bed!" he shouted. "I need to take back my command before I don't have anything to take back!"

The doctor finally agreed to release him if I promised to keep him medicated and in bed. Henderson rode in the jeep's front seat, swaying as the jeep turned and bumped. I sat in the back with Lance, holding him to prevent him from jumping out.

Douglas and I carried Henderson to his cot. It must have been amusing to watch, me slight and short, Douglas a tall, big-boned Scots Highlander. The docs had dosed him heavily with morphine for the ride up to the ridge.

Volkerson, the medic from Carson's platoon, came running.

"Get Lance to a tent, and don't let him have any more betel nuts," I ordered.

*** 

Henderson's moaning woke me early the following day.

"Here, sir. Let me give you some of this morphine they sent up for your pain."

"No. I don't want to be too drugged to do my job. I can't just lie here and do nothing. Report on the patrols yesterday."

I repeated the information I had told him the previous day, adding information about Lance and the Betel incident.

After hearing my report, he sat up and shouted, "I'm down for one day, and we lose two men? I'll take back the command today. You take a squad of Brasseux's men out on patrol. Finish patrolling the area we were assigned."

"But, sir, you need more recovery time."

"I am fully capable of commanding the battery. Take the patrol."

I acknowledged the order and left the tent.

# CHAPTER 19

## PATROL DUTY

**I** APPROACHED **BRASSEUX FROM** behind as he swiped down with his razor.

"Brasseux," I said mid-swipe.

He jumped, cutting himself with the razor. He turned quickly and stared at me wide-eyed.

" I need to take one of your squads out on patrol duty this morning. Can you pick some men and send them to HQ after they've had something to eat?"

"You shouldn't spook a man like dat first thing in the morning. Now, look what you done." He dabbed at the blood trickling down his neck.

His accent seemed thicker than usual. "I wasn't trying to spook you. Sorry. Are you on bennies?"

"Don't need dat to stay awake. De terror of dis place does dat."

I nodded. "Just have those men at my tent in thirty minutes."

"Which men?"

"Choose a squad and have them bring their rifles."

Half an hour later, the squad showed up at my tent.

"We have patrol duty today. We'll be looking for Japanese emplacements and liquidating them if we find any.

As the patrol followed me, they talked loudly, slashing the underbrush.

"Halt!" I ordered. "We're trying to find enemy soldiers before they find us, not inviting them to target practice. Move slowly and quietly. Keep your eyes open and mouths shut."

I recalled something an Indian Scout had shown me—rather St. Clair. I took a few minutes to teach the patrol how to place their feet to make the most minor noise, move slowly to avoid attracting attention, and use several hand signals so I could communicate with them. Nothing difficult. We proceeded silently along an animal track skirting the swamp and headed for a coral cliff. A large cave in the cliff attracted my attention. Creeping as close to it as I thought we could, I held up my hand, and the men stopped.

Inside, men spoke in Japanese. My heart raced.

As I turned to signal the men to move forward, a three-man Japanese patrol emerged from the forest below us. "Look out behind!" I shouted.

Four men pivoted and shot at the Japs, killing one. A rush of adrenaline seized me. I sprinted to the cave and threw a hand grenade as two Japanese soldiers ran toward the entrance. I leaped back, ducking behind a tree. The hand grenade exploded. Coral collapsed, falling in huge chunks, sealing the cave and burying the two at the entrance.

The remaining Japanese crashed away from us through the forest below. The men took off after them. I took another look at the collapsed cave mouth and followed. As I ran, I saw something move in a tangle of brush. Three Japanese soldiers stood as I pointed my rifle at them. I shouted to my men to come and demanded that the Japanese surrender, one of the three Japanese phrases I knew. They pointed their weapons at me. I fired my rifle as machine gun fire tore through the undergrowth, killing two Japanese and wounding one. As I approached the wounded soldier, he drew a knife and slit his throat.

"What the?!" shouted one of the men, but I silenced him with a shaky hand and signaled for the patrol to search the area for other enemy soldiers.

As they searched, I retrieved the ID tags from the fallen Japanese, my heartbeat gradually returning to normal. I thanked the Lord that none of my patrol had been killed or wounded.

We regrouped. For a time, we listened carefully for any other sound. Not hearing anything, we began the trek back to camp, marching too quickly and carelessly.

A native patrol, led by an elderly Australian, emerged in front of us, the Australian calling out in English to ensure we didn't shoot.

"You eliminated those Japs?" asked the Australian.

"Pretty sure we did," I replied.

"My boys thank you. The Japs'd been harassing their village for months. If you come down to the village, the chief can give you a report on local Japanese activity."

"We'd be happy to," I said. "Reed, radio the camp and tell them we're all accounted for and will be making a stop at a native village."

The patrol turned into the jungle on a narrow path. We had missed the village earlier as we marched within about one hundred feet of it. As we entered the settlement, we saw tattooed women rushing around preparing food and picking grass and flowers from the forest. Here, the fully clothed women seemed to fear the men, unlike the Trobriand women of Kiriwina. Some children running around with curly blonde hair surprised me.

The leader of the native patrol led us to a sizeable thatch-roofed building with elaborately carved supporting posts. Carvings also decorated the walls.

"This is the Spirit House. The chief will be along shortly," said the Australian.

Some native men spread woven mats on the floor, indicating that we should sit. I studied the elaborately carved masks on the wall. Salvador Dali could have designed them: long, surreal faces, colored red, yellow, black, and brown, with broad noses and inlaid shells for the pupils of the eyes.

High-pitched drumming and what sounded like a flute approached outside. A large man in an elaborate feather headdress entered. His face was painted to give the impression of a fierce bird above a grizzled beard. He wore armbands of woven grass with flowers attached, a bark cloth loincloth, and a kind of grass fringe tied around his lower legs. We were unsure of the etiquette of meeting a tribal chief on this island, so we all stood up as he came in. He seated himself on a carved wooden throne in front of us, and an assistant motioned for us to sit down.

"We thank you for eliminating the last of the Japanese on this portion of the island. We trust that the Allies will be kinder neighbors than the Japanese. Fighting continues to the east, but your actions have cleared our lands of this scourge today. We have prepared a feast for you. Please join me outside."

He beckoned for me to walk beside him while the men followed behind.

"How did you learn to speak English so well?" I asked him.

"I originally learned English at the mission school on the island's east end. Germans occupied the island then, but there was a small British mission school. I served in the Australian Army in the last war and worked in Australia after that until my father died, and I had to take over the responsibilities of village chief."

"You were willing to return to this little primitive village after living so long in Australia?"

"Like so many, you assume that our existence here is much more difficult and uncomfortable than your so-called civilization. I found quite the opposite to be true. Our food and clothing come mostly from the forests, the sea, our gardens, and our pigs. We work maybe five hours a day gardening, gathering, preparing food, building or repairing our homes, making clothes, and carving canoes and other useful items. The remainder of our time is spent playing with and teaching our children, enjoying the company of our wives or neighbors, celebrating, and relaxing. I find it a much richer and more rewarding lifestyle than the workday life in

Sydney."

"The women seem to be working pretty hard right now," I said.

"They're preparing for a sing-sing in your honor. They're very pleased to be doing it. The Japanese have been very hard on them, abducting and raping."

"Unfortunately, I can't promise the Americans will stay away from them."

"The Americans will come and go and not injure the ability of the women to have children. Sometimes, a man with many wives grows tired, but a man's power will disappear without the women and children to tend the gardens and pigs. He cannot give as many gifts or have great feasts. So, the Americans will help the people of the village. They are even better to women than Australians. We greatly increased the strength of the village after the Australians came in the first war, and we are expecting even greater strength through the Americans."

I squirmed at his casual discussion of what seemed to me the prostitution of the women of his tribe. I felt I had to say something. "So you see this war as a benefit to your people?" I asked as we seated ourselves on grass mats.

"Oh, no. It's definitely not a benefit. But we have learned to take what good we can from everything that comes our way."

I nodded.

Several men positioned bamboo instruments in front of us. Some looked like xylophones, their large diameter pieces of bamboo tied together with leather strips. The men played them with wooden paddles. Others had what looked like pan pipes made from smaller shafts of bamboo. Finally, four men carried in two hollowed-out log drums. The musicians settled in front of their instruments and began to play.

Grass-shirted men in heavy wooden masks danced out of the Spirit house. They darted back and forth, raising sticks with grass, flowers, and feathers tied to them over their heads. It seemed they might be reenacting a series of battles. As villagers sang, the dancers cried out at intervals. The chief did not translate. We sat mesmerized, unaware of the sun going down, until a large bonfire flared behind the dancers. Three dancers appeared in tattered First World War Australian army uniforms. I gathered that they were re-enacting the seizure of the island from Germany in that war. Then, I recognized the reenactment of our attack on the Japanese. The islanders must have been watching the whole engagement. The villagers and our patrol stood and cheered as the cave exploded, a crescendo of loud drum beats and rolling bodies. I felt the exhilaration of the battle all over again. Finally, the dancing stopped, and all was silent. Young women from the village ran to us carrying bead necklaces and crowns of woven grass and flowers. I did not know how to respond, so I bowed to the girls and the chief.

"We are honored by your generosity and entertainment," I said.

The chief clapped his hands, and young men and women ran from the forest carrying roast pig, sweet potatoes, and other fruits and vegetables. They served each of us a wooden platter, heaping the food high. Every time we cleared a portion of the platter, they filled it again. Finally, we could eat no more.

"Your men eat well," the chief told me. "They will be held in high esteem here. One of the ways we achieve status here is through eating contests. You have all fared well."

I didn't mention that we had been subsisting mainly on spam and canned peas for some time because the supply convoys were not always making it through. I suddenly realized the abundance surrounding us while we grumbled about spam and overcooked English peas.

By now, it was pitch dark. I had thought we would briefly visit the village, then return to camp, but now we would have to spend the night. I radioed our base again and told the men to settle down here. A village girl led me to a raised platform under a thatched roof. Woven grass mats enclosed the platform. Several times during the night, a young woman peered into the enclosure, asking if I needed anything. I refused the offer but could hear that other patrol members did not.

We returned to camp in the morning in high spirits.

"We have eradicated the Japanese from this part of the island," I told Henderson proudly.

"And how do you know that?" he asked.

"The Australian coast watcher and village chief said we did."

"We'll still be sending patrols out. How many did you kill?"

"Nine accounted for. An unknown number in the cave that we hit."

"Those limestone caves are all connected. They could easily have retreated down the cave and come out someplace else. Send Carson and Brasseux out with new patrols."

I turned to carry out the orders.

"You know that Edelstein bled out on the way to the hospital?" I nodded. He apparently didn't remember either of my two reports on the subject. "The Doc said it was friendly fire."

"Yes, sir. I reported that to you, sir. You were heavily drugged, though."

"I see," he replied. "I've written a letter to his mother. Take care of the rest of the paperwork and see to anything else that needs doing." He hobbled back to his bed and fell onto it, closing his eyes. I checked the morphine. It was almost gone.

I relayed the orders to Carson and Brasseux and went to my desk, but

I couldn't concentrate. Edelstein was killed by friendly fire! And Henderson showed no emotion at all. Was it the morphine?

Douglas climbed the coral path.

"Got some requisitions for youse," he said. "Too bad about Edelstein. I knew he would come to a bad end the way he treated his men."

"I tried but couldn't get Henderson to do anything about it. He doesn't seem at all disturbed, either."

"He's plenty disturbed but is not about to show you because then he would have to admit he was wrong. He had a major heart-to-heart with the platoon while you were gone. Heard you saw some real action yesterday."

"We did," I replied. "Eliminated the last of the Japanese from this part of the island. Just as we found their cave, a group charged us from the rear. I lobbed a grenade into the cave, collapsing it. The boys behind me shot half the Japs. The others ran off, but we caught them."

"You seem very enthusiastic for someone who didn't want this war in the first place. You should watch that. You might come to enjoy combat."

I realized I did relish the experience. While I was terrified, I was also thrilled. Nothing in my life had prepared me for this. I felt guilty for breaking my promise to Mr. White to remain peace-loving even in war.

"That's a good reaction for a soldier under fire," Douglas said. "Just as long as you don't look for opportunities to kill."

"I'm not that far gone. I'm much more concerned about the battery's condition than about myself. Henderson is overusing the morphine they gave him, Lance is addicted to betel, and who knows what else. Brasseux is so antsy he can't sit still. Edelstein's men are all addicted to bennies, and everybody is on edge."

"We've been in combat zones for almost a year with only one week of R and R. That does things to your peace of mind." Douglas said. "We're constantly concerned about being strafed, bombed, or shot at. And we do our work at night. We haven't had a good night's sleep in ages. Not everybody is as resilient as you."

I resolved to see what I could do to give some men a break. So I took Brasseux's place that night. Toward dawn, a single Jap plane flew over; no bombs dropped, no strafing. At breakfast, Brasseux walked in, laughing, with Douglas.

"Amazin' what a good night's sleep can do for you," he said. "I slept yesterday until about 1400, went down to the beach for a swim, played some cards, and then went to sleep again around midnight. I feel a hundred percent better."

"I'm glad," I said. "Once the men settle down here, I have to meet with the Colonel and confer with the gun battery."

"What do you think you're doing, trying to do your job, plus Henderson's and Brasseux's job?" Douglas asked me.

"Trying to get this battery back on track. You said everybody needs a little R and R."

"That includes you. You'll burn out if you try to be everything to everyone."

"I'm fine for now. I'll get some time when Henderson is up and about again."

When I returned from the gun battery, I found a message from Colonel Squires on my desk. Twenty-five men from the battery would be granted leave to go to Australia for R and R. He promised a rotation so everyone would get there sooner or later, but I was to pick the first group to go. Lance, of course. I would have liked to send Brasseux, but commissioned officers couldn't go this time. It would be a triage situation. I walked around camp, recording the names of those who looked most haggard. When I got to twenty-five men, I typed up the list and sent it to Battalion HQ.

A ship arrived with replacements for the dead and wounded. They would also take the selected men back to Australia. I was lying on the beach after a long swim when I saw Mitchell, the cavalry lieutenant from Will's card game, arrive loaded with gear.

Surprised to see an officer preparing to board, I asked, "Mitchell, are you leaving us?"

"I got leave to go home. My granddaddy's real sick, so they are letting me go see him. I haven't been home in a year and a half. Before that, I'd never been more than fifty miles from home."

"It's been about that long since I saw my family, but it doesn't look likely I will see them again soon. I hope all goes well with your granddad."

The ship brought some very welcome letters. I read the first one during dinner.

January 9, 1943

Dear Gene,

We've heard that Colonel Hobby, the director of the WACs, might tour WAC installations in the European theater. We have been very busy with our work and getting ready for her. She will observe us at work and inspect our quarters. Some of the girls are really worried, but I don't know what we can do about it at this late date if either our work or quarters are not up to snuff. I really think we should be concentrating on the job right now because what we are doing is really important to the war effort.

I did find out what has been happening to your letters. Apparently, there is a massive backlog of mail at the sorting station nearby. They say some of the items there are over six months old. There just aren't enough personnel to keep up with it. Maybe that is one of the things Colonel Hobby will be able to correct.

One of the women in my officer's training group is now in charge of a mail-sorting battalion. Their work is outstanding, and they are dedicated to their jobs. Their motto is "No mail, no morale." I wish they would send them here, but they are an all-black battalion, and that complicates things. According to the rule, they must be housed separately, and the army is having enough trouble finding housing for the all-white troops. As far as I'm concerned, they should put us all together. Those kinds of rules really get in the way when we are trying to win a war.

Everybody around here is really on edge because we have been doing so much work. Arguments always break out, and even when we're not arguing, we are testy with each other. For example, yesterday, I was trying to take out the trash at the same time another girl was. I got to the trash bin before she did, and she just said, "Move." I didn't say anything, but I was really slow getting my trash in the bin, then closed the lid before I left, so she had to open it again. There was no reason for that, and it was really nasty, but I got angry when she demanded that I move.

They are yelling at me to help mop the halls before Colonel Hobby gets here. Keep writing, and maybe someday soon, the letters will get through.

Love,
Sarah Gale

I wondered if managing a WAC unit would be more complicated than managing the men. I remembered my sister's arguments with her friends, always being so emotional and so ridiculous. But that had been when they were teenagers. Surely, grown women would be more reasonable, especially when they knew how important they were to the war effort.

There was another letter, and I sat in the mess tent to read that before going out to check on the platoons.

January 23, 1943
Dear Gene,
Guess what? General Dwight Eisenhower, the new Supreme Commander, came here, and I got to talk to him. He asked me lots of questions about a specific area I have been studying. He is a really nice man. It is interesting how different the supreme commanders in our theaters are. They are both excellent commanders in their own way but very different. Eisenhower is from Kansas. Do you know him? He said he was from central Kansas, and you said you were from north-central Kansas. So you grew up in pretty much the same place. I told him about you, and he said to wish you luck.

Jenny and I were riding to work by a different route the other day, just to get some variety in our lives, and we rode past some searchlights at an RAAF field. They were being "manned" by women. We stopped briefly to talk with them. They

*said that almost all the able-bodied men in the country are in combat positions, so the women protect the home front. They told us the radar gives them the coordinates, and operating the searchlights is not complicated. And I thought your job was hard.*
*I love you and can't wait to see you again.*
*LOVE !!!*
*Sarah Gale*

I would have to tell her that Dwight Eisenhower had left Kansas before I was born, although I had been through his hometown several times. She was obviously teasing me about searchlights being easy, but I stopped again to remind myself how glad I was that I was not in the infantry.

*** 

We continued to see a single Japanese plane every night for three nights. Then, all action stopped. An offensive by the cavalry tanks around the airfield met no opposition. No Jap planes flew over the beaches or the airport. The Japanese were truly gone.

Orders came down to improve defensive positions and continue patrols looking for stragglers. We continued our patrols but didn't see any more action. Finally, we had time to swim at the beach and explore the jungle. Henderson took back his duties, allowing me to join the men on the beach.

Another shipload of replacements arrived as I sat on the beach. Men came from every direction to board the ship, showing their leave passes and trying not to look too jubilant. I said goodbye to the men from the battery, then lay down on the beach again, thinking of Sarah Gale and home.

"Excuse me." A fresh, young second lieutenant stood over me. "I'm Second Lieutenant Lucas. Replacing a lieutenant in the 227th AAA. They told me you're an officer with that unit. His dark hair and deep-set, almost black eyes gave him an intense look. He reached a muscular arm down to help me up.

"Lieutenant Sinclair. Let me show you the way." I felt dizzy. I thought it was just from jumping up so quickly, but it got increasingly worse until I was so tired by evening that I skipped dinner and went to bed, calling on Douglas to take over nighttime command duties.

# CHAPTER 20

## FORT TICONDEROGA

**S**CHUYLER WANTS TO MEET with you as soon as possible," said a lieutenant at my side.

Schuyler? I tried to orient myself. Wearing a Continental Army uniform, I rode a horse through an oak forest. *St. Clair.* Red columbine bloomed at the edge of a nearby meadow. Late spring or early summer. My mind gradually merged with his, like coming out of deep sleep.

"Arthur, how are you?" Schuyler said as he entered. "And how is Cousin Phoebe?"

"She's well. The birth of our little Maggie was tough, but she has recovered nicely. I have the family in Potts Grove. Phoebe would never have been able to manage had they stayed out west."

"You are fortunate. All of your babies have lived. We've had thirteen, but only seven have survived."

"Yes, we are fortunate to have eight beautiful, healthy children."

"What of the fort?'

"Phillip, I don't see any way it can be defended with the men I have.", I said. "Come with me and have a look."

The bright summer sun seemed blinding as we emerged from the stone room with its single window. We crossed the parade ground to a barracks converted to a hospital. "Although there are nearly three thousand here, the fighting force numbers less than twenty-two hundred. That's simply not enough to hold both forts." We climbed to the second story and surveyed the landscape. "We don't know if or when the British will come or from what direction," I said, "They could come down the river or approach overland the way they did in the French Indian War. Half the scouts I send out do not return, and the others are chased back by Indians before they find anything. The woods are crawling with Indians, indicating that Burgoyne may not be far away."

Schuyler looked across the river.

"Perhaps bringing all the men to Ticonderoga and abandoning Independence would be advisable."

"Abandoning Ticonderoga would be more advisable," I told him. "We can see farther up the lake from Fort Independence if they come by water. They will be coming down the west side if they come by land, and it will be difficult for them to cross. Abatis are erected over there, and the cannons are mounted and ready to fire. If we make a stand, it will be on the east side of the river. Even then, we'll be unable to repel a major invasion. We need to plan for retreat."

"Let us retire to your quarters," he said, eyeing the sentries coming toward us.

We settled into the none too comfortable chairs in the cool stone room. "I'm afraid you're correct." Schuyler said. "There are two ways to retreat. You can go by water to Skenesborough, or there is a rather rough road to the northeast through the little village of Hubbardton. But don't give up too soon. Establish a defensive post on Mount Hope. They will probably try to take that position first. It offers them a good defensive opportunity. Hold the fort as long as you can to give us time to prepare for the defense of Albany."

My chest felt like a vice squeezed it. No matter what I did, there was little chance of success. I wondered how Washington seemed to be able to make decisions so quickly. Four months at the man's side had shown me his decisiveness and courage. How did he so often get out of sticky situations like this?

Schuyler left early in the morning for the two day trip back to Albany. After seeing him off, I walked toward the defenses along the old French line. Suddenly, I found myself walking through a Kansas wheat field beside General Eisenhower. We both stopped to pack tobacco into our pipes, lit up, and then strolled on through the rippling wheat.

"You must win the loyalty of your troops and take the action that will be most effective for the future of the war," he told me. "What purpose takes priority in the situation?"

"Defeating the British," I replied. "The trouble is, I don't think we can do that."

"Can you think of a different strategy? Rather than sit and wait, is there a way to divide and conquer?"

Just as suddenly, I was lying on an army cot in a room full of moaning and snoring men. "Our job is to assure that as many as possible survive to fight another day," I heard someone say. "We do that, whatever it takes."

"Always remember, whatever decision you make, you will have to take responsibility for it," I heard Eisenhower's voice.

*\*\**

I woke to sunlight shining through the little window of my bedroom at Fort Ticonderoga, now sure of what I would do. No matter the effect on my reputation, I could not let these boys die here. We would retreat if the British came with more men than I felt we could defeat.

I established a defensive post on Mount Hope and sent more scouts out to discover whatever intelligence they could. A week went by, and they did not return. After two weeks with no intelligence, I figured they had been captured or killed. We were discussing the lack of knowledge as to the British position when Fullerton, the scout I had sent out that morning, bolted into the dining room.

"Sorry to interrupt you, sir. I did want to let you know that I ran into a band of Indians, and they shot rifles at me and chased me back to the fort."

"That means the British are likely agitating them. It's an indication that Burgoyne is nearby," I said.

"You are assuming a lot just because some savages chased this man," said Colonel Marshall.

"The Indians in this country don't generally just up and chase a white man unless they've been paid off by someone," I countered. "Plus, they had rifles and ammunition. Many have rifles from the Seven Years' War, but gunpowder is harder for them to come by. They would not have wasted their powder and shot on scaring Fullerton had they not been given it by the British."

I heard raucous laughter from outside.

"What is that racket?" I asked.

"Oh, that is just Andy Tracy telling stories. His father is an Irish storyteller, and he seems to follow in his father's footsteps. Once the men get their porter, they settle in and listen to his stories," said Major Stephens.

"Assemble your units at sunrise tomorrow. How many fit and able troops do we have?"

"Two thousand eighty-nine, sir."

*** 

A scout approached me at sunrise when I walked across the yard to lecture the assembled army.

"Sir, The British are approaching Three Mile Point. They have two warships, eighteen gunboats, and three sloops. I don't know how many men are on those ships, but they appear to be British, Canadian, Hessians, and Indians."

*This is it,* I thought. I set my jaw and faced the men.

"The British are at Three Mile Point. We will double patrol and be on alert until we find out how many there are. Report to the armory for ammunition. Check your arms and remain battle ready. Dismissed."

The patrols brought word of small units of British building fortifications at Three Mile Point. Around midnight, Livingston woke me and reported that a patrol had brought in two Hessian deserters.

I found two dirty, haggard men lounging in the brig.

"What is your unit?" I asked.

"Major von Barner's light infantry,"

"What prompted you to desert your post."

"We have no provisions. We were hoping for food."

"Bring some of that venison stew if any is left," I called. "And some bread and ale."

When the food arrived, I had the private stand by holding steaming bowls of stew and chunks of bread.

"What general leads the party?" I asked. "And how many troops are there?"

"General von Reidsal leads the Hessians. We have five regiments and one battalion, plus a company of dragoons." One of the men answered.

"You have horses?"

"No. They were planning to acquire those when they arrived."

"Is Carlisle leading this expedition?"

They conferred between themselves. "I think they called him Burgoyne. I believe Carlisle is still in Canada," The soldier who had spoken before answered.

"How many men does he lead?"

"I don't know. The Germans are always in front, so we don't get a good view of the whole army. They said all we would have to do is fire one volley, and you would turn tail and run."

"I heard someone say they were expecting a thousand Indians," the other man said.

"Give them the food," I ordered the guard. They were wolfing it down as I returned to my quarters.

In the morning, I ordered the men at Mount Hope to fall back to the French line. They had barely reached the old French fortifications when the British arrived on Mount Hope. A company of British soldiers and Indians formed and marched toward the Fort. I hurried to the line.

"Hold your fire until they get close enough to see the white of their eyes," I ordered. I'd heard that Putnam said that at Bunker Hill and like the sound of it.

As they moved closer, young Captain James Wilkerson fired. A British soldier fell. On hearing that gunfire, the remainder of Wilkerson's company opened fire. They had fired three volleys of our precious ammunition before I could stop them. As the smoke cleared, we could see the British in a hasty retreat.

"Wilkerson!" I fumed. "When I give you an order, I expect you to follow it."

"General, don't you see that I have killed the first Redcoat of the engagement. They were close enough for us to hit them."

"Your duty is to follow orders, not to seek glory for yourself!" I yelled. Wilkerson stalked off. The British soldier still lay on the ground.

"Retrieve that soldier," I ordered. "We can at least give him a decent burial."

Four men ran out and picked up the British soldier, who lay still on the field. As they approached, he jumped up and swung his musket wildly, trying to club them. He was subdued and brought into the fort, stinking drunk.

"Put him in the stockade until he can answer questions," I ordered.

I called the officers together.

"We are about to fight the British and Hessians. They are trained, disciplined troops. They also have Indians among them, who are exceedingly daring and fierce warriors. Impress upon your men that they MUST follow orders. A great deal of ammunition was expended on this attack, with the only result that we picked up one drunken sot off the field. If we cannot get useful information from him, that ammunition has been wasted."

"Sir, the prisoner is conscious," a sentry called.

The colonels followed me to the stockade.

"What is your name, soldier?"

"Mmm. Name. Um."

"Who is your commanding officer?"

"I cannot tell you that."

"What regiment are you with?"

"I can't tell you that."

"Can you tell me anything?"

"No, sir."

I left the stockade and turned to my aide de camp. "Livingston, get me Major Stevens."

Livingston rushed off, and in a few minutes, Stevens hurried to my quarters.

"Where is that Irish storyteller lieutenant of yours? Get him for me."

"Andrew Tracy, sir," the lieutenant reported a few minutes later.

"Tracy, I want you to pretend you are a Loyalist spy. Put on civilian clothes, and we will lock you in the stockade. Get friendly with the prisoner. See what information you can get out of him. Share this flask of whiskey with him, but don't get him so drunk he'll pass out again. Pump him for all the information you can get."

"Yes, sir. The best assignment I have gotten in this army."

The following day, Tracy came to give his report.

"Once he believed I was a spy, he was willing to answer anything. During the night, he informed me that Generals Burgoyne and Carlton were with the Troops in Canada. Carlton came as far as Crown Point with them. The prisoner himself has been out with scouts these three days past who took six prisoners and killed a number more, which the Indians scalp'd. The enemy is five thousand six hundred regulars strong; they have eighteen sail of vessels coming down the lake, one of which was called the Thunderer and was mounted with eighteen brass twenty-four pounders, two thirteen-inch mortars with three hundred shells fitted for them, and more. They intend to surround us and cut off all communication, for which purpose they intend to divert us by attacking our lines daily to draw off our attention from their actual design. Eight hundred Indians was to harass us continually, joined by the Light Infantry. I think this was the most material part of the conversation."

"Thank you, Tracy. You should get some breakfast and some sleep now."

"Yes, sir."

Five thousand six hundred regulars, three thousand two hundred Hessians, a thousand Indians, and an unknown number of Canadian militia. Over ten thousand men coming at our two thousand tired, weak, and sickly men. Should we leave now, before they had us surrounded?

Some of the Hessians crossed the lake and were within range of the Fort Independence lines. We heard sporadic fire all that day and the next but saw no action on our side. That evening, we had a quiet Independence Day celebration.

"It's hard to believe that less than a year ago, I read the declaration to the men for the first time. So much has happened since then."

"This new nation has had quite a start," said Colonel Hale.

"That it has," replied Cilley. "Wait! What's that? Do I see a campfire on Sugarloaf?"

We all rushed to the window.

"They've occupied Sugarloaf!" I cried. "I fear our mission is doomed. We'll hold a council of war at seven in the morning. Livingston, make sure Fermoy and the colonels on the other side know I have called this war council, and I expect them to be here."

\*\*\*

When I rose in the morning, I could see a cannon on Sugarloaf. Our chance to defend the fort was lost. The only hope I could see now was to try to draw them out and divide their forces.

All the colonels were in my quarters promptly at seven. The only one missing was Fermoy. It would be bad form to start the Council without the only other General in attendance.

"Livingston, can you see what is delaying General Fermoy?"

Livingston returned in about fifteen minutes.

"He is starting across the bridge now."

We waited another half hour, then I began without him.

"This is our situation."

Fermoy walked in.

"It is very disrespectful to begin a council of war when your co-commander is absent."

"There is no co-commander here. I outrank you as much as you outrank these colonels. We waited forty-five minutes. There are urgent matters to be discussed here." I retorted in French.

"Ah, These New England Puritan timekeepers. Every moment must be exact."

"I'm neither from New England nor a Puritan. Please be seated." I returned to English and said, "As I said, Gentlemen and General Fermoy, this is our situation. The British are coming at us with over ten thousand troops—a combination of British regulars, Hessians, Canadian militia, and Indians. They have occupied Sugarloaf and have dragged cannon up there. Likely, they are now fully prepared to open fire on the fort. It is also likely that they will attack both Fort Ticonderoga and Fort Independence simultaneously, meaning that neither fort could come to the aid of the other. They have been repairing bridges and roads on the east side of the lake. We have two thousand eighty-nine able-bodied men, which includes one hundred twenty-nine unarmed artisans and about nine hundred militia who have joined us but can stay only a few days. Our choices are to move the tents lower, out of range of the guns, and fight from Ticonderoga, move everyone to Fort Independence, or abandon the fort. Should we fight from both forts or retreat to Fort Independence?"

The Colonels spoke almost all at once.

"We should retreat."

"If we are to remain, we must move all the troops to Fort Independence."

"That is the only way."

"We can't hold the fort even if we all die, but we will be vilified for losing it."

"I will be vilified. You will be following my orders. Is there anyone who disagrees with that assessment?" I asked.

No one spoke.

"Secondly, once removed to Fort Independence, will we be able to defend it?"

Again, the colonels argued among themselves.

"We are already almost surrounded. It would take little effort for the British to cross the peninsula's narrow neck and cut us off completely."

"A retreat should be undertaken as soon as possible."

"We will be fortunate to accomplish that. The British already have eyes on us from all sides."

I spoke up. "We will retreat under cover of darkness. All the invalids, camp followers, and as many supplies as possible will secretly be loaded on boats. We will do nothing to alert the British. Bring anything that floats to the docks, where they'll be hidden from both Sugarloaf and Mount Hope. We'll begin loading the boats as soon as it is dark. Inform the men and have them prepare secretly and quietly, getting ammunition from the armory and rations from the quartermaster a few at a time. Destroy everything we can't take with us. We must not leave any supplies for the British army. They are already running low, and we don't want to give them any advantage. Fermoy, do the same at Fort Independence. Leave the tents standing until we are almost ready to leave. I will talk to the Quartermaster."

The officers left individually after which I visited the Quartermaster.

"We will retreat under cover of nightfall. Divide the rations among the men, giving them as much as they can carry, except for rum. Leave the rum here. Package anything that remains after the distribution to be put on boats with the invalids and camp followers. Butcher eight of the cattle as quietly as possible and distribute the meat among the men. We will drive the rest into the woods."

"Do you know what this will look like on your record?"

"I can save the army and lose my reputation or save my reputation and lose the men. I know what I'm doing. If all turns out as I hope, it will ultimately benefit the nation."

"We appreciate your willingness to do that."

"Well, get to work, man. There is much to do before nightfall."

The fort seemed only a little busier than usual. Many men were in the yard, but they did not congregate in one location as though preparing for battle or retreat. Soldiers collected two hundred boats and canoes near the docks. Men filled their haversacks with all the supplies they could fit, and the fort had an air of anxious anticipation.

A messenger rode into the fort in the late afternoon.

"Sir, two militia companies are coming from Massachusetts and New Hampshire. The New York Militia from the Albany area is on alert. They should be here in three days."

"That is too late," I told him. "We'll be retreating under cover of darkness tonight. Livingston, send a messenger to find the militia and have them gather at Hubbardton and Skenesborough."

Darkness finally fell, and we began loading the boats. It was mass confusion at first, but everyone did remain quiet. Eventually, the officers sorted everyone out, and loading the boats began to go more smoothly. Then, one by one, they took off into the dark lake. As the last boat shoved off, I ordered the men to strike the tents and begin the march across the bridge.

The doctor came to me. "Sir, it appears we do not have enough boats. We have about ten men in the hospital who can march. They can go with the troops, but four men are quite ill with smallpox. We have kept them isolated and did not want to put them in the boats with the women and children, but now no boats are left for them. At least two of them would likely not survive the trip."

"I hate to leave them behind."

"There is nothing else we can do, sir. They are too sick to travel over-land, and we have no more boats to carry them. One of them pointed out that he could do no better service to his country than to give the British army smallpox."

I nodded and moved toward the bridge as a messenger rode back across.

"Sir, Colonel Marshall wanted me to let you know that they have not started the evacuation of Mount Independence."

"What!" I jumped on my horse and crossed the bridge as quickly as possible without shoving the foot soldiers off. I rode to Fermoy's quarters and pounded on the door. He opened the door, rubbing his eyes.

"What are you doing? The night is half gone, and you have not begun to evacuate."

"You surely can't expect us to march all night without sleep."

"That is exactly what I expect."

I rode to where the regiment was awaiting orders. "Spike the can-nons, strike the tents, gather your supplies, and march after the Massa-chusetts regiment."

I ordered the Ticonderoga garrison to help. After two frenzied hours, they packed as many supplies as they could and destroyed the cannon. I ordered them to move out. Fermoy emerged from his quarters, threw his saddlebags over his horse, and mounted. As he did, I saw flames through the open door.

"You idiot! You set fire to your quarters? What better way to alert the British. Damn you. Damn you all to hell." He galloped away.

I was beside myself with fury. The building blazed, lighting the dark night. The British could clearly see the army's rear guard as they climbed the hill. In the water, the flotilla of boats was lit up by the blaze.

"We have lost the advantage of secrecy! Francis, form a rear guard to hold back any troops that follow us." I ordered.

Cilley pushed the men forward, ordering a fast march. I looked back as I rode over the hill at the rear of the retreating army. Fraser's Highland Regiment, already creating a bridge of flat bottom boats using the old French boom and chain system to hold them, followed us much too closely. Crossing the lake on the boats would be slow, after which they would have to negotiate the marshy ground around East Creek before reaching the Hubbardton Road. We still had a chance of escaping. Yet Fermoy's fire had cost us the four-hour lead I had hoped for. I rode forward, encouraging the men as they went.

Fermoy was not with the column.

"I believe he went down the lake with the boats," Colonel Marshall told me.

"Good riddance," I shouted. "But at least we have divided the British. Some will stay to hold the fort, some will follow us, and some will follow the boats downriver. Let's hope the militia is ready to meet them." To myself, I said Thank you, Dwight.

# CHAPTER 21

## RETRAINING

**I** **WOKE IN A** dark, underground bunker. I lay there for some time, listening and looking, clearing the fuzz from my brain, before I realized I was in the half-buried hospital on the Arawe Peninsula in 1944. A medic slept in a chair at one end of the room, his feet on a desk. A slim young nurse bustled in as sunlight began filtering in around the door flap. As she came toward my bed, I recognized Nurse Morris.

"Sinclair, you're back with us."

"I took my Atabrine," I said. "How did I have another malaria attack?"

"Atabrine isn't one hundred percent effective," she said after she took my pulse. "Particularly against relapses of the type of malaria you have. You're more likely to have an attack when you're stressed. They should get milder with time. You were only out for three days this time."

"I don't know how I can avoid being stressed in the middle of a war zone," I said. "How much time before it gets milder?"

"We aren't sure. You seem to have a severe infection. We suspect that you have two different kinds of malaria simultaneously. That's the problem with moving you guys around all the time. Different islands have different strains."

"How do you and I happen to be moved to the same island so often?"

"Our medical unit is attached to the same division as your AAA unit. So we follow them around just like you do. I'm generally assigned to the malaria ward, so I care for all of our regulars."

"So I'm a regular now, am I."

"Appears so."

As I sipped a bowl of broth the medic had given me for breakfast, I heard Captain Henderson in the distance.

"I need my Executive Officer! They're shipping us to another of these God-forsaken islands, and I need to take him with us!"

"You can't take him out of the hospital until he's coherent," another voice said.

"Go tell them I'm coherent," I told Nurse Morris.

She sent the sleepy medic. Henderson appeared quickly at my bedside.

"We're heading out for Goodenough Island again. Can you walk, or do I need some stretcher bearers to take you?"

"I think I can walk," I said. "When are we leaving?

"Two hours."

Even though the hallucinations felt as real as in the previous bouts of malaria, I was recovering much more quickly. Maybe it was because I had not wrecked a jeep or fallen down a cliff this time. Instead, I'd gone to sleep in my own cot and woke up halfway around the world a hundred seventy years earlier. Then I woke up back in my own war. Corporals O'Neill and Perry came for me. They each took an arm and escorted me to a jeep, which Perry drove up the causeway and directly onto the ship.

They helped me to a deck chair, and Perry handed me a letter from Sarah Gale. I sat in the sun and read as the ship pulled away from the causeway and out to sea.

February 6, 1944
Dear Gene,

It appears you have already taken back half the Pacific based on the map I saw the other day. Keep up the good work down there.

I finally got the letters you wrote while you were on Goodenough Island. I thought that was a funny name for an island. I guess they thought it was just good enough. I also thought it was funny that the Australians would use the name Evelyn for a boy. I have only heard it used for girls. I asked an English girl why calling a guy Randy would be wrong, and she turned bright red. She could barely explain it to me, but now I understand.

We have worked out our differences, and things are improving around here. I talked to the girl who was aiming to take her trash out. We decided to try to turn things around, so we started writing one nice note to someone every day and putting it on her door or at her usual place at breakfast. Now, it seems that everyone is writing nice notes and doing favors for others. It is so much better when we all get along with each other. The work doesn't seem so difficult, and we can come home and relax rather than come home to more stress.

There hasn't been much movement on the Western front. Italy still has a lot of back and forth, but the siege of Leningrad is over. The Germans couldn't take Russia as quickly as they had most of Europe. You told me that the Russians and the Russian weather were the end of many great armies, and you were right. The Russians are pushing the Germans back. If we can put pressure on from our side, I think we might be able to win this war.

Try to stay cool, dry, and healthy. I want you back in one piece.
Love,

*Sarah Gale*

So much for cool, dry, and healthy, I thought as I wiped the sweat off my face, dragged my chair into a patch of shade provided by a lifeboat, and started her second letter.

February 20, 1944
Dear Gene,
Air raids have started up again in London and the surrounding area. We have had to go to bunkers a few nights because of the air raids. We work in a bunker, so the only way we know there is an air raid during the day is that the hallway outside our workroom fills up with people, and it is impossible to get to the bathroom if we need to. We can't let people into our work area because we do top-secret stuff. The raids don't happen as often here as in London, but they do sound the siren if there is the slightest chance of the bombing reaching us.
The weather is starting to get a little warmer. They say spring doesn't really arrive until April. I have found this winter to be really dreary. I am not sure whether it is the weather or working in a concrete bunker. Both are grey or gray, depending on whether you are British or American.
I am starting a new project — a personal one, not one for the war effort. I photograph a specific area of the woods daily from the same spot at the same angle. I hope to make a time-lapse sequence of the coming of spring. I don't know if once a day is good enough. I may have some jumps in the unfolding of things, but I don't have time to visit the spot more than once daily. And I can't always get there at the exact same time. I will make two copies of the sequence and send one to you if it turns out.
Have to go now. Air raid!
Love,
SG

I shuddered, thinking of Sarah Gale running from air raids. Why had I encouraged her to join the WACs? She could be safely home in North Carolina. But still slaving away in the laundry without a high school diploma. That was why.

Sitting on the ship's deck, I felt my energy return. I was ravenous by lunchtime. I loaded my tray in the line and sat beside Tilton and Henderson.

"Why can't we just go into Rabaul and take them on directly?" Tilton asked. "We're fighting all around Rabaul but aren't even approaching the major Jap stronghold. That makes us look weak. How can we win a war if we don't fight the enemy?"

"I know," Henderson said. "This war doesn't even have a front. We're just randomly taking some islands and leaving others."

"There's a definite advantage to avoiding the most densely occupied islands while cutting off their supply lines. Sometimes, a strategy that divides the enemy will get you much further than attacking them head-on," I said. "The Marines are doing some heavy fighting, but it would be worse if we were trying to take every island by ground attack. We don't have as many men as willing to sacrifice themselves as the Japanese."

"Are you trying to say that the Japanese could defeat us if we attacked Rabaul head-on?"

"I think that's a possibility," I said.

"You're still too sick to think straight," Henderson said. "The American forces are the strongest in the world. We can take on anyone in any place.

I shoved a big forkful of mashed potatoes into my mouth in an effort to keep from contradicting him.

***

We found Goodenough Island a changed place. Five months before, there had been tent camps in the jungle up to the base of the mountains. With General Kruger in residence, much of that jungle had been cleared. Several hospitals lined newly built streets near the expanded docks, and the whole place bustled. Barracks had replaced the tents. We were assigned to barracks near the area where we had parked our equipment previously, too close to the barracks that housed several army nurses and WACs for my comfort.

"Assign Tilton to ensure the women are treated with respect," Henderson said.

"That's like having the fox watch the henhouse," I told him.

"Tilton formed relationships with some women when he was hospitalized here. So he will hear if any of the men get out of line," Henderson replied.

Tilton set up a chair and table in front of the barracks, where he and a group of women had drinks every night. Soon, other officers joined them, but the enlisted men stayed away.

Men and women fraternized more freely here than in the States. The tables and benches in the largest mess hall were cleared on Saturday night for a dance. Junior officers, NCOs, and enlisted men danced freely with the WACs and nurses. The opportunity for at least some contact with women eased the loneliness of the men.

***

Captain Henderson returned from a planning meeting at the beginning of our second week on the island. He tossed a packet of mail on my desk. I could see a letter from Sarah Gale on the top, and I wanted to tear it open right there, but Henderson said, "Send the radar men down to the equipment lot with the old radar. We're replacing them all with new SCR 584s."

"Fantastic!" I said. "Do you realize how much easier it will be to transport and set up our equipment with the 584? It's so much more accurate. And we'll need less fuel."

Henderson still didn't seem excited. He resisted any change of equipment. It seemed his mind didn't wrap itself around technology very well.

"The men have to pick up the new equipment on the dock as it comes off that ship out there." He pointed to a giant cargo ship offshore. "We'll have ten weeks retraining before the next invasion."

Tilton walked by, apparently headed for the showers. I called him over.

"Get all the radar men together and take the SCR-268 units to the equipment depot, then go to the docks and pick up our new 584s."

"Aw, I was trying to get a shower while the water was warm."

"In this heat, I don't mind cold showers at all. Better get down there. If I know the army, they haven't delivered enough for all the searchlight units on the island, and it'll be first come, first served."

Tilton ordered, "Perry! Call the platoons and get the radar units down here." He told me, "It will probably take them long enough to get here that I'll be able to shower."

Tilton was right. The men had been scattered all over the camp, swimming or relaxing in the big tent that served as our mess, PX, and enlisted men's club. By the time they assembled, Tilton had returned, freshly scrubbed and ready to go. The twenty-seven trucks used to transport our radar and power units bumped off down the rutted road toward the equipment lot. I needed to set up the new training schedule, but I decided to read Sarah Gale's letter first.

March 6, 1944
Dear Gene,
The air raids are over. At least, we think they are. We have not had any for several days. So I don't want you to worry about me.
Colonel Hobby didn't come here. We don't have a lot of enlisted women here, and the work we do is not done by too many WACs. Our captain said the colonel heard a report on what we were doing but was more interested in how the enlisted women got along. I guess I can understand that. I was still a little disappointed, though.
I am learning to play tennis. I am not learning too fast because I only have

one weekly lesson. I don't really have time for more than one. Soon, I may not even have time for that one. Today, though, I learned about serving. I won't say I learned to serve because I still don't do it right most of the time, but I learned about serving because I know a lot of ways to do it wrong. I don't know if I will proceed to something else next week or if I have to stay on learning to serve until I can do it right more often than I do it wrong.

I have to tell you that my instructor is male. He is a British Air Force Captain. I am not at all interested in him. I am just interested in learning how to play tennis. The other girls say I should not be leading him on, but he had been pestering me for a long time, and I just thought I would use his interest in me to get some lessons. I hope you don't mind. He is tall and skinny with a receding hairline and makes funny faces when he plays tennis. It almost makes me wonder if he really likes the game. He is a good player, though, so I let him give me a lesson once a week. If he seems to have the idea that it is more than a tennis lesson, I will stop going.

I am getting very bored with the food around here. It is not bad, just dull. Gabriella got a job at a restaurant that pays more. Our new cook is about seventy and does not hear very well. I understand she is the best they can find because all the able-bodied young women do other jobs. She is trying to cook with the dehydrated supplies the army is sending over. Generally, she does a reasonable but very ordinary job, except for the cottage pie we have had twice this week. It has a lovely flaky crust, nicely browned, but inside, it combines canned peas, rehydrated mashed potatoes, and spam. It is seasoned with only salt and pepper, and the spam is salty enough without adding any more. I told her she should taste things before salting them again, but I am unsure if she heard me. I didn't want to shout at her. Maybe I should leave a note for her when a meal is not too salty and tell her how much I liked it.

Love
Sarah Gale

I did have a big problem with Sarah Gale taking tennis lessons from an "interested" British Captain. Why would she think I wouldn't? I thought long and hard about how to word that in my next letter so she would understand my feelings without hurting her feelings.

*** 

Three hours after the men left with the old radar equipment, nine trucks drove back into our billet site, each towing a radar trailer and power source.

At roll call, which we still did at 1600 hours, our men were expecting R&R again.

"We will begin retraining on the new SCR-584 units tomorrow morning. Roll call will revert to 0600. Training will commence immediately following chow. Every member of the unit will participate," Henderson announced.

The men groaned.

"Sinclair has set up nine rotations. The roster will be posted in your barracks."

We had nine units, but Tilton, Lucas, and I were the only officers who knew how to operate the new radar. We each took nine men at a time and trained them to set up and calibrate the units. They then had the opportunity to track incoming air traffic, three men to a team, for two hours as we went from one unit to the next, checking out their proficiency. Then we had them fold everything up and hitch it to a truck for the next twenty-seven men. This process allowed each man in the battery, including drivers, mechanics, and cooks, to learn to operate the radar. By the end of the second week, we could step back and let them practice under the supervision of the platoon commanders. I was impressed with Lucas's knowledge and ability to work with the men.

Before I read Sarah Gales's latest letter, I forced myself to catch up on the paperwork I had let slide. I would never get to the forms and other details if I didn't do them first. Finally, I filed the last report and turned to her letter.

March 20, 1944

Dear Gene,

They just passed a law here that female schoolteachers can be married. I always thought teachers could be married. My sixth-grade teacher was married. Are there any laws that teachers can't be married in Kansas? It is only about women teachers. Men teachers have always been allowed to be married in England, but apparently not women. I asked one of my British friends about it, and she said it is because women might get pregnant and because they don't need to work because their husbands can support them. I think I might want to work after the war. Not as a washerwoman but as a photographer. Would you have a problem with that? You keep writing about living in a nice little Victorian house and about the education and work you expect to do, but you never mention your opinion about me working.

The tennis lessons are over. At the very next session, he put his arms around me when he tried to show me how to do a backhand and would not let go when I asked him to. The other girls told me that was what he was after, but I didn't want to believe them. I guess I learned a different lesson. I thought your promise ring would discourage him. I am looking for a female tennis teacher, but I may not find one here because few females have time to play games. Most of them are working at jobs the men have left, raising children, and keeping house. I guess that is another thing I will have to put on my list for after the war.

*Love*
*Sarah Gale*

I was grateful I wouldn't have to write the letter saying I disapproved of her taking tennis lessons from this British officer.

*** 

As planning proceeded for the upcoming invasion, Henderson returned from a meeting with another change.

"We'll be working with three battalions on this island. We only have the equipment to direct one. See if you can figure out how we can do that."

I sat down with Wright, Tilton, and Brasseux.

"We have to figure out a way to direct three times as many guns as the equipment is set up for," I said. "Tilton, you were trained as an electrical engineer, weren't you? Can you try to figure out a way to make this work?"

"It shouldn't be too difficult, although every gun connected to a given radar unit will be directed to the same aircraft. We will have to figure out how to have each radar track a different target in the case of a large attack."

"Wright, can you deal with that? Brasseux, I brought you in to figure out the practical aspects of all this wiring."

Brasseux nodded and began making sketches on a paper napkin he pulled out of his pocket.

Over the next few days, Tilton laid out a communications network to aim the guns and lights, automatically set off air raid warnings, and telephone communication with gun battalions, automatic weapons battalions, and HQ.

"This looks good, but we'll have to move it constantly," I said. "Can we make it so we can just plug it in rather than splicing wires every time something changes?"

"That would be possible," Tilton replied.

"Brasseux, have you figured out how much cable we'll need?"

"Miles. We don't have dat much."

"We can get it. I checked with the Quartermaster yesterday, and they said there's no shortage of cable. We'll have to put spindles on more jeeps to hold the spools."

"Wright, what do you have in the way of a plan to get all the radar to track different targets?"

"Pretty simple, really. If we have several targets approaching, radar unit one will lock onto the far right, unit nine on the far left, unit five on the center, and the others in increments between. We'll post instructions in each trailer, so the operators know exactly where they lock on."

We presented the plan to Henderson. He looked it over, but I don't think he fully understood all the drawings and plans. "We should try this out first. See if you can set up a trial run with the gun battalions."

"We have to rig the connections first," I said.

Tilton and Brasseux spent the next two weeks rewiring the connections on the controller, and then I contacted the gun battalions.

"All well and good, but how are we supposed to know if it really works?" one XO complained. "All the planes around here are ours. Shooting down a squadron of our own aircraft wouldn't be good for my career."

"We're just trying to determine if the guns and lights move. You won't be shooting any ammo," I told them. "If the lights hit the planes, the ordnance will too,"

We set up a training session for the new setup. Tilton demonstrated how to make the connections to the controller. We strung the cable to the light and gun controllers. A flight of bombers returned from a mission, and we followed them in. The lights and guns focused on the planes as they approached the airfield. Our invention worked.

*** 

That evening, we learned that the landing had been moved up. We would be on the island of Biak in ten days, May 24. This was a much bigger problem for the senior officers, intelligence, and supply personnel than for us, but it meant less time retraining on the new equipment.

Intelligence briefings said there were believed to be around 4000 Japanese troops on the island of Biak. The 12,000 troops, 12 big Sherman tanks, and 29 big guns we were bringing should be able to clear the island quickly.

"There are three airfields on the island," General Fuller explained. "We need those fields for our attack on the Philippines. The infantry will take Mokmer field first, then march to the others. Antiaircraft will set up at Mokmer as soon as it's ours and defend it while the engineers bring it up to specifications. By then, we should have captured Sorido and Boroko, and the defenses will be reallocated as needed.

When I returned from the briefing, a packet of letters from Sarah Gale sat on my cot.

April 17, 1944
Dear Gene,
We are busier than ever. They say a picture is worth a thousand words, so I have enclosed a new picture of myself that I had one of the girls take the other day. That makes this one of the longest letters I have sent. Will write more when the workload lets up.

Love
Sarah Gale

I lifted the picture into the light. Sarah Gale stood, wearing the bright green dress her mother had made, her vivid red hair gleaming in a beam of sunlight as she stood before a flowering hawthorn amid a field of daffodils. Her dazzling smile and sparkling green eyes flashed. I could almost feel her standing in front of me. I had seen color photographs before, but Sarah Gale produced one of herself, just for me. Tears formed in my eyes at the extravagance of her gift.

May 1, 1944
Dear Gene,
There was a real tragedy on Friday during a training at a beach near here. I know if I told you about it, it would all get censored anyway. But it was really sad, and I will tell you at the end of the war when I see you again.
Our rides to and from work are much more pleasant now because it is light when we leave our quarters and come back. Summer days are so much longer here than they are at home. Of course, days get longer in the summer in North Carolina, but not as much as here in England. We are as busy as ever, but seeing sunlight every day makes it so much better.
Love
Sarah Gale

# CHAPTER 22

## BLOODY BIAK

**W**E APPROACHED THE ISLAND under an overcast dawn sky. Gladly, no rain fell. In the dim light, the island's jumble of coral rock seemed about twenty times higher than the little hill we had called a ridge on Kiriwina. As the sun rose, a spire of coral rock appeared, growing from the thick jungle. A jagged ridge on the southeast of the spire petered out in a low-lying shelf. From the ledge, sheer cliffs fell to the white sand beaches.

Several men lined the rail of the transport, eager to see the bombardment. Others paced nervously between the vehicles. The ships moved farther east to where the shelf widened, and two stone jetties jutted out into the water from a little village, our landing site. The navy fired the first salvo of shells. Brasseux jumped, then ran for cover as they exploded. I found him crouched behind a truck, his hands over his ears.

"They're just shelling the beach. Nobody's shooting back."

"Dis place is too exposed," he said. "Dere is no place to hide."

"We'll be in the trees again soon. We need you to help us find a place to set up once we get to the island."

He took a deep breath and nodded. Even after years of training, we were captive to our upbringing and experience as we prepared to invade this treacherous island. I felt nervous if I could not see the horizon, and Brasseux felt nervous if not surrounded by trees and swamps.

The smoke from the bombardment thickened, and soon, we could not see the island. Hundreds of shells hit the beach and cliffs, shredding the jungle vegetation and knocking great chunks of rock from the cliffs. Then, after forty-five minutes of noise and smoke, the barrage suddenly stopped. Time for us to move out. Henderson popped a pill into his mouth as he stood and swallowed quickly. Maybe he wasn't getting better.

Landing craft spread out on the water, some already approaching the jetties, others riding the waves over the coral and moving toward the beach. As they neared the island, the first boats, pushed east by the current, disappeared into the smoke. A few minutes later, as the second wave arrived, the smoke had cleared enough that we could see them as they landed in a mangrove swamp west of the landing site. Mass confusion reigned on the beach as the regiments tried to get to the places where they should have landed. Men from one regiment marched through the lines of the other to reach their assigned positions. Even with all the confusion, we faced no enemy resistance. We felt confident as we breached the reef and navigated the inner lagoon.

As our landing craft reached the island, the 163rd infantry marched west toward Mokmer airfield. Automatic weapons fired in the jungle to the east—just a short burst. Otherwise, there was no action. Our automatic weapons battalion, already set up when we drove our trucks off the landing craft, returned the fire. We moved onto the beach and sat, waiting for Henderson to give an order. Instead, he stood staring at the jungle.

"Captain," I prompted, "Where are we supposed to go?"

"Oh. Take the road up the little valley and set up to the right."

I looked around. To our left, the cliffs ended, and a narrow gorge provided access to the shelf above the beach. A road, hardly wider than a cart track, led to the plateau. I turned my jeep over to Perry and climbed into Henderson's, pushing him out of the driver's seat. He willingly relinquished the wheel and pulled himself into the passenger seat. I raised my hand and signaled the men to follow me. Revving the engine, I turned the jeep up the steep track. The drivers gunned the engines of the trucks behind me. Tires spun on the soft sand, digging the trucks in. Men jumped off the trucks and pushed them as the drivers downshifted and ground toward the shelf.

The jungle had been burned and flattened by aerial bombing and navy shelling, creating a clearing at the edge of the cliff where I stopped. The big guns moved into place on the beach fifteen hundred feet beneath us, closer together and closer to the radar and searchlights than usual. Their firepower would be very concentrated until we could move to a more open location. While ideal for protecting the landing beach as personnel and supplies were unloaded, we could not detect anything approaching from the northwest.

Henderson was still contemplating setting up in the new clearing when Carson spotted some approaching aircraft. Unfortunately, we were not yet set up to track them. The big guns were not ready, and the automatic weapons battalion was already moving to a new location.

"Perry, notify the navy that enemy aircraft are approaching at about one hundred ten degrees," I said.

Before he had given our call letters, the planes turned around.

Four Sherman tanks rolled onto the beach. As these tanks lumbered into the jungle, three Japanese light tanks tried to cut them off. The Japanese tanks were no match for the big Shermans. They retreated within a few minutes.

Shortly after that, we were operational. Henderson had overcome his drugged stupor and ordered Brasseux to lead his platoon into the jungle to find a secure campsite. Carson's radar operators took the first shift on the radar, and Lucas' platoon went down to the beach to help with supplies.

Suddenly, the cliffs about a quarter mile to the west exploded with machine guns and mortar fire. The Japs had let us land, then sprung the trap, firing from the mouths of numerous caves in the cliff. Several infantrymen fell as others fired on the hillside. The destroyers offshore fired, but the bombardment from the caves continued. We could see the guns roll out of the caves, fire, then roll back in. Field artillery quickly moved into position and fired toward the caves, too, but the shelling did not stop. There appeared to be hundreds of caves, each with a gun emplacement completely hidden from below. The radar and searchlights were positioned high enough to see the guns as they appeared from the caves, but the big AAA guns were on a lower ledge to protect the beach and could not fire on the caves. We had machine guns, but the caves were out of range around the curve of the bay. If we fired, our bullets would rain down on the infantry. We watched helplessly as the infantrymen scurried for whatever cover they could find.

***

The infantry regiment was pinned down in a defile directly in the line of fire of the Japanese guns with no effective defense and had been for most of the day. Destroyers came as close as they could to the coral reefs and fired on the hillsides, a risky strategy because the American troops hid close to the base of the cliffs, but they took out the guns on one hill. The other two sides were inaccessible to the ships. Many more than the estimated four thousand Japanese troops were entrenched on this island. They continued to fire on the trapped infantry until air support arrived in the late afternoon and fired on the caves while amphibious boats moved in to rescue them.

Our radar warned us of five Japanese bombers approaching the beach. The radar effectively locked onto the targets and directed the guns toward the aircraft. The ninety-millimeter guns fired as the planes came into range, hitting three. The other two dropped bombs near the jetty as the automatic weapons fire hit both aircraft. The bombs did not explode, but one of the planes hit an LCV as it fell. Two PT boats moved in to rescue the crew. From our vantage point, we could not determine the number of casualties. The mangled iron and wood of the bomber and landing craft floated offshore for an hour until another landing craft attached a tow rope and pulled it back toward the ships.

Brasseux's men had located an intact grove of palm trees near the beach. We slung hammocks there and unloaded some of our personal items from the trucks before sunset. I took the night command by default. Henderson had already passed out in his hammock.

Gunfire not far to the west told us the battle still raged in that direction. I ran from unit to unit, slapping at mosquitoes as I ran. I couldn't find my insect repellent in my duffel bag. My trousers were stiff from the salt and sand of wading ashore. Sweat dripped down my temples under my helmet, even as the sunrise brought the sea breeze ashore. We would all, except for Henderson and the mechanics, be up twenty-four hours by morning, and last night's sleep on the ship had not been good. A single plane flew over just after daybreak. All the radar locked on it, and all the guns blazed away when it came within range. It went down in the intense fire. So far, we had a phenomenal antiaircraft kill rate on this island, but the Japanese had a clear advantage in the ground fighting.

At first light, the Japanese launched a full-scale assault. A battalion of Japanese infantry supported by several of their light tanks pinned down most of our troops. The Sherman tanks, advancing overland, suddenly arrived to save the day, like the cavalry movies I had watched at matinees as a child. They came over the hill and moved toward the light tanks of the Japanese, guns blazing. I watched from behind the berm of sandbags we had constructed in front of our position. A Japanese tank on higher ground hit one Sherman's gun turret. The gun turret would not move. The driver backed into a crater left by a mortar and fired at the tank that had disabled its gun turret, demolishing the Japanese tank.

When we came off the lights and radar, Sergeant Martin had a hot meal ready. Henderson looked much better after a good night's sleep. We ate, then rolled into our hammocks, slung among the trees. The infantry started moving forward again as we drifted off to sleep. I woke as an artillery battalion slogged back through our little jungle camp.

"We made it to Mokmer, but they pushed us back," a passing captain told me. "Then the General told us to pull back because we were about to be cut off."

The expected quick capture of Mokmer field had failed. I tried to climb out of the hammock, but my foot got tangled in the mosquito netting. The hammock flipped and threw me to the ground. Men from both the searchlight and artillery units stood laughing at me as anger rose in my chest. I pushed myself up, ready to explode, when Henderson stepped forward.

"Trying to get your calisthenics out of the way first thing, Sinclair?"

"Just checking out the jungle floor," I said, brushing leaf mold and ants off my arms and legs. I realized that getting angry would not serve any purpose, and my antics had probably provided some much-needed comic relief.

*** 

Neither we nor the infantry saw any action on our second night on the island. Then, as we changed shifts the following day, the Japs came at us with their most potent attack yet. Nine tanks led the attack. As Jap land forces approached, six bombers appeared on the radar. The operators locked on them as we had rehearsed. In the concentrated gunfire, only two escaped being hit. One fell into the ocean, and two turned back, trailing smoke. The others dropped their bombs on the field artillery positions.

This attack pushed the infantry and artillery back to our position near the beachhead. Reinforcements from a second wave of landings poured onto the island as the Japanese pushed us back. A stalemate.

The Allies needed these airstrips to move on to the Philippines, and the Japanese were not about to let them go. So, the Allied force's main objective on the island became clearing the caves of Japanese soldiers and weapons. Tomahawk fighter bombers sealed some caves. Infantrymen gained others by crawling up the cliff with flame throwers to drive the Japs back into the caves and throwing hand grenades in.

Even antiaircraft artillery shot their big guns into the caves. They relocated to higher ground and began firing with little success in their first few tries. When I woke from a fitful sleep, I went to their new emplacement and saw how poorly they aimed. I learned their captain had been killed in the fighting soon after landing, and the young unit had grown accustomed to automatically controlled guns. Some had never calculated trajectories for targets that could not be located by radar. I offered my help calculating coordinates, something I had excelled at in the coastal artillery before the war. I sighted a cave entrance, calculated the trajectory, and gave the coordinates to a gunner. He aimed and fired. The shell went right into the cave.

"Got 'em!!!" shouted the crew, clapping the gunner and me on the back.

"Let's try again!"

A second shot missed the cave we aimed for but knocked a good size piece of coral off the hillside so that it partially blocked another cave. The infantry radioed for us to cease fire so they could eliminate survivors.

"Come on up and see these caves," they called after a couple of hours. "You won't believe it."

We scrambled up the face of the cliff on the steep, rugged paths the

Japanese had made. Inside the first cave, a horrific sight waited: men blown to pieces, dismembered body parts all over. Some lifeless Japanese still bled from the nose and ears. Others lay on their backs with their intestines hanging out.

"Look at this place," called an infantryman from deeper in the cave. "Wooden floor, electric lights. There's a kitchen farther back with a freshly cooked meal on the stove. This is a better barracks than we lived in in the States."

We hesitated inside the entrance.

"Come on," he said. "We cleared the entire cave. It goes on and on."

We heard gunshots echoing from deep in the cave.

"Now maybe the whole cave is cleared," he said.

A gunner turned and fled the cave, throwing up until he had nothing left in his stomach. I followed. Outside, an infantry officer said, "What's up? You look like you've seen a ghost."

"At least a hundred of them," I replied.

He shook his head as we made our way shakily down the path.

I reached our newly erected HQ tent just as a private from the radar unit came running up. He saluted as he ran and asked, "Where's the captain?"

"Asleep," I said. "What do you need?"

"We have something funny on the radar."

I returned to the radar trailer with him. The radar showed multiple objects approaching.

"Way too small for aircraft," I said. "Could it be birds?"

"Doesn't act like birds," the radar operator said.

"But there's a huge flight of Zeros and Vals behind whatever it is."

"I bet they are trying to scramble our radar," said the relief radio man behind me.

"Probably. That might work with the old radar, but we can see through it with this equipment."

The radar locked on and aimed the guns. The engines of the planes could be heard in the distance.

"At least twenty-five of them approaching," said the relief radar operator as he slid into position. "They must know when we change shifts and hope to catch us unawares."

"That's why Captain Henderson or I monitor every shift change," I said. "They've taken advantage of shift changes on other islands. I don't know how they find out."

"Probably just watch us from the caves."

We heard the guns firing, and I went out of the trailer. Huddled behind a wall of sandbags with the machine gunner, I watched the planes approach.

"Biggest attack yet," he said.

We watched as several planes were hit and turned away. For the first time, I realized that as each aircraft went down, a crew of men went down with it. I had kept that out of my mind until I saw the carnage in the cave. During my twelve-hour shift that night, the visions of that cave kept coming back to me.

The next afternoon, Captain Henderson woke me up early.

"Sinclair," he called. "Get up. You're going with a group of engineers to check out the little island to the south to see if there is a good site for an air base. You'll assess the site for AAA positions. Find Douglas and tell him he will be temporary XO, get three days' rations, then join the engineers on the beach."

# Chapter 23

## OWI RECON

**I** FOUND DOUGLAS OVERSEEING rod replacement in the lights and sent him to the HQ tent, packed my duffel, and stopped by the hospital for a week's supply of antimalarials. I arrived at the beach at the same time as the boat taking us to the island.

"Are you the Triple-A joining us?" asked the lanky young Captain leading the squad.

"Yes, sir, Lieutenant Sinclair."

"Well, hop on, Sinclair, and let's see what we can find. I'm Pierce Rosen. Meet Lieutenant Peterson and Sergeant George." We shook hands, "We also have privates Lopez, Carter, Lancaster, and Gardner." I returned the salutes of the privates, and we all turned to climb into the boat.

Twenty minutes later, after dropping us on the shore of Owi, a tiny, oval island, the boat quickly took off so as not to call attention to our presence.

"Pretty flat and much less decayed than the coral on Biak," said Captain Rosen

"Is it even big enough for one airstrip?' asked one of the engineers.

"Let's find out. Follow me." Rosen took off, rapidly pacing along the beach.

Peterson, a surveyor, rolled a wheel in front of him, measuring the distance. A civil engineer, George drew a map of the island's features. He stopped to sketch occasionally, then ran to catch up with us. As we walked, I noticed a native boy watching us. I caught Rosen's attention and glanced toward the boy. By now, a man and three other children had joined him. Rosen started walking toward them, but they disappeared into the jungle. As we rounded the eastern edge of the island, we spotted a little shack on stilts in about four feet of water with a couple of dugout canoes bobbing under it. Both canoes had a single outrigger and what looked like barkcloth sails folded in the prow.

"A fishing hut," said Carter. "Must belong to those natives who were watching us."

He started to examine the canoe, but Captain Rosen barked, "We're here to check out the island, not the occupants' property."

We walked on. About an hour later, we found another fishing hut on the island's south side and spotted three men in a canoe a short way off-shore spearfishing. Children from that hut followed us for about fifteen minutes, then disappeared.

Two and a half hours later, we arrived back where we had left our equipment. Someone had gone through it but had not taken anything. As the rest of us double-checked everything, Peterson and George sat down for a little conference.

"Three miles long and a quarter wide," Peterson announced when they finished their calculations.

"Is that big enough for the airfield they want to build here?" I asked.

"Look here," said George, showing me his sketch. "If we put the run-ways diagonally across the island and the buildings over here, we can fit it all, I believe."

"Tomorrow, we'll determine if the runways can be built," Rosen said. "But now we need to set up camp."

We found a small jungle clearing and set up our tents. The engineers pulled out camp shovels and leveled an area in the center of the little camp, dragged some fallen logs from the forest to sit on, and built a fire. We pulled out our C rations and had a superb beef stew, creamed corn, and peaches. Peaches still showed up at least every other day as part of our meals.

***

I watched from the beach as the sun rose over the ocean. Two ca-noes, one family in each, sailed toward another small island to the north-east. Poor families. First, we bombed Biak; now, we were taking over Owi. Where would they go next?

"Were those Japs?" asked Rosen, coming out of the trees behind me.

"I believe they were the families we saw yesterday," I said.

"Lancaster, Carter," Rosen called, "grab the scope and see if you can confirm that those are the natives we saw yesterday.".

The men came running from the camp with telescopes and con-firmed my original assessment.

"Probably got bombed out on Biak, so they came here, then took off as soon as they saw us coming so they wouldn't get bombed out again," Rosen said.

We moved to the interior of the island. As the engineers marked lo-cations suitable for runways and examined the terrain, I checked out lines of sight necessary for searchlights and radar. This would be an excellent place to spot incoming aircraft from the Philippines and New Guinea. It didn't have the spire and ridges of Biak to block the light or radar signals.

"Will it work for your boys?" asked Rosen.

"The island's a search lighter's dream," I said. "A speck of coral surrounded by sea. "How many runways are we talking about?

"The General wants three. We'll know for sure if we can do it when we complete the survey."

We continued to survey the island for the rest of the day.

That night, as we sat around a fire, the smoke from its green wood keeping insects away, we reveled in how perfect the island was.

"The soil is only a foot deep, so the bulldozers will have no problem clearing an area for runways. Also, camps and structures," said George.

"And the coral underneath will crush and pack to support runways with almost no work," put in Lancaster.

"The sight lines will allow the searchlights to light up aircraft in all directions, and the radar will not be blocked by thousand-foot cliffs like on Biak," I added.

"Tomorrow, we'll begin laying out the runways," said Captain Rosen. "Do you have the perimeter calculated, George?"

Sergeant George had been drawing on a portable drafting board off and on since breakfast.

"I've got it," he said. "All set for tomorrow."

\*\*\*

In the morning, we broke camp and piled our gear at the pick-up point. Rosen took half the men to the northeast, where the runways would start. The rest of us walked toward the far end of the island.

Peterson handed me the grade rod and said, "Go stand by that palm over there." I held the rod as Peterson called out measurements, and Carter wrote them down. Then Peterson sent me to stand in another spot, and we did it again. By afternoon, we had laid out three runways connected by taxiways on the island. The two crews met at the center of the island.

"We just need to get our equipment over here and get busy," said Rosen. "We'll have an airbase here in no time. They'll pick us up at 18:00 hours at the drop-off point so we need to hurry to get back there before the boat arrives."

We marched double-time across the little island to arrive at the pick-up point on time. We waited, but the boat did not show up.

"Why don't we radio them?" I asked.

"No radio," replied Rosen.

"I thought engineers thought of all the details," I said.

"We expected the Navy to follow through without being reminded,"

Rosen said.

Behind his back, Peterson pointed and mouthed, "He forgot it."

I nodded. Both Rosen and Peterson thought I nodded to them.

I pulled my shaving mirror out of my kit and tried to signal the island but got no reply.

After dark, we moved back into the jungle and set up camp again in the dark. We skipped the evening meal to have rations for the following day.

"What do you think might have happened over there? Is everyone dead, and they can't come to get us?" asked Lancaster.

"No. See, they're still shooting at the cliffs." We could see the blasts of artillery across the water in the dark. "They'll come as soon as they can," I replied.

*** 

We ate the last of our rations the following morning, returned to the beach, and sat there waiting for the boat. We tried signaling Biak with shaving mirrors. No response.

"What are we going to do?" asked Lopez.

"I'm going to try to get us something to eat," said George. He waded to the fishing hut, where he found a spear the locals had left behind. With that, he waded into the ocean and began fishing.

The rest of us scoured the nearby jungle, looking for food. Finally, I located some ripe bananas. On the way back, I saw a yam plant. I cut a stick and dug three large yams from the soil. I came back, my arms full and my uniform covered with dirt.

"Sinclair wins," Gardner said. "He has the most food."

Just then, we heard a shout from the beach. George had speared a large fish.

"Look, I caught a tuna," George exclaimed as we emerged from the jungle.

"It's a yellowfin," shouted Rosen as George heaved the three-and-a-half-foot-long fish onto the beach.

George and Lopez quickly gutted the fish and cut steaks from the side. I built up the fire, and we threaded the tuna steaks onto sticks and cooked them as the yams baked. This meal beats C rations any day!

*** 

The engineers twisted some vines to form a rope, then used them to lash several hardwood branches together.

"Are you building a raft to get us back to Biak? I asked.

"This would definitely not be seaworthy," Peterson declared. "We're building a lookout platform to mount among those three palm trees."

We hauled Gardener up to the platform by ropes to watch for the boat while the rest of us took an afternoon nap. Still, the boat did not come.

As the sun set, we built a fire on the beach and cooked more tuna steaks. Unfortunately, they weren't as good as the fresh steaks we had eaten earlier.

Even though the troops on Biak apparently hadn't seen the sun glinting off the mirrors, we felt sure they couldn't miss a blazing bonfire. Rosen assigned two-hour shifts to keep the fire burning and continue signaling Biak by lifting and dropping a ground cloth in front of it. Unfortunately, help did not come that night.

The next day, we realized we needed to be prepared to survive on the island until someone finally came for us. We set up a twenty-four-hour schedule assigning us to the watch tower in the palms, fire tending, food scavenging, and sleeping on a rotating basis. From the lookout, we could clearly see Biak, but no boats came in our direction.

George caught an even heavier tuna that morning, and after eating some fresh steaks, we cut up the leftovers and hung them in the fire's smoke.

I used a ground cloth to rig a water collection basin. Daily rain kept us in fresh drinking water, but there was not enough for bathing. All the fresh water trickled away into the porous coral immediately after each shower.

Even smoked, the tuna had a somewhat rancid taste by evening. We cracked coconuts and collected a few breadfruits from a tree halfway across the island, but the tuna George continued to catch every second or third day was still our primary food source. Every day, we expected the boat to pick us up. It did not show.

*** 

On the tenth day on the island, the seventh day of tuna, George failed to catch anything.

"I think the tuna have moved on, "he said. "And they seem to have eaten or scared off all the other fish."

Lopez and Lancaster woke complaining of fever, headaches, a severe cough, and diarrhea.

"Do they have malaria?" asked Captain Rosen

I examined the men, finding numerous small insect bites on their arms and legs.

"This looks more like scrub typhus," I said. "A few of the same symptoms as malaria, but the cough and diarrhea are different. Also, do you see these scabs on their legs? They are probably bites from the mites that carry the typhus."

"What can we do for them?" he asked.

"We'll try to keep the fever down and pray for the boat to get here quickly."

I dosed them with aspirin from the first aid kit and carried water from the ocean to bathe them. The fever of both men would go down as we bathed them in seawater but spiked again to what felt like dangerous heights when we stopped. As the day wore on, they became confused and delirious. Lopez tried to fight anyone nearby, and Lancaster ran into the scrub. We brought him back and tied him to a tree to keep him from getting lost in the jungle. We rotated between watching for boats, tending the fire, caring for the sick men, and sleeping.

Rosen and I stopped eating the smoked tuna, subsisting on coconut and breadfruit. However, Carter, Gardener, George, and Peterson were still eating it, insisting the smoking process made it safe.

The following day, Peterson and Carter were down with scrub typhus. Lopez was unconscious, and Lancaster raged about someone trying to take his shoes. Rosen, George, Gardner, and I agreed on six-hour shifts with one in the tree, one tending the sick and the fire, one sleeping, and one scavenging for food. We had no malaria pills left.

"Do you know what Owi means?" asked George as I climbed into the lookout to relieve him.

"No, what?" I asked.

"Island of Death," he replied.

He climbed down and lay under the mosquito net to get his six hours of sleep. Rosen returned with six bananas, one of which he tossed to me.

"That's the last from that location," he said. "We'll have to see if we can find another source,"

I sat hunched in the afternoon rain, eating a not-quite-ripe banana, watching for a boat that refused to come. Maybe this would become an island of death for us.

George did catch a grouper late that afternoon, which tasted better than two-day-old smoked tuna.

On the morning of the twelfth day, all four men with typhus were comatose. Rosen was coughing and had diarrhea while George and Gardener were puking their guts out. I felt the familiar dizziness of an oncoming malaria episode as I tended them. I had to do something or we would all die here. I made my way back to the southern fishing hut and found a small canoe still tied there. My sailing experience was limited to a little recreational sailing in a small dinghy in Puget Sound with my buddy Tom Morris while we were stationed at Fort Worden, but I was determined to figure this out. I climbed into the canoe and noticed that the outrigger made it more stable than I would have expected. This small canoe, I discovered, had no sail, just a long, leaf shaped paddle. I had paddled a canoe on the pond at my college campus, but his was a whole new experience. I pushed off and began paddling. The outrigger and a twig covered platform between the outrigger and the canoe allowed me to paddle on only one side. I pushed off and started paddling toward Biak. The outrigger seemed to make it go straighter than I would have expected, and I paddled slowly toward Biak, going only slightly sideways. Canoing on the ocean was different from canoeing on the placid pond in Kansas, but after a bit I learned to move in rhythm with the waves and began making progress. About every fifteen minutes I had to move to the back of the canoe and correct my course, using the paddle as a rudder. After four hours of paddling, nearly exhausted, I washed ashore on the Biak, praying that the movement I had seen among the trees was allied forces.

An infantry medic ran from the trees and pulled me to cover.

"Send someone to Owi to pick up the men there," I gasped before passing out.

# Chapter 24

## VALLEY FORGE

I **WOKE TO AN** almost unbearable stench. "What is that smell?' I asked.

"Decaying horseflesh and overflowing latrines, sir," my son David told me. *My son?* "It's warming up, and everything frozen is thawing and rotting. General Washington sent an invitation to join him for breakfast. I believe he has a new assignment for you."

*St. Clair again.*

"He's going to give me another command even before the Court Martial?" I asked.

"Laurens said it had something to do with procuring supplies."

"God knows we need some supplies around here. Has he decided we should plunder the countryside?"

"How should I know? You're the general," David said. I wondered again if having my teenage son as an aide was the best idea. Livingston had been much more respectful, but when he was promoted, I felt it was important to have David by my side.

I dressed, and we walked out of the little house into the miasma. Smoke from the cooking fires hung in the damp air. The sticky mud sucked at my boots. The stench lessened somewhat as I neared Potts House, the General's headquarters, but it did not disappear.

"Arthur, thank you for coming. Sit down," Washington said. "The representatives from Congress are arriving today. Alex has written the statement we will present to them. It includes all the suggestions we discussed. I believe it to be very well written. I would like you to act as host to the committee. Ensure they have ample opportunity to assess conditions here, visit the storerooms, and witness the state of our provisions."

"Could I read that statement you plan to present?" I asked. "I would like to know of what I am to convince them."

Hamilton handed me the thirty-eight-page document, written in his clear hand and nuanced prose. As I read, Washington, Hamilton, and Laurens left to handle other business.

***

I rode to Moore Hall to ensure everything was ready for the Congressional delegation. The first-floor parlor had been set up as the meeting place for the commission. The second-floor bedrooms were assigned to General Biddle and the delegates, while David and I would share the third floor with the Moores.

"You cannot take more of our home," Mrs. Moore harped as David carried our trunks upstairs.

"It's an honor to have a Congressional Delegation in your home," I said.

"This whole bloody rebellion is a fool's mission," her husband declared.

"You are being paid for the rent of your house," David said.

"In worthless Continentals," they countered. For which I had no good response.

Washington arrived a short while later, just a few minutes before the delegation.

"Welcome to Valley Forge," he told the Congressmen as they dismounted. "General Arthur St. Clair will be your host during your time here. If you require anything, please let him know."

"We've come well supplied so as not to further reduce the supplies you say the army does not have," Congressman Morris replied as wagons loaded with trunks, barrels, and servants pulled up behind them.

As their servants carried baggage to the upstairs rooms, the congressmen shared a bottle of port with me in the parlor. The cook they had brought along built up the fire in the kitchen and began roasting a cut of beef, the first I had smelled in over a month.

"Would you care to take a preliminary tour, gentlemen?" I asked. "Simply to observe conditions?"

As we left the mansion, three men pulled handkerchiefs from their pockets and covered their noses.

"Sorry for the smell. The men have been ordered to use the latrines but don't want to walk that far in the cold when they don't have shirts and shoes. You will also note that several workhorses have died. They were all butchered where they fell, and the meat was eaten. Their rotting carcasses add to the odor."

"Where are the storehouses," asked Dana.

I led them to the first storehouse and unlocked the door. Inside were thirty barrels of flour, nothing more.

"How many men are here?" asked Morris.

"With all the deaths and desertions, it is hard to say. Probably around nine thousand right now."

"Washington can't keep the men from deserting?" asked Reed.

"Why should they stay when they have no food, no clothes, and sickness is rampant in the huts? Only because of Washington's quiet strength and constant assurances is anyone still here."

"Where are your other supplies?" asked Dana.

"This is it. We have no other supplies unless General Greene arrives with some soon. The men have been surviving on firecakes and horse meat. We have no fodder for the horses, so they are starving, too."

"Can you show us your clothing stores?" said Folsom.

I opened the door of the next storeroom. One pair of torn breeches hung on a peg in the wall.

"You have no uniforms to clothe the men?" asked Dana.

"No sir, we do not. Do you think the men would be running around like they are if we had clothes for them to wear?"

We returned to Moore Hall, where servants had set the table in the dining room with Mrs. Moore's finest damask tablecloth and good China.

"Won't you join us, General St. Clair?" asked John Reed.

"Thank you. I would be pleased to."

I pulled up a chair and sat down. It had been weeks since I had eaten anything besides cornmeal mush or firecakes. David looked on hungrily.

"Have a seat, young man. There's plenty," said Morris.

He ate the way only eighteen-year-olds can, devouring the beef, bread, potatoes, and carrots the congressional representatives brought. I noticed that they watched him closely.

***

"Sir, drink some broth," I heard a medic coax as he lifted my head. I sipped the warm broth, then lay back.

"Oh, it feels good to have something warm in my stomach," I mumbled.

"I'd prefer an ice cold drink," the medic replied as he stood. "I'll be back later with something more."

As he walked away, I faded back to the muddy paths of Valley Forge. I took the congressional representatives to meet officers from their home states.

Realizing that procuring food came first, the committee sent messages to Congress and the various states' governors that the army's peril was as accurate and dire as Washington had portrayed it. We received word that Governor Wharton of Pennsylvania would send supplies within the week, with provisions from other states to follow.

Late one morning, the sky darkened. By early afternoon, it was almost as dark as night. Snow began falling that evening, and a blizzard engulfed the camp for two days, with snow moving sideways. No one ventured out of their cabins or tents. On the third day, the snow turned to torrential rains, melting the snow and turning the roads into rivers, washing debris and sewage from the open latrine pits through the camp. That night, temperatures dropped again, locking the entire camp in massive ice sheets. The river froze, and the men had to chop through the ice for water.

I suddenly felt warm and feverish as I walked to my room on the third floor of the stone house.

"I told you I would be back," the medic said. "I have some chicken noodle soup. My Grandma always says chicken noodle soup is the best medicine in the world."

"Mine did too," I whispered. "I'm so glad you arrived with the food. How are the men?"

"The men you were with on Owi?" he asked. "We have five of them here. Four down with bush typhus, and one with food poisoning.

"Five?" I said.

"Yes, five."

"There should be more."

"Why don't you close your eyes and go to sleep," he said.

I wanted to find out what happened, but my body had other ideas and I slipped back into unconsciousness.

*** 

In the pale light of a winter's day, I walked to Potts House to report to Washington, not wanting to overtax my undernourished horse. The most incredible sight stood in front of the house: a sleigh decorated with bells, four coal-black Percherons harnessed to it. An African driver sat in the sleigh, and several European and African servants stood behind it. I skirted the large sleigh and entered the great room that served as Washington's office. A portly man in a fur-trimmed black silk robe stood holding a French-style hat. A young man was trying to translate the man's French but was having difficulty due to the man's heavy German accent. Another, dressed in a red coat cut in the latest French fashion, stood slightly behind him.

"Where is Laurens or Hamilton?" Washington asked. "I need someone who speaks French."

"Maybe I can help," I said. "Bonjour."

The man introduced himself as Baron Friedrich Wilhelm August Heinrich Ferdinand von Steuben.

"He would first like to spend some time inspecting the camp to set his priorities," I translated.

"Tell him he can do that."

"He would also like to know the location of his quarters."

"While you're in Moore Hall, can he stay in your rented house?"

"He could," I said tentatively. "It's small for the size of his retinue."

"Tell him," Washington ordered.

I told him where the house was located. Just then, John Laurens rushed through the door.

"John, take the baron to the house St. Clair used to occupy and get him settled in. Tomorrow, you will accompany him on an inspection tour of the camp," Washington said.

John asked the Baron to follow him, and they left the room.

"Who is he?" I asked.

"Franklin sent him. He was a general in the Prussian army. He's here to help us reorganize the army."

"Let's hope he's more like Lafayette than Fermoy," I said.

"That's partly why I suggested that he use your house. By the time the congressional delegation leaves and you're ready to return to it, I may need an excuse to send him back to where he came from.

***

Baron von Steuben wasted no time at all reorganizing the camp. He ordered all the pit latrines covered and new latrines dug downhill on the opposite side of the camp from the cooking area. The officers selected one hundred fit and healthy men from various units, and von Steuben began training them in the drills and maneuvers necessary for an effective army.

"Arthur, you're one of my best recruitment and training officers. I also admire your strategic abilities. I want you to learn everything von Steuben is teaching the men and help with the spring campaign plan. I want to get out of here as soon as this mud dries up, and the army can march."

With the strenuous activity, for both my brain and the body, of following von Steuben around and translating for him, I began to feel my forty years. I slept deeply at night. I woke from one such sleep to a loud discussion near my bed,

"What's happening?" I asked. "Is there a problem with the reorganization?"

"Reorganization? What reorganization?" asked Henderson.

"Oh, um, nothing," I said.

"Well, I'm glad you're awake. You hurry up and get well. We need you."

Nurse Morris appeared.

"Here's that medicine, Captain. Hope your feet get better soon."

Captain Henderson took the bottle and limped off as I dozed off again.

# CHAPTER 25

## BUSH TYPHUS

**I** **THOUGHT THE LATRINE** issues were taken care of. What is that smell?" I asked as I woke, hearing movement near me.

An orderly had just arrived to change my sheets. "Let's see if we can get you into this chair," he said. As I moaned my way out of bed with his help, he explained. "We're fighting a major bush typhus epidemic, malaria, and jungle rot. A few thousand dead Japs are rotting in the caves all over the island, and the bodies can't be removed fast enough. I've almost gotten used to the smell. Not that I like it. We've had to consider the smell normal,"

"I see." After he finished, I lay back down and closed my eyes while adjusting to this new century, asking, "So we've broken through their cave defenses?"

"We captured Mokmer Airbase before you were admitted here. The fighting's still intense, but the men they're bringing in say we're making headway."

"Good," I mumbled and fell asleep.

The following day, I could eat a little bit of solid food. The smell of rotting flesh fought with my intense hunger, but I managed to keep down some of the gruel they gave me.

Captain Henderson came to visit, and I asked him if there were any letters from Sarah Gale.

"No, nothing," he replied.

I lay there, bored, disappointed, and worried. What if something had happened to her? She could have been killed in an air raid. She could have taken up with one of those British officers who were so interested in her. She could have decided she was no longer interested in me. After all, she could support herself now and wouldn't need me to take care of her. What if she had decided to become one of those spinster career women who never married?

Nurse Morris stopped by to check on me, pulling up a chair beside the bed. "I haven't gotten any letter from Sarah Gale," I told her. "I'm worried that something has happened."

"You can relax," she told me. "Nobody's getting mail. This is one of the Pacific's bloodiest battles, and the disease rate is through the roof. To make morale even worse, the mail isn't getting through. I'm sure Sarah Gale writes as often as she always does, and the letters will catch up to you eventually."

She sounded cheerful, but I could see she was exhausted.

"I really shouldn't be bothering you with my concerns," I said. "You need to get some rest."

"Actually, it's been nice to sit down for a bit. Nurses are getting sick, too, so those of us still working pull double shifts. These few minutes sitting down and talking to you is the most rest I've had in eighteen hours." She pushed herself out of the chair and checked on a nearby patient who was moaning loudly.

***

Within three days, I was back in my tent, weak but able to walk. They needed beds in the hospital for those who couldn't. I made my way to the HQ tent.

"They say I'm ready for duty," I told Lucas, who had taken over from Douglas as interim XO. "Can you get me up to speed?"

"You don't look ready for duty, but we can use anybody who can stand around here," he replied as he moved out of the desk chair, motioning me to sit down. . "The infantry just broke through, though. We hold all three airfields. There're still three to five thousand live Japs on the island, but we have them on the run. Their air raids have trailed off. Haven't seen a single Jap plane since last Friday.

"In the battalion, about one hundred fifty men are down with bush typhus, but that's fewer than other battalions thanks to our use of insect repellent. Once the men saw infantrymen dropping like flies, they decided insect repellent was a good idea. It helps cover up the other smells, too."

Lucas spent the next three hours reviewing daily reports, requisitions, and orders Captain Henderson gave for the past twenty-two days.

"There seem to be more supplies than we really need," I said.

"Sergeant Hammond assured me we needed all of it. However, I did notice more requisitions than you generally submitted. I think we must have run out of a lot of things."

I continued examining the reports. There were all sorts of unnecessary statistics, but they were very thorough. After Lucas finally showed me everything and returned to his platoon, Captain Henderson entered the tent.

"I'm so glad you're back. Lucas insisted on following every procedure he could find in any manual he could get his hands on. Nearly drove me mad."

"Yes, sir. I noticed that we used an average of a quarter gallon more fuel per hour in the generators than they are supposed to and that your jeep is fifty-three miles overdue for an oil change," I replied. "If you recall, I was pretty much a by-the-book guy when I was new. I wanted to be sure I did everything right, so I spent the evenings reading the manuals."

"That was stateside, and you had the time," he growled. "Have Douglas change the oil and check the unsubmitted requisitions before you send them to HQ. Lucas has been changing the amount of food and everything else daily based on the number of healthy people in the battery. Spent half his day checking roll calls against requisitions. You probably won't have anything to eat tonight because you were not here by roll call."

"I'll find something," I said. "We just sent two more men to the hospital with jungle rot or something."

"These damned diseases are killing more people than the fighting."

"Four percent of the troops killed in action, twenty-one percent wounded, and twenty-nine percent lost to illness."

"He calculated that, too? How many do we have left?"

"Let's see, that would be about forty-six percent." I checked the stats. "But that's on the whole island. Our battery has seventy-four percent on the job. None were killed in action, and only four were wounded. Lucas must have been having a wonderful time with this desk job."

"Nobody around here is having a wonderful time. This is the worst hellhole I've ever been in," Henderson mumbled.

I mustered some energy and walked through camp encouraging the men. Then, returning to HQ, I spent the rest of the day sorting the papers and round-filing the extra paperwork and calculations. A few I kept: I had a hunch the extent of the non-battle casualties would be of interest someday.

***

Returning from breakfast the next morning, Carson pointed to the sky. A B-25 glided silently over our heads.

"The engines must be dead. Looks like he's heading for Owi. I wonder if they're ready for him. Surely they haven't been able to complete even one runway."

We watched as the B-25 glided onto the island, gear down, apparently able to land.

"They did it. The field's ready for landing."

I slept all day to be ready for my first shift back on night duty. When I woke, several men, including Henderson and Carson, stood in our makeshift assembly area, looking at the sky. A flight of P-38s was approaching the airfield.

"Looks like they had to jettison their belly tanks," Carson said. They must've flown a long way to get here.

"You can tell that from here?" I asked.

"Sure, look at the profile."

As the planes approached, I saw none had belly tanks. Then, finally, the aircraft landed on Owi to several men's cheers.

Just then, the radio crackled with a message from Battery HQ.

"Sir," the radioman said, "Colonel Squires is calling for all COs and XOs to come for an important meeting."

"Get a jeep and pick me up here," Henderson told me.

He pulled himself into the jeep when I parked in front of him. He could barely walk at this point. "This better be worth it," grumbled Henderson.

"I wonder if it's another reorganization," I commented, the memory of Valley Forge still fresh on my mind. Captain Henderson continued to scowl.

At battalion HQ, I offered to help him, but he waved for me to proceed. I entered the tent and waved to the Colonel's secretary.

"Sinclair, I'm glad to see you up and about. Lucas had been bombarding us with so many reports and stats that we've started round-filing them," he said.

The Colonel walked into the tent. He returned my salute and said, "Sinclair, you're up and about! So glad to see it."

"Yes sir, glad to be up. You knew I was down?"

"I've been keeping an eye on you. It pays to know the exceptional junior officers."

"Yes, well, thank you, sir," I said as he went to the head of the conference table.

Other COs and XOs were already at the table. I joined them. When Henderson reached his seat, Colonel Squires began the meeting.

"We're having another reorganization and redesignation," Squires said.

Henderson frowned at me.

"Battery A will become Battery C of the 236th AAA Battalion, Battery B will become Battery C of the 237th and Battery C will become Battery C of the 238th."

"And you, sir?" asked Captain Gill of the former Battery B.

"Lateral move to the 236th. Barton will give you your orders."

Major Barton handed each captain an envelope, and the meeting was adjourned.

"How did you know?" Henderson scowled at me as soon as we reached the jeep.

"It was a dream. I was confused. I didn't know about this."

"Someone in the hospital must have leaked it, and you overheard," Henderson said.

"Completely possible," I replied. "I was totally out of it and don't remember." That was easier than explaining Von Steuben's reorganization of the Continental Army.

*** 

We were ordered to move to Owi Island and set up our radar and searchlights at the airfield. Henderson immediately assembled the officers and NCOs and read the order. Sergeant Hammond blanched.

"We have to pack everything up and move it?" he grumbled under his breath.

But Henderson heard him. "Of course. This is war. We go where we're ordered. What's the problem, Hammond?"

"Nothing, sir. Sorry, sir."

I followed Hammond back to the supply tent. It was packed solid with various supplies.

"Will all of this fit in the trucks?" I asked.

"None of it will. All the trucks are full."

"What have you been doing, Hammond?"

"Just trying to make sure we don't run out of anything."

"The supply convoys are making it through every time now. I'm sure we can get supplies on Owi. How do you expect us to move all this?"

"I wasn't planning on moving until the mop-up was completed."

"Like Henderson said, this is war. You don't get to plan it. So how did you manage to get all this stuff anyway?"

"Lucas didn't know how much stuff we usually use, so I doubled every requisition. You know Henderson never checks them."

"Of course, I know that. I check them. Don't you think someone in HQ will figure this out before long? Think of the other units that won't get the necessary supplies because you've hoarded all this."

"It's my job to ensure our unit has the supplies we need. The other units have their own supply officers. They can look out for their units."

"I'll figure out how to deal with this," I said.

Right after I returned to Battalion HQ, a staff sergeant from the quartermaster's corps arrived to talk to Captain Henderson.

"There seems to be a problem with your requisitions, sir," he said.

"I think I can explain," I said. "I generally prepare the requisitions, but I've been ill. It seems there was a SNAFU with the inexperienced personnel. The extra supplies are here and undamaged."

Henderson frowned at me.

"We'll sort it out," I promised.

"We move out at 0800. Sinclair, can you sort out this SNAFU by then?" Henderson asked pointedly.

"I believe so. Sergeant, can you send some trucks up?"

"I'm really short on men due to this typhus epidemic, but I can get some trucks up here and leave them if you can get them loaded."

"Can do," I said.

As the sergeant disappeared, Henderson shouted, "What the hell was that?"

"Hammond was stocking up on supplies while I was gone. That's why Lucas was working on requisitions every day."

"I'll see both Hammond and Lucas court marshaled."

"Let's just return the supplies. As irritating as this is, Lucas is healthy as an ox. We need as many healthy men as possible. And Hammond may be a little overprotective of us all, but he's efficient with the supplies."

"Get some men on that. And make sure Lucas is one of them."

I ordered the men on duty to break down the equipment and roll up the miles of wire connecting us to the gunners.

I ordered all the men not on duty to report to the supply tent. I hated to keep men up all night when they had just finished the day shift, but I had no choice. None of the men looked healthy, and we would head for the lice-infected island of Owi as soon as we finished this marathon.

When the trucks arrived, Lucas asked, "Can't we just deliver the full trucks to the Quartermaster and fill these trucks with our supplies?"

"Oh no," said Hammond. "These trucks have different serial numbers. Those trucks are assigned to us."

"They probably wouldn't notice," Lucas said.

"The hitches on the empty trucks aren't strong enough to pull our equipment," said Douglas.

"Don't return that insect repellent," shouted Hammond. "We're going to the most insect-infested place in the Pacific. Half the people who go there come back sick. And keep the extra uniforms. The chemicals in the insect repellent rot the material faster than the damned monsoons."

By 0400, the supplies were sorted and loaded into the correct trucks. I assigned eight men to drive the loaded trucks back to the main supply depot and took the rest to the radar installations to ensure the men on duty had completed the breakdown and were prepared to leave. The new radar could be packed quickly, but our fuel, wire, and auxiliary equipment took longer. Fortunately, all the equipment was ready to go. I sent the men to strike the tents and gather their gear as the sun rose. They swarmed onto the trucks an hour later, packs on their back and weapons slung on their shoulders.

The landing craft approached the beach as we cleared the palms. We didn't have to stop the convoy; the first vehicles drove across the beach and onto the landing craft. Almost all the men were asleep as soon as their truck was safely tied down on the landing craft. The seven-mile crossing was too short. It would probably have been better not to have slept at all. The men were groggy as they drove the equipment off the craft less than an hour after leaving Biak.

# CHAPTER 26

## OWI AIRFIELD

**T**HE ENGINEERS HAD COMPLETELY transformed the island since I had last seen it. Three parallel coral runways now ran diagonally across its length from north to south, with parking bays for aircraft on either side of the strip of runways. A complex of large tents lined roads under construction to the northwest of the runways. These would house the hospital, HQ, main supply area, and other common facilities. Medical personnel from Biak scrambled to set up the hospital. I waved to Nurse Morris, who looked about ready to drop as she carried a large box of supplies to the surgical area. She smiled weakly. I feared she might be getting sick.

I walked over and took the box from her arms. "Are you OK?" I asked.

"Yes. Just haven't had any sleep in thirty-six hours. I get three days' leave as soon as we are set up."

We walked to the surgery. I dropped off the box and continued to HQ to get our campsite assignment. She began taking items out of the box and putting them in a cabinet.

Campsites for various units lined the beaches. Unfortunately, we were assigned a site closer to the middle of the island, away from the beach. So we set up between HQ and the runways where the constant take-off and landing of planes would keep us awake at all hours. Henderson supervised the radar and searchlight set up near the runways' south end to provide lights and traffic control for the air base until more permanent lights and radar arrived.

\*\*\*

We had just settled in when the 421st Night Fighter Squadron landed. We would work closely with them, so I went to talk to some of the pilots.

"Excuse me, Captain," I said as I approached one of the pilots.

He turned, and I recognized him.

"Tom Morris! Long time no see! How has the war treated you?"

"Better than you, it seems. You always were a bit small, but now you're downright scrawny. What have you been doing with yourself?"

"Malaria, uncertain rations, a month on bloody Biak, eighteen months of island hopping in the Pacific. It's not the Fort Worden Resort. You gave up artillery to fly one of these?" indicating the planes nearby.

"Decided it would be more fun to chase them down than just shoot at them from the ground. We just got the latest birds. Brand new P-61 Black Widow."

Morris called over one of his men. "Jenkins, let's show Lieutenant Sinclair here the equipment." To me he said, "Jenkins is my radar operator."

"Radar operator!?" I exclaimed. "There's a radar on the airplane?"

"There is. It's an amazing piece of equipment for a fighter. We can find enemy aircraft and follow them wherever they go. Come take a look at it."

Jenkins shook my hand. "Tom Jenkins, In-flight radar operator." He noticed my expression. "The navigator is Tom Millikan. We call ourselves the tomcats."

If they were anything like Morris, the moniker applied.

The radar antennae and screen were even smaller than our SCR-584s.

"The plane's a little bigger than your average fighter because of the radar, but it's very maneuverable," said Morris. "These are great machines."

"Amazing machines," said Jenkins, patting the radar console. "We've had these birds for only a week. I hope they managed to send some profile cards for you guys. Check with the major before you leave."

"By the way, Morris, have you seen your sister yet?"

"She's here?!" he exclaimed.

"Yes. Probably still helping set up the hospital."

Morris ran off in the direction of the hospital.

I walked to the spot where the support group set up the night fighter HQ and approached a corporal.

"Mr. Sinclair," he said. "I mean Lieutenant Sinclair he corrected, saluting."

"Zook! Joseph, right?"

"Yes, sir. We've come a long way since boot camp, right?"

"You look like you've done well. Did anyone ever find out how old you are?"

"It wouldn't matter. I'm nineteen now."

I laughed. "I'm looking for some profiles of the new Black Widows so I can give them to the Skylighters. Wouldn't want to shoot down one of our own."

"I know just where they are."

He dug through a box and found the profile cards. A major approached me.

"You know him?"

"Morris, Zook, and I were all inducted together. I watched out for Zook at boot camp."

"He is a fine young soldier. That boy will go far provided he survives this war."

"That he will," I agreed.

\*\*\*

We were back to regular shifts with very little to do otherwise. On Biak, the infantry continued mopping up, but once our battery was set up, we ate, slept, worked, and spent the rest of our time on the beach, playing baseball or cards.

On our first Saturday there, Morris suggested we go to the movie being shown in the USO tent. The feature was *"The Pride of the Yankees"* with Gary Cooper, but first, they showed a newsreel. The talking and laughing continued during the newsreel's introductory music; we expected the usual boring report. Then suddenly, the word INVASION flashed on the screen. Attention turned to the front. The Allies had invaded France at a place called Normandy Beach on June 6, captured thousands of German troops, and made their way inland. Morris said that was old news, but those of us who had been on Biak hadn't gotten any mail or news in weeks. The crowd cheered. Some threw hats in the air. We watched closely as they showed scenes of the early bombing, the flotilla crossing the channel, and the infantry wading ashore.

I barely noticed the movie, thinking about what this invasion would mean. The entire war effort would be focused on the Pacific if they could achieve victory in Europe. I didn't think we could win with the Europe first policy in place, but victory in Europe would mean all the forces could concentrate on the Pacific.

\*\*\*

One thing about being on an established base is that the mail began trickling in, although it was still a month behind. The fact that our battery and battalion designation had changed seemed to be holding things up. Sarah Gales's first letter brought news I had seen in the newsreel but was welcome anyway.

*June 6, 1944*
*Dear Gene,*
*By now, you probably know that we landed our army on the beach at Normandy and are fighting our way through Europe. I have been working on that for so long, but I couldn't tell you. I must know every grain of sand on that beach and all*

the fortifications and installations within a hundred miles. I looked at it every day for six months, trying to detect the most minor changes. But now it is over. There are still photos coming in that we have to look at, but we are back to working only eight hours a day. It seems downright leisurely after the last several months.

I have been doing a lot of sightseeing in the last week. I went to London. It is safe now, and they are doing a lot of rebuilding. Seeing all these things I have read about in books, like Buckingham Palace and Westminster Abbey, was so interesting. Almost eight million people are living in London. It is by far the biggest city I have ever been to. It is a very friendly city, too, at least for someone wearing a WAC uniform. Several people stopped and thanked us for what we're doing for their country.

Just one more month and I will have been here a year. I never thought I would ever get out of North Carolina, let alone live for a year in England. I think of you all the time and wish you could be here with me.

Love,
Sarah Gale

With all the previous letters she had sent me, I had no idea she was that deep into the war effort. The girl was amazing—right in the middle of planning the most significant invasion of the war and not even a hint in her letter. She just said she was busy, which most of us fighting the war were.

*** 

The Japs ran a few raids on Owi, but the defenses were so effective that they stopped coming after a few weeks. Meanwhile, more planes and personnel continued to arrive. Already over eight thousand men called this little island home base, with more on the way. Movie theaters, officers' clubs, and all the usual facilities were being set up. Before long, the base functioned much like a stateside base. There were rumors that Bob Hope was coming at Christmas, but that was still five months off.

I continued to get Sarah Gale's letters as they caught up with me.

June 26, 1944
Dear Gene,
I got another letter from you. The one where you wrote about Edelstein getting killed. That was too bad. He seemed to be a very troubled man. I do hope things are going better for you now. Keep writing me, even if I don't get the letters right away. Eventually, I will read all about what's happening to you. I imagine the same thing is happening for you with my letters.

I spoke too soon about London being safe. Now, the Germans are sending buzz bombs over. Those are self-propelled bombs flying over and dropping on their target without a pilot or airplane. It is just a bomb with wings. Hundreds have been bombing England, not just London, in the past few weeks. Some have come very close to our location. They are trying to shoot them down with antiaircraft guns but are not getting nearly all of them. It makes me glad I work in a bunker, although right now, I spend less time in the bunker than out of it.

You know what I really want? When we get home, I want to go to a place where nobody will tell us what to do or when to do it. We will eat when and what we want to and sleep as long as we want to. No guards, no reveille, no morning calisthenics. Just a couple of rocking chairs where we can sit and read, you can smoke your pipe, I can play the dulcimer. Do I sound like an old lady just wanting to sit in a rocking chair beside you? I'm barely an adult, and I am ready for the rocking chair.

Love
Sarah Gale

Knowing Sarah Gale, I doubted she would sit in a rocking chair for very long, but the prospect seemed nice. While I was in medical school, she probably would get a job somewhere, and then we would settle down and start a family. I would be in my mid-thirties by then, but Sarah Gale was eight years younger than me, so that would not be too late to start a family.

July 3, 1944
Dear Gene,
Tomorrow we are having a 4th of July celebration. We get the day off even though it is Monday. That shows you how little work there is right now. At work, it is more fun to look at different locations every day rather than analyze and reanalyze the same place day after day. Anyway, we just finished putting up some decorations. We probably won't have fireworks. Not only are they hard to find right now, but they would also scare the neighbors right out of their wits. I did make a cherry pie, though. I asked Mrs. Bell (our latest cook) how to make that wonderful flaky crust she makes, then I filled it with cherries just like gran did and put in as much sugar as I could find. I hope it tastes good. I know it won't be as sweet as gran used to make it.

It does seem a little funny to be celebrating Independence Day in England. After all, they are the ones we won our independence from. I hope you have had a good Independence Day when you get this.

Have you been paying any attention to the elections back home? It will be really strange for me if Roosevelt doesn't win. He has been the President since I was ten years old. I don't really remember any President before him. I don't think it would be too good to change Presidents in the middle of a war, either.

Keep writing.

*Love*
*Sarah Gale*

I kept writing, but couldn't make timely replies to her questions and comments because of the delay in receiving her letters. I was feeling lonelier and more disconnected than ever.

\*\*\*

All of our men recovered from typhus but were weak and assigned light duty. Our duty was light anyway since we weren't in the infantry or firing artillery. We gave half shifts to men just out of the hospital. Everyone willingly used insect repellent now. Everyone, that is, except Captain Henderson, who somehow thought he was invincible. He wasn't. It took a while, but two months into our stay on the island, he came in one morning coughing and holding his gut.

"You should report to sick call," I said.

"I'm fine. I'll shake it off," he said.

"I doubt it," I said, looking at the black scabs on his arm.

By noon, I heard him moaning in the back of the tent. I called the medics, who took his temperature:104 degrees. They carried him off to the hospital.

"They're going to keep Henderson for a while," O'Neill said when he returned. "After they get his fever down, they want to keep him and treat that Jungle Rot of his. He let it get totally out of hand."

\*\*\*

A few days later, I sat in a chair outside our HQ tent, watching the sun sink over the ocean and reading Sarah Gale's latest letters.

*July 24, 1944*
*Dear Gene,*
*There are enough photo interpreters here that they are talking about sending some of us home. I don't want to go home without you, so I'm thinking of putting in for a transfer to the Pacific Theater. We might actually run into each other sometime if I'm there. I plan on talking to the major tomorrow to check out the possibilities.*
*It is so cool here that it is hard for me to believe it is the middle of summer. Mama says it has been over ninety several times at home this summer. It is seldom over eighty here. I didn't get a garden started because we were so busy when it was time to create one, and now I am considering asking to transfer, so I guess it will be a while before I begin gardening again. From the letters I have gotten from you, it appears that I will not be chilly at any time of year if I do go there. I don't know anything about gardening in the tropics!*

*I do hope you are still healthy. I am reading more and more about tropical diseases. There seem to be an astonishing number of them.*

*I love you.*

*Love,*

*Sarah Gale*

Was the girl crazy? She had a chance to go home, see her family, be safe, live in a place where she understood the language and culture, and have an easy life, and she was asking to come to the South Pacific. I immediately wrote and told her to forget about coming to the Pacific.

She didn't get the letter in time.

*August 14, 1944*

*Dear Gene,*

*I didn't get a transfer to the Pacific Theater. I did get a transfer, though. It should be great fun, and I look forward to it even though I am disappointed that I will not be in the Pacific with you. I had been studying up, reading everything I could find about the Pacific, then they send me somewhere else. So now I have to study parts of Asia because I know almost nothing about them. They had no WACs in the theater until last month. The general did not want us there. Even now, the WACs are with the air corps only, not the regular army.*

*I have lots of things to do before I go. I have been wearing my winter uniform almost all year here, and it has not been too hot. Depending on where I am, I will probably need a summer uniform. I have also acquired several things I will send home, so I don't have to lug them around. They are souvenirs and photos mostly. I also need a few more immunizations. I want to be safe from as many tropical diseases as possible.*

*You probably won't get any letters from me for a while. I promise to keep writing, but I won't be able to send the letters while I am on the ship. So don't worry about me. I will be back in touch as soon as I can.*

*Love*

*Sarah Gale*

She must be going to China. General Stillwell had been adamant about not having WACs in the field. He insisted it was too dangerous. Why were they sending her to the most dangerous place in the war? Why had she agreed to go?

The men loitering around the tent snapped to attention. I stood and turned to find Colonel Squires approaching the tent.

"You've been doing a good job with your command here, Sinclair," he said.

"Thank you, sir.

"Captain Henderson was to accompany me on a little excursion. As his replacement, you'll come. Whom would you recommend we put in charge while you're gone?"

I thought quickly. "Either Lucas or Douglas could handle it. Lucas will enforce all rules and regulations. Douglas will come up with creative solutions if any problems arise."

"Douglas, then. Be at HQ at 1500 hours."

# CHAPTER 27

## GENERALS, COLONELS, AND CAPTAINS, OH MY!

**I** SENT PERRY FOR Douglas, quickly packed my duffel and backpack, and rushed to HQ, arriving just in time to follow Colonel Squires to the airfield. We boarded a transport plane with a profile something like a B17, following two brigadier generals and their aides. I was by far the most junior officer on board. The senior offices occupied wide cushioned seats, three facing the tail and three facing forward with a table between them. Their aides occupied single seats across a narrow aisle, The plane was only half full, but I was directed to a narrower seat near the back with two captains, who turned out to be reserve pilots. I settled back and struggled to fasten the seatbelt. Trying to appear nonchalant, I watched the pilots. Then, as the plane started moving, I gripped the armrest.

"First flight?" asked the pilot next to me.

"How could you tell?"

"First, you didn't know how to fasten the seatbelt. You had to watch us. Second, you're extremely nervous, and we're only taxiing. Just relax. This is a luxury liner for VIP transport, with three pilot/copilot crews on board. It's an easy flight over territory we've already taken. Nobody will be shooting at us, and we're taking the long way to avoid the highest mountains. Here, sit by the window."

We quickly changed seats, and I looked out as we sped down the runway, then felt a strange momentary sensation in my stomach as we left the earth. As we turned, the island receded beneath us to a small peanut shape. Before long, we climbed above the clouds into bright sunshine.

Not too long after takeoff, some corpsmen started serving a meal to the generals at the front of the plane. One of the captains got up and walked to what seemed to be a tiny kitchen in the middle of the aircraft. He returned with three beers and a small package of cheese and meat.

"Are you allowed to drink and fly?" I asked.

"No problem. We won't be flying until the third leg of the flight, hours away," he responded.

"The third leg?" I asked. "Where are we going?"

"Brisbane. They didn't tell you?"

"No. I'm only here because my CO got sent to the field hospital. So I had about an hour to find an acting CO and get on the plane."

We chatted as the plane flew over New Guinea. It was dark by the time the corpsmen brought us our meals. Two pork chops, mashed potatoes with gravy—the real thing, not dehydrated—garden peas and coleslaw. I forced myself to eat slowly and deliberately. This was the best meal I'd had in a long time. When I finished, a corpsman brought a large slice of chocolate cake. Seeing the grin on my face, the pilot next to me said, "It pays to travel with the VIPs, doesn't it?"

"Sure does!"

There was a sudden change in the feel of the airplane. It seemed to be falling. I looked at the pilots for reassurance.

"We're about to land at Port Moresby to refuel before we start across the ocean," one said.

After we landed, the plane's pilot emerged from the cockpit.

"Gentlemen," he said to everyone on board, "this stop is for refueling, checking the plane, and taking on additional passengers. You may deplane if you wish, but we will depart in exactly one hour. Please be on board at that time."

Colonel Squires motioned for me to join him.

"Do you have Captain Henderson's report? It doesn't seem to have been packed in my portfolio."

"No sir, which report is that?"

"On the number and type of planes we've seen."

"I compiled and typed that report. I can probably give you most of the information you need from memory."

"I'm glad you remember it. I don't need it; you do. You'll be giving the report."

"Yes, sir. To whom"

He turned to me and raised his eyebrows. "The General!"

"Which General?"

The colonel's head reared back a little, and his eyes widened. "THE General! MacArthur. He's got this idea up his butt to get reports from field officers all over the theater. Thinks it will give him a better picture of what's happening."

"Um. Yes sir. I guess it might."

"Let's see if we can get a nip at the officer's club before we get back on that infernal machine," the Colonel said.

I followed the Colonel to the Officer's Club, where most other officers from the plane had already ordered drinks. The Colonel joined the senior officers while I sat at the bar, trying to remember all the facts and figures in the report. I scribbled what I could recall on a napkin.

"What's up, man? You look like the fate of the war is in your hands," said a young first lieutenant next to me.

"It may be," I replied and explained the situation.

"Hey, I work in communications. We'll just radio your people at Owi and get the data you need. What unit are you with, and who is your radio man? By the way, my name is Grant Marshall."

"Gene Sinclair, 236th AAA Searchlight Battalion. Battery C. Ask for Perry"

We ran to the communications office, where he flipped on a machine and called our HQ.

"Howdy, Perry," he said when he got through. "We have a situation. Lieutenant Sinclair here needs some information. Can you locate a report for us?"

He handed me a pad of paper for my notes. I put on the headphones and sat in front of the microphone. I considered how to get the information without compromising security. Douglas came on.

"We found the report. What do you need?"

"Read me the last number of each entry in the first column on page three," I said. That would identify the type of plane we had seen. I wrote down the information.

"Now read me the numbers in the second column." That was the number of planes that had been detected in May.

"Now read me the fourth column," That was July.

"Now, the last column." That was the total number we had shot down.

I picked up the pad and ran out of the communications shack.

"Thank you! You saved my life!"

"Hopefully, it saves a lot more lives than yours!" Marshall shouted after me.

They were about to close the plane as I ran up the tarmac. The soldiers moving the stairway away from the aircraft pushed it back as I shouted to them. I ran on board, and they slammed the doors behind me. Three new generals in the front of the plane frowned at me. I waved the paper at Colonel Squires, who nodded, then returned to my seat at the back of the aircraft, getting the seatbelt fastened just as the wheels left the ground.

Corpsmen converted the seats the generals and colonels occupied into bunks as we flew across the ocean to Australia. The sound of snoring grew almost as loud as the engines when the senior officers dozed off. The aides and off-duty crew slept in their seats.

Trying not to disturb the sleeping pilots, I reconstructed the entire report as best I could, using the light of my flashlight. The finished product was shorter than the original report, but I was confident it contained all the most critical information.

I managed to grab some sleep before the plane landed at a little airbase in the wee hours of the morning. I stood to let my pilot companions out.

"Almost there. We're in Australia now," my seatmate told me. "Port Moresby to Brisbane is just a bit too far to go on one tank of fuel, especially with all the 'heavy' big brass on board. We'll refuel and then go on to Brisbane. This last bit is only about an hour."

***

A convoy of vehicles lined up on the tarmac carried us to the hotel near where MacArthur kept his headquarters. We arrived as the sun rose and were assigned rooms to freshen up. I quickly washed, shaved, and changed into my dress my uniform.

"Name, rank, and unit," an armed soldier demanded as I entered the briefing room.

"Lieutenant Sinclair, 236th Antiaircraft here for Captain Henderson," I replied.

After checking his clipboards, the officer beside him waved me to a row of folding chairs against one wall. The room was poorly lit, but I could make out the red flocked wallpaper and massive red velvet curtains covering the windows. As more people filed in, an assortment of captains and one major joined me in the folding chairs while generals and a few colonels filled the cushioned chairs around the big conference table. We all sat silently until the guard at the door called, "Attention!"

Everyone stood as MacArthur entered the room, and bright lights came on above the conference table. He was tall, and his ramrod-straight posture made him seem even taller. I knew he was in his sixties, but he didn't look it. His strong lower jaw was firm, his eyes bright, and his long stride firm. Fully aware of the theatrics, MacArthur strode into the light and said, "Let's get this started."

First came the reports by the folding chair set. One by one, the major and captains stood in the spotlight at the front of the room and read their briefs, taking half an hour to forty-five minutes each. As my turn approached, I realized I had a much briefer brief. My hands shook as I came to the spotlight. I began talking, mostly from memory, because I could barely read the scratching I had made on the vibrating plane in the middle of the night. I summarized the situation when we arrived at Biak and the current situation and read the numbers. I offered Captain Henderson's opinion and thanked the officers. Twelve minutes in all.

"That," said General MacArthur, "is how to give a briefing. All the pertinent facts in the most succinct way possible. It is, after all, a briefing."

His staff laughed at his wit, and the other officers politely joined in. I returned to my seat, walking a little taller.

The two remaining officers quickly tried to edit their reports and gave stumbling summaries of the information, and then we were all dismissed.

"Sinclair," called one of the captains as we left the room, "Want to come with us to the bar."

"At ten in the morning?" I asked. "I didn't get any sleep last night because I had to recreate my CO's report. I am going back to the room for some shuteye."

"See ya later," they said and headed to the hotel lobby. I went up to my room.

I only slept until noon, when my hunger overcame my fatigue. I went downstairs to find the Captains still in the bar, more like a British pub than an American bar. I ordered a meat pie and dark ale and joined the Captains.

"The senior officers are meeting for two days. Want to join us at a movie tonight, Sinclair?"

"What movie?"

"So far, it is a tie between *Casablanca* and *The Desperadoes*. You can break the deadlock."

"I say *Casablanca*," I replied.

"But *The Desperadoes* is in Technicolor," complained one Captain.

"Just wait and see. *Casablanca* will become a classic, and *The Desperadoes* will be forgotten," countered another.

"I really like Katherine Hepburn," I said. "Do they have a matinee? We could see one in the afternoon and one in the evening."

"This man is brilliant!" declared the captain, who seemed to be the group's ringleader. I just hadn't been drinking beer all morning and could still think clearly.

Outside, the sun shone brightly, a light breeze blowing. After months on steamy tropical islands, the fifty-degree weather and humidity below eighty percent chilled me a bit. Still, winter in Brisbane wasn't winter in the Midwest. We walked to the nearby theater to see *Desperadoes* in Technicolor, a first for all of us. After the movie, the usher directed us to a barbeque joint, where I ordered a mixed plate of sausage, lamb, and kangaroo.

"You really are a risk taker," laughed Hildebrand.

After we were served and eating, he asked me what the kangaroo tasted like.

"Reminds me of venison," I replied.

"Didn't eat much venison growing up in New Jersey," he said.

We hailed a taxi to the theater across town showing *Casablanca*. By midnight, back in the hotel bar, we were totally relaxed, the war and privations of the island momentarily forgotten. Hildebrand pried me with drinks until I became totally sotted. Sometime in the early morning, I stumbled into the room I shared with Colonel Squires.

"Best have some fun and get some sleep while you can, boy," he mumbled. "We're in for it when we get back to the theater."

I flopped into my bed and slept more soundly than I had in months.

\*\*\*

The sun was well up and shining brightly when I awoke. I met Captain Hildebrand and his buddies in the bar. Most were desk jockeys, but Brisbane had much more to offer than the island bases. We'd been ordered to return to the hotel by 1400 hours, and I intended to fully enjoy our liberty until then. So, I embarked on a tour of the town with the captains, concentrating on eating and drinking establishments.

As the alcohol slowly wore off on the seven-hour flight back to Port Moresby, I wondered what had possessed me. I had not realized the toll the war had taken. I could hold it together in the field and keep going, but when the next problem wasn't staring me in the face in Brisbane, it all came crashing down on me, and I drowned my woes in beer. Knowing full well the problems that could cause, I vowed not to let it happen again.

We spent the night in Port Moresby, dining in the officers' mess. Better than Owi, but still not Brisbane. As I finished dinner, Morris slipped into a chair beside me.

"What are you doing here?" I asked.

"One of our Black Widows got shot down last week. I'm picking up a replacement. I could ask the same of you." I explained my recent mission.

"Want to ride back with me?"

"I'll have to clear it with the Colonel," I said.

He jumped up and dragged me to Colonel Squires' table.

"Sir, would you mind if I borrowed this guy? I'm flying a new Black Widow to Owi in the morning and need a radar operator."

"By all means, take him. He's one of our best."

Morris had us off the runway speeding through the air in seconds, it seemed, unlike the long runway time of the passenger plane. The climb plastered me to my seat as we shot up.

"Watch this," he shouted above the roar of the engine. He did a few quick maneuvers that had me so dizzy I didn't know up from down, and then he sped off on a straight shot to Owi. We arrived two hours before the passenger plane carrying the Colonel and other officers.

When I got back to camp, I saw that Henderson had returned from the hospital and taken back command of the battery.

# CHAPTER 28

## LEYTE

**W**E'VE BEEN ATTACHED TO the 24th Infantry Division!" Henderson announced. "We're joining MacArthur on his return to the Philippines!"

Hearing him talk, it sounded like we were going in on the same ship as Himself. Instead, we boarded an old transport, obviously not the flagship. The ship steamed north, joining a convoy out of Hollandia, New Guinea, that carried the 24th Infantry. The 1st Cavalry from the Admiralty Islands, about eight hundred miles to the east, joined us later that afternoon.

At sunrise on October 20, our convoy approached the eastern side of Leyte Island, one of the biggest islands in the Philippines. We could see Japanese planes coming from the northeast.

"What are those?" asked Douglas. "They look like the old Oscars."

"The Japs must be running out of aircraft," I said.

The ship's guns opened fire on them, hitting three. As they fell, the pilots did not seem to be ejecting.

"Look, dey tryin' to drop der planes on de ships," shouted Brasseux.

An Oscar crashed into a supply ship behind us and burst into flames as we watched. Two escort cruisers moved in to rescue the crew. The other planes all headed for other ships in convoy. We tumbled to the deck as our transport ship swerved. An obsolete fighter plane crashed into the water just inches from our bow, rocking the ship even more.

"Damn," said one of the navy men lying on deck near me. "They're using their planes as bombs."

"In a way, that's a good thing," I said. He looked at me like I was crazy. "It means they're short on ammunition." I added.

As we pushed to our feet, two other planes narrowly missed a troop transport and a PT boat. A destroyer was hit but not sunk. When the last aircraft dove into the sea, the navy men took stock of the situation, and we moved toward the island again.

\*\*\*

The infantry began the invasion of Leyte at 1000 hours. We watched as they crossed the beach under light fire from the Japanese, then got mired in the deep swamps beyond. Wave after wave of infantry landed, making slow progress inland, but the Japanese fire stopped altogether. Then our turn came. We drove off the landing craft onto the beach amid the chaos. Unfortunately, the entire division of infantry slogging through the swamps in front of us blocked our way.

"Sinclair," Henderson called to me. "Damned radio is malfunctioning. Go tell the beach master that we're on the beach."

I ran down the beach to where the beach master stood, shouting into his radio microphone.

"Walk in—the waters fine," he said.

He turned to me. "236th Search Lighters are on the beach, sir," I said.

He gave me a thumbs up, then turned back to his radio. All I heard was "Engineers."

I looked toward the sea and spotted General MacArthur striding through the water with his entourage, scowling and saying something. On shore, reporters photographed him as he strode up to a set of microphones on the beach.

"People of the Philippines, I have returned. By the grace of Almighty God, our forces stand again on Philippine soil," he announced as photographers clicked more photos and reporters scribbled furiously.

I returned to my unit, its trucks and trailers mired down at the edge of the swamp. The men pushed and rocked the trucks as drivers gunned the engines, slowly moving the vehicles forward. We had arrived in a little village just over a mile inland by nightfall, the Filipinos indeed glad to see us, greeting us with flowers.

In the morning, we followed the infantry up Leyte Valley. The valley appeared to be an agricultural plain. The hills and mountains on either side were as steep as New Guinea but covered in forest rather than jungle. These lovely forests, where they had not been destroyed by shelling and bombing, were filled with orchids, and many species of wild animals ran helter-skelter through them, disturbed by the war that had arrived to destroy their homes.

The Japanese opposition seemed somewhat disorganized initially but soon figured out where we were, and the infantry and cavalry had to fight for every inch. Waves of enemy aircraft moved in. We moved as close as possible to the infantry positions during the afternoon, set up the radar, and watched all night for enemy aircraft. The move was easy because a paved highway went up the middle of the valley.

My job, keeping track of platoon locations and who needed support and providing it, was difficult within the winding valley because of poor radio reception. We pitched our HQ tents close to the road, but the radar had to be as high on the ridges as possible. Often, the men would take cart trails through the forest and be out of radio contact until they were set up and had placed antennae on the top of their selected ridge. On our second day of this, a Filipino man approached me and identified himself as a leader of the Philippine Guerrillas.

"Sir, I know you are having difficulty staying in touch with your units. Therefore, I would like to offer the services of some of our guerrilla forces who can act as runners to get messages to them."

I hesitated.

"Please, sir. These boys have been running the trails of these mountains all their lives. They all learned some English in high school and are determined to fight for their country. As their teacher, I prefer they deliver messages for you rather than fight on the front lines."

I radioed Henderson and cleared the idea with him.

"Very well. Have your boys here by 1800 hours tonight."

He waved his arm toward the woods, and fourteen teenagers ran into camp. He spoke briefly to them in their native tongue and then introduced them to me.

"Thank you for your willingness to help. I'll assign you to different units the next time we move forward," I told them.

The battle grew fierce as we made inroads into the island. Massive air attacks matched the ferocious fighting on the ground. We located up to sixty enemy planes a night, and the gunners shot down about a third. Another ten percent or so were hit but managed to fly home.

At sea' another fierce battle raged. A reporter Perry knew, embedded with the 24th Infantry, kept us posted. Hundreds of ships and planes fought it out all around the island. He reported that the Allies were victorious within three days, and the Japanese navy was decimated.

Their army, however, put up heavy resistance as we pushed into the Leyte Valley east of the central ridge of mountains. We seldom moved forward more than a mile a day, with severe casualties to both sides. Estimates said we killed four or five of their men for every one of ours. Still, over three thousand allies were wounded and about twelve thousand injured by the time we reached the head of the valley.

Early November found us within sight of the port of Cariaga, now in allied hands. We established a more permanent position while the infantry moved over the ridge toward Ormoc, the only port city still held by the Japanese. There was little action in the air, and our stable position allowed us to relax a bit.

As we stayed at the head of the valley, mail finally found us. I carried a huge packet from Sarah Gale to my cot after roll call. I opened the first, an overstuffed envelope filled with sheets of the flimsiest paper I had ever seen, her spidery script covering both sides.

August 21, 1944

Dear Gene,

This has been quite a trip so far, and I haven't even left the United Kingdom. The first thing I had to do was go to London for processing. And boy, was I processed. In addition to getting immunizations and two new uniforms, I got a complete physical and psychological evaluation. They asked me in every way possible why I wanted a transfer from the European Theater. They could not believe I did not want to be sent stateside. They said I was passing up a strong possibility of promotion. I don't want to make the army my career, so I am not interested in a promotion. I just want to have one more adventure before we settle down and start a family. So they finally approved me for the transfer.

Then, I had to travel to Belfast, Ireland. I took a train to Carlisle. I spent the night there and had a chance to visit Carlisle Castle and Cathedral. They are ancient. The Cathedral has an arched ceiling set with gold stars on a blue background. I don't even know all the words to describe it. It also has a very old, very beautiful stained-glass window. Someone said it was about five hundred years old.

The next morning, I took a bus to Cairnryan to catch the ferry. We rode through a deep, dark forest that could have come from a fairy tale. I saw a herd of red deer led by a stag with the most giant antlers ever seen. That old man put the little white tail deer back home to shame. I don't know how he managed to walk through the forest without getting all tangled up in the branches.

On the ferry, we sailed through the Loch of Ryan. It was beautiful—smooth, deep blue water surrounded by green hills, a light breeze, and perfectly smooth sailing. Then we got out into the Irish Sea. The wind blew something fierce, and the waves bounced us all around. A couple of old men on the ferry told me it was like that more often than not. Then they started talking about my hair. One of them said it was Scots red. The other said it wasn't red at all. It was chestnut and was French. They asked me what my surname was, and when I told them Simmons, they started arguing about whether that was Scottish or French. When I told them I was American, but my ancestors came from England, they said I was too young and pretty to know anything and should keep my mouth shut. They didn't say it in a mean way. The man said it with a twinkle in his eye. They seemed like old friends who just enjoyed arguing and being difficult.

Now, I am on board the ship, ready to leave Belfast. I am the only WAC on the ship, but a group of nurses will be boarding in a little while. That is why I had to come here. The army would not consider sending me halfway around the world without any other women on the ship. I will be glad for the company because if it is like the ship we came to England on, I will be locked up in the cabin a lot of the time.

*August 24, 1944*

We are underway now, and I was right. We spend almost all our time in the staterooms or dining room. At least we have our own dining room, so we are not always shut up in the staterooms. Fortunately, I have a stateroom with a porthole, which I share with the ranking officer of the nurses. She is a major, and I thought I would be intimidated to be rooming with a major, but Major Thomas is very nice. She has been very interested in what little I can tell her about my job. We went out for a walk on the deck late last night. It was fabulous. We could see every little star glowing brightly with no other lights around. All the stars were reflected in the water while a full moon lit the waves in a fascinating pattern.

We sailed between Great Britain and Ireland for the longest time, then turned into the open ocean. I wish I knew if we were going through the Suez Canal or all the way around Africa. Of course, I can't ask the ship's officers. They aren't allowed to tell us anything.

*August 26, 1944*

I enjoy traveling with the nurses. They are all very adventurous as well as compassionate. Once I got acquainted with some of them, I started taking portraits of them. I am also trying to get some candid shots to show something about life aboard the ship. One of them asked if I planned on being a photojournalist after the war. I told her my only plans are to be Mrs. Eugene Sinclair, but she said I should keep more possibilities open.

*August 30, 1944*

Now I know which way we are going. Yesterday, we sailed through the Straits of Gibraltar. It was actually less exciting than I thought it would be. When we read about the Pillars of Hercules in school, I thought the strait between them was a much narrower space, and it would be almost like riding rapids through a canyon. Instead, we just steamed through without any turbulence. We could see land on both sides—they let us come out on deck to see—but it wasn't like going through a narrow passage with cliffs on either side.

We are in the Mediterranean now. It is not as rough as the Atlantic, although the Atlantic wasn't too bad. Both times I have sailed on the Atlantic, it has been summer, so I don't know how bad it might be in the winter. Every once in a while, we see some islands or the far-off shore of Africa.

*September 5, 1944*

We are now in Egypt. Staying in a hotel. We aren't doing any sightseeing because they say it is much too dangerous, but we can see the desert from one window and the Red Sea from another. The ship we were on was only coming this far, and the one that was supposed to take us the rest of the way was delayed for some reason, so now we just sit. I found some ten-year-old American magazines downstairs and enjoyed reading them, but things have changed so much since 1934 that it seems like a different world. Has there ever been a time that the world changed so dramatically in such a short time? I finished the magazines and passed them on to some nurses. I have been wandering around with my camera taking pictures of different patterns. I have taken close-ups of the tile on the hotel's courtyard fountain, a big pile of watermelons, palm leaves looking down from a balcony above and up from below, and several other interesting shapes. I can't wait to develop them and see how they look.

### September 8, 1944

We are back at sea again. This Captain is more open to communicating and letting us know where we are. We will sail through the Red Sea, then into the Indian Ocean and land at Bombay. That will take eleven days.

We don't have our own dining room. We eat in the same place as the army and navy men. The result is that we end up spending more time in our rooms. There are several shifts to feed everybody, so we can't be in the dining room all day or go out on deck when all the troops are there, like the previous ship. So we just stay in. Major Thomas and I have a lovely stateroom, but any small space gets very confining after so many days.

### September 19, 1944

At long last, we are in India. I met up with four other WACs who had just arrived from the US and were also going to the same place. We are still very far from where we are going, even though we are in India. Tomorrow, we will get on a train and begin the trip across northern India. That should be fun.

### September 24, 1944

I have never been so hot, tired, sticky, and sweaty in my life. Trains in India are not the same as at home or in England. We were crowded into way overloaded cars. Military personnel and civilians traveled together, and the civilians sometimes brought chickens or plants or any number of other things along. We slept on wooden seats with very thin padding, and that was in first class. After changing trains five times, we were finally dropped off in a town at the foot of the Himalayas. Now, we are waiting for the jeeps to take us to the air base.

The jeeps finally showed up. We are now driving on a narrow road beside a river to get to the air base from which, we discovered, we will fly over what they call the hump. This is pretty country, but I am so tired I just wish we were at the nearest shower.

Sorry for the sloppy writing. It is tough to write in a jeep on a bumpy road.

*September 26, 1944*

*After sixteen hours of bumping along that dusty, rutted road, we arrived at the air base. It was almost midnight when we got here. They had beds set up for us in a little grass hut. All night, I kept hearing what I assumed were mice scuttling through the thatch over our heads. As I left the hut in the morning, a giant snake slithered down the post on the porch. I screamed, and our native escort came running.*

*"Oh, it is just a little python. Not big enough yet to swallow you. Just a baby."*

*That baby was longer than I am tall. I am not too confident it won't eat me. You have no idea how happy I was to get on the plane and head for China. The flight over the hump was unbelievable. We were at least five hundred miles from Mount Everest but still in the Himalayas. The mountains had snow on them, and it's only September. Even the shorter mountains are pretty tall.*

*Finally, we are at our base in China, and I can send this. Hopefully, your letters will catch up with me.*

*Love,*
*Sarah Gale*

One of the Filipino boys ran up to me and slid to a stop. He saluted, and I stood and acknowledged the salute.

"What is it, soldier? I asked.

"Sir, it's the Captain, sir. Something is wrong with the Captain, sir."

"One sir is enough, son. What happened to the Captain?"

"The Captain has fallen out of his chair, ss—. Oh sorry. No more sir."

"The Captain has fallen out of his chair? Did he get back up?"

"No. The Sergeant said to come get you."

By the time we got back to the HQ tent, Captain Henderson was back in his desk chair, a morphine bottle clutched in his hand.

"Do you need to go to the hospital again, sir?" I asked.

"I can handle it. We have got to get through this war. Look how close we are to Japan. I'll be fine," he insisted.

I took the morphine from his hand and called O'Neill. When he arrived at the tent, I handed him the bottle. "You need to take charge of this situation. Treat Captain Henderson's jungle rot every morning and evening and ration the morphine. Give him enough to sleep at night and the smallest amount possible to keep him functioning in the morning."

"Yes, sir," O'Neill said. Captain Henderson just stared at me, a mixture of sadness, anger, and relief on his face. He didn't say a word.

O'Neill and Sergeant Hammond took Henderson to his cot for treatment while I stayed at the desk dealing with the day's business. About an hour later, O'Neill was back.

"The captain is on his way back," he reported. "I have never seen anything so bad. I don't know how he walks at all. I'll see what I can do, but we may need to send him to the hospital.

Keep me up to date on his condition," I said.

When Henderson returned, I relinquished his desk and went back to my cot, where I opened Sarah Gale's next letter.

October 9, 1944
Dear Gene,
I absolutely love this job. I could not believe the beauty of the mountains we flew over on our first photo expedition. When we came over the hump, I knew it was beautiful, but I was so exhausted that I didn't look at any details. On photo expeditions, we generally fly at a lower elevation, and I see things much more clearly. By now, the higher peaks are completely snow-covered, but it is still warm around the air base and to the east. They say it is always spring here—not too cold in winter or too warm in summer.

We fly in all directions, and the differences in the terrain and climate are huge. Everything from rainforests to glaciers. We cover a lot of territory, but the changes sometimes happen suddenly.

I am not getting really good pictures. There is too much turbulence, and the pilots keep changing our route to avoid mountain peaks, updrafts, or antiaircraft artillery. I don't want to crash or get shot down, but I want some good pictures. I wish there was some way to know how clear the images are before we leave an area, but I can't very well set up a dark room on the planes. The chemicals would be all over the place.

The colonel I work under doesn't seem to be too upset. We are getting enough intelligence that he can tell where enemy installations are, but I know it is possible to get better photos. So, I will keep working on it. There is one area in particular that I would like to get clear images of, but the pilots say it is very treacherous.

I actually have my own personal maid here. I was a little embarrassed about it, but the colonel told me that all the officers have maids provided by the Chinese government. They sort of insist upon it. Anyway, her name is Chen Ling. I can't really tell if she understands English. I think she does, but I am not supposed to know. I think I could get used to someone cleaning my house and washing my clothes, though. Will you make enough money for me to hire help when we get home?

Just kidding. I don't know what I would do with my time if I just sat around waiting for you to get home and had someone else do all the housework.
Love
Sarah Gale

# CHAPTER 29

## PRISONERS

**S**UDDENLY, IN EARLY **D**ECEMBER, the Japanese air attacks ceased. While information filtered back to us that the AAA battery attached to the 11th Airborne Division had fended off an attack by Japanese paratroopers, we saw no action at all.

A messenger arrived with new orders. Henderson opened them, frowned, and reread them. Then he said, "Lucas's platoon will light the port so the Quartermaster's Corps can unload supplies day and night. Brasseux will light the airfield. And you will take the remainder of the battalion and set up a POW camp,"

"What? I know *nothing* about how to set up a POW camp."

"Well, you better learn fast because your first prisoners arrive this afternoon."

.I found the isolated valley where the engineers said we should make the camp, laid out a rectangular area, and assigned Douglas to have his men build a fence around it. Sergeant Hammond took some men down to the port to requisition some tents. The men, who would act as guards, cooks, and maintenance for the camp, set up their tents uphill from the prisoner enclosure and started digging latrines. By noon, we had a makeshift POW camp set up that could house about a hundred prisoners. I had no idea what to expect.

The enemy had thousands of casualties, but the 24th Infantry had taken only fifteen prisoners. I felt a bit embarrassed at the size of my enclosure. A few days later, a dozen more prisoners arrived from other units.

Four of our Filipino runners spoke Japanese as well as English. We enlisted their help as interpreters and questioned the prisoners through them. The Japs, even the officers, seemed surprisingly willing to give up whatever information they had. They were so forthcoming that I wondered if they were feeding us false information.

O'Neill dropped by to tell me that he thought the progress of Henderson's jungle rot had been stopped. The slightly drier weather and twice-daily medical treatments were having an effect.

"I know I have the bacterial infection under control, but he also has a fungal infection. Those fungal infections go deep and are resistant to our medicines, so they might not completely disappear. However, Henderson ordered me to report to the prison camp and discontinue treatments. I would have liked to have continued treatment for another two weeks, but Henderson threatened me with insubordination."

"We can definitely use you here, but I wish Henderson was more willing to complete the course of treatment."

I sat in my office contemplating what to do when a messenger brought the mail. I quickly found Sarah Gales's latest letter and forgot about the prisoners and Henderson as I caught up on her adventures.

October 23, 1944

Dear Gene,

I am getting news of what happens in the Pacific Theater much more quickly now. In England, we only heard about the biggest, most decisive Pacific battles; the news usually came days after they happened. I hear most of what happens there, usually within two or three days. Even if I don't know exactly where you are and I have to wait at least a week for a personal letter, it makes me feel closer to you.

I am not getting nearly as much information about the war in Europe, but things seem to be going well there. Casualties are much higher than I would like—of course, I would like zero casualties best of all—but we are taking back territory.

Still no luck on those pictures I have been trying to get.

I did find out that Chen Ling speaks fluent English. I told the Colonel I was surprised that someone with her skills and education would be a servant. He told me that they assign educated people to these jobs so they can learn more about Americans. Knowing that, I am careful not to say too much to her. We are allies, but she does not have top-secret clearance.

Having someone close to my own age in the house makes me want to talk about everything, and I know I can't. However, we are becoming close friends, and she is teaching me about Chinese culture. The Chinese are not really all one people. The Han Chinese are by far the biggest group, but the area where I live is mixed with only a few Han. Before the war, I barely realized that the Japanese and Chinese were different, let alone all the other Asian countries and peoples. It really is good to get out and see the world. I am not at all the same person I was in the backwoods of North Carolina.

That makes me think you and I will have to get reacquainted after the war. But, of course, you won't be the same person either. I have always thought you would be the same, but since I have grown and changed so much, I am sure you will have, too.

Love

Sarah Gale

As mopping-up efforts continued, prisoners arrived in rapidly increasing numbers. Within a week, we had to enlarge the size of the camp. Ultimately, we had 821 prisoners, outnumbering our guards by more than ten to one. They didn't seem to have any intention of causing problems, for which I gave thanks every time I looked at the vast camp. I marveled at the difference between the fierce fighters we had encountered on every island and these docile, compliant prisoners. How could they be the same people?

O'Neill told me that many seemed to be exhibiting drug withdrawal symptoms, so that could explain part of it, but there had to be more to it than that.

We hadn't had any training to do this, so I generally flew by the seat of my pants when making day-to-day decisions. I regularly referred to the Geneva Accords to ensure we treated them appropriately. I had no intention of getting accused of war crimes.

Feeding the prisoners became increasingly difficult. Many appeared near starvation when they came in, and our supplies didn't stretch far enough to feed them well.

"Japanese supplies have been left behind all over the island. Why don't you let me take out a few prisoners and collect the rice and other supplies?" one of the Filipino interpreters suggested.

I hesitated because we had so few guards. Sending enough guards to manage a foraging expedition would thin our ranks. However, I needed the food, so I selected a few prisoners who had provided reliable intelligence and sent them out with two trucks under a few guards led by Carson and two Filipino boys. They returned in about two hours, both trucks loaded with sacks of rice, boxes of other Japanese rations, and a complete Japanese camp kitchen. We recruited cooks from among the prisoners, and they soon served meals the prisoners relished.

We sent the trucks out at least twice a week, and they always managed to return with at least one truck full of food, mainly rice. I worried the prisoners ate more rice than meat or vegetables, but one of the Japanese officers told me through a Filipino interpreter that the Japanese usually eat rice at every meal and lots of it, and meat or fish less often.

We discovered a few officers among the prisoners spoke English. I visited them daily, checking how the men were doing and asking if they needed anything. They wouldn't tell me anything, and if I made suggestions, they refused all I offered. I provided paper for them to write home, but most would not do that. They said to be captured disgraced them, and they did not want to dishonor their families. As crucial as Sarah Gale's letters were to me and mine to her, I struggled with their refusal to write.

Sarah Gales's letters continued to arrive, but they didn't come any faster from China than from England.

> November 13, 1944
> Dear Gene,
> I am still trying to get some good pictures of the places I am assigned to study. Yesterday we flew there but didn't get good photos. It was amazing to look at, though. We flew over the tall, snow-covered mountains in freezing cold, then down to a lower elevation over the jungle on the other side. It was hot, wet, and miles and miles of green. The terrain and vegetation changed so suddenly that I almost couldn't believe it. The jungle is beautiful. To think you have been living in this kind of place all along.
> Over the weekend, I got out and looked around the city a little bit. The Japanese bombed this city, and it seemed worse than London. The Chinese have not done as much rebuilding, and almost every building in the urban center is damaged. It is sad that so many cities have been destroyed by this war. I knew that Europe would never be the same after all the damage there, but I did not realize that so many other places have been damaged, too. You told me about the air raid on Darwin, and that seemed like an extension of the bombing in England because Australia is part of the British Empire. I don't know why I did not think of the war destroying places in China, Burma, New Guinea, and the Philippines. Probably because I was in England.
> Chen Ling took me to meet her family earlier today. Sunday is her day off, and this particular Sunday was an auspicious day for meeting relatives. Every day seems to be auspicious or inauspicious for doing any number of things. It is really amazing how they figured all these things out based on their calendar, zodiac, or something. They go by the lunar year, and we go by the solar year, so it never comes out exactly the same. By their calendar, it is the ninth month, and by ours, it is the tenth.
> I think it is wonderful that Macarthur returned to the Philippines just like he promised he would. He looked so determined in the pictures, striding ashore. It was a big moment for the Allies. I assume that you were somewhere close to there at the time. You have been moving along pretty close to the front lines since you arrived in the Pacific.
> I look forward to your letters even more now that they are arriving within a few weeks of you writing them.
> Love,
> Sarah Gale

I wished her letters were arriving more quickly, but I was always glad to get them whenever they arrived.

Before I could start her next letter, a Japanese man in a US Army uniform entered the tent.

"Who are you?" I asked.

"Lieutenant Ken Sato," he said in perfect English. "I'm here to act as interpreter."

"How did you learn such good English?" I asked.

"Born and raised in California, as was my father and his father."

"Oh, sorry," I said. "I bet you get a lot of suspicion, given how much antagonism there is toward the Japanese."

"You don't know the half of it," he said. "They took our farm away, sent us to a camp at a little fairground in Southern Colorado, and made us work in fields run by German-speaking farmers so they could keep an eye on both of us. The Germans at least got to keep their property."

"I wasn't aware of that," I said. "I've been out of the States too long, and I guess they don't report those things in Stars and Stripes."

"No, they wouldn't. Then, after taking everything they owned, they came and asked all the young males to join the army and defend our country."

"Why did you do it?" I asked.

"Despite the mistrust I run into, this is better than living in a dusty camp surrounded by barbed wire. I save my salary to buy a new place for my family after the war. There's no way to go back. You have to move forward from where you are, and my Dad asked me to join the army to help my family do that."

"I, for one, appreciate it. Our interpreters have been Filipino high school boys for whom neither English nor Japanese are native languages. Communication has been a bit difficult."

"I have spoken both since infancy. That's how I got placed in the interpreter program. Where do you want me to bunk?"

"Things are a bit temporary and primitive here. We're really short on tents because of the recent influx of prisoners. I guess you will have to sleep at the back of the HQ tent next to me."

I called to Perry.

"Check with Sergeant Hammond and see if he can find another cot for Lieutenant Sato here."

While Sato settled in, I returned to Sarah Gale's letters.

November 27, 1944
Dear Gene,
We had quite a Thanksgiving here. I told Chen Ling that we usually ate a roasted turkey for Thanksgiving and had a big feast. She did not know what a turkey was but promised a big feast. So she got together with the other officers' cooks (The higher-ranking officers have a whole house full of servants.) They made a feast for us that made our Thanksgiving look skimpy. Everything seems to have a traditional meaning based on what the name sounds like. I lost track of all

the meanings because there were just too many of them. Also, you don't eat an entire dish. Instead, you make sure there are leftovers so you will have food for the coming year.

The feast's main dish was Peking duck. I don't know the recipe, but it takes a long time to prepare. It doesn't taste like the ducks my brothers shot, which Mama roasted in the oven. It seemed much richer. It came from a larger duck than the mallards and scooters they used to hunt, but they still had one for each officer. I think the symbolism was to show off the abundance of their resources. I secretly shared some of it with the children who hang out on the streets begging. At least, I hope it was a secret. I wrapped it in smaller packages than the one they sent home with me and wrapped them in plain brown paper rather than the red they had used.

I have formed a relationship with the begging children. We pretend it does not exist because I am not supposed to associate with people of their class, but I can't bear to see them starve right in front of me. So I casually drop packets of food or other things in the bushes as I walk past, and they pick them up.

I also make sure to personally deliver all my letters to you directly to the US Army mailroom at the base. It is conveniently next to the photo shop where I develop my pictures. I could give them to the messengers who are always ready to take care of such things for me, but I think they read them before posting them. I let the messengers take letters to my brothers so they don't get suspicious, but I don't talk about the same things I do with you.

Love,
Sarah Gale

Lieutenant Sato and I went on a tour of the camp as soon as he had his things in order. He spoke with several of the prisoners.

"The men say the camp is run very effectively, and they have been treated exceptionally well," he said after the brief tour.

"I'm surprised by that. I still have no idea how a POW camp should be run." I replied.

"They had been told they would be tortured and starved if they surrendered. That's what's happening to our men in Japanese POW camps. It came as a complete surprise to them that they had good food and no beatings."

"They were very forthcoming with information about enemy strength and movements, most of which turned out to be true," I told him. "Was that to avoid torture?"

"Possibly," he shrugged, "to a certain extent, but also, being captured is the ultimate disgrace for a Japanese soldier. Once captured, they've lost face. They don't want to return to Japan, so they're trying to ingratiate themselves to you, hoping to find a place in American society, even in the lowest echelons."

"Won't we ship them back to Japan after the war?"

"Yes. I'll explain that to the prisoners. But, while we're still at war, they'll be shipped to official allied prisoners of war camps. So, I'm here to sort out the men who might have useful intelligence information and get them sent to the States. The rest will probably go to Australia."

Every ship that brought supplies took a group of prisoners back with them. Each of the ships had more guards than we did. I wondered how they expected the prisoners to escape when they were in the middle of the ocean.

You'd be surprised," one ship's captain told me. "They could commandeer the lifeboats or even jump overboard hoping to swim to some island."

Before they went, we had each group strike their tents and police the area. Lieutenant Sato sailed with the last group of prisoners, those he had selected for interment in the United States. By the time they left, we had only about half a day's work to remove the last few tents and temporary kitchens, take down the fence, and roll up the wire. Then, finally, our battery came together again. We rejoined the 24th Infantry, heading to Mindoro Island, a mountainous island on the opposite side of the Philippine chain 250 miles to the north.

# CHAPTER 30

## MINDORO

**W**E LEFT THE HARBOR wary of potential Kamikaze attacks. Our best spotters stationed themselves around the deck, watching the skies in all directions. Captain Henderson and I walked the deck, keeping our eyes and ears open. As we emerged from the straight between Leyte and another island into an expanse of open sea, Tilton approached us.

"Should we set up one of the radar units on deck?" he asked.

"The escort boats have good radar," said Captain Henderson. "I don't think that will be necessary."

"No, it definitely will not," I said, pointing north. A squadron of Japanese planes approached us. Captain Henderson scrambled to the bridge to alert the crew.

We could identify them as a mishmash of older aircraft as they drew closer. Kamikaze! The convoy spread out to allow for evasive maneuvers. Sailors manned their guns on every ship. Our machine gun and automatic weapons batteries brought out their weapons. The captain ordered the rest of us to take cover if possible. I led a group of men to a deck sheltered by the lifeboats.

The planes came in and immediately began aiming at the ships. The explosive sound of the ships' guns shattered the air. Planes crashed into ships, and both exploded. The escort planes above were helpless. They could not fire on the enemy without hitting our craft. We watched as a tank landing craft almost crashed into our transport ship in an evasive maneuver, then veered off. Moments later, a Japanese fighter plane crashed into her side. A light cruiser came to her aid, but she sank quickly, taking several men and tanks down with her. Some men bobbed to the surface, where a PT boat picked them up. We were unable to determine how many might be dead or injured. Then, we saw a plane heading straight for us.

"Run!" I yelled, pushing men in either direction.

We scrambled away from the line of attack. The machine gunners fired directly at engines and propellers, and the plane exploded, scattering debris across the deck. I felt a sharp sting in my elbow.

"Sinclair's hit!" cried Brasseux. He immediately fell to the deck.

Stretcher-bearers appeared and carried Brasseux off. Two men grabbed me, one by each arm, and the sting became a searing burn. They dragged me away from the debris on the deck.

Then suddenly, everything went quiet except for a few shouting men and rumbling ships' engines.

"Anyone injured, report to sick bay immediately," the captain called over the loudspeaker.

I looked around to see if any more of my men were injured. I didn't see any injuries among the men around me.

"You better report, Sinclair," said Carson.

"What?" I said.

"There's blood running down your arm and dripping on deck. I assume it's yours."

The pain had disappeared in the rush of adrenalin.

***

In sick bay, a medic bent over Brasseux, who lay on a cot.

"We can't find any injuries. What happened to him?"

"He fainted at the sight of blood," said O'Neill, who was helping with the injured.

The medic broke a capsule of smelling salts and held it under Brasseux's nose. He opened his eyes but just stared straight ahead. Even when the medic slapped and shook him, he didn't get a response. Brasseux seemed conscious but not aware.

"Have you noticed any previous behaviors that might indicate battle fatigue?" the medic asked.

"More than once," I replied.

"I think he's catatonic. Doc, take a look at this guy." meaning me.

The doctor approached and lifted my arm. "What happened to you?"

"I think I have a piece of shrapnel in my arm," I told him.

"Front of the line," he said.

"Shrapnel in the arm is the worst injury?" I asked. "Brasseux is totally out of it."

"Not much we can do there other than send him to the psych hospital in Australia," he said. "You, on the other hand, could bleed to death or at least get an infection that could lead to amputation. " Go over there," he pointed, "and let me look at it."

"Good God," I mumbled, pushing past sailors with ice packs and a soldier with a burn on his arm.

The ship's doctor numbed the area, dug around in my elbow with forceps, and finally pulled out a chunk of metal. He plopped the metal in a vial, capped it, and gave it to me.

"There you go, your own little war souvenir," he said.

I pocketed it, thinking Sarah Gale might find it interesting or something.

He wrapped a bulky bandage around my arm, put a sling around my neck, placed my arm in it, and motioned to the door.

"Can I have a pain reliever?" I asked.

"You didn't seem to be in much pain when you came in. You can't handle a little scratch?" he said.

"It didn't hurt much until you started digging around with the forceps. I think the remedy was worse than the injury." It hurt a lot!

"You wouldn't think that if I left it in and it got infected," he said, handing me a small bottle of aspirin. "This should take care of the pain when the anesthetic wears off."

I made my way to the officer's mess. Despite the attack, the galley crew had a delicious roast prepared with generous helpings of carrots and potatoes. It was even better than the food at the officer's mess on Owi and far better than the C-rations we'd subsisted on before, not to mention rancid smoked tuna.

Eating was a little awkward with my right arm in a sling, but several officers came to my aid, carrying my meal, cutting the meat, and so forth. I was a hero, being the most seriously injured person on board. Soon the scuttlebutt claimed I had saved all the men on that side of the ship. I hoped they would have had the sense to run if I had not told them to, but I didn't say so. I relished playing the hero.

"Word is General Dunkel was injured when the Nashville went down," Captain Henderson said as he joined us. "They're evaluating the damage, but I don't think it was bad enough to abort the mission."

The convoy soon reassembled, on its way again. One transport ship left the convoy to return the seriously wounded and recovered bodies to Leyte. The medics transferred the still catatonic Brasseux onto that ship.

***

By morning we were in position to begin the invasion. The naval bombardment started early, clearing the way for the landing. Despite heavy antiaircraft fire from the ships, two Kamikazes got through and hit two of the landing craft. One craft reached shore, where several injured men were carried off. A destroyer, USS Moale, came alongside the other landing craft and rescued the men.

"That LST was carrying a full load of fuel and ammunition," said an Ensign beside me. "They had better get out of there quickly."

Just then, a massive explosion sent a fireball high into the sky. As the smoke cleared, we saw gaping holes in the destroyer's hull, and the LST quickly sank.

***

The men of the 24th Infantry Division crossed the narrow coastal plain unopposed but met with heavy fire when they first penetrated the forest. As they disappeared into the trees, the battle seemed to be moving quickly toward the mountains in the center of the island. By the time we came ashore in the late afternoon, the Japs had retreated into the mountains. We still heard the echoes of guns from far above us, but no bullets whizzed around our heads, and the mortars were distant thuds, not deafening blasts.

With the engineers, we moved to the location selected for the airfields and set up our equipment. By the end of the day, the engineers had laid out the first airstrip. They worked through the night in the light of our searchlights, and the runways had taken shape by morning.

The fighting was out of earshot within forty-eight hours, although we knew there were still Japs on the other side of the island. The infantry continued to comb the rugged mountains as daily monsoons kept us all damp and miserable. Engineers worked round the clock, except in the worst rainstorms extending the runways for long-range bombers. From here, they could reach Japan itself. We expected the Japs to attack at any moment.

I had just gotten off duty at dawn on our second morning on the island when I saw the first of a flight of bombers emerge at a low altitude from behind the mountains.

"They're coming in low behind the mountains where the radar won't see them," I shouted. "Alert the guns."

The gunners quickly loaded their guns and fired, shooting down ten of the eighteen bombers. We watched as the planes fell from the sky, and the others turned and fled behind the mountains.

"That was amazing," I said. "I am going to talk to the gunners."

I approached the commander of the nearest gun platoon.

"That was some shooting!" I said.

"We have that new ammo. It has something called a proximity fuse. It doesn't go off until it's near the target. We only get three per gun per day, but that was enough today."

"Let's hope it continues to be," I said.

Raids came every day after that, almost always low and behind the mountains, at night, dawn or dusk. The gunners hit more than half of them. Then, after a small raid shortly after New Year's Day, the air raids stopped.

The skies remained dark and silent all night. We continued to watch, but the Japanese had apparently given up their efforts to recover Mindoro.

"We shot so many of them down that they didn't think it worth the effort to keep trying," said Captain Henderson.

"Do you think they've run out of bombers?" asked Wright as we assembled for roll call.

"They're using those old planes in their Kamikaze attacks, but we've seen fewer new ones."

"I think they no longer consider this island worth the cost," I said.

Henderson insisted I wear the sling much longer than I thought necessary. I don't know if it was because of concern for me or in retaliation for my insistence that he get treatment for his jungle rot. He did have me continue my usual duties and the sling became exceedingly irritating, particularly when I could move my elbow without pain, but he insisted on its continued use.

Mail was handed out at roll call, and I took my letter from Sarah Gale to my tent to read.

December 11, 1944

I will be thinking of you on your birthday tomorrow.

The Japanese attacked us by air the other day. They did a great deal of damage in the nearby city but much less on the airbase. I don't know if they thought the base was in the city or if they were targeting the civilian population. At any rate, several people were killed, including three of the children I had been giving food to. I was really upset by that, but I could not mention it to any Chinese people around me because that would let the cat out of the bag, and they would try to keep me from feeding the children who survived. I don't know why they are so opposed to that.

The high command here has changed. The theater has been split, so India and Burma are one, and China has its own theater. What that means for me is that I don't fly so far on my photo expeditions. I am still in China, but I may go to Burma or India if I'm needed there. The new commanders are still sorting things out.

The other day, I realized I was beginning to understand some Chinese. Chen Ling has been teaching me Mandarin words, and I am finally putting it together and understanding some of the language. I'm still not sure which Chinese language I hear most of the time if it isn't Mandarin. There are hundreds of them. The kids in the street speak something different from Mandarin. I tried to say something to them the other day, but they didn't understand. Language is very complicated in China, and it is all tied up with class problems I don't understand.

I hope you are well and your men are working together.

Love,

Sarah Gale

My command worked together better than ever. By now, the men knew what they were doing. Our only job now was monitoring and lighting the airstrips, so we didn't have to constantly set up and tear down our equipment. Though we missed Brasseux's congenial banter, our stationary position made it easy for Tilton to manage Brasseux's platoon and his own duties as a searchlight officer.

A squadron of Black Widows landed at the base late on the afternoon of January 8, 1945. Morris showed up at our HQ tent a couple of hours later.

"We're about to retake Manila," he said.

"You know that?" I asked.

"Well, they brought us up here, along with several squadrons of bombers. When they do that, there's about to be another big landing, and the only likely place is Manila. We aren't ready to attack the Japanese islands themselves, and there's not much more of New Guinea or the Philippines that needs taking."

"You're probably right," I said. "How soon do you think we'll be going?"

"Won't be more than a day or two. They don't like to have us just sitting around."

We got our orders the next day. We were going to Luzon to take back the capital.

# CHAPTER 31

## LUZON

**W**HEN WE BOARDED THE transport, I noticed that this convoy included more destroyers than any I'd been shipped on previously. Our battery was split among several ships.

"In case of kamikaze attacks," a sailor told me when I asked. I understood their desire to ensure that some members of each unit survived, but what a much more difficult landing project!

So far, naval, air corps, and Filipino guerrilla activity had been concentrated in the southern part of the island, near Manila, to lure the Japanese defenses there. But we moved toward Lingayen Bay to the north. As we entered the bay, shore batteries fired upon us from all sides, and kamikazes attacked every ship. We hadn't fooled them.

Two battleships and three heavy cruisers fired back on the enemy positions onshore while aircraft from the Third Fleet strafed and bombed Japanese gun positions. On all the ships, AAA gunners fired on the kamikazes. Amidst all this, heavy winds came up, and the surf became very rough. Soon, about half the army men on board seemed to be barfing over the side.

After an hour of shore bombardment, the first landing craft headed in. They stopped about a hundred feet from shore.

"They're grounded on a sandbar," an Ensign shouted.

The infantry men on board leaped off the landing craft and slogged to shore in the rough water, their heads barely above the waves, rifles held high. The lifting of the weight allowed the landing craft to get some buoyancy, and they moved back to the ships for the next wave. They tried another approach but grounded again this time, and the men and equipment unloaded into five-foot-deep water.

The bombardment abated, but the Kamikazes kept coming. The escort carrier *Ommaney Bay* went down, and a kamikaze hit a cruiser while it tried to come to their rescue. As we watched, a destroyer and three battleships were also lost to kamikaze attacks. Many sailors swam for shore or clambered aboard the landing craft as the artillery moved off.

By midmorning, enemy fire on the beaches had stopped, but the wind had picked up even more. Our ship pitched and rolled as we moved equipment to the landing craft.

"Wait here," the ensign in charge of the loading process said. "We are setting up a pontoon bridge from the sandbar to shore. Once that's secured, we'll put you on board the landing craft and get you ashore."

About an hour later, his radio crackled, and he motioned for the first radar truck to board the landing craft. We jammed men and equipment on board and waited. Then, finally, the engines rumbled, and we headed to shore. The pilot of the landing craft carefully maneuvered it to line up with the pontoon bridge. The drivers got behind the wheels of the trucks and started their engines. With the rest of the unit carefully directing his every move, the driver moved the first truck onto the pontoon bridge. He drove slowly on the bobbing bridge toward shore, the team walking in chest-deep water in front of and beside the truck. Half an hour of tortuously slow driving brought them to the beach. The next truck, a searchlight unit, moved onto the bridge, Private Anderson at the wheel. As he moved out, a wave almost bounced him off the bridge. He had made it to the bridge's center when another rogue wave tore the bridge from its moorings and swept it aside. Anderson gunned the truck and drove off the bridge into the water, creating a great splash that sent the bridge scooting farther away. By some miracle, both truck and light stayed upright, and he drove through the water to shore.

"That was some driving," the pilot said.

"Amazing," I replied. "Look, our equipment is all waterproof up to six feet. Can we just drive the trucks off the craft into the water and drive them to shore? What is the bottom made of?"

"It is actually pretty solid sand," he replied. "Some coral outcroppings, but if the truck can make it up mountain roads around here, it should be able to make it over those outcroppings. If you're willing to risk another rogue wave, you can give it a try."

"Jenkins," I called. "The sea is about five feet deep here. We are waterproof to six. Do you want to risk driving to shore without the bridge?"

"Certainly, sir. I'd prefer that, as a matter of fact. I didn't trust that floating bridge one bit in this surf."

Several men climbed on board, clinging to the slats corralling the fuel barrels, and Jenkins rolled down the ramp at the head of our mini convoy. I jumped into the truck beside him, before he drove into the water. The truck was almost buoyant in the sea, but we had enough traction to move slowly forward. Suddenly, we fell into a hole, and water began leaking into the truck. I cranked the window down and crawled out.

"Come on, men, we need to get this vehicle to shore." Everyone dropped into the ocean and began pushing as waves washed over us. Anderson unhitched the searchlight, backed into the water, and we tied a rope from his truck to ours. Jenkins and Anderson both gunned their engines and got some traction. Jenkin's truck lurched back into shallower water, and both trucks leaped toward the shore. Lucas, the tallest man in the battery, stood by the hole and waved the other trucks away. The rest of us swam or waded to shore.

By the time we reached the shore, two landing craft carrying the big guns had arrived at the sandbar. The gun battery drove off the ramps into the sea, and we waved them away from the hole, indicating Anderson's path.

The landing master greeted us, saying, "You'll set up camp along the road to the north of those rice paddies." He pointed. "Leave your radar and lights on the beach. We'll need them here."

We unhitched the lights and trailers where he indicated and drove the trucks to the rice paddy. We pitched our tents on one side of the road, trying to leave space for a jeep to pass. The first thing that came through was an oxcart. By nightfall, we had three searchlights and two radar units operational. Half a battery of 90 mm guns and several automatic weapons were on shore. We set up for action. There was none.

***

As the sun rose, I stumbled across the sand. The landing craft, docked endwise against the transport ships, were again being loaded. Overnight, the wind had died down, and the sea calmed. No more rogue waves threatened the pontoon bridges, and low tide meant these men would come ashore in only about two and a half feet of water.

About ten percent of the invasion party made it to shore the day before. Hopefully, the command had figured out how to get more men and equipment onto the island today. Some Filipino guerrillas had arrived with small motorboats and canoes; they were waiting by the sandbar to bring men and small pieces of equipment in.

"Sinclair," called the landing master, "We have more landing craft on the way. Could you have your men help unload? We are way behind and need to get everyone and everything ashore as quickly as possible."

I roused the men, who had just gotten to their cots, and we returned to the beach.

"We'll need four men to signal the drivers to avoid the holes we discovered yesterday. Those should be your tallest men because the tide is coming back in. Only some of the vehicles can come ashore through the water. The rest will be coming on the pontoon bridges. We have a few engineers ashore who will be setting those up. We need about six of your best swimmers beside each bridge. The remainder will be needed to unload and stack supplies."

I assigned the men to their duties and went into the water myself to help with the pontoon bridges. Some more men from the battery rolled off the landing craft in the second wave. I waited until the supply truck on the pontoon bridge had passed my station, then swam to shore. I met the trucks as they came ashore.

"Everybody off. They need us on landing duty."

I picked the twenty-four strongest swimmers and sent them out to relieve the men on the pontoon bridges. Four of the tallest men in the battery were with this group, so I sent them to flag in the vehicles. Then, I turned to the remaining men.

"Everybody except the drivers, go relieve our men who are unloading supplies and send them back here. Drivers, wait here."

When the men who had been up all night arrived, I ordered them onto the trucks. "Park those trucks along the north side of the first rice paddy, behind the others, and get back here ASAP," I ordered. The trucks drove off to our camp, and the drivers were back within twenty minutes on foot. I stayed onshore, directing the vehicles as they arrived from the landing craft.

A supply truck drove slowly up the pontoon bridge late in the afternoon. The wind had picked up again, and the bridge bobbed precariously. High tide had come only an hour earlier, and the water was deep. A rogue wave bounced the truck off the bridge. The driver was not as fortunate as Anderson and the truck tipped sideways.

A shout arose from the men alongside the bridge, "Fenton is trapped under the truck!"

The men acted quickly, looping a rope around the truck and fastening it to a LST in the bay. It managed to lift the truck enough for the men to pull the man out.

They dropped him on the beach, and I began doing chest compressions. O'Neill and I traded off doing chest compressions for several minutes before the man choked, vomited, and took a shuddering breath. He groaned and grabbed his chest. Two medics arrived right then. They loaded him on a stretcher and took him off to the area where the hospital would soon be set up.

A doctor came by several minutes later to report that he had two cracked ribs but would recover.

"You acted quickly and effectively. Have you had any training beyond what is offered in Basic?"

"I trained as a pharmacist at Fort Worden just before the war. During the beginning of the training, they had medics, orderlies, and pharmacists all in one group for anatomy, physiology, and emergency care before we went on to specialized training. Pearl Harbor happened the weekend after I finished training. The army decided I should be an AAA officer rather than a pharmacist since I had a college education and high scores in math and science."

"A loss to the medical profession," he said, shaking his head.

"I still hope to attend medical school after the war," I told him.

I returned to camp for a two-hour nap and a quick meal before returning to command the night shift. Again, we watched empty skies through the night, providing light for the exhausted quartermaster's corps to unpack, sort, and repack supplies.

***

Men and supplies kept coming despite the difficulty of the landings. Ships and landing craft ranged up and down the gulf beaches as far as the eye could see.

"How many troops are they landing here?" I asked Captain Henderson as we trudged past each other at sunrise.

"More than any other invasion force in the whole war."

"More than Normandy?"

"That's what the rumor is."

I looked at the masses of men running like ants on the beach, swarming the roads between the rice paddies and lining up outside mess tents in all directions.

It took a week to get everyone ashore—not exactly the Normandy invasion—then for two more days, the generals argued over whether we should quickly move south to recapture Clark Air Base or clear the mountains to the north and east. Ultimately, the long column of soldiers moved south along the road to Clark Air Base and Manila without the flanking protection in the mountains that General Krueger had argued for.

Compared to the jungle warfare in New Guinea, driving between rice paddies and green fields down the paved Highway 1 through the island's center was easy, but moving an army is always slow. MacArthur drove up and down the lines, inspecting units and making suggestions for faster movement. It reminded me of George Washington, but MacArthur was much louder and brasher than Washington.

I had devised a leapfrog plan with the other searchlight and gun batteries. When the rear of the column passed a given battery's site, they would wait two hours, then break camp and move past the positions of the other batteries to the front of the column, where they would set up new positions. In this way, the entire column could be continuously protected from potential air strikes.

One morning at about 1000 hours, we were breaking camp. There had been no action for the past two days; the sun shone brightly, and the men were in a good mood, joking around. Some tossed baseballs around with the gunners, others folded up tents, stowed equipment, and hitched lights and trailers to the trucks. MacArthur drove into the camp, slammed on his brakes, and jumped from the jeep. While the rest of us looked like we had just emerged from a grueling battle, MacArthur's shirt was neatly pressed, and his pants still held their crease. How did he do it?

"What's going on here?" he barked. "Where's the CO of this unit."

A staff sergeant pointed to the HQ tent, where we had finished packing the contents and just begun to strike the tent.

MacArthur strode up to where Henderson sat in a camp chair studying a map.

"Do you realize, Captain, that the army is miles ahead of you? This army is moving slowly enough without having laggards! Get your asses moving! I'll have a word with your Colonel!"

He turned, marched back to his jeep, and sped out of camp.

Henderson was mortified.

"I'm sure Colonel Squires will explain the plan to him," I said. "But we'd better get on the road."

Henderson limped to his jeep. His jungle rot must be back. He drove around shouting at people to get their asses in gear.

"We move out in fifteen minutes! Be ready!"

***

We realized the combat units had reached Clark as we approached the front of the column. Gunfire broke out, and progress halted. The fighting sounded heavy. We could hear almost constant shelling even though we were still a few miles from the base. I approached Henderson's jeep. Anderson sat behind the wheel with Henderson on the passenger side.

"Should we find a good location to set up?" I asked.

"No orders yet," he said. "Hold tight until we know what's happening."

For some reason, he seemed reluctant to get out of his jeep and just sat in the middle of the road waiting for orders. Nothing seemed forthcoming from the front lines. Word came back that the artillery was engaged in a pitched battle.

# CHAPTER 32

## CABANAUTUAN

**T**OM MORRIS SKIDDED HIS jeep to a stop in front of the newly erected HQ tent as we set up camp on a hillside overlooking the airfield on the second day of the battle for Clark.

"Found you, Sinclair. I have new orders for you!"

"What?"

"There's a prisoner of war camp about thirty miles from here. They're holding the men captured on Bataan at the beginning of the war. The Japs have been killing whole camps of prisoners whenever we get close, so the Rangers decided to liberate this camp. The pharmacist who was going to assist just got deathly ill. I told their colonel I knew a pharmacist who could do the job. Your orders are to come on this mission."

I stared at him. "They need a pharmacist to liberate a POW camp? And what are you doing bringing the orders?"

"Seems they do need one," Morris answered. "It's a unique mission, put together very rapidly. I'll be involved too, and since nobody else could find a pharmacist this close to the front lines, I volunteered you. So you're to come with me immediately." He handed me a copy of the orders.

"Where's Captain Henderson?" I shouted at Jenkins, who was driving by in a supply truck.

"Haven't seen him in hours," he replied.

"Just show the orders to his second in command and come now," Morris said.

"Second in command would be me," I said. "Perry, get Colonel Squires man on the radio so I can check this out."

A minute later, Perry brought me the walkie-talkie. Squires already knew. "Sinclair, get a move on. I got word from Hank Mucci that he needed you for a special mission six hours ago. What are you waiting for?" Colonel Squires shouted.

"Just found out and am confirming," I replied. "On my way! "

I ran to the communications tent. Wright was always where he was supposed to be.

"I have a special assignment. Take over as XO. Figure out how to let Henderson know. I'll be back—when will I be back, Morris?"

"Should be about a week," he said.

"Always taking off and leaving us to fight this war," mumbled Wright.

***

"What does Wright mean about taking off?" asked Morris as we sped between the rice paddies and tents.

"I tend to get a few more special assignments than most lieutenants. Don't know why. They all have to do with fighting the war, but things besides watching a radar screen or setting up searchlights. Wright believes we are all cogs in this great army machine, and if one cog slips out of its assigned space, the army will crumble. If I slip out to do a secret mission or a high-level briefing, he feels I overburden the men doing their assigned jobs."

Morris looked at me. "High-level briefing? You in with MacArthur or something? Is that what that trip to Brisbane was all about?"

"Something," I said. "To tell you the truth, watching for air attacks has become downright boring. I think the Japs are running out of aircraft."

"I can tell you they are," Morris replied. "At the beginning of the war, the Jap pilots were twice as effective at taking out their targets. They had some ace pilots. But we got better, and our planes got better. The Japs built some new aircraft, but not nearly as many as we did. We've been attacking their airfields for several months and taking out most of their aircraft at each one. I piloted a Flying Fortress over Rabaul and the Jap force there was decimated. That's been happening all over the theater. And the navy destroyed almost all their aircraft carriers in the Philippine Sea and Leyte Gulf battles. They don't have much firepower left anywhere. We've been making raids on the Japanese islands from China for the past few months."

So that is why they needed Sarah Gale in China. I watched the Philippine countryside flash by as I thought about her.

We reached the Sixth Army HQ at sunset, where we slipped into a large tent. At one end of the tent, a Lieutenant Colonel was conferring with several Rangers and some lieutenants with the patches of Alamo Scouts—a special reconnaissance unit attached to the 6th Army. Across the room was a man with medical insignia on his uniform. Morris signaled to the doctor, who was analyzing some maps with the Rangers. He broke away from the group and came to us.

The doctor looked at my bars and AAA insignia and frowned.

"He's a bona fide pharmacist," Morris claimed.

"I trained as an army pharmacist before the war," I said.

"Captain Jimmy Fisher," he said, introducing himself softly. "Let me fill you in on this little trip we are about to take. First, look at the maps and pictures to get an idea of the lay of the land."

He explained as we examined maps, then moved to another table covered with photos. "At one point, there were over eight thousand prisoners in this camp, but the able-bodied were shipped out to do forced labor in other parts of the Japanese-occupied territory, and many of the sick have died over the past two and a half years. Reconnaissance estimates that only about five hundred remain, with around one hundred Japanese guards. Two advance parties of scouts will leave this evening to meet up with the Filipino guerrillas and make sure everything is ready. We'll go in tomorrow. The raid will take place at dusk the next day. Your friend here," indicating Morris, "will create a little diversion with the night fighter so the Japanese look the other way. The Rangers will take care of the guards and get into the camp. Then we must get the prisoners out quickly and get them on the road. Guerrillas are collecting ox carts to move them."

We joined the officers and a few Alamo Scouts and Rangers, looking at the maps and planning.

"This road will be one of the danger points," said Lieutenant Colonel Mucci, the Ranger CO. "If there's Nip traffic on it, we'll have to find a way to evade them."

One of the Rangers said, "This ravine might provide some cover."

"You sure that's a ravine?"

"Looks like a ravine to me, and whatever it is, there's a bridge over it on the road right here."

"You're right. Be prepared to take cover in the ravine if necessary. Does anyone else see any potential pitfalls?" Nobody did.

"Scouts, head out," said Mucci. Some of the Rangers backed away from the table of maps. "The rest of you get a good night's sleep tonight."

Two small groups of scouts took off along different paths as the Rangers drifted toward their tents.

"Come with me," said Doctor Fisher to me. "Medic, join us." A corporal ran to catch up. "This is Romero, my surgical assistant. We can expect most prisoners to suffer from disease and malnutrition. We'll provide medications for only the most immediate needs during the evacuation."

He took us to the back of the field hospital, where he handed me a backpack and a red cross armband. "Put the armband on. Put these in the backpack. Vials of morphine, some sulfanilamide, aspirin, 325 milligrams; Atabrine, 100 milligrams; Benzedrine, five milligrams. Here's a list of the names of the Rangers who will be going into the camp with us."

"Into the camp? Aren't we going to let the Rangers bring the prisoners out?"

"No. We're better off with the main body of highly trained men rather than on our own behind enemy lines. If we stick with the Rangers all the way, we're much more likely to get out alive. Ensure every one of them gets an Atabrine daily and Aspirin on demand. Give out the bennies as needed, but make sure no one soldier gets more than six in twelve hours. That's what the list is for."

"Six?" I asked.

"We need these men to be at peak alert. Lives depend on it, including yours."

"Very well."

"Here's a wound kit and a basic first aid kit."

I checked and repacked the kits.

"I see you've packed a medic kit before," he said as I put the items in the backpack.

"Romero, get as many surgical kits as possible into your pack. Make sure you have plenty of morphine, too. Let's see if there is anything else you might need." He looked around. "Nope. That's it. Fill the rest of the pack with chocolate bars. Hand them out to anyone in the camp who can walk. They'll need all the energy they can muster. We'll probably have to march fifty miles after the rescue to get them to safety."

"I thought we were going to be thirty miles from HQ."

"You were talking to your flyboy friend. Thirty miles as the crow—or Black Widow—flies, fifty by road. The guerrillas will line up as many ox carts as they can, but there won't be enough for everyone."

"Here's a pistol and take that carbine over there."

"I thought medical personnel were not supposed to be armed," I said.

"Everyone, even the photographers, will be armed for this mission." He looked at the expression on my face.

"Lieutenant Colonel Mucci thought documenting the raid would be a good idea, so we have both still and movie photographers in the group. Now we'd better sleep. We leave at 0500 tomorrow."

I followed Romero to the tent where we would sleep. What had Morris gotten me into now? Neither Pharmacy nor AAA training had prepared me to go behind enemy lines armed to the teeth, ready to invade an enemy POW camp. Would I be able to kill someone at point blank range? Would I even come back alive? Would any of us?

*\*\**

The night was entirely too short. Before sunrise we climbed into trucks and bumped along dirt roads between rice paddies and palm groves. The Ranger beside me looked at the medic armband, the first lieutenant bars, and AAA patches on my shoulder.

"Just who and what are you?" he asked.

"Most recently, XO of Battery C, 236th Searchlight Battalion, but I'm also trained as a pharmacist. Tom Morris, the pilot creating the diversion, pulled me in when the other pharmacist got sick. I'm carrying the Atabrine and bennies."

"A valuable member of the party. Can I have a couple of bennies now?"

"No bennies until we get behind the lines."

"That's why they brought in an officer to hand out bennies, Arnold. So you couldn't bully him into giving you too many too soon," laughed another Ranger. He turned to me. "Arnold here loves those bennies. He's why we have a pill pusher coming along with us instead of everybody carrying a bottle of bennies in their pack. Best shot in the unit, but if he gets strung out, he can jeopardize the whole mission."

Arnold glared at the other Ranger.

Most men propped themselves up with their packs or leaned against the truck's sides and tried to get more sleep. I followed suit. The trucks slowed and stopped just after noon in a little village. A band of Filipino guerrillas met us and motioned for us to be quiet as we jumped from the truck. We were directed to various homes, where the villagers gave us food and thanked us for coming. This village was at the very edge of American-held territory. From here, we would hike through enemy territory to the prison camp.

*** 

At first, we walked across open grasslands. The Rangers walked quickly but quietly through the grass, keeping a close watch in all directions. The photographers trotted up and down the line, taking still pictures and movies as we marched. We crossed a shallow river, the sun low in the sky, pulling out some K-rations and eating as we walked. Our pace slowed only slightly after the sun went down until we reached the first road crossing. Some scouts went ahead and reported a tank on the road.

"Into the ravine, quickly," they whispered down the line. I was amazed at how quickly and quietly the large band of Rangers and guerrillas disappeared into the ravine. We kept moving silently, passing under the bridge, stopping momentarily as the tank went over, then resuming the march. We emerged from the ravine after several hundred yards, crossed a field, then followed another river for about an hour to a point where it could be forded. We followed paths between rice paddies, walked through sugarcane fields, and several times through quiet villages where the guerrilla bands in front of us had muzzled all the dogs and put the chickens in cages.

We marched through the night and, by morning, arrived in a little farming settlement where we stopped for breakfast. I joined the other officers in a small cottage. The leaders of the guerrilla group waited inside.

"About a thousand Japanese troops are camped within a few hundred yards of the POW camp. They should move on tomorrow. There are around seven thousand Japs in Cabanatuan village. We should delay the attack until the Japanese leave," the guerrilla leader said.

"But they may kill all the prisoners before they do that," Mucci said. "We should go in tonight as planned."

"No, these are retreating troops from the south with no responsibility for the prisoners. They'll move on tomorrow."

Captain Prince of the Alamo Scouts came into the cottage. "It's going to be a difficult approach. There are also retreating Japanese troops camped by the river. They're just passing through and should be gone tomorrow."

"You must delay the mission," insisted the guerrilla leader.

Lieutenant Colonel Mucci nodded his head and turned to the radio man. "Notify headquarters' Mission delayed twenty-four hours."

"There's a village a few miles south of here where you can hide until the Japanese have moved on," the guerrilla leader said, drawing a rough map of the village's location, our area, and the camp. "It is called Platero."

The hike to Platero took less than an hour. The Rangers settled in for a nap. Captain Fisher called me over. "We'll set up a makeshift field hospital in the schoolhouse," he said, leading the way. Romero was already inside.

In an upstairs classroom, he said, "Take all the desks out of here and bring a library table up. This room should have the best early-morning light. We'll use it as an operating room if we need one. Push the desks aside in all the other rooms. Make sure everything is scrubbed down."

Several village women, already recruited by Romero, arrived with buckets of water. Romero instructed them in Spanish, giving them soap, and they began scrubbing.

I fell asleep on the operating room floor at dusk and slept more deeply than I had in a long time. I awoke at dawn. From a window on the second-floor field hospital, I could see Japanese troops moving along a road to our south. I watched until the last soldier marched out of view, then joined the other members of the party for breakfast in the school lunchroom.

The villagers provided boiled eggs, rice, and sweet, dense coconut bread. We ate sparingly, knowing that feeding us all created a hardship for them. The rest of the day was just a waiting game. I checked and rechecked everything in the makeshift hospital, paced the schoolhouse hallways, and spent hours staring out the upstairs windows. I could see guerrillas massing oxcarts and Rangers cleaning their guns. Finally, Captain Prince called us for a briefing.

"The ground is flat, and the Japs have cleared it of all vegetation within several hundred feet of the camp. We'll have to crawl approximately a quarter mile. If anyone is detected, we'll stand and rush the camp. Otherwise, stay as low as you possibly can. We have one hour between the time the sun goes down and the moon comes up. The moon is nearly full, so it'll help us liberate the prisoners, but it'll be disastrous if we're not in camp by the time it comes up.

"Murphy will lead thirty men around the back of the camp. They'll fire on multiple positions at the rear of the camp at 1930. That's the signal to attack. As soon as you hear gunfire, rush the front gate. Simultaneously, a Black Widow fighter will be creating a distraction overhead. That's for the Japs. Don't let his antics distract you.

"The prisoners have been alerted. We had some local boys throw rocks over the fence with notes telling them to be ready to go out. However, the prisoners haven't been treated well, and many are sick. So be prepared to carry them out. We'll be cutting the telephone lines at 1930, but there are about seven thousand Japanese troops close enough that they might hear gunfire. Guerrilla groups will hold them off with landmines and bazookas as long as possible. Get those men out and back to this village as quickly as possible."

At 1700 hours, one of the Rangers handed me a white cloth. "Tie that around your left arm," he said.

"Why?" I asked as I tied the cloth.

"So nobody mistakes you for a Jap and shoots you in the dark."

I nodded, but my mind began to wonder how dangerous the mission would be. I handed out bennies then followed the Rangers out of the village. At first, we marched through sawgrass that cut at any exposed skin and ripped a few uniforms, but it hid us well. About forty-five minutes later, one guerrilla group moved out to the east and one to the west. Murphy's men skirted the camp while the rest of us lay down on our bellies at the edge of the grass, waiting for darkness. I lay trembling, my rifle over my forearms, my elbows dug into the leaf litter at the edge of the grass. Finally, as twilight fell, the man beside me whispered, "We're in luck. No searchlights."

Soon, we heard the sound of a plane overhead. The man next to me mouthed, "The Black Widow."

I nodded. Suddenly, the engine cut out, then restarted with a loud backfire. It swooped low over the camp, then rose and flew toward the hills nearby, clearing them by only about thirty feet. Morris was putting on quite a show. Then, the signal came to move out. I was a bit slower than the Rangers. They had more practice. Fortunately, no one expected me to be at the front of the attack.

The first men reached the front gates and stopped. The Black Widow flew low toward the hills, looking like it had crashed, then turned, rose higher, and dived toward the camp. Morris pulled up, barely clearing the guard towers, then headed for the hills again. I continued my slow crawl toward the gate. 1930 came and went with no sound from the back of the camp. We waited nervously in front of the entrance as Morris continued his acrobatics, appearing to crash into the hills two more times.

Finally, around 1940, the back of the camp erupted in gunfire. Most of the POW guards ran toward the back of the camp. A sergeant rose and shot the lock off the front gate. We rushed through the gate, and the Rangers ran toward the barracks. Doctor Fisher, Romero, and I ran to the hospital. An orderly wearing a tattered Norwegian uniform met us at the door shouting, "Don't shoot, don't shoot. They're all dying anyway!"

"We're Americans, here to rescue you!" Fisher responded loudly. Romero pushed the orderly aside and entered the ward where men lay in the throes of malaria or dysentery. The conscious patients shied away from us as we ran in.

"Look!" Romero pointed to the red cross on his arm.

"A real medic would not be armed," one of the patients said to me.

"No way I'm coming into a prison camp unarmed, medic or no medic," I said.

"Your uniform," he whispered as a group of Filipinos rushed in the door.

"No time to explain," I said. "These fellows will load you into oxcarts and take you away. You're free! You're going home!"

The men were so light we could easily carry them to the waiting oxcarts. I picked up a man in fragile condition and took him in a fireman's carry to the oxcarts. As I moved him to the oxcart, he clutched his chest, shuddered, and died in my arms. Dr. Fisher came to examine him as I laid the body in an oxcart.

"Looks like a heart attack," he said.

"Oh shit!" I cried. "A hundred feet from freedom."

I laid my head on the dead man's chest and began crying. Dr. Fisher put his hand on my shoulder. "There is nothing more to be done for him. Go back for another patient."

It took only minutes to evacuate the hospital. From there, we went to the center of the camp, where everyone madly dashed about. As I ran to help carry some of the weaker prisoners out, I heard the scream of a mortar behind me. I turned to see the mortar slam directly in front of Fisher. Shrapnel tore into his body, ripping open his abdomen. His intestines spilled out as he fell into the dust. Romero and I rushed to his side. He was still breathing. I quickly pulled a morphine syrette from my backpack and jabbed it into his thigh.

"Save that," whispered the doctor.

Romero rinsed the doctor's intestines with water from his canteen and stuffed them back into his abdominal cavity. We wrapped strips of gauze around his entire abdomen as tightly as possible. The doctor was conscious the whole time. I took off my field jacket, we slipped our rifles through the sleeves, buttoned the jacket, and lifted Fisher onto it. We placed him gently in an oxcart and started to climb in after him.

"Stay with the boys," he whispered, "they need you more."

Reluctantly, Romero and I climbed out of the oxcart, and it moved out. We returned to the camp, helping other prisoners find their way out. The camp soon cleared out, and Captain Prince fired a flare, signaling our departure. I glanced at my watch and realized we had only been in the POW camp for thirty-five minutes. It had seemed like an eternity.

\*\*\*

A little under an hour later, Dr. Fisher was the first patient in the operating room of the schoolhouse hospital. I acted as an anesthesiologist under the direction of the Filipino doctor guerrillas had dragged in while Romero assisted him. The doctor removed as much shrapnel as possible then stitched the abdomen shut.

"He must be evacuated by aircraft as soon as possible and be operated on in the American hospital," he said.

I reported the doctor's condition to Lieutenant Colonel Mucci. He immediately assigned several Rangers to clear an airstrip long enough for a C-46 twin-engine evacuation aircraft to land. A few of the released prisoners volunteered to stay behind and help. They immediately found a level area in the sawgrass and began chopping with machetes.

"We'll be moving out in ten minutes," Mucci told me. "See to the needs of the men."

It was difficult to join in the jubilant celebration of the prisoners after watching the doctor's abdomen being blown to bits and realizing how slim his chances of survival were. Regardless, after three years in captivity, the prisoners were ecstatic. The Rangers celebrated with them.

I stood at the front of the column as it moved out, distributing Atabrine, Aspirin, and bennies to anyone who requested them. Then, I followed the last man out of the village, trotting forward to distribute pieces of chocolate to the prisoners. Many wore only a pair of undershorts, ribs were bluntly visible, and arms and legs skin and bones. As we walked, their bare feet bruised and bleeding, many stumbled.

The guerrillas commandeered more oxcarts and drivers as we went through other villages. We loaded more prisoners into them. The oxcarts moved sluggishly, and the prisoners who still walked clung to them for stability. At the front of the line, having given a square of chocolate to each man, I had only three candy bars left.

***

The moon had passed its zenith and dropped toward the western horizon. I stood passing out additional bennies, then turned to follow the column again. I could barely force my legs to move. No way I would make it back to the front of the column this way. I popped a benny myself. It jolted me. My eyes popped open; the warmth radiated through my body. My heart raced, and I was ultra-awake. I jogged forward, congratulating all the freed prisoners as I did. My body began trembling. I continued walking, holding onto one of the carts while the temperature turned colder. Then, I wasn't aware of anything anymore.

# CHAPTER 33

## MIA

**S**INCLAIR! **S**INCLAIR! **O**VER HERE for a photo," yelled someone off to my right. I looked that way and heard the click of a camera shutter.

I shook my head and realized I was still clinging to an oxcart that was now stationary. I looked into the newly risen sun. US planes flew over the column of Rangers and oxcarts, and the freed prisoners cheered. I joined a group of Rangers, and one of the photographers snapped our picture.

"Where are we now?" I asked.

"We're heading toward a village called Talavera. The allies have taken it and will have trucks there to take us back to HQ," a corporal told me. "It is still about five hours away at this pace, but we won't have to walk all the way back."

Dizzy and disoriented. I grabbed the nearest oxcart and clung to it as we walked. A few Rangers came to me for bennies. I gave them out without checking my list.

When we finally reached the village and climbed onto the trucks, I passed out almost as soon as I climbed on. They had to shake me hard to wake me when we reached HQ.

I assisted in getting the freed prisoners into the hospital, where they were deloused and given hot showers and new clothes. With the prisoners safe, the Colonel asked me to participate in the debriefing as senior surviving medical officer. I was filled with grief and shame over my inability to save even one person, yet they considered me the senior medical officer.

I sat in on the debriefing session and reported on Dr. Fisher's injuries when asked. Unfortunately, someone had told me he died before the plane dispatched to pick him up arrived. After the briefing, I dragged myself out and went to the officer's mess. Not interested in eating, I just sat. My chest felt hollow, and I had never been so tired in my life.

A young corporal entered the mess.

"I'm looking for Lieutenant Sinclair. Is there a Lieutenant Eugene Sinclair here?"

"Here!" I mumbled.

The corporal trotted over and handed me a sealed envelope. He stood there waiting.

"Sir," he said, finally.

"Thank you, corporal," I said, flipping him away with the back of my hand, halfheartedly returning his salute. He walked out.

I opened the envelope and discovered orders to report to Clark Air Force Base. "Get it together,'" I said to myself. "There's no reason to treat the corporal that way."

"The scuttlebutt is that you're off to Clark," said Tom Morris, coming up behind me.

"Yeah," I said. "We must've captured it."

"Yup. Just before I took off to do the decoy flight. I'm going back there. Why don't you hitch a ride with me? I only brought one crew member, so we have room."

I grabbed my gear and followed him to the jeep he had commandeered.

"That was quite something," Tom said as we drove toward a makeshift airstrip. "I was a bit worried when it took so long for the firing to start. I almost left before it did. Then I kept flying around to see how things went, but you probably didn't notice. What was it like on the ground?"

"Terrifying," I said. "And once we got into the POW camp, it was a wonder any of them could stand, let alone walk out. I've never in my life seen men so emaciated. Nothing but skin and bones. Most of them in their skivvies. It took every ox cart in the countryside to get them out."

"This is one for the books! I don't think there's ever been a rescue like this. Take the radar position," he continued as we reached the plane.

After everyone strapped in, Tom spoke through the headphones. "This strip is a bit short. We'll have to get up to speed quickly. Hold on."

Tom pushed the throttle, and the plane burst forward. We shot almost vertically into the air at the end of the runway, barely clearing the trees. An alarm sounded, and Tom dropped the nose a bit, still climbing. Then he made a farewell loop of Sixth Army HQ as men below waved their hats, and we were off. I was so dizzy by that time I saw spots before my eyes.

It seemed we had barely gotten to our flight altitude before we began descending again.

"Are we there already?" I asked.

"It's less than 45 miles. Doesn't take long in one of these."

"Right. A bit different from traveling by oxcart," I said.

The landing on Clark's long, wide tarmac differed significantly from the takeoff. We touched down gently and braked for what seemed a mile or so before taxiing to the hangar where Morris parked the plane. My legs were still wobbly as I climbed out of the Black Widow and walked toward the terminal the flagman had directed me to. Lieutenant Wright greeted me there, wearing first lieutenant bars.

"Congratulations," I said, noting the bars.

"Congratulations are in order for you, too," he said.

"It was quite a mission," was all I said.

"The Colonel asked to see you," Wright said.

Wright drove me to Colonel Squires' headquarters.

I walked into the tent. The Colonel immediately rose and came from the back.

"Sinclair, glad to see you back safely. We heard the team met with great success."

"Yes, sir, proud to be a part of it."

"We have some new things in store for you. Henderson's foot problem took a turn for the worse. Gangrene. They flew him out yesterday and amputated both feet this morning." I flinched, thinking of how that would affect an active man like him. "You'll take over command of the battery. It comes with a promotion to Captain." He pressed the new insignia into my hand since I had no jacket to pin it to. "However, more antiaircraft troops are in the field than we can use. What we need now are MPs. Japs are surrendering or being captured all over the islands. People are needed to guard them. Your battery will move out in the morning for Finschhafen to retrain."

"Yes, sir, thank you, sir," I replied with all the energy I could muster. I stumbled back to the jeep.

"I'll need to requisition a new field jacket," I told Wright. "The old one is soaked in blood and probably still sitting in a little village schoolhouse," I said.

"Were you injured, uhm, Captain?"

"No, used it as a stretcher for someone who was."

"I'll take care of that, sir."

"I, oh. Yes, Wright, please do," I said, realizing that I was now the CO and would no longer be filling out requisition forms. I would name Wright as my XO.

In my battery HQ tent, I untied the white cloth, pulled off the red cross armband, peeled off my shirt and pants, and lay down on the cot that had been Henderson's. The men had already brought my trunk and duffel bag in. On top of the trunk was a letter. I was exhausted, but I opened the letter and read it, without reading the return address or looking at the postmark. It was not from Sarah Gale but from her twin brother, a Marine cook who had lost his thumb in a kitchen accident in North Africa and been sent home.

*January 16, 1945*

*Dear Gene,*

*I am very sorry to have to give you bad news. We received a tele-gram that Sarah Gale is missing in action. The plane she was in went down over Burma…*

The rest of the letter went unread. My world went grey, and the letter fluttered to the floor. Then everything went black.

\*\*\*

I woke before dawn feeling cold and empty. I rolled off the cot; standing upright took almost more effort than I could muster. I didn't immediately remember why. I only knew that all was not right with the world. Had I experienced another hallucination? I didn't remember one. Was I suffering from another strange tropical disease? Then I saw the letter from Jeb, the orders to Finschhafen, and the Captain's insignia all fallen to the floor at my feet. I let out a deep cry from the center of my being, waking Wright, sleeping on my former cot.

"Sir, is something wrong?" he asked, suddenly upright.

"Everything is wrong," I mumbled, walking toward the latrine.

When I returned, Wright had picked up the items off the floor, placed Jeb's letter next to Sarah Gale's picture on the trunk, taken the orders to the desk in the front portion of the tent, and pinned the insignia to a new field jacket he had somehow managed to procure during the night.

"Sir, we should be boarding the ship in another hour. But, first, you will need to give an order…"

"Order the men to move out," I said, stuffing things into my duffel bag.

Somehow, everyone assembled and got onto the ship in good order. Word had spread about Sarah Gale, and many men expressed their condolences, but I was too numb to hear most of it. I sat and stared at the ocean for three days on the ship. Wright and the platoon leaders took care of anything that needed to be done.

Then, I overheard a conversation between two naval officers.

"Did you hear what that new VH-3 squadron did?"

"You mean the rescue of those two B-29 crews at Saipan?"

"Yes. They didn't lose a man. The rescue squadron got in there before the Japs could even figure out where the planes went down."

"Did I hear you say they rescued downed crews at Saipan?" I asked.

"Sure did. The Corps has so much invested in training those pilots and crews that they put a lot into recovering them."

I pulled out the letter from Jeb. No, not Saipan. Burma.

"Would the same be true in Burma?" I asked.

"I would think so," the Lieutenant said. "Like I said, they hate losing those highly trained pilots."

Then suddenly, I knew what I had to do. Sarah Gale was missing, not dead. She had to be rescued. I would not rest until I had found out what had happened to Sarah Gale and the crew of that surveillance plane.

# About the Author

Lynn Doxon was born in the same little Colorado town as Ken Kesey, although the Keseys had flown the coop and moved to Oregon by the time Lynn came along. She grew up in an average 1950s family. Father a World War II vet turned schoolteacher, stay at home mom who bred chickens, one younger brother and one older.

She started writing in second grade, although she made up stories from the time she learned to talk. Each of her books – fiction and non-fiction – relate to a different part of her life. The Greatest Generation Series is loosely based on her father's experience in World War II. The latest book in the series follows Gene Sinclair's adventures while island hopping through the Pacific, and Sarah Gale's time as a photo interpreter in England.

Lynn lives amid a permaculture food forest in Albuquerque, New Mexico with her husband, the three youngest of their six children, her 98 year old mother, four cats, three dogs, two fish and one hermit crab.